Wintry Night

Modern Chinese Literature from Taiwan

Modern Chinese Literature from Taiwan

EDITORIAL BOARD
Pang-yuan Chi
Göran Malmqvist
David Der-wei Wang, Coordinator

Wang Chen-ho,
        Rose, Rose, I Love You
Cheng Ch'ing-wen,
        Three-Legged Horse
Chu T'ien-wen,
        Notes of a Desolate Man
Hsiao Li-hung,
        A Thousand Moons on a Thousand Rivers
Chang Ta-chun,
        Wild Kids: Two Novels About Growing Up
Michelle Yeh and N.G.D. Malmqvist, editors,
        Frontier Taiwan: An Anthology of Modern Chinese Poetry

Wintry Night

LI QIAO

Translated from the Chinese by
TAOTAO LIU & JOHN BALCOM

COLUMBIA UNIVERSITY PRESS
NEW YORK

3 1969 01199 8423

Columbia University Press wishes to express
its appreciation for assistance given by the
Chiang Ching-kuo Foundation for International Scholarly Exchange
in the preparation of the translation and in the publication of this series.

COLUMBIA UNIVERSITY PRESS
Publishers Since 1893
New York   Chichester, West Sussex

Library of Congress Cataloging-in-Publication Data
Li, Ch'iao, 1934–
         [Han yeh. English]
         Wintry night / Li Qiao ; translated from the Chinese by Taotao Liu and John Balcom.
           p.   cm. — (Modern Chinese literature from Taiwan)
         ISBN 0–231–12200–4
         1. Li, Ch°'ao, 1934– —Translations into English. I. Title. II. Series.
PL2877.C519 H2913 2001
895.1'352—dc21   00–035882

Contents

$\mathcal{F}$oreword

The publication of the English version of *Wintry Night* is a great dream come true. This saga chronicles the ups and downs of a Taiwan "Hakka" family of three generations from the late nineteenth century to the end of the Japanese occupation in 1945. Recounting this family's adventures, struggles, frustrations, and expectations amid endless natural and man-made trials, it vividly records the time when hundreds of thousands of Chinese immigrants tried to relocate themselves on the island of Taiwan and redefine their cultural and political identities. Most of the plot elements are based on records left in the archives of the Japanese governor of Taiwan.

The author, Li Qiao, is one of the most prominent writers in Taiwan. As he explains in his original preface, this ambitious trilogy is based on the story of his mother, "the woman who not only gave birth to me but is also the embodiment of our native land." Li Qiao's tender reminiscences about his mother and motherland enable him to invoke an unusual lyricism throughout his narrative. His rendition of the morals and manners of Taiwanese society under colonial rule is full of piety and compassion.

I am sure that this novel will inspire the coming generations of overseas Taiwanese who may not be able to read Chinese. They will find in this book their own families' history vividly portrayed with affection and eloquence. More important, *Wintry Night* will also serve as a compelling introduction for general readers interested in the cultural and historical dynamics of Taiwan over the past century. The novel is well translated by Professors Taotao Liu and John Balcom, to whom I wish to express my heartfelt thanks.

Pang-yuan Chi

Wintry Night

John Balcom

Li Qiao's novel Wintry Night (Han ye) is accorded the near sacred status of a classic by many readers in Taiwan. Written over a five-year period from 1975 to 1980, it is a three-volume saga detailing the lives of three generations of Hakka settlers in the mountainous village of Fanzai Wood near Miaoli over fifty-five years. The story focuses on the Peng family, their foster daughter, Dengmei, and her husband, Liu Ahan; their struggles in opening up unsettled mountainous lands in the last decade of the nineteenth century during the Qing dynasty (1644–1911); and their lives during the Japanese occupation period (1895–1945). The first volume, titled Wintry Night, is included in abridged form as part 1 of this book; it describes the dangers and hardships of the first generation of Hakka settlers and their children. It ends with the arrival of the Japanese after the imperial government of China was forced to cede Taiwan and the Pescadores to Japan as part of the Treaty of Shimonoseki that ended the Sino-Japanese War of 1895.

The second volume, titled The Deserted Village, which has not been translated here, recounts the anti-Japanese activities of Liu Ahan and ends with his death shortly after being released from a Japanese prison. Liu Ahan and Dengmei are members of the second generation of settlers who arrived with their parents and elders of the first generation.

The third volume, titled The Lone Lamp, is included in abridged form as part 2 of this book. It deals with the sufferings of the third generation of settlers, those actually born in the settlement areas. Liu Mingji, the youngest son of Liu Ahan and Dengmei, is the central character. The novel ends with the defeat of the Japanese in World War II and the deaths of Dengmei, by then an aged grandmother, and Liu Mingji, conscripted by the Japanese for their war efforts in the Philippines.

Because Li Qiao's saga is so imbued with the culture and history of Taiwan, the series editorial board felt that an introduction to explain its cultural and historical background for readers with little or no knowledge of Taiwan was essential. The editors also felt that adding an introduction was preferable to encumbering the text with footnotes. The introduction is divided into seven parts on the following topics: Qing-dynasty Taiwan; the island during the Japanese occupation; the Hakka; the aboriginal peoples; religion in Taiwan; festivals in Taiwan; and the historical and literary significance of the novel.

Qing-Dynasty Taiwan

The historical connections between Taiwan and China go back to the Three Kingdoms period (A.D. 221–263). But significant settlement by the Chinese did not begin until about the fourteenth century. Most of the early settlers came from nearby Fujian province. The island had also provided ports for fishermen and pirates. The first Westerners—the Portuguese—arrived in 1517. As regional trade increased, armed Portuguese, Japanese, Chinese, and Spanish ships regularly passed through the Taiwan Strait. Everyone became aware of the island's strategic importance, and Chinese settlement continued. The Dutch actually took Taiwan in 1624, with little opposition from its few thousand Chinese inhabitants, most of whom were farmers, or from the aborigines living on the coastal plains. The Dutch established an outpost in Anping, on the coast west of Tainan city. There they built a stone fort called Casteel Zeelandia, the ruins of which can still be seen today. As the Dutch expanded and tried to tax the local inhabitants and Japanese traders, they met with resistance.

The collapse of the Ming dynasty in 1644 was to have a profound effect on Taiwan. The chaos on the mainland drove many people across the Taiwan Strait to seek a new life. The Ming loyalist Zheng Chenggong (also known as Koxinga) fled the mainland and landed in Taiwan in 1661. By 1662, he and his followers had expelled the Dutch. Over the next two decades, Zheng and his close followers and relatives set up their own government and ran the island, collecting taxes on local agriculture and on trade. Taiwan fell to the Qing in 1683. The government really did not want to deal with the island, but retained it so as to keep it out of the hands of foreigners and dissident Chinese elements. In 1864, Taiwan was made a county in Fujian province, and remained so until 1887 when it was made a province in its own right.

In the period after Taiwan fell to the Qing, the imperial government imposed a partial quarantine on the island, prohibiting immigration by

Han Chinese. The Qing government was more concerned about preventing dissidents from gaining a foothold than developing the island. The government was also concerned about the effects of Han settlement on the local population of aborigines, fearing conflicts. Civil and military offices were established in the southwest part of the island to regulate immigration and exports. The government continued Zheng Chenggong's practice of taxing the coastal aborigines, known as "cooked" or "civilized" aborigines, but could do nothing with the "raw" or "uncivilized" aborigines who inhabited the mountainous areas beyond government control.

The Qing quarantine policy remained in effect until Han settlers took up arms to rebel against heavy taxation in 1721. The rebellion threatened Qing control of the island. In its wake, the government strengthened the quarantine policy, but gradually it was seen as ineffective and ultimately counter to Qing interests. In 1731 another rebellion occurred, this time by the aborigines who opposed the corvée labor policy of the government, which was actually another remnant of Zheng Chenggong's time. In the aftermath, the government began an assimilation policy through education. It was only after yet another rebellion of Han settlers that the quarantine restrictions were at last removed, allowing Han settlers to immigrate; by 1740, entire families were finally allowed to immigrate. The easy availability of open land attracted large numbers of settlers. In 1735, the population of Chinese immigrants was tallied at 415,000; by 1756, that figure had risen to 660,147 people.

The period from 1680 to 1770 is generally considered one of a pioneering and frontier society. An intermediate stage in the development of Taiwan occurred between the 1780s and the 1860s, just prior to the opening of Taiwan's ports to foreign trade. Immigrants continued to pour in; the number in 1824 was listed as close to two million. It was during this time that the complicated land tenure system depicted in Wintry Night was introduced. It was also during this time that a significant and powerful landed gentry emerged.

The land tenure system evolved for a number of reasons. The island's Han settlers were prohibited by the government from encroaching on aboriginal lands. To get around this, many Han entered into private tenancy agreements with the aborigines. These agreements became even more complicated with lands officially opened for Han cultivation. A landlord class emerged that actually owned the land and was responsible for paying property taxes. They in turn leased the land to tenants, who, if successful, also became landowners. Many of the more successful tenants actually never farmed but sublet the land to a host of sharecroppers. In many cases, a system of dual ownership evolved, with a landlord who owned the land and a major tenant who owned cultivation rights.

After Taiwan's ports were opened to foreign trade in 1860 and until the island was ceded to Japan in 1894, it again underwent many changes. The Taiwanese became more involved in both the cultural and the economic currents sweeping through all of Asia, as well as in local government and defense. Instead of simply producing rice and sugar exports for the mainland, the island now began trading internationally in other commodities such as tea and camphor. The camphor trade produced a great deal of wealth, especially for the Hakka settlers in the mountainous areas, such as those depicted in *Wintry Night*. By the early 1890s Taiwan was supplying two thirds of the world's camphor, used in the production of celluloid and smokeless gunpowder. It was also during this time that foreign consuls, merchants, and missionaries began to settle in Taiwan, strengthening the island's international ties.

In 1884, Taiwan became a province, and Liu Mingchuan, the island's first governor, arrived. Under him, the "raw" aborigines of the mountains were finally forced to submit to Han rule. Liu also embarked on innovative infrastructure projects, including a telegraph system, a railway system, a postal service, and a local steamship service as well as the expansion of roads and harbor facilities and the mechanization of a number of key industries. Under Liu Mingchuan, Taiwan grew from a marginal backwater of the empire to the most technologically advanced province in the country. Liu left Taiwan in 1891 and was replaced by Shao Yulian, who left in 1894 after Qing China and Meiji Japan had already gone to war.

Taiwan Under the Japanese

China went to war with Japan in 1894 over Korea. The war ended the following year with China's defeat. The Qing government signed the Treaty of Shimonoseki on April 17, 1895, ceding Taiwan and the Pescadores to Japan.

The Qing court recalled all its officials from Taiwan on May 20, 1895, and in anger and frustration at having been abandoned, the Taiwanese came out and burned the governor's *yamen* in Taipei. The first Japanese arrived southeast of Keelung harbor, five days before the official transfer. Resistance had begun, and the island's first Japanese governor-general knew from the shelling his ships received at Tamsui that military occupation would be necessary.

It took until 1915 to quell all major armed resistance. Tang Jingsong, the last Chinese governor of the island, rather than turning Taiwan over to the Japanese, declared it a republic, the first in Asia, with himself as the new president. The Taiwanese, led by a Hakka scholar, rallied a defense force, but to no avail. Tang turned tail and ran as the Japanese pushed into Taipei. Rebellions continued to occur. "Black Banner Liu," a Chinese general loyal to the Qing court, declared a second republic, but he too fled the island, taking the treasury with him as reward for his efforts. The Japanese continued trying to put down Chinese and aborigine rebellions for many years.

Within a year and a half after the Japanese stepped ashore in Keelung, sixteen thousand Japanese civilians had come in to manage the island. But colonial rule only began to improve under the fourth governor-general, General Kodama Gentaro. Kodama restricted the power of the military in Taiwan and turned domestic affairs over to his chief of the civil administration, the competent Goto Shimpei. Goto sought to make Taiwan an agricultural appendage of Japan, and to that end, he revamped the entire agricultural sector. He also introduced extensive improvements to Taiwan's infrastructure, laying the foundation for economic development and modernization of the island. By the time Goto left in 1906, the total number of miles of roads had tripled, major rail lines were operating, the postal and telegraph systems were greatly expanded, the first modern newspapers had been established, the first hydroelectric plant was running, and accounting and banking systems along with Japanese corporate enterprises had been introduced. The Bank of Taiwan, which had been founded in 1899, began issuing currency. Also, having received Western medical training, Goto brought advances and reforms to the area of public health and sanitation. Rule of law was imposed, and China's complicated legal system was brought in line with Japan's modern one. An extensive police system was implemented.

But Goto's reforms had to be financed, and the Japanese were not going to take the burden entirely upon themselves. Local taxes were the answer, but the Chinese land registers were inaccurate. Goto and his administration undertook a census, which took five years to complete, largely due to local resistance. According to Chinese records, there were 867,000 acres yielding revenue, but according to Goto's fact finders, there were actually more like 1,866,000 acres! The Japanese Land Commission had its work cut out for it, because of the complicated ownership system under the Chinese. In addition, much of the land was held in aboriginal areas outside the jurisdiction of the Chinese government. Under the Chinese, land claims were always settled according to the personal interests of all involved, including local government officials. The Japanese grew impatient with the complicated litigation and finally set terminal dates for all cases. The Japanese officials decided that if a claimant was not able to produce proof of ownership, his land would be confiscated and sold. This made the Japanese very unpopular—some farmers lost lands opened by their ancestors, and many landowners were reduced to tenant and sharecropper status.

In 1919, Den Kenjiro was selected as Taiwan's first civilian governor-general. He and the eight civilian governors who succeeded him until 1936, the eve of the outbreak of war in China, all emphasized the need for the cultural assimilation of the Taiwanese, using a variety of strategies. Den focused on education and proper training for all Taiwanese. Language was a problem, and translators were needed badly. The Japanese language and Japanese textbooks were used in school to indoctrinate the locals. Government-sponsored associations were also formed to bring about social and cultural change. Many of these practices were also implemented in aboriginal areas. The local population was encouraged to change their lifestyle and learn Japanese. Education did allow social mobility, and by 1922, 2,400 Taiwanese students were studying in Japan. Many ended up working as doctors, government functionaries, and corporate agents.

In 1920 reforms were introduced to the government, which enabled more local autonomy through councils at the lower levels of government. The councils were appointed by the colonial authorities, but this did allow for marginal participation in government by the local elite. Taiwanese political movements and organizations learned to work within the system; home rule was proposed, and liberal elements within the Japanese government went so far as to request Taiwanese representation in the Diet in the late '20s.

But the increasingly liberal political climate was to change in 1936 after Admiral Kobayashi Seizo became the seventeenth governor-general. To prepare for Japan's military expansion in Asia and the Pacific, Kobayashi instituted an industrialization policy and an assimilation policy, both of which were strengthened by the governors-general who succeeded him. New factories were built, volunteer labor was mobilized, and by 1942, an army volunteer system was implemented, as is well detailed in *Wintry Night*. By the end of the war, 207,183 island residents had been conscripted for military duty—80,433 servicemen and 126,750 civilian employees. Most were sent to Hainan island in China, Southeast Asia, and the South Pacific.

The assimilation policy involved a number of measures, including making Japanese the only official language for media use. By the end of the war, about half of the population was literate in Japanese. In 1940 there was a name-changing campaign in which local residents were encouraged to take Japanese names. By the end of the war, only about 7 percent of the population had complied. All those who took part were given Japanese rations.

With Japan's surrender in 1945, at first no one was sure what Taiwan's status was to be—colony or province of China. Japanese officials were reviled, and many collaborators were attacked. Overseas, Taiwanese army volunteers were abandoned. Many were killed; others died from disease or starvation before they could be repatriated, a process that took months, during which volunteers were kept in prisons. Those who returned home did so without fanfare or honor. It is on this note that *Wintry Night* ends.

The Hakka

Wintry Night is a novel of Taiwan's history, but perhaps more specifically, a novel of the role played by the Hakka in that history. Li Qiao, the author, is himself a Hakka.

But who are the Hakka? The term "Hakka" literally means "guest people." They are a Chinese ethnic group who, like all Han Chinese, are believed to have originated in north central China, but who migrated south in the fourth century in conjunction with the flight of the Jin dynasty. By the fourteenth century, they had populated China's southeastern provinces, especially Guangdong and Fujian. Today, most of them live in southeast China, Taiwan, and Southeast Asia.

The Hakka are somewhat paradoxical: they consider themselves preservers of traditional Han culture, but they also consider themselves a distinct ethnic group. Their customs and language—they speak their own dialect of Chinese—distinguish them from their neighbors. Language has been one of the most important differences, but even when the language diminishes, as is happening today, the identity persists. There are in reality few cultural differences that set the Hakka apart from other Han Chinese. They perceive themselves as different, and this apparent clannishness is a typical sterotype. But in the People's Republic, they are simply considered part of the Han majority.

Self-perception of identity is the key. The Hakkas' identity was first formed when they existed as a poor underclass of peasant laborers in southeast China, and later in Taiwan. Their unique experiences in Taiwan, for example, account for many aspects of their identity. Many came late to Taiwan and were forced to settle in the less promising hills and mountainous regions, where they worked as woodsmen, often intermarrying with the aborigines. They are known for a pioneering spirit; in fact, they were responsible for opening up much of Taiwan's mountainous interior during the Qing dynasty and for developing such industries as Taiwan's lucrative camphor trade. It has been estimated that most of the mountain frontiersmen and as much as one quarter of the entire frontier population were Hakka; nowhere else in China did the Hakka ever make up such a large proportion of the population. Today they account for approximately 5 percent of Taiwan's population.

As pioneers they were often seen as poor, hard-working farmers able to withstand the dangers and deprivations of frontier life, much as they do in Li Qiao's novel. It is also widely held among Hakka and non-Hakka alike that Hakka women are especially hard-working. In Qing times, they were certainly different from other women: they participated in agricultural work alongside the men, they did not bind their feet, and they had a degree of freedom generally seen only among non-Han minorities. This attitude is borne out in the depiction of women in Li Qiao's novel.

Fiercely independent, the Hakka are also known for steadfast loyalty and readiness to fight. They fought the aborigines as they opened up Taiwan's mountainous interior; they fought antistate rebels and foreigners in the eighteenth and nineteenth centuries; and they offered the most resistance to the Japanese occupation. In fact, it took the Japanese years to quell Hakka armed resistance.

The stereotypes of the Hakka as clannish, thrifty, loyal to each other, and ready fighters are integral features to characterization in *Wintry Night*. The main characters—Peng Aqiang, his wife, Lanmei, their foster daughter, Dengmei, her husband, Liu Ahan, and their son Liu Mingji—all exhibit these characteristics. They work hard and live frugally for a small bit of land to call their own. Also, they have a strong sense of justice, and fight for what they believe in: they fight against predatory landlords as well as the Japanese invaders. The idea of clannishness, or ethnic unity, is also strongly developed. So, when Huang Huosheng takes on the Japanese name of Nozawa Saburo during the Japanization campaigns, he basically rejects his ethnic heritage, forsakes his language, and opts to become Japanese. Of course, he is depicted as a traitor, not only to Taiwan but to his own ethnicity.

The Aboriginal Peoples

The aborigines of Taiwan are Austronesian peoples, and evidence suggests that they have lived in Taiwan for at least fifteen thousand years. There are three theories as to their origins. The first, called the theory of southern origin, suggests that they originated in Southeast Asia and spread north and east. The second, called the theory of northern origin, suggests that they originated in China. A third and more recent theory suggests that Taiwan itself is the Austronesian homeland. This theory rests largely on linguistic evidence: Taiwan has the greatest concentration of Austronesian languages—about a dozen extant and a dozen extinct.

Taiwan's aborigines are generally divided into two main groups: the plains peoples and the mountain peoples. The plains peoples, who are now all extinct, once consisted of fourteen tribes. They lived on the coastal plains and were exterminated, assimilated, or driven into the mountains by the Han Chinese. There are eight mountain tribes, all of which still exist in Taiwan—the Saisiyat, Atayal, Ami, Bunan, Tsou, Puyuma, Rukai, and Paiwan. (The only surviving nonmountain tribe is the Yami, a tribe that lives on Lanyu Island, one of Taiwan's offshore islands.) They live largely in the mountainous regions of the island and have been able to maintain their cultural identities.

The Atayal tribe is the one tribe of mountain aborigines that is mentioned in *Wintry Night*. The Atayal people lived and still live primarily in central Taiwan in dispersed villages or hamlets known as *she*, a word that has simply been rendered as "village" in this translation. In general, their homes were made of wood, bamboo, and reeds. They lived by hunting and gathering and practiced agriculture by shifting methods— that is, they would burn off a piece of land and cultivate it for three to five years, then move on to another area. The Atayal were also known for a number of social initiation customs. For example, when young people reached puberty they would receive tattoos signaling their official entry into tribal life. Young men and women would also have their two upper lateral incisors knocked out. The reason was said to be that since they were no longer children, they must cease to resemble monkeys and dogs.

The Atayal were the most resistant to Han, and later Japanese, incursions into their territory. They were famous for their warlike nature. In fact, the Atayal practiced head-hunting, not just as a form of fighting enemies but also as a rite of initiation for young men. It is said that a man was not allowed to marry until he brought in a head. Often, though, dispensations were granted for killing deer and boar. Of the many uprisings led by the Atayal, none is more famous than the Wushe incident, which occurred on October 27, 1930, during the Japanese occupation. The incident arose over a cultural misunderstanding. Japanese officials at Wushe were invited to participate in a party but refused, saying the utensils were too dirty. Feeling insulted, the Atayal were angered and ended up thrashing one of the Japanese. That night, the Atayal men discussed the matter and decided that since they would probably be punished by the colonial officials they should make a preemptive strike against the Japanese. Eleven tribal villages attacked the Japanese at Wushe, killing 135 and injuring 215. The Japanese responded by sending in the police and the army. The villagers withdrew to a well-fortified place in the mountains, where a force of 1,163 policemen, 800 soldiers, and 1,381 mercenaries using cannon and machine guns could not dislodge them. The siege lasted about 50 days. Finally, the Japanese resorted to poison gas. In the end, more than 900 tribespeople were killed, as well as 49 Japanese and 22 aboriginal mercenaries.

Religions

The three religions mentioned in *Wintry Night* are the Taoist, or folk religion; Buddhism; and Japanese Shinto.

When the first settlers came to Taiwan from the coastal provinces of Fujian and Guangdong, they brought with them their diverse gods. These form the pantheon of Taiwan's so-called local religion, also termed Taoist. All together, it is said that there are approximately 250 gods worshipped in Taiwan. The pantheon exists in a heavenly bureaucratic hierarchy that mirrors the old imperial system. Naturally, certain gods are more widely worshipped than others. Of the seven deities mentioned in *Wintry Night*, the City God, Matsu, the Earth God, Guan Ti, and Guang Yin are among the ten most widely venerated.

The local religion is the most colorful, and it is certainly one of the most striking aspects of life in Taiwan today. Religious festivals, especially the birthdays of deities, can be gigantic affairs with prodigious quantities of food as well as opera performances. Local gods are given offerings and are regularly petitioned by worshippers to solve problems and, through divination, to foretell the future. Many are worshipped for specific reasons or by specific occupational groups.

The gods mentioned in the novel include:

1. The City God: The tutelary deity of the capital and all provincial and major counties and towns. A temple to the City God can be found in all large towns. His temple is considered a celestial yamen, and counterpart to the actual city yamen. Thus in the novel, Miaoli, an important city, is depicted as possessing both a county office and a City God temple. The City God is supposed to bring prosperity to urban dwellers, bring rain, drive away disease, and control evil spirits.

2. The Righteous Lords: The wandering spirits of the dead who have no wives or descendants to carry out ritual sacrifices for them. In general, these are the spirits of the earliest settlers in Taiwan, who died alone in frontier conditions. It is widely considered a Taiwanese, but also Hakka and Cantonese, cult. Temples to the Righteous Lords are extremely common in the Xinzhu area of central Taiwan, the setting for *Wintry Night*.

3. Matsu: Probably the best-known guardian deity for seafarers. Given Taiwan's close connection with the sea, it should come as little surprise that she is widely considered the patron goddess of the island. As a virgin goddess, she is a maternal protectress of women and a fertility deity of sorts. Worship of Matsu began in Fujian, one of China's southern coastal provinces, in the tenth century, and her position was sanctioned by imperial order during the Qing dynasty. From Fujian, her popularity spread to Guangdong province and to Taiwan, where hundreds of temples are dedicated to her today. The mother temple for the worship of Matsu is located in Beigang, in central Taiwan, and is host to one of the island's largest religious festivals celebrating the goddess's birthday.

4. The Earth God: One of the most widely encountered of all local deities. His temples are found throughout China, and small shrines to him can be seen in fields and farming communities throughout Taiwan. He is prayed to as the bringer of prosperity, fortune, and wealth.

5. Guan Ti: Also known by his personal name of Guan Yu, is one of the three heroes of the Three Kingdoms (221–263). He is all things to all people: prayed to for protection and prosperity and to solve all problems, personal, domestic, national, and universal.

Buddhism is also mentioned in the novel, as are a couple of bodhisattvas. The Buddhist practice depicted in the novel involves the recitation of popular sutras such as the *Amithaba Sutra* and the popular twenty-fifth chapter of the *Lotus Sutra*. Millions have sought release from human suffering by chanting these sutras. The Pure Land Sect, one of the most popular in China, emphasizes salvation by faith, and the recitation of sutras is central to devotional practice.

Two bodhisattvas, Buddhist deities who have renounced nirvana to help save all sentient beings, are also mentioned in the book:

1. Kuanyin bodhisattva or the Goddess of Mercy: Certainly one of the most widely worshipped Buddhist deities. She is so popular that she has become a goddess to handle all problems: she is the giver of male children, a comforter of the sick and dying, and also the protector of seafarers, farmers, and travelers. But one of her most important tasks is to care for the souls of the dead, and in this capacity she is also invoked in Taoist ritual. Perhaps the most important Buddhist text devoted to her is chapter 25 of the *Lotus Sutra*, which is titled "The Gateway to Everywhere of the Bodhisattva, She Who Observes the Sounds of the World."

2. Earth Store bodhisattva: The savior of souls in the underworld; one of the more popular Buddhist deities. He is said to have overcome

death and devoted himself to helping others do the same. Like Kuanyin, he is a compassionate deity and a protector of the dying and the dead, especially chldren. It is said that he roams the underworld preaching Buddhist doctrine and that when he encounters a repentant soul, he can have its punishment reduced. Worshippers pray to him on behalf of recently deceased relatives so that he might quickly lead their souls through the court of the underworld. There also is a popular sutra dedicated to him.

In *Wintry Night*, Japanese Shinto is mentioned only in a passing reference to a Shinto shrine at Great Lake Village. During the last decade of the Japanese occupation, Governor-General Kobayashi intensified efforts to establish the Japanese state religion, Shintoism, on Taiwan. Local religion was suppressed in some cases and religious statues were removed from temples and the buildings torn down. The Taiwanese were encouraged to maintain household Shinto shrines and worship amulets from the Ise Shrine in Japan, and there was a great deal of pressure to revere Shinto shrines and the imperial palace from afar. Rituals were practiced on an increasingly more massive scale throughout the period.

Festivals

China and Taiwan are rich in traditional festivals. Just a few appear in *Wintry Night*, and they include:

1. The Lantern Festival: This takes place on the fifteenth day of the first lunar month and is also called the "small new year." Traditionally, the day is used to honor the gods. Families prepare sacrifices and worship the gods, asking them for blessings. People also worship their ancestor tablets. In some areas, the Earth God statue is placed in a sedan chair and carried from business to business for blessings.

2. Birthday of the Earth God: A holiday of great importance for merchants and anyone else concerned about prosperity. In general, a family will make offerings, set off firecrackers, and eat a meal to celebrate the god's birthday. Merchants make an even bigger deal of the occasion, often inviting their employees to dinner.

3. The Dragon Boat Festival: The fifth day of the fifth month; generally a large festival. At mid-day, every family prepares various offerings, especially a special type of steamed dumpling called a *zhongzi*. With these, the family prays to the gods and worships their ancestors. The festival takes place as spring is turning to summer, a dangerous time when many evils lurk.

4. New Year's Eve: The biggest and liveliest occasion in the Chinese calendar. It is about as important as Christmas in the West. In general, a family will gather for a huge meal that will hopefully set the tone for the new year, making it one of abundance and good fortune. After the meal, it is time for gift giving, which generally means distributing coins to the younger members of the family.

Literary Value and Historical Significance

This introduction began with the statement that *Wintry Night* is one of the classics of contemporary Taiwanese literature. It has been accorded this status for a number of reasons. It was one of the first modern novels to deal with the uniqueness of the Taiwanese experience and to explore the nature of Taiwanese consciousness and identity as it has emerged through history. In some ways the perceptions in the novel tell us as much about Taiwan in the early eighties as they do about the island's history. *Wintry Night* also appeared at a critical juncture in contemporary Taiwanese history. The island had always been treated as a marginal area, first during the imperial period and then during the colonial period, and it was again stifled under the KMT. Li Qiao's work appeared just when the Taiwanese were really starting to reconsider their past during the liberalization of the late seventies and early eighties. This gave the novel a political and historical significance that some believe far outweighs its literary value.

To understand the significance of the novel as a literary work, it is necessary to understand something of Taiwan's literary and cultural heritage. Until Taiwan was ceded to Japan, classical literature and the imperial exam system were the foundations of education and culture for the island. After Taiwan became a colony of Japan, that system was abandoned in favor of modern education in which science was of paramount importance, and, of course, instruction in modern vernacular Japanese.

Through the medium of Japanese, Taiwan's intellectuals came to know more about what was going on in the world than their compatriots in mainland China. But Taiwan still felt the shock waves of the founding of the Republic of China in 1911 and the May Fourth Movement of 1919 and the new culture movement. Overnight, China's moribund imperial system was overthrown, and its educational system, which was geared for the imperial exams, was scrapped. The modern vernacular became the new medium for writing as well as for education. Writers in Taiwan had the luxury of being able to write in Chinese or Japanese, and some even toyed with using the local dialect.

However, as the Japanese embarked on a course of military expansionism in Asia, they sought to consolidate support by placing restrictions on the use of Chinese. Eventually the language was banned. Local writers responded in two ways: they took part in international avant-garde movements such as surrealism or they focused on literary nativism, attempting to articulate what it meant to be Taiwanese and criticizing the Japanese. More often than not, this meant looking to rural society, because it was seen as a last bastion of traditional Taiwanese values. But in both cases, writers used the language of the colonizer: Japanese.

After the war, with the arrival of the Nationalist government from mainland China, Japanese was soon suppressed, as was the local dialect, in education, government, and the media. This effectively silenced a generation of writers who had received Japanese educations. The political climate did not allow for activism, so most literati looked to the West for inspiration.

But as some of the older writers made the transition to Chinese and a younger generation of Chinese-educated writers emerged, resistance to the westernization trend grew. Local writers began investigating their own heritage, and literary nativism was reborn. By the 1970s Taiwan was in a lower position in the world—it lost seats in many international organizations and was "derecognized" by the United States when formal relations were established with the PRC. These failures abroad forced the Nationalist Party (KMT) to begin a process of Taiwanification—opening the party to more local participation. As this occurred, the Taiwanese began to demand a more equitable system. Soon many local writers were involved in politics. Literature and politics dovetailed in the heated debate on nativism in the late seventies. The status quo saw nativist writers veering too far to the left, and the nativist writers saw the KMT as unwilling to relinquish its dictatorial power and allow local self-determination. In 1979, the Kaohsiung riots occurred to protest KMT meddling in election results. In the end, a number of local writers were imprisoned.

It was against this explosive backdrop that Li Qiao wrote his trilogy *Wintry Night*. In the three decades after the arrival of the Nationalist government, local intellectuals began trying to define what it meant to be Taiwanese, to articulate a Taiwanese identity. By reexamining Taiwan's history from the Qing dynasty through the Japanese occupation, Li Qiao was making an ambitious attempt to textualize, once and for all, what it meant to be Taiwanese. His was not the sole attempt; several other massive historical novels had appeared earlier, such as Wu Zhuoliu's *Asia's*

Orphans (*Yaxiyade guer*) and Zhong Zhaozheng's *Taiwanese Trilogy* (*Taiwanrende sanbuqu*), but none of them was as successful as *Wintry Night*. Li Qiao's success is to some extent attributable to the ideological position afforded him by the increasingly liberal political climate of the late seventies and early eighties. *Wintry Night* is often regarded as a defiant attempt to create an autonomous identity for Taiwan. Even later historical novels such as Yao Jiawen's *The Spectrum of Taiwan: A Record* (*Taiwan qiseji*) were never able to capture the imagination of Taiwan's readers the way Li Qiao's novel did.

Although the work represents a breakthrough of sorts, the Taiwan identity or consciousness articulated in the novel is still largely a masculine construct, and to some degree it is quite reactionary with regard to women and non-Han peoples. Traditional stereotypes inform the depiction of women: while men rule the world, make decisions, and contemplate human destiny and identity, the women rule the roost—they raise the children, provide the food, and live out their lives without ever questioning the religious and social dogmas that govern them. Women are all perceived by the male characters as being weak and in some cases lascivious. Most of the female characters seem to lack consciousness beyond their animal instincts for eating and reproduction, while men seem to be the sole vehicles for consciousness. In the novel—and in traditional society for that matter—women tend to lose their identities after marriage; rarely are they referred to by their own names once they take a husband. Or, perhaps more accurately, their identity is defined by their husband. For example, after Dengmei, the only character—male or female—who plays a major role throughout the entirety of *Wintry Night*, marries Liu Ahan, she is referred to as "Ahan's wife," and after she gives birth to a child she is sometimes called "Mama Ahan." As time goes by her husband dies and she grows old, but she is referred to as "Auntie Ahan" and "Granny Ahan" by younger members of the family. However, in order to make this translation more readable and less confusing, we have generally used her name, Dengmei, or a phrase like "Ahan's wife" in place of her many and varied titles. We have adopted this practice for all the female characters in the novel.

The aborigines tend to be portrayed as just one more impersonal force of nature, much like storms of earthquakes. They too are lacking in any consciousness. Ironically, the Chinese characters in the novel just never seem to understand why the aborigines would want to harm them for taking their land. But with the arrival of the Japanese, the conflicts between Han and non-Han peoples are resolved in their struggle against a common enemy.

For these reasons, some critics suggest that the novel's political significance far outweighs its literary significance. But for other critics, Li Qiao's novel, with its epic scale and historical dimensions, is comparable to great works of literature such as John Steinbeck's *The Grapes of Wrath*.

Maui/Monterey, 1999

Bibliography and Suggested Reading

Qing-Dynasty Taiwan

Our summary of Taiwan during the Qing dynasty is drawn directly from John E. Willis, "The Seventeenth-Century Transformation: Taiwan Under the Dutch and the Cheng Regime"; John R. Shepard, "The Island Frontier of the Ch'ing, 1684–1780"; Chen Chiukun, "From Landlords to Local Strongmen: The Transformation of Local Elites in Mid-Ch'ing Taiwan, 1780–1862"; and Robert Gardella, "From Treaty Ports to Provincial Status, 1860–1894" in Murray A. Rubenstein, ed., *Taiwan: A New History* (New York: M. E. Sharpe, 1998).

Taiwan Under the Japanese

Our discussion of Taiwan during the Japanese occupation is derived from Harry J. Lamley's excellent "Taiwan Under Japanese Rule, 1895–1945" in Rubenstein, ed., *Taiwan: A New History*, and George H. Kerr's outstanding *Formosa: Licensed Revolution and the Home Rule Movement, 1895–1945* (Honolulu: University of Hawaii Press, 1974).

The Hakka

An excellent study of the Hakka is Nicole Constable, ed., *Guest People: Hakka Identity in China and Abroad* (Seattle: University of Washington Press, 1996). We found Constable's introduction, "What Does It Mean to Be Hakka?," Myron Cohen's article, "The Hakka or 'Guest People': Dialect as a Sociocultural Variable in Southeast China," and Howard J. Martin's "The Hakka Ethnic Minority in Taiwan, 1968–1991" particularly useful and have freely drawn on them in this discussion.

Aboriginal Peoples

On Taiwan's aborigines, we have found Michael Stainton's essay, "The Politics of Taiwan Aboriginal Origins," in Rubenstein, ed., *Taiwan: A New*

History very useful. Chen Chi-lu's *Material Culture of the Formosan Aborigines* (Taipei: Taiwan Museum, 1968) remains essential reading on the subject.

Religions

To us, the best book on local religion in Taiwan (and in much of China and Southeast Asia) is Keith Steven's *Chinese Gods: The Unseen World of Spirits and Demons* (London: Collins and Brown, 1997). We have drawn heavily on it in our descriptions of the gods, both local and Buddhist. Another very good book is *An Introduction to Taiwanese Folk Religions* by Rev. Gerald P. Kramer and George Wu. The book was privately printed in Taiwan in 1970 as a handbook of sorts for missionaries. For more information on Buddhism in China, the reader is referred to Kenneth Ch'en's standard *Buddhism in China: A Historical Survey* (Princeton: Princeton University Press, 1964), as well as the second edition of *Sources of Chinese Tradition*, compiled by William Theodore de Bary and Irene Bloom (New York: Columbia University Press, 1999). On Shinto, see Professor Lamley's article, "Taiwan Under the Japanese, 1895–1945" in Rubenstein, ed., *Taiwan: A New History*.

Festivals

The standard work on festivals, religious and secular, in Taiwan is *Wine for the Gods* by Henry Wei Yi-min and Suzanne Coutanceau (Taipei: Ch'eng Wen Publishing Company, 1976).

Literary Value and Historical Significance

For information on Li Qiao's historical milieu and more on the literature of the postwar period, the reader is advised to see: Thomas B. Gold's *State and Society in the Taiwan Miracle* (New York: M. E. Sharpe, 1986); Jeannette L. Faurot, ed., *Chinese Fiction from Taiwan: Critical Perspectives* (Bloomington: Indiana University Press, 1980); and Sung-sheng Yvonne Chang's *Modernism and the Nativist Resistance: Contemporary Fiction from Taiwan* (Chapel Hill: Duke University Press, 1993).

PART ONE

Wintry Night

The Peng Family
Make Their Way to Fanzai Wood

In the second year of the Qianlong era (1737) of the Qing dynasty, Hakka people from Meixin, Zhenpin, and Lu Feng in Canton province settled in Miaoli, Taiwan. Within ten years, Miaoli became a Hakka market town of moderate size, and it was made county seat in the fifteenth year of the Guangxu era (1889) of the Qing dynasty.

The County Office was on Miaoli Road; down the street stood the City God's temple. Miaoli Road led south to the Cowpat Hills, the highest peak of which was Miaoli Mountain; southeast of it lay Tortoise Mountain. The Tortoise Mountain watershed drained into a large river filling Great Lake. Miaoli Road was a yellow dirt track that ran through a pass on Tortoise Mountain and then down the slope following the course of the river. It was traveled by rickshaws and oxcarts, and the twin peaks of Miaoli and Tortoise mountains stood always before the eyes of those journeying up the road.

A basin extended from the foot of Tortoise Mountain to Guard Post; the central part of the basin was inhabited by settlers from southern Fujian province. The area to the southeast, known as Stone Walls, was inhabited by Hakka who were employed as farm workers. The men were away from home much of the time, so the doors and walls of their homes were fortified against attacks by the native tribespeople. The area got its name from the sturdy stone wall that surrounded the settlement.

The villages of the tribespeople were located in the mountains beyond Stone Walls. The deeper one ventured into the mountains, the greater the numbers and strength of the natives. There was also a corresponding increase in the danger to travelers. The oxcart road from Miaoli ended at Stone Walls and became a small footpath of yellow earth that wound its way up the slope between the boulders through Bamboo Grove, Mine Pit, Wen Shui, and Water's End Flat, and finally to the Chinese settlement at Great Lake. The aboriginal villages of Sheyata, Bali, Yeyu, and Mawa were located in the forests on either side of the trail. There were aboriginal lookout posts throughout the area. The land around Great Lake had only just recently been opened to cultivation by the settlers from Meixin, Canton province.

Early one winter morning, just after the sun had risen, when the mountain wind was particularly cold, Peng Aqiang's family of seven males and five females and two armed escorts left Stone Walls and set out for Great Lake Village.

Peng Aqiang placed the spirit tablets of his ancestors into a small basket and lit three sticks of incense. "Ancestors, we are on our way now," he prayed. "Protect us from all harm on our journey." He picked up the basket, glanced at his family, then, turning abruptly, led the way, striding out of the house.

It was very cold. The wind picked up, giving the sun a yellowish cast. On the dirt trail, the wind whipped up the yellow dust raised by the sandal-clad feet of the travelers, making it difficult for them to keep their eyes open. It was the first day of the period known as the Little Cold in the Chinese solar calendar, but the west wind unexpectedly had grown strong. As the folk song says:

> Livestock will perish during the Little Cold
> > when the west wind holds sway,
> And all the vegetables and all the grains
> > will be put in harm's way.

It was not the best of times to be moving, but the time of their departure had been appointed by the Righteous Lords—the lost spirits of the earliest immigrants to Taiwan, who had died without wives or children to carry out postmortuary rites for them—and could not be changed. Even tigers, leopards, dragons, and snakes had to respect their wishes. With the blessings of the gods, a way would be found through the mountains and the rivers would be bridged. What was there to fear?

Huang Aling, one of the armed escorts, was also the younger brother of the husband of Peng Shunmei, Peng Aqiang's eldest daughter. Taking the gun he had recently been issued, he hurried to assume his position as advance guard at the head of the column, in front of old Peng Aqiang. Behind their father came Renjie, Peng's eldest son, and Renxiu, his fourth son, who pushed a wheelbarrow filled with sweet potatoes on top of which all the bedding had been piled. Atop the bedding sat Renjie's two-year-old son, Dexin. Renjie's wife, Liangmei, carried Defu, their baby, on her back and walked with one hand on the cart to steady Dexin. Then came Renxing, Peng's third son, and Renhua, his second son, both of whom carried large baskets. Behind them was Qinmei, Renhua's wife, who was well on in her pregnancy. She was often out of breath and carried nothing. Lanmei, Peng Aqiang's wife, came next; she carried three chamberpots with wicker covers over her arms as well as a number of odds and ends in her hands. Trailing behind was Dengmei, the Peng's foster daughter, who had been purchased at birth for future marriage to one of their sons, as was the custom. She had trouble keeping up with the others because she was carrying the heavy iron cook pot, the earthenware rice pot, and other cooking utensils. Bringing up the rear was Liu Ahan, who, like Huang Aling, was in uniform and carried a long rifle.

Peng Aqiang was a tall farmer with a full head of white hair, and though getting on in years, he was still hale and hearty. Lanmei, Peng's wife, was four years his junior. At fifty-four, she walked with a robust stride and was still energetic. Now and then she would take note of how her daughters-in-law plodded along wearily; seeing signs that they were faltering, she shook her head disapprovingly, convinced that they wouldn't last two hours. "Oh, these women really are useless!" muttered Lanmei under her breath. "If they are like this now, what will they do when we start tilling the new fields in the mountains?" She saw that Renjie and Renxing were both strong as oxen, just like their father when he was a young man. But Renhua and Renxiu were not nearly as strong.

Looking as if she could go no farther, Qinmei stopped, turned, and spoke to Lanmei. "I don't think I can go on. Can we stop and rest for a while?"

"Here?" asked Lanmei, glaring at her.

"Not here! We only have to pass the mouth of Wen Shui, and Water's End Flat will be just ahead," said Renxing.

"Hey! Hurry up, Water's End Flat is straight ahead," said Huang Aling loudly, turning to tell everyone. Summoning all the strength she had, Qinmei picked up her pace. The others, young and old, all pushed on as quickly as they could. In a short while they had reached Wen Shui. The upper reaches of the Wen River were part of the territory of Shabulu and Henglongshan villages. The Shabalu villagers were among the fiercest and most bloodthirsty of the Atayal tribespeople.

Water's End Flat was a scant five hundred paces ahead. The people of Shuiwei village lived in two groups there: one in cave dwellings on the cliff above the path along the river, the other in the dense forest that extended up the steep slope to the left of the path. The malakajimu, or head-hunting expeditions, took place without any apparent regard for ritual or season. It was courting disaster to pass through the area; rifles had to be loaded and ready to fire. No one ever considered stopping for a rest there.

"We've almost reached Great Lake Village," announced Peng Aqiang. "We'll have our noonday meal there."

"I'm exhausted," complained Liangmei. She had carried one child on her back and had to constantly look after another. All along the way she had gritted her teeth in silent resentment.

Lanmei wanted to say something to comfort her, but when her eyes fell on her pregnant daughter-in-law's big belly, she didn't know what to say.

"I don't want to go on, Mom," shouted Weimei, the Pengs' youngest daughter. "I don't want to walk anymore."

Everyone was dumbfounded. The women burst into laughter at this, and the pace slackened. But when Peng Aqiang turned around and gave them a stern look, they all stopped smiling and walked faster.

"Be quiet. If you yell like that again, you'll be left behind."

"All right, all right," said Weimei as if she were going to make a fuss.

Lanmei glared angrily at her husband, and as Weimei turned to start walking again her mother gave her one shove, then another. Eighteen-year-old Weimei was pretty as a flower, but rather simple-minded.

Shunmei, their eldest daughter, had been married to Huang Ajiang, but he had died before his time, leaving her at Stone Walls with a son and daughter. She wondered whether her hardships would ever end. Liangmei, their eldest daughter-in-law, was the sister of Huang Ajiang and Huang Aling. Having exchanged daughters, the Pengs and the Huangs were bound by marriage. For generations, "marriage exchanges" such as those practiced by the Pengs and Huangs had been common practice among farm laborers. It worked well, everybody did it.

Renjie and Renhua both had wives and children, and Renxing was a strapping young man. If Weimei were not a half-wit they might have been fortunate enough to find a family willing to do a marriage exchange. It was intended that Dengmei be the wife of Renxiu, the youngest son. She was not an appropriate match for Renxing because the difference in their ages was more than six years: he was twenty-three and she was seventeen. However, she was a perfect match for Renxiu, who was only nineteen. Lanmei was always preoccupied with these troublesome family matters.

"Hey, the village at Great Lake is just ahead," shouted Aling, urging everyone on.

A hillock divided the village into two parts. At the entrance to the lower village, halfway up the hill, was the Temple of Myriad Benefits. It stood alone on a grassy expanse of ground. The temple was dedicated to those who had died defending the Hakka from their enemies and to the wandering ghosts—the spirits of those who had died without descendants and whose remains could not be sent back to their ancestral homes on the Chinese mainland.

On the slope where the lower village began to rise, a watchtower had been constructed. After nightfall, the villagers would take turns keeping watch. The tower, which held two guards, stood thirty feet above the ground on six huge bamboo posts. The walls were made of two layers of tightly woven bamboo strips and twigs, with loopholes left for firearms. A large gong hung on the wall.

Burdened as they were with all their worldly goods, including potatoes, that basic necessity, the procession of fourteen people climbed the slope with difficulty. They rested and ate their noonday meal under two large beech trees by upper Great Lake Village.

Their meal, which had been provided by Uncle Shanqing, consisted of the best white rice, fried shrimp, and garupa fish, the kind of food normally eaten only on festive occasions such as New Year's Eve.

The whole family had been invited to a banquet held as much to see them off as to celebrate their newfound independence. Uncle Shanqing had made a speech in which he said, "You and your sons who have worked for us for more than twenty years are now setting off on your own to make your way in the mountains. I haven't got anything of value to give you, but I will provide you with five hundred catties of potatoes to see you through while you are getting settled. Also, I make you a gift of this meal of the best white rice for your journey."

"Your generosity . . . ," Lanmei had said, tears running down her face.

"Now, now. I told you once that new fields do not produce very quickly. The only thing I can do for you is to give you some potatoes so as to keep hunger from your door. If you run short of grain before your mountain lands produce anything, please, Lanmei, don't hesitate to come and help yourself. There is no need to stand on formalities."

Such generosity, Lanmei had thought, would certainly be hard to repay in her lifetime. She and her husband would have to count on Renjie and his brothers.

Lanmei raised her head and looked at her husband, who was holding a glistening ball of white rice. He too was lost in thought.

"One day, after we become rich, we'll come and live in Great Lake Village," said Renhua.

"One day? When?" asked Renjie's wife wearily.

"I don't think we have that kind of luck," said Qinmei, Renhua's wife, her voice loud and shrill. She seemed angry.

"Not necessarily," objected Renxiu. "That's not necessarily so. Wait till we get to Fanzai Wood. As long as we don't lose our heads first."

"Qinmei, as long as there is good food, eat up and don't talk nonsense," said Renhua, quickly changing the subject to keep his wife from talking wildly.

Such inauspicious talk was generally considered taboo. Everybody suddenly became very quiet, and all eyes turned to Qinmei and then to the two armed escorts.

Lanmei gave Qinmei a stern look. Qinmei's face went pale.

"Have you all had enough to eat?" asked Peng Aqiang.

"Yes, enough," they all replied.

"Dexin and Defu! Don't throw your food on the ground!"

"They can't eat any more," said Renjie's wife.

"Whoever wants more to eat, take it. And be quick about it!" said Lanmei.

No one said a word or moved. Lanmei looked at Dengmei, her foster daughter. Dengmei was a thin, young girl with brownish hair—a sign of less than robust health. She always seemed to be staring straight ahead, never blinking. Her impassive appearance was like Weimei's, but unlike Weimei, she didn't drool.

"Dengmei, do you want more rice?" asked Peng Aqiang.

At Peng Aqiang's words, Dengmei got up and went over to little Defu. His mother took the half-eaten ball of rice from his hands and gave it to Dengmei. Dexin threw what was left of his riceball on the ground. Dengmei was just about to walk away when Renjie's wife gave her a hard look. She realized that everyone was looking at her. Then she understood. She picked the rice up off the ground, wiped it on her clothes, and began to eat it. Renxiu quickly glanced at her, then immediately, as if out of shyness or disgust, looked away again.

The only person besides Dengmei who was not part of the Peng family was Liu Ahan. He was a very quiet young man, and watched everyone in silence. His gaze had fallen on Dengmei several times in the last four hours, and he had vaguely sensed that she was a lonely person and that they were alike in their apparent detachment from the people and things around them.

Having taken about an hour to eat and rest, everyone stood up, stretched, and rubbed their legs. By the time they started walking again, the sun had already begun its descent.

The settlement of the area around Great Lake began in the twenty-second year of the Jiaqing era (1817) of the Qing dynasty, when Chen Ahui, a native of Quanzhou, made an agreement with the indigenous people that allowed the forty-five members of the Chen clan to build houses and to clear and work the land.

In the third month of the eleventh year of the Guangxu era (1885), Liu Mingchuan assumed office as the first governor of Taiwan province. In governing the indigenous people, he adopted a number of measures: he pacified the recently opened areas, set up schools, strengthened the guard post system, and was generally beneficent in his rule. After three years of a combination of peaceful and punitive measures, the indigenous people finally submitted. Around that time, the number of Chinese settlers in the Great Lake region gradually increased. Most were engaged in collecting rattan, making potash, distilling camphor, and other such "mountain" occupations.

Fanzai Wood, located in the hilly area east of Great Lake, was in the process of being opened up. Since it was still under the control of the indigenous people, tacit permission was needed before the land could be opened. There were already five Hakka families living in Fanzai Wood; Peng Aqiang's family would be the sixth.

But it was not the best time to move to Fanzai Wood. Only a couple of weeks before—in the tenth month of the sixteenth year of the Guangxu era (1890)—Liu Mingchuan had resigned due to ill health. In no time at all, the tribespeople began making incursions along the fortified border region.

However, families like Peng Aqiang's had no choice but to brave the dangers, for in the fourth month of the same year, there had been extensive flooding throughout the island, and 60 to 70 percent of the rice paddies around Miaoli and Guard Post, which had been under cultivation for more than twenty years, had been destroyed. In one night, twenty of Uncle Shanqing's prime paddies had been swallowed by the river. Thirty years of blood, sweat, and toil had been wiped out by a natural disaster against which there was no defense. Peng Aqiang and his sons and eight or nine other workers who had witnessed the disaster knew at the bottom of their hearts that "when the forest burns, the monkeys will scatter." Everybody voluntarily asked permission to leave.

In any case, thought Peng, to go on being someone else's hired hand meant never leading a settled existence. Although he himself didn't have much of a future to look forward to, he was anxious for his sons Renjie, who was twenty-nine, and Renhua, who was twenty-eight. Both were married and both had children. And if they remained laborers working for someone else and didn't make their way in the world soon, they would fail their ancestors.

Yes, Peng Aqiang thought, there was truth to the old saying that "life and death are fated, as is one's fortune, and there is no escaping disaster." Other people were brave enough to settle in Fanzai Wood and work the land. Was he, Peng Aqiang, any less courageous?

After making certain that his line of reasoning was correct, Peng Aqiang set about trying to convince his wife. Lanmei was a traditional Hakka woman, strong in character, tough, and tenacious. If she had had her teeth knocked out, she would have just swallowed them, blood and all, and kept on going. She could do anything her husband could do.

Their sons, daughters, and daughters-in-law would say nothing in opposition. Although the Pengs were not from the aristocracy or the landed gentry, the rules of their family were strict. The head of the family was the undisputed leader: when he gave an order, no one would hesitate for even a second, regardless of fire or flood. This was an unchanging rule passed down from one generation to the next.

Thus the Peng family decided to face the dangers and hardships of relocating. They challenged fate, gambling with the lives of young and old alike.

From this point on, the Pengs' difficulties would mount. The crooked path wound its way from Great Lake to Fanzai Wood amid cliffs and boulders and high undergrowth where even a wheelbarrow was useless. Peng Aqiang continued to carry the ancestral tablets while his sons carried sacks of potatoes. There were not enough sacks, so Peng Aqiang had used some old bedding (which actually had been made by unstitching some old sacks) to make packs to throw over his shoulders. They couldn't do without the potatoes.

Aling and Ahan were helpful above and beyond the call of duty. They too carried potatoes, in hemp rucksacks used by the indigenous people. But unlike the aborigines, they didn't use the head band.

Upon leaving Great Lake, they followed the path eastward toward a small hill known as Upper Slope. After crossing it they descended a small declivity called Kiln Corner. Huge camphor trees grew throughout the area. It is said that the Chinese first began to process camphor in the area around Great Lake. But most of the camphor kilns seemed to have been abandoned; only two were apparently still in use.

"Strange! Are those the Great Lake kilns?" asked Renxiu, who had never been to the area before.

"Hadn't Governor Liu been successful with the aborigines?" asked Renhua, puzzled.

"I heard that Liu Mingchuan resigned!" said Renxing.

"But that just happened. From the look of things, the kilns were abandoned years ago."

"Look at the size of the trunk on that tree," said Renhua, pointing to the left in front of them. There stood a tree about as big around as a tub. It branched about ten feet above the ground; its limbs were as thick as a man's legs. The smaller branches rose another ten feet or so. How strange that a tree of such girth should grow only about twenty feet high, and that the only leaves should be clustered ridiculously at the ends of the branches.

"Is that a camphor tree?" asked Renxiu.

"No, it's a kulian tree," answered Peng Aqiang.

"It sure looks strange."

"The women mustn't look at it," added Peng Aqiang suddenly.

"Is that what they call the 'hanging tree'?" asked Qinmei in a loud voice.

"The hanging tree?" Weimei cried out. "Is that where people go to hang themselves?"

"Uh, yes," replied Peng Aqiang, somewhat exasperated. Now that the tree had been mentioned, he decided to tell them about it. "Years ago, a young couple failed in farming and hanged themselves here. Later—every year—others hanged themselves on the same tree."

"Why?" asked Renxiu, who was younger and more inquisitive.

"Listen to me. We Pengs are going to Fanzai Wood to farm. We must succeed. We can't fail; we musn't fail. There's no way back. If we fail. . . ." With these words, Peng Aqiang was on the point of looking at the hanging tree but restrained himself.

"All right, all right! Let's be on our way," said Lanmei. Her words put an end to that fruitless line of thought.

"Hurry along! Hurry along!" said Ahan. This was the first time he had taken the initiative to speak up and say anything. His voice was deep, resonant, and forceful. But he also seemed to be speaking to himself, as if to rid himself of some anxiety.

Many indigenous people lived at Kiln Corner; they were "cooked" or "civilized," meaning that they lived on friendly terms with the Chinese settlers. They did not head-hunt anymore, but they themselves could be the victims of "raw" or "uncivilized" head-hunting aborigines in times of conflict. They might also be pressed into spying on the Chinese. Danger still lurked there.

Between Kiln Corner and Garrison Camp was a row of towering gray crags that looked like hundreds of monstrous horses rearing up on their hind legs, their heads thrust high into the air. When the wind blew from the northwest, it made a weird howling sound. The crags rose from a pool of deep blue water—the famous Blind Man's Pool. Its name derived not just from the blind man who fell in and drowned but also from the feelings it evoked in passersby. All who walked the narrow trail between the crags and boulders, amid the howling wind and the sounds that apparently rose from the deep pool, would begin to feel dizzy and be sucked down against their will.

"I'm not going on," said Weimei, the first to speak.

The two daughters-in-law looked reluctant as well, and Dengmei seemed to step back.

The sky had darkened. The sun was already low in the west, hidden behind the trees beside Blind Man's Pool. A northwest wind, each gust of which seemed stronger than the last, pushed at them from behind.

"How are we going to go on with all this bedding?" Renjie and Renhua were worried because all the women who were taking care of children or pregnant were carrying huge loads of bedding. If the hempen covers were to get snagged on a rock or twig or were caught by the wind, the bearer might lose her balance and fall, becoming yet another ghost in the waters of Blind Man's Pool.

It was then decided by general agreement that the men should first carry the potatoes sack by sack around the pool, then come back and carry the bedding and the household utensils for the women.

Everybody seemed to have overlooked Dengmei and had left her standing there holding the cooking pots. She glanced around at nobody in particular, her eyes wide open and panic stricken.

"Hey, Renxiu! Go and fetch the things for your Dengmei," said Renhua winking at him.

"Not me," said Renxiu, shaking his head, as he glanced at his mother. Lanmei had lowered her head as she tried to remove the sharp pebbles that had lodged in her straw sandals. She did not see her son's inquiring look.

Since his mother gave him no indication, he remained standing where he was. Lanmei often had reminded him that he had to assert his superiority before his woman and not be too pliant; otherwise, after marriage she'd walk all over him. Only by being a little heartless and a little stern would he be able to keep his wife in line.

Liu Ahan seethed with anger as he watched in silence. He wanted to help Dengmei, but his feelings made him hesitate. He had made up his mind that if worse came to worst, he would do something. When Renhua made the joke at Renxiu's expense, he dared not move. After all, he too was a young man.

"Hurry up!" Peng Aqiang finally shouted.

"The pots are too big and heavy. I can't," replied Dengmei.

Perhaps Renxiu simply didn't have the courage to face Blind Man's Pool. Aling handed his gun to Renxiu and took a big steamer and a pot cover, among other things, from Dengmei. Ahan realized that he could also help out now. He picked up the cast-iron pot and the earthenware rice pot and carried them down the narrow, dangerous path through the rocks.

After passing Blind Man's Pool, they continued up the slope to Garrison Camp. More than fifty armed guards had been stationed at the garrison, the outpost deepest in the mountains near Great Lake. Aling and Ahan had both been stationed there for three months prior to being sent to the garrison at South Lake, itself a tinderbox of hostility.

There was no real path from Garrison Camp to Fanzai Wood. One just had to struggle along the meandering river, picking a way through the shallows and crossing bamboo footbridges over the rapids. It was a difficult trip. This part of their journey tested their strength and endurance. Full cooperation was needed to safely complete the trek. When faced with such a crisis, the Pengs demonstrated their steadfastness and courage. Only when it was nearly dark did they leave the river and make their way up a short but steep slope to Fanzai Wood.

Uncle Ajin, their friend, had already lit a torch of cassia bamboo and was there waiting for them in front of the Peng's mud-and-thatch hut. The mud-walled, thatch-roofed hut had been built facing east with the mountains behind it. It consisted of a large hall and three rooms laid out in a row; the kitchen was a small open space surrounded by a wall of reeds on three sides.

Uncle Ajin greeted them warmly while his two sons, Yongcai and Yongbao, brought out a tub of potato and ginger soup.

"Come and have a bowl of soup and get your blood moving again."

"Many thanks, brother Ajin."

"Supper is also ready. Sorry, but it's just a pot of steamed dried potatoes and taro soup."

At this point, Ajin's wife arrived, accompanied by Xu Shihui, Chen Afa, Chan Agu, and Xu Rixing, the heads of the other four households at the Fanzai Wood settlement. Everyone showed up to help the Pengs get settled and stow their belongings.

Afterward, the Pengs sat down, their bodies covered in sweat. Soon they began to feel a chill. The doors and windows were made of bamboo lattice, and the piercingly cold winds swept through the gaps.

Renjie and his family, Renhua and his wife, and Peng Aqiang and his wife were to occupy one room. The others were to sleep on the floor of the hall. This arrangement had been decided upon long ago, but as there were now two men from outside the immediate family with them, Peng Aqiang decided that the women and children should take two rooms, he would take the third room along with Aling and Ahan, and his four sons would sleep in the hall. The rooms were all empty of any furnishings; beds would have to wait until the family could cut the cassia bamboo and construct the bedframes themselves.

There were no lamps in the mountain villages, as kerosene was too expensive. Split cassia bamboo or pitch pine torches were the most common form of lighting. When the torch that Uncle Ajin had brought was extinguished, the entire house was plunged into utter darkness. The sky was raven black, and not a speck of starlight was to be seen on winter nights. When the mountain winds blew through the roof thatch, it made a sound not unlike ocean waves. Peng Aqiang wondered if he was hearing the sea or the wind.

Half asleep, Peng Aqiang could no longer clearly distinguish the sounds that came to his ears. The sounds seemed to come from all around him, from outside and inside. The sound of the wind, which had already taken on a certain familiarity, seemed at once to come from both near and far. The wind continued to blow through the doors and windows, growing colder and stronger.

The women shared two quilts; Peng Aqiang and the two escorts shared another, while Peng's four sons shared another. There really were not enough blankets. All they could do was feel around in the dark for the sacks of potatoes, which they emptied in the corner. They then used the emptied sacks as bedding to keep the cold away. That had been part of their plan for getting through the winter.

It was cold, very cold, without a glimmer of lamplight to be seen.

That was how the Pengs spent their first night in Fanzai Wood. It was the twenty-fourth day of the eleventh month in the sixteenth year of the Guangxu era (1890) by the old calendar.

Days on Guard

*D*eep in the mountains, a cock crowed, distant and clear. The light of dawn broke through the hazy sky. Peng Aqiang and his wife got up.

In the reed-walled kitchen, water from a spring ran out of a bamboo pipe, forming a small pool in the corner. They really ought to have a water pot, but they had to save where they could. Anyway, the small pool was perfectly serviceable. Peng Aqiang scooped up a gourdful of water. He then rubbed his hands vigorously for a while to get his blood flowing; then he rubbed his eyes, forehead, cheeks, and nose. Only after he felt somewhat warm did he splash the water on his face. After drying off with his sleeves, he lit a stick of incense and placed it before the ancestral tablets.

This had been his unvarying routine every morning. He wasn't likely to ask anyone else to light the incense unless he were going to be away from home or he were ill. When necessary, only Renjie, his oldest son, was allowed to take his place.

As soon as the senior member of the family started moving around, everyone else got up. Despite being very cold deep in the mountains, mornings were quite invigorating once the wind died down. When the family arrived the night before, their surroundings had been shrouded in darkness, but now, looking out from the doorway of the thatched hut, they found themselves in the midst of myriad mountains and lush, untamed forests.

The thatched hut faced west. Behind it, a deep green primeval forest rose steeply along a rocky cliff that half concealed the sky from view. Directly in front of the house, terraced fields were in the process of being constructed, and the area to the left of the house was already under cultivation. Beyond the terraced fields and cultivated plots, the upper reaches of Great Lake River flowed into a narrow gorge at the base of the cliff, then past the terraced fields directly in front of the house and on to Blind Man's Pool.

The land allocated to the Pengs for farming was in two sections. One part was located on the wooded slope behind the house; the other was between the house and the rest of the settlement. It was said that they could get a *jia* and a half of terraced fields. If their luck held, in three years' time, they would no longer have to eat potatoes at every meal. Their first step in opening up the land was to slash and burn the vegetation to make potash. The second step was to plant potatoes and beans.

Peng Aqiang had long been trying to persuade Aling to give up his dangerous occupation as a soldier, bring his family, and set them up as farmers. After a breakfast of sweet-potato soup—the first meal had to be sweet for luck—Aling and Ahan prepared to leave.

"Think about it again, Aling. Farming is a proper way of life," said Peng Aqiang.

"I'll consider it," said Aling, who seemed to have more problems on his mind than anyone else.

"The Huangs all look to you." Then he looked at Ahan, who was cleaning his rifle. "Ahan, that goes for you too. You ought to get out of this business. You're not yet twenty, are you?"

"I just turned twenty."

"Farming is the only proper occupation for a man. All other jobs are just a sham. That's doubly true for being a soldier: you're always in danger."

"I've no family. I'm not afraid."

"You shouldn't say things like that. You are your parents' child; you have to take even greater care of yourself in order to carry on the family line." The more Peng Aqiang spoke, the more carried away he became. Ahan listened, somewhat at a loss.

Ahan and Aling left only after the sun had risen above the thatched roof. Standing in the doorway watching them go, Peng Aqiang had to force a smile.

The two friends, rifles slung over their shoulders, walked, absorbed in their own thoughts. Several times Peng Aqiang had wanted to say something to Aling, but he always forced himself to keep silent. Lanmei too had wished to speak to Aling, but her eyes filled with tears, and she was a woman not easily reduced to tears. The entire family stood by the door and watched them depart. No one said a word, as if a weight pressed down on their hearts.

Their friends were gone; only the settlers at Fanzai Wood remained.
The days, the months, and the years that were to be spent at Fanzai Wood
had truly begun.

Urgent news from South Lake was awaiting Ahan and Aling when they
arrived at Great Lake Village. Headquarters had ordered them to proceed
south as quickly as possible. However, Huang Qian, Aling's father, had
sent word that there was an emergency at home and that he should stop
at Stone Walls before leaving.

"I'm not going," said Aling, changing color.

Aling's attitude came as a surprise to Ahan. He was normally so
calm and level-headed. What made him behave in a manner so out of
character?

True, Aling had indicated that he was afraid to go home. That was
understandable. Aling's elder brother, who had been making potash for
someone in South Lake Village, had died from an illness the summer
before. He had left behind three children and a wife in poor health. This
June, his mother and another brother had perished after being swept
away in the floods as they worked in the new fields, which were still
mostly sand and gravel. Aling's second brother, who had been married to
Shunmei, the Pengs' daughter, had left a daughter and a son who had
been born forty-nine days after his death. Also living at home were
Aling's aged father and a younger brother. That brother was an invalid
whose legs had withered; the only way he could get around was by
crawling.

"What's the matter, Aling?" Ahan asked, looking closely at his friend.

"Nothing." Aling sighed.

"I'll go with you to Stone Walls. We can still make it to South Lake
before nightfall."

"I'm not going home. I'm not going home," said Aling, filled with
anger. His face darkened and he hung his head dejectedly. "You don't
understand, Ahan! You don't know the unhappiness I feel."

Regardless of what Ahan said, Aling was determined not to go home.
Nor did he discuss his unhappiness.

Despite a ten-year difference in their ages and enormously different
temperaments, they had strangely become the best of friends in a short
time. Aling regarded Ahan as a younger brother; Ahan, for his part,
regarded Aling much like an older brother. Ahan had no idea what afflict-
ed Aling. Suddenly he recalled their departure that morning and how the
elderly Peng couple had seen them off, and he thought it strange.

The two men had lunch at a small food stand at Great Lake Village
and, after a brief rest, proceeded directly to South Lake. The road south

from Great Lake was a narrow yellow dirt track that ran through Bamboo House and Little Joint Gate before winding through a gap in the high cliffs known as Door Bolt Gap, then down a slope to South Lake Village. Arriving at Door Bolt Gap, they found themselves in the brilliant light of the sun sinking in the west.

We've arrived safely, thought Aling.

The guard post was at the bottom of the slope, to the left of the temple dedicated to the Righteous Lords, the gods of the just. The temple sat near South Lake River, which wound almost completely around the village. South Lake Village was deeper in the mountains than Great Lake Village, and had much less level land. And although the area had been opened for cultivation as well as camphor and potash making later than Great Lake, it was more developed and the people there were far more successful.

The village also marked the farthest extent of armed protection for the Chinese settlers. The situation at South Lake was complicated. Many native villages with large populations and considerable power were located in the mountains to the east, south, and southeast of South Lake. The closest was Jialihewan, directly across the river from South Lake Village. Other nearby villages included Manabang and Sulu; a little farther on were Demoponai, Xidaobang, Luben, Mabihao, Jinmuyi, and Tiangou.

At the beginning of the Qing dynasty, the government had attempted to restrict the indigenous tribes to certain areas. These were known as *fandi*, or "aboriginal lands." A series of armed guard posts were set up to form a defensive perimeter along these lands. The most important one was established to the west of Taiwan's central mountain range, running from Taoyuan in the north to Southern Taiwu Mountain in the south. The mountains marked the border between the indigenous inhabitants of the island and the Chinese settlers, but the division was in no way clearly delineated. There was a considerable amount of contact between the two populations. Groups of indigenous people, normally women and children, would visit the Chinese markets for daily necessities. The sacred lands of the indigenous people were likewise open to visits by the Chinese.

The Miaoli area was inhabited mainly by Ayatal tribespeople. The tribe was subdivided into three groups—the Saikaokikeya, the Ze'aoliya, and the Saidekeya. The area around Miaoli city was Ze'aoliya territory. Of the Ze'aoliyas' villages, Demoponai was the strongest. At one time the villagers had lived in the area around the upper reaches of the Big Peace River, but they had recently moved to the area known as Sima Line, east of Xidaobang village. Sima Line was some distance from South Lake Village.

The Demoponai villagers were numerous, and many smaller villages, recognizing their superiority, had joined in an alliance with them. This alliance had become a threat to the security of the area around South Lake and Great Lake.

Babo Endo had ruled this alliance, but as he was getting on in years, it was decided that Beidu Babo, his third son, would lead. Babo's first two sons had died in battle, and Beidu was very ambitious—a leader of outstanding mental and physical abilities. He was also the village's best deer hunter. Twelve tufts of human hair hung on the scabbard of his *gebutimi*, or long-handled battle sword, glorious reminders of the twelve enemy heads he had taken. The harvest festival had just passed, marking the beginning of a time of leisure before the Sowing Festival. Liu Mingchuan had resigned, making this an ideal time for training the men and sending them out head-hunting.

The guard post at South Lake Village was directly under the command of the headquarters at Great Lake. Twenty permanent guards and forty patrol guards were stationed at South Lake. The recent security threat meant that another twenty-five patrol guards had been dispatched from Great Lake, bringing the total number of troops at South Lake to eighty-five.

On the fifth day after their arrival at South Lake, Liu Ahan and another guard by the name of Du Shuihuo had been sent out on patrol. As they arrived at Door Bolt Gap, the alarm bells at the outpost began to sound the alert.

"Let's climb up to the lookout post and have a look," said Du Shuihuo. "We can avoid everything."

They managed to get to the heights above Door Bolt Gap, where a small lookout post that could hold four or five people was located. During the day two guards were stationed there; at night, the number was doubled. On duty were Shameless Wang and Drunkard Yu.

"What's the situation?" asked Ahan.

"What situation? They are coming out of the brush."

A surprise attack by the indigenous people was referred to as "coming out of the brush." These attacks were a form of psychological warfare by which the aborigines were able to instill fear and panic in their enemies. They would attack when least expected and retreat quietly without leaving a trace. After all, in an open assault, they would stand little chance against a battery of guns.

"Hey, you see that row of things on the other side of the river?" asked Drunkard Yu, as always sounding a little tipsy.

"There are twenty of them over there sharpening their swords! My god, they're sharpening their swords!"

Ahan and Du Shuihuo were dumbstruck. Understanding the situation, Shameless Wang and Drunkard Yu smiled as they looked at Ahan. An expression of fear and helplessness seemed to pass over Du Shuihuo's face, followed by a look of depression and indifference, or so it appeared to Ahan. It was a common expression among the older soldiers.

"I've been a soldier for six years, and I've never seen anything like this," said Shameless Wang.

"Quick, go tell Three Chops."

Three Chops was the commander of the troops at South Lake. He was coming their way. Before they could open their mouths, he was giving them orders. "Get back to the village. From now on, you are not to go more than fifty paces from South Lake Village. Be sure to get enough to eat and plenty of sleep, and no alcohol."

"They, they are down by the river sharpening their swords."

"I've known about it for a long time. It doesn't matter. Get enough to eat and plenty of sleep. And no alcohol!"

Three Chops was a short, squat, middle-aged man. He had a square face, a sharp nose, a small chin, and a headful of stiff hair that stood straight up in contrast to his curly beard. Oddly, he had no eyebrows above his round, oxlike eyes. His was a strange and fearsome face. Three Chops was an unusual person. There were many stories circulating about him. For instance, it was said that he had come directly from Changshan, and that he was a deserter from Liu Mingchuan's army. It was also said that he had been a bandit operating alone up north in Yilan until he joined the army after his wife was killed by the indigenous people. An even wilder tale had it that he was actually a native or, even worse, a half-caste. Three Chops had two unbeatable skills: he knew a bit of the Taiya language and he was good at martial arts.

Judging from the seriousness of Three Chops's orders, the situation must indeed be grim. After giving the matter some thought, Ahan decided to have a talk with Aling.

From the look of things, the tribespeople of Jialihewan Village were not preparing a surprise attack. Perhaps they were drawing the lines of battle and would "cleanse" the village. Nearing the temple of the Righteous Lords, Ahan was certain that Aling would be there.

Aling was to be pitied. Two elder brothers had died, leaving him widows and five children as well as a crippled brother to support. Aling's father wanted him to marry his younger sister-in-law, but he couldn't. He had become a soldier to escape, and now he was in danger of losing his head.

When Ahan found him, Aling was the first to speak. "Ahan, you ought to be able to sneak away."

"Me? I don't have any place to go."

"What about Fanzai Wood?" Aling suggested. "I'm really worried about my sister and her husband, Renjie."

"I have no blood ties with the Pengs," said Ahan, smiling. Aling also smiled absent-mindedly.

Ahan's thoughts turned to the Pengs. An image of Fanzai Wood floated vaguely through his mind. Then a thin and lonely figure flashed across it. Who was it? It was Dengmei, the Pengs' foster daughter. Startled, he broke into a sweat.

He wondered why out of the blue he had thought about the girl. She had nothing to do with him. She was a foster daughter who had been purchased by the Pengs. A bought girl. She wasn't an orphan, but she was the most insignificant member of a large family. She was an ill-fated woman. Ill fated? He reminded himself the he was an orphan too.

He had no clear memory of his father, who had died when he was only three. He clearly remembered the kindly, wrinkled old face of his grandmother. As for his mother—he always referred to her as "the person who bore me"—he had no memories of her, either. That was because he had done his best to banish her face from his memory.

I have no mother or father; I'm an orphan! he cried in the depths of his heart hundreds of times each day. There is someone just as alone in the world as I am in Fanzai Wood, he thought. He fell into a deep reverie.

THREE

*P*lanting Potatoes, Making Potash, Death

*S*pring began on the twenty-fourth day of the twelfth lunar month. The early morning cold made the Pengs shiver when they got up. But once the sun had risen, their fingers lost their numbness and clumsiness.

It had been a month since they arrived at Fanzai Wood. They had eaten all the potatoes they had brought with them. Those lasted as long as they did only because they had combined them with wild greens. After breakfast, Peng Aqiang and Renxiu, carrying poles and sacks over their shoulders, climbed the slope to buy potatoes from Xu Shihui.

Renjie and his wife went to make potash on the newly cleared land behind the house. Qinmei, who was ready to give birth any day, remained at home with Lanmei to look after the two grandchildren, Dexin and Defu. The rest of the family had gone off to plant potatoes in the new fields behind the house.

Xu Shihui was the local "potato king." Anyone who was short of food could buy or borrow from him. He had the most land in the area under cultivation, because he had the most manpower: two wives and nine sons, four of whom were married, as well as three unmarried daughters still at home and a number of grandsons who were still young. In all, he could count on twenty pairs of hands to do the work. He himself, though past sixty, was still as strong as an ox and capable of working from morning till night.

Peng Aqiang still remembered his first meeting with Xu Shihui. "Do you have enough people for the work?" the old man had asked. "Can everyone use a hoe?"

"We're twelve in all, young and old," replied Peng Aqiang. "Ten, not including one unborn and one still crawling." He felt that Xu Shihui was a man of no nonsense, a man after his own heart.

"That's good. In Fanzai Wood everyone must work. The bigger the family, the better."

Peng Aqiang was determined to follow Xu's example. But for now, all thoughts of making money were in the back of his mind: the problem of food had to be solved first. Thus all the land that they cleared had to be planted with potatoes.

After father and son returned, they went to plant potatoes in a newly cleared field at the base of the slope. It was a field of black soil with brown flecks, furrow after furrow of loose, rich soil that emitted a strong, earthy aroma.

"How much food will this field yield?" asked Renxiu.

"Enough for several months," replied his father.

"That won't be enough. What are we going to do?"

"That's why we've got to clear some more land. We will get two crops, though."

"Let's plant buckwheat between the potatoes."

"Sure, why not?"

"I think millet would be better." said Renhua. "What I wouldn't give for a bowl of millet gruel right now."

"Barley is the best!" interjected Renxiu. "I haven't had my fill of barley in ages."

They talked of their hopes as they worked. The sound of the large mattocks at work along with the talk and laughter combined to create a lively rhythm.

"Listen, everyone," said Peng Aqiang with a wave of his hands, "we can plant anything we like—this is our land." His elation knew no bounds.

"Ours?" asked Renxiu. "Ours in what way?"

"All we have to do is pay the taxes on it one day."

"Don't we have to pay rent to the landlord?"

"Our landlord is the state. What other landlord is there?"

"Land for our family? Our own land?"

At that time, Renjie and his wife were already putting the fifth load of vegetation into the furnace to make potash. This was the only thing the family could do to make money.

The best material for making potash was wild taro, mountain bananas, mountain palms, papayas, ferns, and other alkali-rich plants. But the supply was limited; such plants couldn't be picked for long without growing scarce. Moreover, the time it took to transport them made it more economical to gather plants nearby, though they contained less alkali.

They used a simple earthen furnace in making potash. Two pots were sitting on the ground next to the furnace. One was half filled with a cooling gray-brown liquid—the liquid potash undergoing sedimentation. The other was full of boiling-hot liquid that gave off a good deal of white steam that floated high into the air. The smell of the acrid liquid filled the morning air. It didn't seem like a winter's day.

Two other large cauldrons sat atop the furnace, which was six or seven feet high. One contained the leach water and the other was filled with spring water from a reservoir next to the furnace. The water was piped from a mountain spring above their newly cleared fields to the reservoir via a duct made of split cassia bamboo. The same clear, limpid spring supplied water for the six families living in Fanzai Wood.

Renjie's face, like that of his wife, was covered with dirt and ashes and smeared black with charcoal. Their lips and noses were pitch black. The knot of hair that Liangmei had done up behind her head had come loose a long time ago, and aside from a few strands blown by the wind, her hair was plastered with sweat to her neck and face. She was busy stoking the furnace to keep the fire burning bright. Renjie was wearing a gray shirt, and his long queue was wound untidily around his head. His knee-length pants were soaked, and his whole body was covered with ash made sticky by his sweat.

Heaps of still-smoldering ash lay scattered over the recently cleared field, which was about one fifth of an acre in size. Bluish smoke rose from some of the piles, flames from others. Renjie, moving as quickly as he could, was carrying the ashes from the field to the large pot of spring water. The ashes hissed as they hit the water and gave off an acrid smell.

"How's that pot doing?" asked Renjie, indicating the cauldron cooling beside the furnace.

"It was boiling when we got here. Who knows?" said Liangmei, sounding very tired.

"Can you taste it and see?"

"Taste the leach water? You want me to put a hole in my stomach?" said Liangmei, glaring at him, which made her very attractive. He didn't know if she was really angry or if she was playing the coquette. Renjie's heart skipped a beat. Generally, in the company of others, she was quite gentle and yielding, but when the two of them were alone together, she was ferocious. As he looked at her covered in ashes, disheveled and dirty, her glare seemed positively enticing. He felt a strange sensation. When he saw her tired and panting, covered in sweat, and could smell the scent of her body, he grew as agitated as a large rooster when it mounted a little hen.

"Why are you looking at me in that way?" she asked, her temper flaring.

Renjie jumped down, picked up the bamboo ladle, scooped up some hot liquid and ash mixture, and, after letting it cool a while, pinched the mixture between his thumb and forefinger. He smelled it and rubbed it between his fingers, testing it. The liquid was thickening nicely.

"Not bad. Good. It'll do."

Liangmei looked at him disdainfully. She moved several feet away from him and sat down on a grassy spot sheltered from the north and west winds by two bamboo racks for drying grass. That was the place to rest. Liangmei heaved a sigh and lay down, pillowing her head on her arms.

Her breasts were full; it was time to feed little Defu again. She cupped one of her breasts in her left hand. Turning around at that moment, Renjie caught sight of her gesture. Liangmei instantly turned her back to him. Renjie laughed with pleasure as he remembered how the two of them had rushed there before the crack of dawn. The furnace had scarcely been lit when he himself felt all aflame. Who could blame him? Twelve of them shared that house, and the only thing that separated him and his wife from the others was a thin wall of bamboo and yellow earth. But their children slept there by their side. How were they to manage? They had no choice. That fire was inextinguishable; he had half forced her. But there was no other way. Women were like that: willing and at the same time unwilling. Surely she wasn't angry.

But when he had risen from her, he let escape a cry of regret, for her breasts were dripping wet; he had squeezed out little Defu's breakfast! He touched his own chest. . . . What about Liangmei? Her face was red, her eyes were half-closed, and she sighed with resignation.

Thinking of Liangmei, he threw another glance at her raised breasts. It was clear to him that everything before him was filled with beauty and love. A spring filled his heart; he was full of life. White clouds floated in the blue sky, and the earth was so solid and felt so new.

He climbed to the top of the furnace and dumped more ashes into the cauldrons, after which he stirred them. Then he decided to change the cauldrons. He scooped the liquid out with a long-handled bamboo ladle and into big-bellied clay pots through filter-fitted funnels. He threw the sopping ashes that remained at the bottom of the cauldrons into a gully where all the weeds and underbrush had withered or been singed. Then he would run the filtered liquid through a bamboo pipe to the cauldrons at the base of the furnace.

Peeking over the tall trees of the dense forest, the sun revealed its face to the little field. It was a cool, liquid red in color, and shone weakly. The cliff was bathed in the soft light; the nearby slopes and peaks were tinged a dreamy yellow. They were in the bosom of the mountains, the vast hall of the great earth, secure and solid. The forest united with the arching sky; the arching sky and the earth were melded together; and men seemed to be part of both earth and sky.

Renjie was busy climbing up and down the furnace. He felt exhausted; perhaps their morning activity had taken too much out of him. His eyes were red from the smoke and the liquid. Tears ran together with his sweat. He felt sticky, and his mouth was dry and parched. He walked over and lay down to rest beside Liangmei. As the sun shone on the tip of his nose, he shut his eyes. The wind blew coldly from the northwest.

"Here," said Liangmei as she handed him a ladle of spring water.

The news that eight or nine Chinese had been killed at South Lake by indigenous people spread quickly through the system of guard posts via headquarters at Big Lake. It also spread to all the villages near the lands of the indigenous people. Strange reports came to Fanzai Wood from the furnaces to the south: some said that the southern villages would be attacking on New Year's Eve; others said that the Tabeilai villagers were going to drive all settlers out of the area; still others said that the Tabeilai and the Moponai were headed their way to join up with the Jiaheliwan, who were coming from the shores of South Lake, for a joint attack. It was also said that the tribes were competing to see who could take the most heads.

The Peng family was frightened but didn't know what to do. On the afternoon of the 30th, Peng Aqiang went to see Xu Shihui to get his opinion. The six families living at Fanzai Wood had long considered Xu Shihui the village head. He himself felt that the situation was serious and decided to call a meeting of the heads of the families.

"What can we do?" Xu Rixing asked. "We have to defend ourselves from attack and also build levies against floods." Fifty-year-old Xu Rixing was the only literate settler; he was considered an important person and was addressed as "sir" by the others. He knew how to choose auspicious days and was a spirit medium as well.

"The problem is, how do we go about defending ourselves from attack while also working to protect ourselves from flood waters?" asked Xu Shihui.

"I don't see a problem. We just do what we have always done."

"Brother Aqiang, do you have a gong at home?"

"No. Why do you ask?"

Xu Shihui then outlined for him their emergency response plan. Every family had a gong for sounding the warning and a long-handled machete or scythe to use as a weapon. Xu Shihui and Chen Afa both had old rifles. When the gongs sounded, the women, children, and elderly would seek protection at Xu's house. A mud wall surrounded the house and courtyard, providing excellent defense against attack. The men would go out in groups to head off and fight the enemy. If the situation were really pressing, everyone would rush to the scene of conflict with their weapons.

"We have to post sentries at night," said Su Ajin.

"This time, according to the reports . . ." Peng Aqiang was reluctant to show how afraid he was.

"Yes, yes." Everyone seemed to be in agreement.

"The area might be evacuated, right?" continued Peng Aqiang.

"You mean evacuate the entire village?"

Peng Aqiang nodded slightly; his face flushed red and he lowered his head. He was certain that he was not afraid of death, but in the last month he had come to realize that everything in that wilderness was a struggle and that he lacked the strength to protect the women and children of his family.

"I'm sure it won't be necessary to evacuate," said Xu Shihui after careful consideration. "However, we should decide if we should get together as a group in one place for the New Year or not."

"You mean for New Year's Eve, I believe. . . ."

"Go and make haste with the New Year sacrifices. After you've eaten, return here."

The suggestion met with heated discussion. In the end, everyone except Peng Aqiang agreed that staying together in one place probably wasn't necessary. After all, rumors about attacks by the aborigines and the taking of heads were rife at least once a year. But Fanzai Wood was a good place and had always been spared by the indigenous people; no harm had ever been done to it or its inhabitants. Being careful would be enough; there was no need to overreact. So it was decided. Since the Pengs did not have a gong, they had to make do with a metal hoe. The hoe was removed from its handle and hung with twine under the eaves to be struck in the event of an emergency.

"There's nothing to worry about, Brother Aqiang. Don't worry about anything and enjoy the new year."

"On the third day of the new year, you and your wife must come and eat with us."

"Don't worry, don't worry. They won't come here to Fanzai Wood. We are much the same—the same vintage. Ha ha."

Peng Aqiang was somewhat reassured. After listening to his account of the discussion, his family also felt as if the sky had cleared.

This was to be the Pengs' first New Year's celebration since they had set up on their own. Although they were beginning to look thin and wan after more than a month, as people who had worked for others for years, they now had an irrepressible gleam in their eyes and a sense of exhilaration. Lanmei had with some difficulty managed to steam rice balls with radish. "If everyone can just work together in peace and harmony," she said with great confidence, "then I guarantee that we will have sweet rice balls to celebrate the next new year."

The rice for the midnight meal was in actuality half rice and half sweet potato. In addition, there were two catties of kaoliang wine. The only shortcoming was that their rough-hewn table, which could hold all the dishes, could only seat eight people. There were only five stools, so most of them stood, squatted, or sat on the piled firewood. That night they also lit their new lamp for the first time. Burning the lamp oil was an extravagance, but the soft glow of the oil lamp at this frugal but happy family occasion gladdened the hearts of one and all.

After the meal, Peng Aqiang gave everyone a New Year's gift of money, as was the custom. But on receiving hers, Lanmei pressed the red packet back into her husband's hands.

"The best place for all of this is in father's safekeeping," said Renjie as he handed all four packets back to his father. The other members of the family did as the eldest son had done. Then they all burst out laughing.

Flushed, Peng Aqiang also laughed. In years gone by, his wife had always returned the New Year's money to him. "I can't take this, you keep it," she had always said. And he, for his part, had adamantly refused, but the money had always ended up stuffed into his pocket. As for the children, they had always kept their gifts. This year, however, Peng Aqiang gritted his teeth, lowered his head with an embarrassed laugh, and accepted the money. He told himself there was no other way; he had to swallow his pride and take the money back because they needed every cent.

After the ritual, Peng Aqiang made an announcement: "Renxiu is now twenty and Dengmei eighteen; I have decided that at the Lantern Festival in two weeks' time, they will be married."

"Congratulations, Renxiu!"

"I told the ancestors at the sacrifices we just held that Dengmei is as good as a member of the family."

"Renxiu, what do you say? You're blushing," they teased him.

"Ha ha. Congratulations, Renxiu," Renxing's loud voice rang out.

That night the Peng family decided to take their bedding and sleep at the Xus' house.

The worries at Fanzai Wood around New Year proved groundless. Spring was late in coming to the mountains. In the valleys lay a sheet of mist that rose to cover the forest in opaque gauze, hiding the few thatched houses halfway up the slope. The milky white mist in the east quickly turned a bright yellow and then an amber color. The mist began to shift; it moved, floated, and finally began to thin somewhat. In the amber-colored east, the faint outline of the sun had risen in the sky above the tree branches. People vaguely could be seen moving around on the slopes, and the loud voices of men were punctuated by the crowing of cocks and the barking of dogs. Spring had been slow to come, but finally it had arrived.

The elders of the Peng family thought of little else but the upcoming marriage of Renxiu, their youngest son, and Dengmei, his bride-to-be. The Pengs couldn't provide the sort of banquet demanded by the occasion, but it was an important moment for the family. Since arriving at Fanzai Wood, they had not yet invited their neighbors for a meal, something they found embarrassing. They would have liked to invite everyone over for a glass of weak wine, but that would mean spending money, something they couldn't afford to do.

Peng Aqiang had always wanted Dengmei to have her moment in the limelight. In truth he was very fond of the girl. It was her story, first and foremost, that touched the old man. Dengmei had been abandoned as a baby. She had been thrown into a pigsty shortly after birth—her umbilical cord had not even been cut. It was the Huang family that had rescued and named the infant and then sold her to the Ye family, who had lost a three-month-old daughter. Dengmei took the place of the Yes' dead daughter, who had been buried without ceremony. Not long after she had been adopted by the Yes, the family experienced a number of mishaps. Through divination, an astrologer told the Yes that they were astrologically incompatible with their new daughter and that she should be sent away as quickly as possible. He further predicted that the girl would have a total of three fathers and three mothers. The incompatibility could only be resolved if she were adopted by someone else. "Once the incompatibility is resolved," said the astrologer, "the girl will make a good wife with the right family and the right house."

The Pengs had purchased Dengmei for one piece of silver and ten catties of brown sugar to be the future bride of one of their sons. Although unfortunate from birth, she had never brought the Pengs any bad luck. She had always been hard-working, skilled, and of gentle temper. Dengmei was actually superior to the Pengs' own daughters in many ways. When Lanmei favored one of their daughters or was unfair to Dengmei, Peng Aqiang felt unhappy but knew that he shouldn't say anything. He was the head of the family and as such could not openly support younger female members. But now Dengmei was coming into her own. When she and Renxiu were married and she took her rightful place as the wife of their youngest son, she would no longer be the purchased child bride, no different from a dog or a cat.

The thought of this gladdened Peng Aqiang, but he also suffered inwardly because he couldn't afford to buy her a new set of clothes for the wedding. As for Renxiu's needs, his mother had obtained a piece of bright blue Fuzhou silk five years earlier, and just after the New Year, she had asked Xu Shihui's second wife to sew a jacket with knotted silk buttons. Renxiu's leather wedding shoes were to be supplied by Renjie. In fact, it was the same pair Renjie had worn six years earlier and only once or twice since. He let everyone know that he was giving them to his brother and not merely lending them to him. The preparations for the wedding were more or less complete. There was no help for what couldn't be obtained, so they decided to make do with what they had.

For Dengmei, the wedding, which had always been a vague, unimaginable event, was now taking shape and becoming a reality. She ate and slept very little. Her eyes were wide open and she always seemed preoccupied. She kept telling herself that she was going to become the Pengs' daughter-in-law, a reality she would soon have to accept. She was only now beginning to take the idea seriously; it was something she could not accept as a matter of course. She was eighteen and had her dreams, but they never included a young man like Renxiu. When she was young, Renxiu had always bullied her; as she grew up, he never treated her well. When she had been scolded or beaten by Lanmei, it was always on account of Renxiu. And he was to be her husband? She could never see him in that role, but he would be in a matter of days. She wondered why it couldn't be someone like Yongbao, Uncle Ajin's second son, or the soldier, the one called Ahan, or even Renxing.

Suddenly she was startled by her own wild thoughts. Peng Aqiang had told her that she should now address third brother Renxing as "younger brother." That would make her his elder; that was impossible! She silently scolded herself for being so shameless.

She let her thoughts wander to Yongbao and Ahan. Ahan was quite handsome. His gaze was deep, and it had seemed as though he wished to speak to her. Those were the eyes of someone who had a lot on his mind. They were lonely eyes that could penetrate the depths of one's soul. He must be very lonely, she thought; we are the same. Her eyes began to itch as she thought about her loneliness and solitude. Then everything before her began to sway.

Lost in thought, she called out for her mother, but the very sound of her voice brought her back to herself. She immediately corrected herself and said "Not this one, my real mother."

Thoughts of her real mother were something she always kept to herself; her real mother existed only in the realm of her imagination. But it didn't matter. By carefully and patiently conjuring the image over time, revising it, redoing it, she had made it more vivid.

She consoled herself with the fact that her real mother did exist. She didn't blame her for what she had done; there must have been no alternative when they had thrown her into the pigsty. Surely she had too many siblings, especially sisters, and this made it impossible for her mother to raise her. Her mother must have been afraid that she would suffer too much in life, so she had released her to find another womb in another incarnation.

Dengmei could not find it in herself to blame her mother, especially now that she was going to take her place in life as a woman. She didn't want to be a woman, and she didn't want to marry Renxiu. But that was her destiny, and she had to accept it. She thought that happiness might be hers if her mother were to know of her marriage. How she wished her mother could be there for the ceremony, but that was impossible. But if only she could know. . . .

She also seemed absent-minded during the day. When Liangmei and Qinmei teased her, she merely blushed and smiled faintly.

"Oh, Dengmei looks so pretty these days."

"That's only natural; after all, she will be married in a few days."

"Marriage will be so interesting."

She was going to be married day after next, that was the day of the ceremony.

When the sun was sinking in the west, Renjie and Renhua brought home the glutinous rice and ritual objects for the ceremony. The rice was put into a pot to soak overnight. The next morning, bright and early, Renxiu and Renxing would take it to Xu Shihui's house and mill it there. Renxiu looked very happy. He said that it was not because he was going to be the groom, but because he'd have a fine meal of rice balls.

"Hey, I'd say that you are just stupid," said Renxing with a smile.

"Renxing, is your horoscope compatible with Azhi's?"

Renxing laughed so hard that he almost let the grindstone slip.

"What are you laughing about? It's no laughing matter."

"Yes, it is important," said Renxing seriously. "Yours is compatible with Dengmei's."

"That's what Mother said," replied Renxiu, quite unaware of Renxing's apparent sadness.

"So your future looks good." Renxing glanced at Renxiu and was about to say something but held back. He concentrated on turning the grindstone and said nothing more.

I don't really like her. She is not as good as Uncle Xu Shihui's young daughter, Azhi, thought Renxiu. But he knew that everything was set. Dengmei was going to be his wife; she was the woman with whom he would spend the rest of his life. I have to be hard on her, he thought. It's best to be hard on one's wife. He clearly remembered this rule that his mother had taught him. After the wedding, I'll put on airs; I'll make her wait on me, make her suffer. That'll make her obedient and gentle. She won't dare disobey me, he thought to himself as he laughed aloud.

I might not be able to do it, he thought. I do like her. . . .

Dengmei's face had grown thinner, but she was fair and quite pretty. And her breasts. . . . Once, he had glimpsed her pert breasts. It was in the bathroom; she had just finished bathing and was wearing a thin undergarment when the wind lifted a corner of the rush matting that curtained off the bathroom. Normally when he looked at her from the side, her chest looked so flat, but suddenly there were her lovely breasts. After the wedding the following day, he would not only be able to see Dengmei in a thin undergarment, but . . . just like those dirty guys said.

As he was thinking, his body grew hot all over and his stomach began to ache terribly. His lower abdomen pained him greatly.

No one had seen Renxiu's illness coming. Around noon the day before the wedding was to take place, the dull ache became a searing, gut-rending pain. Renxiu lay in bed, his hands and feet jerking spasmodically. Then he screamed and sobbed without stop as if he were being torn apart from inside.

Many of their neighbors had crowded into the room. At some point, Dengmei returned from Uncle Ajin's potato patch, where she had been picking potato sprouts. She too had most likely heard Renhua shouting unusually and returned home in spite of the fact that she risked a scolding or a beating. She trembled at the scene before her eyes; her legs felt weak. She wanted to move forward but didn't dare. Finally, Qinmei gave her a shove; only then did she approach Renxiu's bed. She didn't feel grief or pain but a terrible fear and an uneasy sense of isolation.

"Go away," said Lanmei, pushing her.

Dengmei was so startled that she nearly jumped. She covered her mouth with her hand and, in tears, hid in a corner of the room.

The crowd of people parted to make way for Xu Rixing, the geomancer. Aside from being able to pick lucky days and petition the gods, he was the only person in Fanzai Wood who knew anything about medicine. The news of Renxiu had reached his house, and he had hurried right over.

Renxiu continued screaming, but everyone else in the room was absolutely silent as Xu Rixing attempted to diagnose the illness. After looking at the patient and asking a few questions, he closed his eyes and thought for a while. He reached out to press Renxiu's stomach, then solemnly announced, "It's an illness called 'heaven's hook.' He has been hooked by heaven." Heaven's hook was fatal. Aside from the torment of an inhuman pain, the illness was considered a punishment from heaven. A person was hooked like a fish by heaven for doing something wrong; it was a form of divine retribution, a shameful affliction.

After announcing his diagnosis, Xu Rixing turned to go. As everyone else started to leave, he turned to Renjie and said, "We'll be here to help when you need us."

As their kind-hearted neighbors departed, Renjie couldn't help wondering what Xu Rixing's words implied. He turned away from his family to wipe his tears.

From that day forward, Dengmei was excluded and forgotten. On several occasions, after hearing Renxiu's screams, she could not control herself and went to see what was happening, but Renxiu's parents and brothers shouted at her and would not let her in the door. Why me? she asked herself over and over again.

All she could do was hide. When she was beaten or scolded, she always hid in the small space between the kitchen and the sheer rock face behind the house. It was a safe place cut off from the outside world. She did her best to understand her situation and work through what had happened to her over the last two weeks. She forced herself to consider her predicament and how she had ended up there.

Husband, wedding, wedding night . . . a man, Renxiu, a woman, herself . . . Renxiu hooked by heaven. When a person is hooked by heaven, they will surely die. Her husband dead; what about herself? What was the meaning of death? All these things were linked together. What did they mean?

Did she have something to do with Renxiu being hooked by heaven? This thought had been going through her mind since morning. She avoided it, she resisted it, but to no avail. The idea grew, took voice, and took hold. As she pondered the connection, tears ran down her face.

It had grown dark and suddenly she felt cold, colder than she had felt all winter. She was numb to the cold now. She started to squat, but before she knew it, she was kneeling. The ground was freezing cold and damp. Her tears were like ice on her face and the cold wind blowing off the mountain penetrated her bones, but she was oblivious. She lifted her head and glanced around at the matted walls of the house, which were nothing more than a dark outline. Behind her the high cliff, the forest above the cliff, and the sky beyond them were all pitch black. Everything was shrouded in darkness. Even the wind off the mountain and the cold itself seemed black.

Just one time, Renxiu suddenly came out of his delirium. His face was flushed and his eyes were bright and alert. He seemed at ease as he turned, apparently looking for someone.

"What is it, Renxiu?" asked Peng Aqiang.

"Where is Dengmei? I want to see her."

Renhua went and got her and pushed her before Renxiu. Renjie, Weimei, and the others all crowded around.

"It's no good. I'm not going to get better. Mom, Dad, I am an unfilial son. . . ."

"What nonsense. You are getting better."

He gave them a sad smile. His eyes swept over the room and lit on Dengmei's face. Unconsciously, Dengmei knelt but dared not look at him.

"Dengmei," said Lanmei, pinching her arm, "lift your head and look at Renxiu."

Dengmei lifted her head and fixed her gaze on Renxiu. She understood him; no one needed to tell her; she knew. Renxiu's eyes burned with a gentle flame, and although it lasted but a moment, she saw it quite clearly and understood. Renxiu had never looked at her with such an expression. No one had ever looked at her in that way before. She felt as though her heart, her whole body, was going to break into pieces.

"Dengmei, you must look after yourself. It's all over with me; I can't . . ."

Dengmei, who had been biting her lower lip, suddenly burst into sobs.

"Mom and Dad, I heard you. . . ."

"What's troubling you? Tell us."

"Treat Dengmei well. . . . Dengmei . . ." His face was suddenly contorted with pain. "Dengmei has done nothing wrong. Don't blame her."

"Oh, Renxiu," Dengmei cried out as she knelt, putting her head to the floor.

Renxiu seemed to want to say more. Then came the sound of violent sobbing. It seemed as if he were seized by some powerful force and pushed aside—no, not pushed aside but discarded. Then he fell into a breathless fog and lost consciousness.

Renxiu died, hooked by heaven. The next morning, with Xu Rixing acting as priest, they conducted the funeral ritual. At noon, the body, wrapped in a specially woven mat, was buried at the end of a newly opened field. The graveyard already contained the graves of half a dozen other settlers.

On the afternoon of the same day, Renhua conveyed a piece of news to Liangmei that sent her to her room in tears. The news was from the garrison: Aling had been severely wounded and had lost his left ear.

$\mathcal{T}$he Unexpected

$\mathcal{A}$lthough Liu Ahan had been at South Lake for more than six months, he had never taken the time to really look at the place or the surrounding scenery. Though he had some trepidation about the future, Liu Ahan really felt less burdened now that he was about to leave. Not knowing if he'd ever have the chance to return, he decided to take a look around. He climbed to the summit of Door Bolt Cliff for the panoramic view it offered.

From his vantage point on the cliff, he could see the mountains, layer after layer, stretching off in all directions. The high mountains near at hand seemed to lie in the lap of even higher and more massive peaks, and the highest mountains were a barely visible line on the horizon. Below lay South Lake and the lakeside settlement, beyond which ran the river, on the opposite bank of which were the newly opened fields. Above the fields were the orchards, a green belt that formed a decorative base to slopes that rose precipitously in successive masses of peaks that receded into the distance, each layer a slightly paler shade of blue.

Looking at the mountains on that bright and beautiful summer day, Liu Ahan felt exhilarated as his heart was filled with the view. For a moment he seemed to step beyond himself and felt completely at one with his surroundings. Then in a flash he came back to himself. His breast was filled with warmth and tears welled from his eyes. Never had he been so moved; never had he shed such tears of joy and happiness.

He felt a boundless love for the mountains and trees, for all of nature, for that great and limitless land. He decided then to leave the post at South Lake and visit Huang Aling at Stone Walls.

The camphor convoy left Big Lake for Miaoli only in the full light of morning. Camphor oil was the economic mainstay of the people there, and for the sake of security the convoy was provided with an armed escort. Each convoy had a large number of followers including local settlers, peddlers, itinerant merchants, and traders. Liu Ahan had already given up his rifle, so he had no choice but to join the convoy followers. With such a large and mixed group, progress was naturally slow, but their strength in numbers provided a sense of security. In any case, Liu Ahan was in no hurry. He felt very much at ease talking with his fellow travelers as they walked along. It was nearly noon before Stone Walls appeared.

Stone Walls was situated to the left of the road, down in a hollow. Behind the protective wall of gray slate were about fifty houses of varying heights with thatched roofs. The Hakka town had been established in the twenty-second year of the Jiaqing era (1817) by Wu Linfang with imperial permission. Along with Tongluo Bay and Miaoli, it was one of the earliest Hakka settlements.

Liu Ahan began to think about his home in Tongluo Bay. He thought about his father and wondered where his grave was located. He had heard that his mother, the woman who bore him, was living in one of the big houses over in Tongluo Bay. But her face was an indistinct blur; it was something his heart refused to see. Only his grandmother was clear and vivid in his mind. She was his anchor in a sea of emotional turmoil.

But his grandmother had already been buried. Before she passed away, she had said: "Ahan, be a good man. The spirit tablets of the Lius are at your aunt's place. You must go and get them and make sacrifices to them yourself. You must do your best to send my bones and those of your father back to Changshanmei. Also, you must have nothing to do with that hard-hearted woman who deserted you when you were but four years old. You must make a life for yourself and provide for a family." Liu Ahan felt ashamed of himself; he had turned out badly. He shook his head and headed off for Aling's house. Aling's house, which was behind the Earth God's temple, was a long, low, rickety structure. The roof and walls were made of woven straw.

"Brother Aling, I'm here."

The doors of the house were all open. Outside, beneath a papaya tree, sat three children. He called again. Still no one replied. He approached the central hall. Someone was struggling to crawl out over the threshold to greet him.

"Are you Aling's brother?" Ahan couldn't remember his name.

"Yes. So brother Ahan, you've arrived."

"Where is Aling?"

A middle-aged woman walked unsteadily out of the house. Ahan felt nervous and stumbled over his words, scarcely able to speak. This was the woman he most feared. How should he address her? Mrs. Ajiang or Mrs. Aling?

"Ahan, would you like to come in and sit down? Why are you just standing there?"

"I . . . Where is brother Aling?" He wanted to see Aling right away. He would feel better after he saw him.

"My brother Aling and the others have gone to Great Lake for a month."

"The others?"

"My brother Aling, Shunmei, and the two children of my brother Ajiang."

So she wasn't Aling's wife. Was she the widow of his older brother?

They chatted politely for a bit, then Ahan left. He had considered taking the road to Miaoli upon leaving Stone Walls, but on his way he ran into a group of people headed for the mountains. Why not return to Great Lake with some company? he thought. He would be able to see Aling that very evening. It was decided. At Great Lake he bought a catty of wine, some dried bean curd, some peas, and dried fish. He even bought some candy for the children.

Leaving the village at Great Lake, he followed the valley to Kiln Corner. To his left was a luxuriant wood of camphor trees bathed in the beautiful light of the westering sun. There was a row of five camphor kilns, behind which rose a mountain. And there was that huge, strange tree, the hanging tree, looking as monstrous as ever.

"Hey, isn't that brother Ahan?" It was Aling who was shouting.

A man suddenly stepped out from behind one of the camphor kilns. He didn't bother taking the small winding path but made a beeline straight for Ahan, ignoring the undergrowth and creepers that came up to his waist.

"Careful, Aling!" shouted Ahan as he stepped forward to meet him.

"Ahan! Ahan! you're here. You're really here," said Aling.

Ahan suddenly felt his eyes grow moist and his nose tickle. He quickly lowered his head. Aling grasped him firmly by the shoulder and also lowered his head. Ahan was embarrassed by his excessive emotions and weakness. He was afraid that Aling might laugh at him. In any case, he was reluctant to show his feelings, and did his best to suppress them.

The two of them, arm in arm and shoulder to shoulder, made their way to the third kiln.

"How are the children?"

"They are at Fanzai Wood," said Aling, raising his voice. "I was just going to fetch you."

"Why?" he asked wryly. "Is there a good job here?"

"Yes, there is; it's great."

There were three other workmen at the kiln. They were all around forty and experts at their work. Only Aling was new on the job. Aling showed them the food and wine that Ahan had brought. They greeted the new arrival with smiles.

"What's so great? Anything for me?"

"It's a long story," said Aling suddenly. "Why don't we go to Fanzai Wood?"

Ahan couldn't help laughing. Aling had changed a great deal. He used to be such an emotional and impetuous man. Could he have changed so much in just six months? Ahan actually felt calmer seeing Aling in such a state of restless exhilaration. He told him that whatever it was, it had to wait until after they had had the food and drink. After all, he hadn't had a bite to eat since his morning porridge.

But they had no chance to talk after eating. The camphor was being distilled and the kiln had to be refired three times. In the first half of the night, one man had to sit in front of the furnace and stoke it with firewood. In the second half of the night, the fire was allowed to slowly go out.

In the middle of the camphor kiln was a square platform five feet high and seven or eight feet across. A four-foot-high cauldron was set into this platform. A steamer, the base of which was a metal sieve, was set on top of the cauldron. The steamer was a cone-shaped affair made of wooden slats and about eight feet in height.

To make camphor oil, the large blocks of camphor wood had to be whittled into small chips by hatchet-wielding workers. The chipping process was time consuming. Since there was one firing each shift, this meant that the chipping went on day and night without stop. Three or four workers were assigned to each kiln, but even so the work was hard and few people were willing to tackle it.

Once the camphor wood was chipped, it was poured into the steamer, and one worker had to climb in and tread it down to fit as much wood in as possible. The lid was then shut. A fire had to be lit to boil the water in the large cauldron, which would send the scalding steam into the steamer to extract the oil from the wood chips. On the side of the steamer, about a foot below the top, was attached a bamboo or metal tube. The oil-laden steam would rise and flow out through the tube and down to a tank a few feet away. The tank contained clear mountain spring water. The steam passed through the tube that curled like a snake through the tank of cool water. The cooled steam passed out of the tube as a liquid into leather containers. The leather containers had two spouts. The camphor oil flowed out of the upper spout into clay jars; waste water was drained out of the larger, lower spout. The waste water was still warm and made excellent bath water, because insects would avoid anyone who bathed in it.

Once the batch was done, the steamer lid was opened, allowing the remaining steam to evaporate. Then a door in the base of the steamer was opened and the steamed wood was raked out with a special five-pronged rake. By the end of the shift, all four workers were covered in sweat. By the time they finished bathing, it was pitch black save for the blood-red flames in the kiln furnace. The chips left over after the steaming were used as fuel. The air was heavy with the smell of camphor. From the peaks behind the kilns were heard the cries of gibbons, owls, and pheasants.

Some weeks earlier, the people of Fanzai Wood had seen four strangers in the fields. They were gesticulating and measuring the terraced paddies and fields. The people were at a loss in the face of this unusual event. They hastily informed Xu Shihui, the nominal head of the village. When he heard the news, Xu's usually ruddy face went ashen white. Xu followed the others to the field.

"Gentlemen, may I ask who you are? Are you officials?" asked Xu, his voice trembling.

"Master Ye Atian sent us," the visitors replied coolly.

Master Ye Atian was one of the settlers in the Great Lake area who had received official tenure for land. But the land in Fanzai Wood belonged to the indigenous people. By what right had they come to survey other people's land?

"Gentlemen, excuse me, but this is not part of Master Atian's estate. I must ask you to stop your surveying," said Xu, panting heavily.

"Who said it's not? Master Atian has obtained official permission to cultivate the area around Fanzai Wood."

"Little Southside is included," said another.

"No, no. This land is our livelihood. We have poured our sweat and blood into it. It has cost us lives. No one . . ."

"What are you saying, you old fool?"

"I'm saying that I represent the people of Fanzai Wood. You can cut off our heads, but you can't take our land. Never!" Xu became more agitated as he spoke, scarcely realizing that he was striking his chest, preparing for a fight.

"Oh no? Are you bandits?"

"Only those who take the land of others are bandits."

"Hey, do you have tenure on this land?" asked another.

"What tenure?" asked Peng Aqiang.

"Ha, ha, you don't even know what tenure is. It's a official certificate that gives you the rights to a piece of land."

"If you don't have tenure, then you are just squatters. Squatters have no rights to the land."

"Nonsense! We have an oral agreement with the indigenous people to cultivate this land. What do you mean by squatting? Who cares?" Having had his say, Peng Aqiang felt a pain to the roots of his teeth.

"Do you obey the indigenous people, or do you obey the Emperor of the great Qing dynasty?"

Master Atian's people departed. The hearts of Xu and all the people of Fanzai Wood had been dealt a blow. They had sweated blood, survived on the worst of diets, and eked out a livelihood, and were even prepared to sacrifice themselves for a pitiful inch of land. But now, faced with officials who held their fates in the palms of their hands, they felt fear and helplessness. Everyone asked Master Xu Shihui to think of a solution.

Thus, with one change of underwear, Xu set off for Great Lake, then to the government office, and then to Miaoli. After several days, he found a way: they would have to apply for land tenure. Only after they had received tenure patents from the government would their land be safe. With five pieces of silver, a hefty sum contributed by the eight families at Fanzai Wood, Xu was able to ascertain that Master Atian had not yet obtained a land tenure patent.

The eight households—the Fans and Xies had arrived after the Pengs—then decided that Xu Shihui's name should go on the land patent. But they still had to find a captain of the guard. Xu himself was too old, and none of the younger men had any experience. It was for this reason that Aling was so anxious to get hold of Ahan.

"Brother Aling, you must be joking!" exclaimed Ahan as he burst out laughing.

"No, not at all. That's the idea we came up with after many days of consideration."

The qualifications required for being a captain of the guard were that a person be honest and hard-working and have an unblemished past. He also had to be a family man, be familiar with military duty, and know about life in the mountains. He also had to be young.

Ahan, a penniless young man, wondered if he was really qualified. He had no family, no wife. Thinking about the situation, he laughed.

"You are more or less qualified," said Aling. Lowering his voice, he continued: "If we get you a wife, then you'll have a family."

Ahan laughed so hard he could hardly catch his breath, and tears ran down his cheeks. Aling gave him a serious look until he stopped laughing. Then he told him something Ahan never dreamed of hearing. At first he thought Aling was just having fun with him, but gradually he listened to what his friend was saying. He was left speechless and somewhat confused.

The next day they hurried off to Fanzai Wood. Only Qinmei had been left at home to take care of all the children. The Peng family had mobilized to cultivate the newly opened fields. Before they could receive official title to the land, they had to do their best to improve it. Only if they made improvements would things work out in their favor. They had to have proof for their claims. On account of this, the eight families at Fanzai Wood had spent the last two weeks taking precautions against the indigenous people, chopping down trees, and opening new land for cultivation. They constantly put their lives on the line.

Ahan and Aling walked over to the newly opened fields to have a look. Seeing that Ahan still looked somewhat dazed, Aling sighed.

"Ahan, what a state you are in. I'm sorry. We had better go. Go home and think about it for a few days, and then come back." Aling smiled regretfully. "It's my fault, I should have given you some time to think it over."

"I have no family; you are my only family."

Aling thought seriously for a long time before speaking. "I can't decide for you. If it were me, I wouldn't dare accept; on the other hand, if I were Liu Ahan, I would."

"I can do guard duty, even fight for my life." Ahan shook his head. "What I mean is . . ."

After a pause, Aling again told him that the Pengs were willing to give him their youngest daughter for his wife. She could live with him in their own place, or he could live with the Pengs and throw his lot in with them. If he chose to set up on his own, then his wages for the first year as captain of the guard would be paid to the Pengs to pay the bride price in installments.

"Weimei isn't quite right in the head, is she?"

"She's simple-minded. Well, for a woman that's not a bad thing, and she is pretty."

"I don't want a half-wit for a wife." After a long, embarrassed pause, Ahan suggested that the foster daughter might do.

"No, that won't work. Don't you know about Renxiu's death?"

"I'm suggesting her because I do know it."

"He was done to death by her. The woman can't be a wife to any man."

According to Aling, the Pengs had decided to give Dengmei to Ahan, but Aling had opposed the match to keep his friend from marrying a woman with an evil fate. It was commonly known that Peng Renxing was to marry Xu Azhi, but old Xu had demanded that Renxing live in their house for three years. Naturally, the Pengs were not happy about losing the most productive member of the family. As a result, both families were upset. After Renxiu died, the Pengs let it be known that they would like to exchange Dengmei for Azhi, an idea that the Xus strenuously rejected. Later the Xus considered taking the half-wit, Weimei. At that point the possibility of Ahan taking the position arose, but because Aling had opposed the match with Dengmei, the marriage exchange idea was dropped.

"Brother Aling, do you really think a woman can do her husband in?" asked Ahan, his gaze fixed on Aling. There was a strange look in his eyes, and a fleeting smile passed over his lips. Aling was confused and felt a bit uneasy.

"Fate exists; it's undeniable. Why would you want to tempt fate for a woman who can harm you?"

"You can't say that about a foster daughter."

Aling was taken aback.

"A person can't be born just to do someone else harm."

"That's fate."

"Heaven would never intend such a thing."

At a loss for words, Aling stared at him.

"If a person were to have such a fate, heaven would never allow them to be born."

Aling decided that he himself would tell Peng Aqiang of Ahan's intentions. After Aling left, Ahan's agitated mind calmed. He was surprised by his own readiness to express his true desires, and wondered where he got the courage. He wondered if he really had any doubts, or if they had arisen due to Aling's comments. Perhaps he had made up his mind long ago.

Don't pretend to be an idiot, he told himself, you've wanted her ever since you laid eyes on her. He laughed with embarrassment.

At noon, Peng Aqiang made a special trip home to have lunch with some guests. After the meal of dried potato and bamboo shoot soup, Peng Aqiang took them to see Xu Shihui. Xu was not at home, so the three men sat down in a cool spot to talk.

"Did you quit your job, Ahan?"

"Yes, they took my name off the rolls."

Then they discussed the duties of the captain of the guard. They concluded that there was no one else suited for the job.

"Be the captain of our guard. You can choose three other guards."

"You mean I can recruit outside?"

"No, choose them from the village. They will all be part-time, because they will have other responsibilities. All the families will provide them with something. You will be the only one working full-time."

Then they discussed the marriage. Peng Aqiang said, "There are legal obligations that have to be met." At this, Ahan relaxed a bit. Peng Aqiang seemed to be considering the situation like any other business. "Aling told me about your wishes this morning—I don't foresee any problems."

"I mean, is there any other way?" Ahan suddenly felt his cheeks flush. "You all know me—I don't have a penny to my name."

"Are you still going on about that?" Peng Aqiang turned to Aling. "Haven't you cleared things up with him?"

"I have, Ahan; all you have to do is choose the girl you want."

In silence, Ahan look beseechingly at Aling.

"You mean Dengmei?"

Peng Aqiang heaved a sigh as he spoke. "Fine, you can marry Dengmei."

"Marry in the proper way?"

"Sure. We'll even help you build a house nearby."

Then they began to discuss the work involved in building a house. Aling readily promised to undertake the task. He also decided to give up working at the camphor kilns and settle there too.

"That's great, Aling! I've been hoping you would for a long time," said Peng Aqiang. Aling was happy, but as soon as they touched on the issue of the location for the house, Peng knit his brows. "There is less and less land every day."

"I'm not sure I want to till the land."

"Then what do you want to do?"

"Pick palm leaves, cut rattan, and fish for shrimp and crayfish."

Peng Aqiang was against the idea. Ahan suggested that they both take up duties as guards, but Aling was unwilling. In the end, they decided to settle and occupy as much land as possible. They figured it would be pretty easy to find some hilly land on the steeper slopes of Upper Fanzai Wood to live off of. Otherwise, they could rent a piece of land from Xu Shihui or Chen Afa that would keep them in potatoes until they decided.

They also decided that Ahan and Aling would build a house together, with each family occupying one half. They would share the use of the kitchen and washroom. Once the plans were made, the discussion was ended.

As the sun set, Peng Aqiang led them off to the left of the village, over a grayish-brown outcropping of rock, and along a path to the southeast.

The path was the one used by the Tabeilai villagers when they went out on the warpath. The outcropping was the boundary marker between Little Southside and the aboriginal lands.

Although most of the indigenous people of the area were sinicized, they were still under the sway of Tabeilai village. Little Southside lay by a river and a small path. Three latecomers had planted pumpkins and gourds there and later vegetable plots. There were also a field of buckwheat and some potato patches.

Peng Aqiang's intentions were clear: although there was danger from the indigenous people, the land would be safe from grasping settlers. Peng Aqiang explained to them that this was the kind of place where Ahan and Aling could get a piece of land.

The Peng family stopped working only when darkness had fallen. Lanmei, like the rest of them, wore a black sash around her waist and a palm-leaf hat, and carried a machete. One could not tell if she were a man or a woman, and certainly no one would have guessed she was an old woman. As the Peng family came together, there was no sign of Dengmei.

"I saw her in the kitchen," Aling whispered to Ahan.

The cassia bamboo torches had been lit. The evening meal, which still consisted mainly of potatoes, simmered in a pot with some beet sugar. There was also sweet potato soup to replenish them after their long, hot day. The Pengs made a point of treating the two men like honored guests: a dish of shredded turnips and egg and a plate of beans with dried fish were also produced.

"I'm sharing in your glory," said Aling, winking at Ahan. Dengmei carried in a huge pot of soup and quietly tiptoed back to the kitchen. The pot was filled with greens in broth.

Dengmei's face was red, perhaps as a result of working over the stove. As she came out of the kitchen, her lips were open slightly; her eyes were half shut and her eyelashes motionless. When she turned to go back to the kitchen, it was as if neither her eyes nor her neck had moved.

The meal was eaten in silence. Aling seemed to be the only one talking. Renhua was usually the most talkative, Renxing was usually ready to chime in, and Weimei always giggled like a half-wit. But that night there was none of that. Ahan observed their faces. Indeed, the whole family, young and old, all seemed to be behaving quite formally. There was no other movement except for eating. Their faces were all expressionless. Strangely, all the small children were also silent.

Ahan trembled; the atmosphere in the room made him nervous. He was also tired, and then there was Renxiu's death. He thought about death. What was a man's life? What was there to life but the worries of earning a living, conflicts with others, unavoidable matters no one asked for, and the elusiveness of things desired? His views were beginning to change: when a man died, perhaps he had nothing, but he left behind many things without shape or form. Life was full of worries, responsibilities, and helplessness. He had managed to avoid most of that, but now that Renxiu had died, was he to take his place?

As he ate, he decided to take a close look at Dengmei. The truth was that he had never had a good look at her. But strangely, ever since he first met her, he always thought of her when he considered his own life. He always thought of her vulnerable expression. However, after his talk with Aling, he was no longer able to visualize her; whenever he tried, she disappeared. And now the entire Peng family was there before his eyes, all but Dengmei. It wasn't fair.

Had she eaten? Perhaps not. What if there was nothing left for her? That should never happen—even a foster daughter is a human being. He thought of how well he would treat her. Indeed, Dengmei was nearly his. After that, she'd no longer be a foster daughter; instead, she would receive the respect due a married woman. He was pleased with these thoughts and grew more satisfied with his decision.

Xu Shihui arrived just as they were clearing the table, and soon they were joined by Xu Shixing, Su Ajin, and Chen Afa. As they discussed the matter of land tenure, Fan Qian and Xie Atan hurried in. Fan and Xie were both tanned and robust farmers just thirty years old. The room couldn't hold the eight family heads as well as Peng's three sons and Ahan and Aling. The room seemed about to burst.

It was decided unanimously that Xu Shihui was to apply for the land patent under his name and that Liu Ahan was to become captain of the guard. The sum and method of payment for the captain were quickly decided upon. Liu Ahan didn't have much say in the matter; at any rate, he had decided that if the pay was enough for him and Dengmei to live on, he wouldn't make a fuss. Everyone else had probably come to a similar conclusion. Ahan just focused on the discussion of the various other problems.

From their conversation, Ahan gradually learned about the acquisition and taxation of land in Taiwan. In the past, the land of Taiwan had been held in common by the civilized and uncivilized indigenous people, and by law was considered "uncultivated land without owners." When Koxinga took Taiwan, his clan and followers, both civil and military, were officially awarded land. In the early days, under the Qing government in China, people were prohibited from crossing to Taiwan, but it was an empty edict. Beginning in the mid-Qing there was a change of policy: the government actually encouraged people to go and open up the land. That was the origin of the land tenure system. Apart from the official lands that were passed on, those who obtained land patents were the first to legally own land in Taiwan. But they did not actually have to till the land themselves; they could recruit farmers to do it for them. Thus tenant farmers emerged. In the beginning, then, the actual tillers of the soil were tenant farmers while the land patent recipients were the landlords. That's how the feudal system came into being on Taiwan.

By law, the tenant farmer had to pay a certain amount of his crops in tithes. If a tenant prospered or a landlord fell on hard times, property rights could be sold or mortgaged. As such, a landlord's direct connection to a piece of land often grew more tenuous. In turn, a tenant farmer who prospered could lease land to other farmers and in this way eventually become a landowner himself. Those who rented farmland from other tenant farmers were referred to as sharecroppers. Thus one piece of land could be used by three groups of people—landlords, tenant farmers, and sharecroppers—paying two kinds of rent. As far as the government was concerned, the landlord was ultimately responsible for all taxes, regardless of what kind of private arrangements he had made with others. If he could not pay the taxes due, he might be forced to mortgage his land.

The feuds between families at that time were largely between land patent holders and resulted from struggles for land. The tenant farmers and sharecroppers had no choice but to side with the landlords. The power of major Taiwanese families was greater than that of typical landlord families in mainland China.

Once Fanzai Wood had a land patent holder, the status of the families as squatters on idle lands would become that of tenant farmers. Fan and Xie barely cultivated enough land to feed their families. They would most likely become tenant farmers on Xu Shihui's land, which was considerable, or become sharecroppers, paying rent to other tenant farmers. If Huang Aling and Liu Ahan were to settle there, they too would face the same fate.

Chen Afa was related to Master Ye Atian and would probably be able to look after the recently opened fields on behalf of his relative. Therefore, he was not very enthusiastic about the village plan for obtaining a land patent.

For the other seven families, the advantages and disadvantages were equally balanced, especially for the latecomers like the Pengs, Fans, and Xies, and perhaps even Ahan and Aling. All had the same ultimate goal of complete independence. In the end they decided in favor of the plan and to complete the process as quickly as possible. However, they insisted on three conditions. First, Xu Shihui had to draw up an individual contract with each family stipulating that he as land patent holder would not seek to collect rents from the families that farmed the land and that the families would pay the taxes on the lands they cultivated. Second, they would draw up a contract for sharing the expenses for the captain and the guards. Third, they all agreed to go to the temple of Guan Ti, the god of war, at Great Lake Village and swear that if any one of them should act to the detriment of the others and go against the agreements, the god would punish them by depriving them of descendants and by striking them dead with lightning. And so their meeting was brought to a successful conclusion.

*L*ove

*W*ork started on the house for Ahan and Aling and their families on a small plot of land between the Pengs and the Sus. One member from each of the Peng, Su, and Xu families was dispatched to help.

The Pengs had built a pigsty near their threshing ground and directly across from the house Ahan and Aling were building. It had been a big step for the Pengs, because any family with a place in society had to keep pigs. One day, as Dengmei was carrying a pail of pig swill out to the sty, Ahan spotted her.

He tried not to look at her but couldn't help himself. Her slight figure dressed in gray was always there before his eyes. Even when he closed his eyes and shook his head, her slim figure remained. Dengmei was feeding the pigs. Her head lowered, she watched as the piglets greedily gobbled down the food. She always felt that many eyes were fixed on her, all of them reproving, contemptuous, and ill-intentioned.

The previous morning, Lanmei had curtly told her of her upcoming marriage. Dengmei was confused and bewildered for a long time. Although Qinmei and Shunmei had already informed her, she thought they had been joking with her for their own amusement. She had been mocked enough recently to make her immune to it. But Lanmei was telling her that it was indeed true. In a whole year, Lanmei had not uttered so many words to Dengmei, much less consulted with her about anything.

It can't be true, perhaps they're just ... thought Dengmei, desperately trying to clarify things to herself, to find the real meaning behind those words. *If it is true, it will never happen,* was her first thought. It was clear that she was going to be a married woman from the Peng family and no longer a foster daughter. It would be a change for the better, but such changes had never been Dengmei's lot in life. She did prefer Ahan to Renxiu, and she would be marrying outside of the Peng family—it was too good to be true.

"Dengmei, you can help your sister-in-law at home for the next few days," said Lanmei in a friendly tone of voice. "There's no need for you to go up in the mountains."

"I ought to go work in the fields," she insisted. Ever since Renxiu's death, Lanmei had glared at her and scolded her through clenched teeth. Not once did she have a kind word.

"Idiot! Once the house is built, you'll be married. Don't you want to get some rest?"

"There's no need. I can work in the fields."

Lanmei heaved a sigh and looked closely at her for a long time. Her expression was kind and friendly, something Dengmei was not accustomed to. It was the same expression she wore when speaking to Renxiu, Defu, and Dexin. Dengmei had seen it only from a distance; it had never been directed at her. But that was only natural; after all, she was just a foster daughter, someone who had been purchased. Therefore, her foster mother's behavior left her at a loss.

She suddenly felt warm all over and trembled. She wanted to rush forward and seize her foster mother's hand or fall into her arms.

"Dengmei, you're crying. What's the matter?" Lanmei was taken aback, and her expression changed to one of indifference. Dengmei gave a start and shuddered. She felt she had been too presumptuous. Once again, she lowered her head and assumed an air of timid obedience.

"Witch!" grunted Lanmei. Her expression changed from indifference to anger and disgust. She turned and walked away.

Why was her foster mother like that? Would she never understand? Was it always to be an issue without resolution? But there was an answer; the mistrust had always been there, and she herself had already accepted it. But she could not rid herself of that feeling of resentment, even when she was consciously aware of it. And so it went, back and forth, round and round, never ceasing.

I'm only eighteen, she would think to herself. A widow at eighteen? But whatever happened, she would never acknowledge that Renxiu was her husband. Her foster mother and sisters-in-law had indicated that she belonged to Renxiu and that she had been responsible for his death. Now she was Renxiu's wife—widow. I'm not a widow, she thought, and her gentle, timid heart began to swell with courage. It was as if she were looking for a fight, but with no one but herself.

She recalled what had happened the night before the third weekly ritual after Renxiu's death. It was an evening like those preceding the first and second rituals. Standing before his grave, dressed in her hemp mourning garments and hat and holding three sticks of incense, she had implored the departed soul to return. "Renxiu, Renxiu, get up! Renxiu, it's the third week, you must return!"

At Renxiu's grave, she bowed and "called his soul." Xu Rixing had taught her, and after imitating her foster mother, she learned quite quickly how to do it properly. Renxiu had died after reaching adulthood, so someone had to burn incense for him. Since he had no children, his wife had to call his soul home. Without a wedding ceremony, her status in the family had been fixed. "Renxiu, turn the corner, take care. Renxiu, cross the bridge, take care. Renxiu, climb the slope, turn the corner, don't fall. Renxiu, you are home, don't step on the threshold, come in."

From within the house came the sound of weeping. Her chest felt so constricted that she could scarcely breathe. As she took a breath, she too wailed. Why was she crying? Was she sad? Did she feel grief? Was she resentful? Was she afraid? Perhaps it was all of these feelings, perhaps none. She developed a fever that lasted several days, and she couldn't stop coughing. Before dinner she sat in front of the stove dozing. She knew she needed a long quiet sleep if she were to get better. But she couldn't lie down; all she could do was lean against the wall and doze.

"Dengmei, it's time to light the incense."

The soft sound of sobbing continued to be heard from the main room. Several smoking sticks of incense had already been placed in the bamboo incense burner. Dengmei hurried forward, lit three sticks, and, holding them before her, knelt and kowtowed nine times. Then she stepped back and stood in a corner of the room.

"Dengmei," said Lanmei in a clear voice, "tonight you must sleep in Renxiu's room, in his bed."

After Renxiu died, her foster mother insisted that she must spend the night in the "bridal chamber" and sleep in Renxiu's bed. Dengmei didn't have the courage for that; nor did she have the courage to say no. She could only hide in the kitchen and lie near the stove as everyone else went to bed. Her "improper" act was discovered and resulted in a severe scolding, but no one forced her to stay in Renxiu's room. However, that night Lanmei was insistent.

"Dengmei, did you hear me?"

"Yes, but I'm afraid."

"Afraid? Afraid of your husband?" Lanmei then ordered everyone to go to bed early. "Off to bed. If you hear footsteps or some other sound, don't make a fuss. Just watch quietly."

"What are we going to do?" asked the half-wit, Weimei.

No one answered her, but Renhua's wife whispered to Dengmei, "Don't go to sleep. He'll come back at the end of the third week. If you go to sleep, you will surely see him." Spirits of the dead always manifested themselves at the end of the third week.

"Oh!?" Dengmei's eyes grew round with fear.

"You won't do it? Are you afraid?" The pain in Lanmei's heart turned to anger. "Those who ought to die, don't. Renxiu will appear tonight. He'll appear. He'll seize you and kill you!"

"Ma . . ."

"Enough, enough of such goings-on," said Peng Aqiang, stamping his foot and glaring at everyone.

"Cry? You dare to cry? Your crying will be the death of the Peng family." Lanmei herself was in tears now. "Get in there, get in there this minute!"

"I can't."

Peng Aqiang could no longer tolerate his wife's behavior. Renjie also intervened. In the face of such opposition, Lanmei became even more distraught. No one could stop her as she forcefully shoved Dengmei into the bridal chamber.

Already feverish, Dengmei could not cope with the situation any longer. Everything went black, and she collapsed in a heap in the doorway.

When she came to, it was pitch dark all around. A faint light could be seen from the slatted bamboo window. A wave of despair swept over her and tears flowed down her face.

I must be lying in Renxiu's bed, she thought. She recalled the entire scene just before she fainted. Strangely, she now felt no fear, as if her fainting spell had changed everything. Her poor foster mother, she thought. Each time after Dengmei was beaten and the pain had subsided, she would feel nothing but pity for Lanmei. She only had to see her foster parents' grief and she would feel sad herself, and guilty. Maybe Renxiu really will appear any moment now, she thought. Hadn't he told everyone before he died that she was not to blame and that they shouldn't persecute her? She knew if he were to appear, she would see him. From the look in his eyes before he died, she knew that he did not hate her and perhaps actually loved her, just a little. If he appeared, maybe he would take her with him. Living was so hard; everyone suffered. If she went with Renxiu, perhaps there would be an end to the pain. As she considered the idea, her fear vanished, replaced by a mysterious sense of longing and hope, a hope that he really would come and take her away. But all was still. Time seemed to move like the wind over the grass, coming in waves and disappearing, leaving nothing.

Lanmei's admonition was still fresh in her mind: "If anyone wants to die, do so far away. Don't pollute this place." Peng Aqiang had also told everyone that if they no longer wished to go on living they should leave and die far away where no one could find their body. It looked as if Renxiu was not going to appear that night. Could it be that her calls had been inadequate? Perhaps his soul had lost its way. She decided that she would find it herself. She was determined to take her own life. The vague idea of suicide must have been in the back of her mind for years, but after Renxiu's death, for which she had been blamed, it had been brought to the forefront. But she thought of death with a mixture of fear and trepidation. At the bottom of her heart she realized that a huge gulf separated the idea and the fact. She had considered the idea of death to take her mind off the persecution.

She sat up on the bed and remembered that there was a mirror on the wall. With no light, there would be no reflections except those of spirits and ghosts. She knew that Renxiu's spirit would not appear that night. She felt something was missing, but she also felt as though she had achieved a small victory. She rubbed her face with both hands and touched her disheveled hair. The meager plaits of her dry hair had come undone, so she pulled off the ribbon and let her hair hang down.

I expect ghosts must look the way I do, she thought, smiling. She pushed open the door and went down to the threshing ground. The sliver of a new moon was hanging from the branch of a tree. Even in early summer the nights were still cold. She heard a fox bark behind the house. Foxes were spooky animals. She seemed to smell their musky scent and broke out in goose bumps, which were a sign of fear; but her fear was tinged with a certain pleasure, strangely alluring. After a moment of hesitation, she pulled open the gate and stepped out. She walked down the slope and paused for a moment in front of the temple. Putting her hands together, she bowed several times. For no apparent reason, tears welled up in her eyes and flowed down her cheeks.

"God and goddess of the earth, protect my foster parents and make them successful," she said. "Protect my mother, whom I've never seen, and my father, wherever he is. Dengmei is leaving, please guide my spirit." She clearly heard the gods grunt in assent. She averted her eyes at the graveyard, and she did not have Renxiu in mind. Leaving the path, she stepped into the river and headed toward the deep pool.

Suddenly, she heard shouts from behind her. She gave a start and waded on. The sliver of the moon was just in front of her, at her feet. The new moon seemed to waver in the corner of the sky. She was determined to head toward the dark sky. Behind her the shouts grew louder and louder, mixed with the sound of a shrill, scolding voice. Her mind was clear, and she knew that all she had to do was clench her teeth and jump with all her might toward the moon.

In the end she was rescued. Apart from the Pengs, no one else knew about the incident. From then on Dengmei was kept locked in the bridal chamber.

She was going to be married. Liu Ahan really did exist, and he wasn't far off. He was young and good-looking. She had heard that he too was an orphan. There was nothing wrong with that; it was a perfect match. He was so handsome. And how could she, a young woman, steal looks at him and even think about the marriage bed? Her cheeks flushed and her heart leaped. She felt what could only be called a sweet feeling. Never in her life had she experienced anything like it. Suddenly the breeze felt cool, the sky high, and the earth broad; her surroundings were delightful. But how could such good fortune be hers? She was once again overcome with fear and despondency.

The new house was completed in six days. Ahan helped Aling bring some furniture from Stone Walls. As soon as they came through the gate, they realized something was not right. The children were all out of sight and the main room was full of people. Xu Shihui, Xu Rixing, Su Ajin, Peng Aqiang, and his wife were all there, and apparently they were quarreling about something. A man was sitting motionless under a group of lu trees in the gully to the left of the house. They couldn't make out his features, because the sun had already dropped behind the hills and everything was fairly dark, but his burly figure told them that it was probably Peng Renxing.

"What's the matter with Renxing?"

"Go and ask him yourself." Shunmei giggled mischievously.

"Stop monkeying around and tell me," said Aling, a bit cross. "Does it have something to do with young Azhi?"

Aling motioned with his head to Ahan that they should go ask him. As soon as they had walked out the gate and taken a few steps, Renxing suddenly seemed aware of them. He waved at them, turned, and leaped down the gully through the long grass.

"Hey, Renxing! Renxing!" But Renxing paid no heed and plowed on through the long, thick grass. The underbrush there consisted mainly of couch grass, long, swordlike leaves with serrated edges that easily cut a man's exposed hands or feet. Renxing ignored the slashing leaves and charged on. He felt the tingling sensation from the leaves as they swept across his face and neck, followed by a searing pain. He seemed more like a wild boar, angry and desperate after being wounded. He wanted to yell and to laugh, but a huge weight pressed down on his chest. He could only charge through the grass and roll around in it until his misery passed.

Had what happened between himself and Azhi been a crime? Was such a relationship prohibited because they were not married? Wasn't it all the same? It was all the same, it was! The more he thought about it, the angrier he became. He tried to dispel his worries with anger. True, he was bad. He had let his parents down; he had let his family down by doing something so disgraceful. How could he ever look anyone in the eye again? And Azhi? As soon as he thought of Azhi, his heart ached all the more. When word got out, how would Azhi cope?

Was she all right? Had they tied her up? Azhi, that delightful girl. Her image was chiseled in his heart, every little detail was there, clear and precise. Her slim figure, her slender hands and feet, her fine skin so unlike that of a girl who labored in the sun and wind all year long. But her ruddy health seemed to shine through her delicate nature.

The first time he saw her, she had her back to him. He found that lithe figure in coarse clothing pleasurable to look at. He broke out in a sweat unlike any he had experienced. His whole body trembled. It was precisely at that moment that she had turned around. Their eyes met instantly. He found hers beautiful and strong, filled with an untamed spirit.

"Good morning," he had said, thrown off guard.

"Good morning. Your name is Renxing, isn't it?" She actually said his name.

"Yes, that's me. What's your name?"

"Xu Zhimei, Azhi." She laughed in that clear, sparkling way of hers. From that moment on, he was lost. He longed for her, painfully and in secret.

It was easy for hearts to meet in the mountains. Gradually they fell in love, bitter and sweet. Sex between young people before marriage was considered immoral. Their meetings were soon discovered and they were forbidden to see each other, but all in vain. Soon the two families tried to arrange a marriage exchange, but they were unable to come to terms. Azhi and Renxing didn't want to break off. She was scolded, beaten, and kept at home. Renxing was warned to keep his distance.

That afternoon, what had been feared occurred. A violent storm had arisen and rain had fallen unabated for about an hour. The mountain streams swelled and flooded the low-lying fields that had recently been cultivated. No more work could be done that day, so most everyone had gone home in the rain. Renxing remained behind to keep an eye on the flooded fields. At about four, the storm ceased and the rain-washed vegetation glistened under the sun and the clear blue sky.

Renxing was lying in the wet grass. He had removed his wet shirt, and the grass transmitted a cool, prickling sensation to his back. He suddenly felt a part of the earth, as if he too were planted there in the soil. That bundle of sensations known as Renxing had melted away into the chaos of nature.

After that, everything was like a dream. In those days his dreams were his only source of pleasure. In them he always met Azhi. Face to face with her, he was always wooden and silent; he felt dull and stupid, unable to speak. Azhi said she understood him, understood his heart. That was enough. But he hated himself for his inability to talk. In dreams all his difficulties were resolved. He was fluent and bold, doing forbidden things.

Azhi appeared once again in his dream. Her clothes were dry. She must have slipped out after the rain. She smiled at him fondly. He beckoned to her. After a moment of hesitation, she approached and gently pressed herself against his chest. Her movement was entirely natural because whenever they met these days, they would spontaneously move toward each other, but as soon as they touched they would step back, blushing furiously. This time, though, Azhi also seemed to be in a trance. It really was a dream—no wonder she pressed herself against him for such a long time. She was so warm and felt so good against him. I don't have my shirt on, he thought in alarm.

Oh no. One morning while Renjie and his wife were making potash, Renxing had seen them at their games on the ground in the open air. The sight was indelibly etched in his mind. At the time, he had moved away, then come back for another look. As he thought of that scene, his body trembled.

"Don't," Azhi cried tenderly.

"Azhi, will you marry me?" he said, his throat dry.

"Yes."

"Now, Azhi, marry me now."

"Now? How can I marry you now?" He could not see her; how shy she had become. It wasn't right that she was on top of him. How could a woman be on top of a man? It didn't look right; his brother and her wife didn't do it like that. Azhi turned and lay on the ground beside him, her eyes tightly shut, her face flushed the color of the setting sun. He was both confused and excited, very excited. Azhi seemed to be trying to stop him, but her voice was so weak. She couldn't be heard above the raging mountain torrent.

"Renxing, you . . ."

"Azhi, it's all right."

"Renxing."

"Azhi, I love you."

Suddenly the vegetation near them began to move; it was a strong wind, no doubt. It was not the wind. The sound of footsteps could be heard approaching, and there were curses and oaths. Stones began to fly; one hit his shoulder. Then the sticks began to fall on him. He did not defend himself. Heavy blows fell on his chest and back, but he did not defend himself. His only thought was to let them beat him to death.

In the end, he was taken to Xu Shihui's house. He was the "trophy" taken by the Xu brothers in their "hunt." The old man was very calm; he put an end to his sons' violent behavior and untied the ropes that bound Renxing. Xu then went in search of Xu Rixing and Su Ajin; they would then go together to the Pengs' for a talk. Renxing had already decided to abide by whatever decision was reached.

Out of necessity, the Xus and the Pengs now had to come to some sort of agreement. It was decided that Renxing would live with the Xus for two years and work for them. His two years of free labor would count as the bride price; after that, he and his wife would be allowed to return to the Pengs. At first Peng Aqiang held out, wishing instead to exchange Weimei for Azhi, but the Xus would not agree. Xu made it quite clear that he would not exchange his clever daughter for a half-wit, and that they would never admit an idiot into their home. They were all the more adamant because their second son's wife was somewhat slow in the head. She had borne three sons and two daughters, but the third son was just like his mother. Also, under no circumstances would the Xus take Dengmei, because it was universally acknowledged that she had been responsible for Renxiu's death. Moreover, Dengmei had already been promised to Ahan, who was to become the captain of the guard. There was no room for complications in that area.

"My son Renxing can live in no man's house except his father's," said Lanmei, her voice trembling.

"Then what do you suggest?" There was no other way out. If an agreement could not be reached, Renxing would be driven out of the village, and that would be wrong too.

"You are not being fair to your Azhi," said Peng Aqiang.

"For the sake of this shameless, impudent . . ." Xu Shihui's anger flared again.

"All right, all right! What is the point of everybody getting bent out of shape," Xu Rixing intervened. "In any event, two years in a wife's home never did anyone any harm. Renxing is as strong as an ox, and he can do a lot in two years. As for the Pengs, they will just be lending their ox for two years, and then they'll get him back, leading a cow and perhaps a couple of calves. Ha, ha!"

"Rest assured that I won't keep the calves and they will not bear the surname Xu."

"Brother Aqiang, you'll be much better off when that day comes."

Thus it was decided. But the Pengs were left in a serious position. How were they to make up for the loss of Renxing's labor? There was only one way, and that was to have Ahan live in their house in the same capacity.

"No, not that wretch. I won't have him in my house." Lanmei's old grudges and new pains all surfaced at once.

"I don't think it's such a good idea. He's been a soldier, and they are all lazy. He can't use a hoe or plant potatoes, can he?" said Renhua.

"Renjie, you're the oldest; what do you think?" asked Peng Aqiang.

"It's not a bad idea, but I don't think he'll agree."

"Not agree? We can persuade him," said Peng Aqiang, smiling mysteriously. "But do we want him or not? Everyone must agree; otherwise, after he moves in there will be a fight for sure, and that would be disastrous."

"I agree, Father." Renxing had been hiding in the corner not daring to make a sound. Now he took heart and offered his opinion.

"You agree? This whole mess is your fault."

"Renxing, you wretch. If I had known this would happen, I would have strangled you at birth."

"Don't put all the blame on Renxing," said Renjie.

"I must have done something wrong in my last life. How could such a hard fate have befallen me?" Lanmei could not control her tears. She had never been like that before; Renxiu's death had changed her.

"Ma," said Renjie, gently rubbing his mother's shoulder, "let Liu Ahan into our home. In a couple years, Renxing will be back with a wife. It will be fine; we'll have another pair of hands."

Taking Ahan into their house was the only way. It wasn't the best solution, but they had to accept it. They really didn't want someone unrelated living in their home. Because of this, the seeds of discrimination and conflict were sown.

"They really have got the better bargain."

"You can't say that, we need the labor."

"There is also Ahan's pay for being captain of the guard."

"On that count, old man, you must get his money," said Lanmei, her eyes fixed on her husband.

"Father, you seemed pretty confident just now. Do you think he will really be willing?" Renjie asked quietly.

Peng Aqiang smiled again with that mysterious air. From his expression, everyone knew that Peng Aqiang knew where to hoe without even looking.

It was decided that Aling would tell Ahan of the new arrangement. When the news was broken to him, Ahan seemed to be at a loss, but unexpectedly he nodded without even considering.

"Don't make up your mind so fast. Is it worth it? Three years . . ." Aling seemed to disapprove.

"It's okay."

"You know with this kind of marriage arrangement you'll come out with nothing."

"It doesn't matter. I haven't got my eyes on anything the Pengs have." He smiled wryly and said nothing more. Could he tell Aling the real reason? It wasn't a very good one. Aling wouldn't understand. Sometimes he didn't understand himself. He knew that he was doing it all for Dengmei. In the last few days, his heart had been stirred by the swift glances they had by chance exchanged.

That evening after dinner, when the night sky was bright with the moon, Aling asked Ahan to accompany him to catch shrimp in the mountain stream. The best nights for catching shrimp are those when the moon is bright, when the shrimp gather in large numbers among the stones in shallow waters. The men would use the stalk of a palm frond as a fishing pole, to which they would attach a small shrimp as bait. At the end they would tie another piece of palm frond with which to hook the tails. When a shrimp struggled with the bait, they'd give the pole a sharp jerk and catch themselves a large, jumping shrimp.

Their catch that night had been small. Ahan wanted to go down to the lower pool to try his luck; Aling wasn't interested, so he set off alone. As he was going down the stream, he saw someone get up from the washing stone. It was Dengmei. He knew her at a glance, but he didn't know if she had seen him. As she bent down to pick up the large basket of laundry, he coughed softly so as not to frighten her. Dengmei paused, but she was not startled. She turned to look at him as she lifted the basket. Whether because the stone beneath her feet was slippery or because she had misjudged the weight of the basket, she slipped.

Ahan immediately rushed forward to help her up, but Dengmei had already recovered her balance. She stood up and gave him a faint smile. In the moonlight, her smile disappeared as quickly as it had come. Again she turned to pick up the basket and leave.

"Dengmei." He had recovered from his momentary confusion and rashly addressed her by name.

"Yes?" It was only after a suitable pause that she replied. She seemed about to say something but remained standing there silently.

"Dengmei, I'm Liu Ahan."

"Yes." Dengmei turned her head and a smile flickered on her lips once more.

"May I carry your basket for you?"

Dengmei's eye grew round with surprise. She shook her head and briskly climbed the steps. At the top she turned and said, "Don't go down to the deep pool, it's unclean."

"Unclean" meant that it was haunted by ghosts and demons. Even in her confusion and nervousness, she was concerned about him. He forgot to reply and stood there for a long time.

It was the first time that he and Dengmei had exchanged words. In his excitement he felt an inexplicable pleasure. His rough and impetuous heart had suddenly softened, but something bitter also roiled his stomach with a senseless anxiety. He had already made a decision that was impossible to change; that was why he had agreed to live with the Pengs.

He had to go back to Tongluo as quickly as possible to find a senior clan member to act as "elder." He set off without being entirely certain about what he had to do. When his grandmother was alive she had told him about his relatives, but all of that was a blur now.

In recent years he had been determined not to set foot in Tongluo even if it lay on the route he was traveling, except to sweep the tombs of his father and grandmother on the sixteenth day of the first lunar month each year. Now he was on his way home to see the members of his clan, who were strangers to him, to ask them to do something no one would be willing to do.

When he arrived in Tongluo he first prepared offerings of spirit money and incense at the graves of his grandmother and father.

Ahan first addressed his father: "Father, Ahan has come to see you. To tell you that he is going to live in his bride's house. Although it is a disgraceful thing, Dengmei is a good woman. In three years, after we are free to go, we will fetch the spirit tablets from Auntie's house and make offerings to you and Grandmother."

Then he spoke to his grandmother: "Grandma, Ahan has grown up. Without Grandma there would be no Ahan today. Ahan is going to be married, but he will live in his bride's house. Please forgive me. I am doing it for the sake of Dengmei, who is so vulnerable. She is a good woman, and you will like her. In three years. . . ."

After he had prayed he returned to his old home in Tongluo village. A family surnamed Qiu now lived in their old mud-and-thatch house. He asked where his aunt was living. The man told him that his aunt's husband had recently died and had been buried just the day before. This being the

case, Ahan dared not visit her. He went around to visit several Liu clan elders, who flatly refused his request. He knew that people looked down on
men who went to live with their brides' family. It was generally believed
that such men were either lazy or physically deformed.

He wondered what he should do. Should he call the whole thing off?
For Dengmei's sake he had willingly become the butt of everyone's contemptuous jokes and had shamed his relatives, even if they were worthless. If his father were alive there would be no problems. He would not
be in his present predicament. But if his father were alive he probably
would not have met his lovable Dengmei. If only his mother had not
abandoned him, a child without a father, to marry another man. But
what was he thinking? Why was he thinking of that shameless woman
again?

He hastily reined in his wandering mind to avoid that still-festering
sore. He had been here three days now and should have returned to
Fanzai Wood a long time ago with someone to help him complete the
business of the marriage. He was at a loss. He decided that if he could-
n't find anyone to help him, he would leave in the night, go to South
Village or North Shore and enlist as a soldier, and never again for the rest
of his life return to Great Lake.

The day passed, hot and frustrating, long and humiliating. At dusk,
he took one last look at his old home, then walked toward the main road
out of town and the setting sun.

"Ahan!"

Who had called his name?

"Ahan, come back!" It was an old woman hobbling along, trying to
catch him, beckoning to him. It was Auntie Agui, who had already
refused to help him.

"Come back to my house, right now." She half cajoled him, half
pushed him back to her home. He scarcely had time to ask her what it
was all about when he saw a stranger standing in the doorway to the
main room. It was a middle-aged woman, her eyes dim and her mouth
open, looking somewhat dazed.

Who is she? he wondered. He had a strange feeling, then he gave a
start.

"It's him. He's a grown man now. Don't you recognize him?" Auntie
Agui said to the woman.

In silence, the woman shook her head but fixed her eyes on him.

"Looks just like his short-lived father."

He took a step back.

Actually, as soon as he was face to face with the woman he knew
who she was. He had no clear childhood memories of her—he had done

his best to forget her—but he could feel who she was. In his heart he always carried an idealized image of her, and now that motionless woman before him seemed to be the realization of that image, even if she was frail and careworn and much older.

"Ahan, aren't you going to greet her, your own mother?"

He regained his presence of mind and quickly turned away and lowered his head.

"Ahan!" That husky voice.

His head felt so heavy he couldn't raise it. His throat was dry and burned. He couldn't speak a word.

"Ahan, I'm your mother."

He still could not raise his head.

"I heard that you are getting married. Shall I be your witness?"

"It's not a proper marriage; he will be living in the bride's house," Auntie Agui reminded her.

"I will still go and be his witness."

"You!" he said finally, looking her straight in the eye.

"Shall I go?" she said, lowering her head.

"No!" he replied. He turned to leave, but Auntie Agui's unsteady figure barred his path.

"I understand." His mother turned to Auntie Agui and said, "Then you must go in my place as you promised."

"Ahan! How can you treat your mother that way?"

"She is not. . . . Let me go."

Auntie Agui latched on to him and wouldn't let him leave. In his mind he told himself over and over that she wasn't his mother. His grandmother's words came back to him: "That woman married again before you were five and then abandoned you. She is not your mother. You must never acknowledge her as such. You must set yourself up on your own and provide for your family, and make sacrifices for the Lius."

He thought of his grandmother and faintly uttered her name.

"What did you say?"

He shook his head, threw out his chest, and said, "I thank you, Auntie Agui. Let go of me, I'm leaving now."

"Agui, I beg you." His mother seemed to be sobbing now.

"Is that what you are like? Are you so hard-hearted?"

"Hard-hearted! Hard-hearted, indeed." He sneered.

"What if I go in her place?"

"Go in her place for what?" His resentment gave way to something like relief when he thought about it. "Auntie Agui, I came to ask you for your help. If you are just going to take someone else's place then forget it."

"If you don't have a witness from your family, how can you get married?"

"I won't get married. I don't want her to do it. Forget it, it's not a matter of life and death."

"Agui, look at him, he's just a child. Please go!"

"I'm not getting involved! I'm not going!" said Auntie Agui crossly.

"No! Come back, Ahan," she called to him.

"Why should I listen to you?"

"Do I have to kneel before you to make you listen?"

"You . . ."

"Your mother is truly sorry. I know you hate me, I don't blame you. Let Auntie Agui go to your future in-laws and affix her seal to the document, I beg you. If you don't agree I'll kneel before you; see, I'm kneeling."

"What a scene. Get up." Auntie Agui prevented his mother from kneeling.

He stood there like a stone, but his mind was in a turmoil. He was despairing and ready to explode. He wanted to call her "Mother." He wanted her to be his witness. He wanted her to meet Dengmei, because Dengmei would be her daughter. But his feelings scared him.

Auntie Agui finally "volunteered" to go with him to Fanzai Wood to act as his witness in the marriage arrangement. His mother stood by the roadside watching them depart. It seemed that many people were watching from behind their doors and the high grass. He tried not to look at his mother, but he couldn't help himself. He gritted his teeth and with a great effort turned around to face her. Her face was contorted, her eyes welled with tears, but a smile seemed to play at the corners of her mouth.

He couldn't bring himself to say a word. Auntie Agui had already walked ahead. He hurried after her.

On the morning of the fourth day of the fifth month, Peng Renxing and Xu Azhi were married. Liu Ahan and Ye Dengmei were married at noon the following day, the festival day of the double fifth. The times for both ceremonies had been carefully selected by Master Xu Rixing, who had secretly informed them the day before.

"At noon the male element is at its strongest, which is good for you."

Ahan didn't understand the nonsense that Master Xu Rixing was spouting.

"Normally noontime on the double fifth ought to be avoided because the male element would be too strong for the bride."

"That sounds well and good, but can you explain what it all means?"

"Just what I said. Such an hour is good for you."

"But didn't you say it was bad for the bride?"

"Yes, but with Dengmei . . . you know," said the Master in all seriousness.

"What about her?"

"Dengmei has a strong fate, so . . ."

Ahan sighed.

"At noon, when the male element is at its strongest, the malevolent female influence will be kept at bay."

"Nonsense," Ahan burst out.

"What did you say?"

"Nothing. Nothing at all. I just . . ."

"You're scared, aren't you? And well you should be," said Xu Rixing, smiling knowingly. He was full of arcane explanations. "Did you know that women with strong fates can harm their husbands at three critical places? One is at the wedding ceremony; the others are at the entrance to the bridal chamber and during consummation. We can neutralize the harm with charms to turn the malevolent influences to good."

He was bewildered by all that was said about Dengmei's strong fate. He couldn't rid himself of the fear that gnawed at him; he could only hide it.

Hakka wedding ceremonies preserved the ancient custom of six rituals, but when the husband took up residence in the bride's home, the rituals were dispensed with. The Hakka had always looked down on a groom who lived with his in-laws. When a branch of a family was without heirs, a man would make the son of one of his brothers his heir. But when the Hakka began emigrating to Taiwan, they had a hard time finding members of their own clan for heirs. As a result, they had to find a husband for a daughter to continue the family line. Generally it was a man without the means to pay the bride price who took this route. The Hakka all regarded this form of marriage as something shameful and to be avoided.

But the two marriages at Fanzai Wood were exceptions. The Xus did not require that their grandchildren take the name Xu, and the Pengs agreed that all Dengmei's male children should bear the surname Liu. They did stipulate, however, that the first two daughters take the surname Peng and remain in the family. Male children might one day inherit family wealth, but daughters could be sold as brides to other families or contribute to the family's labor pool. Ahan had initially rejected the Pengs' demands with regard to the first two daughters. Later it was agreed that Ahan could buy his daughters back for the same price as a bride.

It was widely considered that the Pengs had struck a good bargain. Ahan felt the arrangement was unfair.

The ceremony was performed in the Pengs' house, but the bridal chamber was in the new house built by Ahan and Aling. This ran contrary to the customs for such a marriage, but Lanmei had insisted on the arrangement. No one was much interested in adhering too rigidly to custom. But when Ahan had expressed the desire to hang a strip of red paper to honor his ancestors in the main hall, everyone was opposed to the idea.

The bridal chamber was newly furnished with a round mirror, a pair of pillows with cotton print covers, a table with bamboo legs, and a fine-looking red wooden chest. The chest was one of a pair that had been prepared for Renxiu, and on the morning of the wedding, Peng Aqiang had delivered it himself. With the chest, they had a place they could put their hastily sewn garments, which had been placed on their bed. They had used Auntie Agui's gift of money to buy the clothes and a pale green blanket.

"It's not my generosity. Your mother pushed the money into my hands."

The nicest touch was the bamboo mat that Aling and his wife had helped Ahan make in the course of a couple of nights.

"Do you think people will find me extravagant?" Ahan asked.

"We made it ourselves instead of sleeping. Take no notice of what others say," said Aling.

Ahan had used what little money he had saved to buy cloth shoes for Peng Aqiang, Lanmei, and Dengmei. Dengmei's shoes had velvet uppers. After a great deal of consideration, he had purchased a pair of leather shoes for himself. In addition, he had a silver ring made for Dengmei. He did have the money for a pair of earrings, but then he noticed that Dengmei's ears had not been pierced. He told no one about the ring because he wanted to surprise Dengmei. It symbolized what was in his heart and that was for Dengmei alone. He put the ring in his pocket.

His wedding suit, a short coat and trousers, though made of coarse cloth, fit him well, and with his leather shoes, he was quite handsome. Aling and his wife had helped him dress his queue the night before. For years he had not concerned himself much with his hair, and like most young working men, he had simply combed through it with his fingers and twisted his queue around his head. In order to keep his hair in place, he had wrapped it in a broad piece of cloth in what was referred to as a reformed hairstyle. Now Ahan's hair was also barely shoulder length, a characteristic peculiar to soldiers in Taiwan. Those who had witnessed the attack of the indigenous people had seen how they had grabbed their

Chinese prisoners by the hair, yanking their queues to expose their necks to the sharp blows of battle swords. This had struck terror in the hearts of all the soldiers, and they had disregarded the official warnings and cut their queues.

I can do away with this new queue in a few days, thought Ahan. Formal dress was also new to him. Washed and well groomed, he looked at himself in the mirror, and his appearance made him feel somewhat ridiculous. His face was flushed due to the heat and all the clothes he was wearing. An itinerant fortune teller had once told him that he had a handsome face, but one that did not foretell many blessings.

Just then Aling appeared, chasing away his idle thoughts. Ahan collected himself as Aling said, "It's time."

Auntie Agui was already waiting outside. They looked at each other without saying a word and then walked over to the Pengs.' The sun was blistering hot. Many people were on the threshing ground, but the main room was quiet. Xu Rixing stood in the doorway.

The Pengs had just completed one wedding ceremony. No decorations had been hung; the expected pleasure on people's faces was absent, and the scene was pervaded by a desolate atmosphere. Ahan felt dizzy. He blinked hard, wanting to greet everyone by name as manners dictated. But all the sweat coursing down his face got into his eyes, making it hard for him to recognize anyone.

"Everyone rise," said Xu Rixing, who was to conduct the ceremony. "Ahan, Dengmei, all the elders and witnesses, Aling, and Ajin step forward and affix your seals or make a print of your thumb." Everybody did as instructed. Dengmei had no seal, so she made a print with her thumb.

"Aqiang, as elder of the Peng family, you light the candles." Peng Aqiang lit three sticks of incense and then the two small red candles on the table. As he lit the candles, Peng Aqiang intoned four auspicious phrases to bring the newlyweds luck in their life together:

> Light the candles;
> A lucky match is made.
> Bright the candles;
> The Peng family fortune is made.

Dengmei was dressed in pink and wore her velvet shoes. Her head was bare; her usual small plaits had been done up in a bun at the back of her head. She looked small and dainty, and everyone murmured with approval. She kept her head lowered, and it looked as if someone had applied powder and rouge to her face.

"Make offerings to the ancestors! Light the incense!" said Xu Rixing.

Aling gave the bride and groom each three sticks of incense. After they had placed their incense in a burner, they knelt to complete a series of nine kowtows. At that point, Peng Aqiang intoned:

> Ancestors of the Peng clan,
> Mighty and manifest,
> A son is taken in
> Willing to work in your interest.

Peng Aqiang's voice was not very loud, but it was clear. And although Ahan was somewhat confused and nervous, he did understand the intent of the words.

The ceremony was quickly completed, and at the call for the bride and groom to enter the bridal chamber, Ahan and Dengmei walked the thirty yards to their new house. Ahan breathed a sigh of relief and was just about to take a long look at Dengmei when Aling burst in and said, "Come and give us a hand with the tables and the utensils."

Ahan wondered if he had heard correctly.

"That's the way it is, Brother. Things have to go back to normal. If you're obliging, people will think more highly of you."

Think more highly of him? A bridegroom fresh from the wedding ceremony moving tables?

"Go," said Dengmei quietly and unexpectedly. She looked at him as he turned to leave.

"You are not to come, Dengmei," he said, his voice tensing. "I'll go."

Leaving the house, Aling kept close to him, holding him by the hand. Ahan understood what Aling meant. Turning his head, he saw Dengmei come out of the house and Aling's wife approach her and say something. In addition to the Peng family, there were at least two members from each family at Fanzai Wood at the banquet.

Auntie Agui was the guest of honor. She sat to the left of Peng Aqiang. Ahan and Dengmei sat obediently across from Peng Aqiang and ate together. That day white rice mixed with a small amount of potato was served. It was a rare treat. Everyone gulped down the rice, forgetting about the many dishes on the table. Dengmei's bowl was heaped with food, but she barely touched it. She just sat there, her head lowered and hands folded before her, not daring to pick up her chopsticks or look at anyone. She seemed confused and on the verge of crying. She was worried that she might cry. She wasn't sad, but she couldn't explain the desire to cry. She didn't listen to what anyone was saying.

Ahan, on the other hand, was quite calm. He paid attention only to the food in front of him, which he gobbled down. But he soon noticed everyone staring at him so he slowed down. He continued to hold his chopsticks and bowl in a pretense of eating, but he ate no more. Inwardly, he was filled with sadness. Dengmei was sitting right next to him, but he couldn't see her because he just looked straight ahead.

The banquet came to an end, and Auntie Agui was on the point of leaving. As she would not have enough time to get back to Tongluo, she said she would visit some relatives at Great Lake. Aling was charged with escorting her.

"Thank you, Auntie Agui," said Ahan. Please tell my mother . . ."

"Tell her what?"

"Give her my thanks. Tell her to take care of herself," he said, starting to weep.

That afternoon his eldest sister-in-law came to tell Ahan that the couple could rest in the bridal chamber and not work. Ahan was too embarrassed to stay indoors long. He went to join the others in conversation in the main room. Since the Pengs had been busy the better part of the day, they didn't have dinner until the evening. Peng Aqiang told Ahan that he and Dengmei could stand and eat a little.

The time had come to feed the pigs, which was Dengmei's job. She wanted to change out of her new clothes and do her chore, but Ahan said he would do it. Dengmei shook her head. In the end, Aling's wife came to their rescue and fed the pigs. When the sun slipped behind the hills, a wind came up and rain began to fall. The rain ceased after a short time, but soon it began again, throwing everything into darkness. Ahan took out an oil lamp he had bought; at the time, Aling had warned him that everyone would see it as an extravagance, but he bought it nonetheless. As the wind picked up outside, the draft of cold air through the bamboo door increased, threatening the flame, which flickered furiously. They were at last able to look at each other. He gazed calmly at Dengmei, but in the flickering light her expression was not well defined.

"Dengmei," he whispered cautiously. She did not reply and sat there motionless. This woman is my wife, he thought. He wanted to protect her and love her properly. He wondered if Dengmei felt the same way. He was confident that she did. She too was a lonely, vulnerable person.

"Dengmei, you must be tired."

"No, not at all."

"Dengmei, go ahead and sleep."

"No."

"Do you dislike me?"

"No."

"Then, do you . . ." He could not bring himself to ask her if she liked him. She looked at him in surprise. "I will work hard, and not let you suffer."

"Ahan . . ."

"I will do my best for our family. I will keep you warm and fed." He had more to say but didn't know where to start. Suddenly he felt the silver ring in his pocket. He summoned up his courage and gave the ring to Dengmei.

"Oh, Ahan."

"I could only buy you a small ring; you must not despise it."

"Thank you, Ahan," said Dengmei, breaking into tears.

"One day I'll buy you a gold one."

"Yes. No. This one is enough; just this one. It will be enough for all my life."

The wind outside picked up. It was stronger than usual. The oil lamp flickered.

"It's getting late. You had better get some sleep."

"What about you?" she replied weakly.

"I'm going to sit up a while before going to bed."

"Then I'll stay up too," Dengmei said decisively.

"Good. Then we'll sit a bit longer." Saying the word "we" made him feel warm all over.

"The sound of wind and rain at night scares me."

"I don't like it when it's too strong, because it makes me feel lonely."

"That's the way I feel," said Dengmei excitedly.

"From now on you won't have to be afraid."

At some time, the lamp was blown out. He suggested again that Dengmei get some sleep, but she made no reply. He could imagine her embarrassment because he himself was so excited. Dengmei seemed to get up and move. He so much wanted to take hold of her pitiable little hand, but he couldn't move. Dengmei walked over and sat on the edge of the bed. In the darkness, everything in front of him seemed as clear as at noon. He felt he could see Dengmei's every move, even her expression. He was glad that the lamp had gone out. He walked over to the bed, telling himself that he must not be shy. He sat down on the edge of the bed next to Dengmei.

Death and Disaster

Soon after the Double Fifth festival, the mountainous areas of central Taiwan were filled with the sound of cicadas. Three days after the marriage of Ahan and Dengmei, the people of Fanzai Wood sent the land patent application in the name of Xu Shihui, with the supporting documents for appointing Liu Ahan as captain of the guard, to Great Lake. The officials at Great Lake passed the application on to the local land office.

The settlers at Fanzai Wood continued to lose no time in clearing land. They began at the break of day and left off only after nightfall, sometimes working even through the night. Aling and his wife cleared a plot of land near the river at Little Southside. Ahan, as part of the Peng family, went to clear land with the Peng brothers at Upper Fanzai Wood.

Clearing land and plowing were new to Ahan. As a child he had herded cattle and gathered fodder for them. He had also looked after ducks, but using a machete to clear vegetation or a hoe or other farm implements such as a mattock were all new to him.

Renjie and Peng Aqiang wielded the mattock quickly and efficiently, as if it were a lightweight bamboo pole. Seeing them the first time left him astonished and feeling quite weak.

"Weakling! What good are you?" complained Renhua. Renhua wasn't much better himself, but for some reason he had taken a dislike to Ahan.

"I've never done this kind of work before," said Ahan, gritting his teeth. "I'll learn."

"That's right," interjected Peng Aqiang, "strength will come as you work. Take it slowly."

"Everyone else will have grabbed all the land, and you still talk about going slowly."

"Don't forget that Ahan is captain of the guard and he is just help-ing out now." What Peng Aqiang said was as much for Ahan's benefit as anyone else's. "As soon as our land patent comes through . . ."

Ahan knew exactly what the people of Fanzai Wood expected of him and what the Pengs wanted from him. He knew now what it was to eat at someone else's table; he was a weakling. But he had never done heavy physical labor in the past. At first bean-sized blisters appeared on his hands. He should have stopped working, but he couldn't. He went on, steadily wielding the hoe but not daring to change his grip for fear of breaking his blisters. But break they did, with a stinging pain. He gritted his teeth but could not help groaning. He kept at his hoeing even as the blisters broke. Exposed to the air, his tender pink flesh stung. One of the broken blisters began to bleed, staining the hoe with wet, red blood.

He put down his hoe and stared at his palms.

"Hurt your hands?" Renjie smiled. "It happens."

"So quickly?" asked Peng Aqiang. "Just ignore it. It always happens. You just have to keep on hoeing. The blood will dry and when they heal, calluses will form."

"But it hurts."

"Is that what all the noise is about?" said Peng Aqiang, clearly dis-pleased.

True, a bleeding blister wasn't much. But why had he been willing to give himself over to such torture, ignoring the pain, the cold, and even the discomfort of his own flesh just for a bowl of rice? He was an orphan fated for a hard life. He was a stranger in another man's home, brought in to risk his life fighting the natives. It was ridiculous that such a little bit of pain troubled him.

"Chop, slash, and kill. This is all pointless."

The old man stopped working and stared at him. Renjie also cast a surprised glance in his direction. Renhua seemed to be smiling; no, he was sneering.

"Take a rest, Ahan," said Renjie.

Renjie was the oldest son and the kindest member of the Peng fam-ily. Ahan thought for a moment, then grunted. He wanted to stop but was not willing to do so. There was really no way he could stop. He car-ried on hoeing.

"Stubborn young fool."

"It's hard for him. He has never done this kind of work before."

They stopped working when the sun fell behind the hills. Ahan went to put down his hoe, but it was stuck to his hands. The old man and his sons started off down the hill, but Ahan remained behind, saying he wanted to rest first.

When he looked up, it was dark all around. His hands were still stuck to the hoe and at the slightest effort to remove them he broke out in a sweat at the pain. What was he going to do? He had to get back or he would be scolded. He struggled to his feet, but lost his balance and fell. His tears flowed.

"Ahan! Ahan, where are you?" Someone was calling him from the lower fields. Dengmei's small form appeared before him. In the dark he could only see the outline of her slim figure and the movement of her eyes.

"What are you doing?" she asked as she reached out to take the hoe from him.

"Nothing. Leave the hoe alone, you might hurt yourself."

"Is something wrong?" asked Dengmei. "Why are you holding the hoe that way?"

"I can't get rid of it."

"What?" Dengmei reached toward the hoe that he was unable to let go of. Dengmei gripped his hands. They were both at a loss. Dengmei didn't even come up to his shoulders. She leaned against his chest and groaned.

"What are we going to do, Dengmei?" he said, snuggling against her.

Dengmei was the first to straighten up and step back. She gently stroked his hands as if she were thinking about something. Then she bent toward one of his hands and began to lick it.

"No Dengmei, you mustn't do that." He stepped away from her, but she stubbornly clung to one of his hands. Again the soft tip of her tongue licked at his hand. He couldn't bear it, but he was grateful. Finally, he ripped his right hand from the handle and felt a bone-piercing pain.

He yelled as he wrenched his left hand from the handle. The hoe fell to the ground.

"Ahan, are you all right?"

"I'm okay. Let's get back."

Dengmei remained standing there, as did he. The two of them embraced. It was love, fondness, the embrace of life itself. Their faces were wet with tears, their hearts full of sweetness and love.

"Let's get back."

"Yes, it's late," said Dengmei, picking up the hoe.

Dengmei strode off, and he rushed to lead the way. Dengmei claimed she knew the way better than he; he said he knew it as well as she. She claimed to have better eyes; he said his were up to the task. She cautioned him, saying they'd get a scolding; he said it didn't matter. She said it would be bad for him; he said he didn't care as long as she was nice to him. She gave no reply. The two of them made their way, each one trying to lead. They squeezed close together as they went down the narrow mountain path in the dark.

There had been no word regarding the land patent application or the one for appointing Liu Ahan as captain of the guard. One morning, as Peng Aqiang and his family were taking a break in the fields, they heard the alarm gong ringing. Renjie, Renhua, and Ahan picked up their tools and descended the slope together. They saw all the other men of Fanzai Wood leaving their fields and hurrying toward the temple. By the time they arrived, the temple was already crowded.

Before them stood six strangers. Two of them were middle-aged. One was tall, the other short; both were thin and pale. The short man was wearing a bright blue gown and a black velvet waistcoat. He wore a skullcap and held a long, thin pipe that gleamed with gold. The tall man was whispering something in his ear. Behind the middle-aged men stood four young men, who, judging from their clothing, were laborers or hired hands from a large estate.

It was Ye Atian and his steward, Renxian. Although the people had never seen them before, they recognized them from Xu Rixing's descriptions. Ye Atian was a big landholder, and he had been awarded a patent for the land at Fanzai Wood. That was the reason for his visit.

Peng Aqiang, flanked by Xie and Fan, stood facing them. Their faces were expressionless; they were all still holding their hoes. Xu Shihui, who had always been regarded as the village headman, stood to the left. He carried a pitchfork. Half concealed to the right was Chen Agu, who was carrying a rifle.

Glancing around him, Ahan noticed that with the exception of Chen Afa, all the grown men of Fanzai Wood were present. The Xu sons, a burly bunch, stood behind their father. Some of the women were also present, standing next to their husbands. Was it to be a struggle that might end in bloodshed? Ahan trembled. Were the people of Fanzai Wood doing the right thing?

But a land patent was just a piece of paper. How could Ye Atian own the land without having shed his own blood and sweat? He was the legal owner, and that meant that the people at Fanzai Wood were squatters. How could the law work in such a way? How could it be so arbitrary? The law itself was lawless.

Renxian the steward cleared his throat and addressed the people of Fanzai Wood: "As everyone can see, before you stands Master Ye Atian, your new landlord."

"We've never had a landlord."

"You have all been living as squatters, which is against the law."

"We have never broken the law."

"We are not concerned about the past."

Ye Atian whispered a few words to his steward and pointed to the parcel he carried under his arm. Renxian quickly opened it. Inside was a pile of documents.

"Here, these are your rental agreements," said Renxian, handing the documents to Peng Aqiang. "There are two copies for each tenant. After you have affixed your seal, return one copy to the master."

"We can't accept them," said Peng Aqiang, refusing to take the documents.

"You will regret this," said Renxian.

"Master Atian," said Peng Aqiang, taking two steps forward and pushing the steward away.

"Give the agreements to Chen Afa," said Ye Atian.

Renxian handed the pile of papers to Chen Afa. Peng Aqiang turned and snatched them away, saying, "Master Atian, can't we work something out?"

"I as landlord have nothing to discuss with tenants about conditions, especially those who are armed."

"I have no weapon."

"Then what do you call that in your hands?"

"It's a hoe. I use it to clear the mountains and earn a living."

"Why do you need it right now? Are you trying to intimidate me?"

"Put your tools down," said the steward to all those assembled.

Peng Aqiang turned to give his hoe to someone behind him; Renjie stepped forward to receive it. When the others saw Peng Aqiang lay aside his hoe, they also laid theirs down. Someone breathed a long sigh of relief.

"Master Atian, great men forgive their inferiors their mistakes. Let us discuss the matter."

"If you have anything to say, you can say it to my steward."

"No, I must beg that you yourself . . ."

Ye Atian turned his back to them.

"We beg you not to ask rent of us for the land we have just cleared."

"Where in the world can you find land for which rent or taxes do not have to be paid?"

"We will, of course, pay the taxes on the land."

"I am the holder of the land patent, and I have the right to demand rent from you," said Ye Atian, laughing.

"What we mean is that you can't just come and ask us for rent for nothing."

"Who said it was for nothing? I had to pay in silver to get the land patent. Now I will have to establish a guard post for the protection of my land from the natives. I will have to pay a lot of money to hire guards."

"We beg you. We entreat you," said Peng Aqiang, sounding ever more submissive. "Master Atian, you have scores of paddy fields and hundreds of acres of land. Do you really care for this little bit? Please be generous and let us have the land we have opened."

"No! And that is final," Ye Atian firmly refused.

"Can't we discuss this?" said Peng Aqiang, his voice quavering. "Do you really mean what you say?"

"I said no, and I mean what I say."

Ye Atian walked about twenty yards down the slope to where his sedan chair was waiting. It was a wonder that the four bearers had been able to carry him up the winding mountain path.

"Heroes are made of those who know their duty," said Renxian as he walked away. "You must plow well. All tenant farmers in the world are in the same position. You have to accept your fate. You were born for it."

"Stay where you are," said Peng Aqiang, as if he had just awakened from a dream. He turned for his hoe, but Renjie refused to give it to him. Instead Peng snatched a machete from Fan's hands, and clutching the rental agreements in the other hand, he took off down the slope, brandishing his weapon. Immediately, Renjie and his brothers, along with Ahan and Aling, rushed after him. Grabbing him by the waist, they wrested the machete away and held him back.

Only after Ye Atian's sedan chair had disappeared around the bend at Blind Man's Pool did Renjie release his father. Chen Afa had slipped away. Everyone else just stood where they were, rooted like trees. It was as if they had sprouted from the ground and would one day die there.

The sun had long since been obscured by the clouds. A warm rain had begun to fall, but still no one moved. The rain gradually grew heavier, and it looked like a real tempest was on the way. Then it poured. Everyone was soaking wet; even the women and children came out to see what was happening. Were the people of Fanzai Wood accustomed to the wind and rain, or did it just not matter anymore? Once again the sun appeared, hotter than ever. It was as if the sun also wanted to escape the storm and dry the land.

His head lowered, Peng Aqiang silently stared at the sopping-wet rental agreements. The anger that burned within him suddenly erupted, and he tore the documents into pieces.

"You're crazy." Xu Shihui sighed. "There is still Heaven; we must just leave it to Heaven."

"Heaven? Who can Heaven help?" snorted Peng Aqiang.

The sun vanished again and a burning wind sprang up, raising goose bumps on everyone's skin. A black cloud arose from the cliff, followed by an unpleasant cawing—a flock of crows.

It was another scorching day. The weak sun wore a halo. Near and far, a pale yellowish mist floated over the hills and woods. The air was filled with huge, yellow-winged ants. They scurried aimlessly, rushing around falling over one another, but looking weak and exhausted. Still they fluttered about. No one knew why the ants were fleeing. Rows of termites also appeared on the thatched roofs. They were smaller and more frail that the winged ants, but they too were fleeing. No one could explain why.

Red and yellow dragonflies were seen hovering above the paddy fields below the temple and above every threshing ground. Their numbers continued to increase until it looked as if half the sky were filled with them. They formed a funnel that rose and sank, shrinking and expanding.

No one went up the slope to work that afternoon. The village was silent; not a peep was heard from the children, who seemed to have vanished.

By dusk a fine drizzle was falling. The eerie shrieks of gibbons were heard from the cliffs above Fanzai Wood. Gibbons were generally only heard in the winter, when they were suffering from cold and hunger. But now they were complaining in midsummer.

Ahan and Dengmei couldn't remain at home, but there was no work at the Pengs' house. The apathy was intolerable. Dengmei finally began knotting grass for kindling. Knotted grass was essential for starting fires in their stoves, and large piles were common in every household. Ahan helped her with the task.

"Father, what are we going to do?" asked Renjie from inside the house. "Our plan has come to nothing, as has Ahan's job."

"Lower your voice," said Renhua.

"Everybody knows. What's the problem? I suggest . . ."

"What do you suggest?"

"I suggest we keep Dengmei and get rid of Liu."

"Shut up, Renhua. If you keep talking that way, I'll get rid of you."

"That's fine. But you won't have to get rid of me, I'll leave myself," said Renhua, his voice growing louder. "There's no future in Fanzai Wood! And I've been wanting to leave for a long time."

Suddenly the room grew silent. Renjie must have taken his brother outside.

Ahan raised his eyes to look at Dengmei. Their eyes met. Dengmei hastily lowered her head; her thin face was flushed.

Dengmei was so small, her back so thin. Dengmei must feel as if her heart were being cut with a knife, thought Ahan. She must be overcome with panic, but she couldn't show it. She was a pitiful purchased child; his own pitiful wife. But he didn't want her to worry. He would never leave her, regardless of how he was mocked, cursed, or beaten. He would put up with all humiliation for her sake. And if need be, he would run away with her, steal her away. He swore to always be with her. And although he couldn't provide her with meat to eat or silk to wear, he would never let her go hungry. He would look after her, grow old with her, share their hard life. They would never be lonely or afraid.

That evening a strong wind blew, but around midnight it ceased and all was calm. At first it was generally thought that a typhoon was coming; later they thought that they had perhaps avoided the disaster that time. But the air was oppressively hot and everyone was sweating uncomfortably. Lying down, Ahan seemed to feel his bed sway. No, the whole house was shaking. Cries came from Aling's room. It was an earthquake, a small one. It sounded as if Aling and his family had run outside. Dengmei remained calm, not even getting up. Nor did Ahan move. He knew what Dengmei was thinking and she certainly knew what was going through his mind—wonderful!

Smiling to himself, he drifted off to sleep. As he dozed off, he felt a sudden prod that made him sit up with a cry. There was only Dengmei, who was smiling gently, sitting there. She was so small, but her eyes seemed so large at times. But that was just fine, it was something that he alone could enjoy.

"What's the matter with you? It's light outside already."

He laughed loudly. "Really?"

"I'm afraid there's going to be a typhoon. Hurry and get up."

It was already quite light. The sun had not risen very high, but the air was unusually bright: the light of the sun was refracted through the moisture-laden air. The forest and the mountains seemed to lack weight and float in the air. The insects had all disappeared and the air seemed to have been washed clean.

"I'm afraid it's going to be a big one. Can the house take it?"

It was true. All signs over the last two days indicated to anyone brought up in Taiwan that a huge typhoon was imminent. There would be no work that day. Nor would the stove be lit. People would have to eat raw potatoes.

After eating, Renjie summoned them to help tie the house down by roping the roof to tree trunks and boulders. Everyone in Fanzai Wood was occupied with taking precautions against the typhoon. Since Ahan and Dengmei had been called away by Renjie, it fell to Aling and his wife to secure the house they shared.

Just as they finished tying down the Pengs' house, the bright sky was suddenly obscured by masses of black clouds streaked a dirty yellow. As the black clouds passed over the cliffs to the north of the village, they were shredded apart in wisps like cotton floss and then blown away to the south. The thick black clouds high above continued moving ever faster, roiling into huge masses as they rolled away to the south. The vegetation, which had been deathly still until then, began to sway. The swaying increased with the wind.

The usually inaudible stream by the village suddenly seemed much louder than normal, as though it had been swollen by a mountain torrent. Actually, the sound was the wind through the woods. The clouds grew thicker and began to press lower, and soon the cliffs were concealed. It was as if the cotton floss of the clouds had been stopped there by a giant fist. The black clouds curled upward, arching into the sky.

As the clouds ascended once more, the sky seemed to brighten just a bit. The mountain peaks suddenly appeared in perfect clarity, as if the sky had just been washed by rain. At that moment the rain began to fall in the area around Blind Man's Pool, where the sky was brightest. The rain looked like bamboo poles connecting the sky with the earth. It fell almost vertically and drifted southward. There was a short lull and then it began to fall even harder; the streaks of rain fell faster and closer together. Such rain was known as a "bamboo tide" and a sure indicator that a typhoon was about to strike.

Gusts of wind following the stream swept low across the ground. The wind seemed to take life from the earth and grew stronger and more violent as it rushed the trees and the roofs. The rain was falling at a forty-five-degree angle and had lost its resemblance to bamboo poles. The raindrops took on a crystalline appearance as they fell. This type of rain was popularly referred to as "salt rain" because it resembled the salt scattered by a Daoist priest to cleanse the air. It lasted but a few minutes. The wind seemed to double in speed with each gust, giving the rain real weight and force. Whipped by the wind, the bamboo began to break and the roofs began to groan.

The full force of the typhoon arrived around noon. It was the twenty-seventh day of the seventh lunar month in the eighteenth year of the Guangxu era (1892). It was the worst typhoon to hit Taiwan in thirty years.

Aling and Ahan's house, being one of the smallest and newest, looked as if it might survive the storm. Aling told Shunmei to keep the children on the bed. Shunmei was noticeably pregnant and could not lift anything heavy. He reminded her that if the house started coming down, she should get under the bed, press the children close to herself, then curl up and try to protect her head.

"I wonder how they are doing over there." Dengmei was worried about the Pengs.

"Their house is a bit older," said Aling.

Ahan said nothing, but he was in a turmoil about what to do. He knew his house was safer than his in-laws' and that it faced no immediate danger. He felt he ought to go over and see how they were, but when he thought of them, the bitterness rose in his heart.

Dengmei threw him a worried glance. "Go have a look," she said, her voice betraying her anxiety.

The sky was dark and they had lost track of the time. Ahan sighed, told his wife to take care, and left through the kitchen door at the back of the house.

He was caught by a violent gust and swept along for several feet, then thrown to the ground. He picked himself up only to again take a drubbing from the wind. There was no way for him to stay on his feet. Having taken his bearings, he crawled on his hands and knees toward the Pengs' house.

It was no good: he could scarcely breathe. He could not make his way over the rocky rise that lay between him and the house. The wind forced him back, and he knew that the longer he remained exposed, the greater his chances of being struck by a flying branch or stone. He could no longer make his way on his hands and knees, so he pressed closer to the ground and tried to move forward on his belly.

The bamboo fence at the Pengs' house had long since been blown away. A few feet of fence had caught on the woodpile. But the knotted grass that he and Dengmei had prepared had disappeared to heaven knew where. The newest layer of thatch, the one added just that year, had been torn away. The older part of the roof seemed intact, but it looked as if the entire roof would be lifted off and blown away.

"Open the door! Open the door!" he shouted. But his voice couldn't be heard over the wind. He crawled over to the side door, but it was no use. He then tried the kitchen door, again to no avail.

He pounded on the door.

"We can't open the door!"

"Open the door! Open the door!"

"No. You must find a way yourself." He couldn't tell whose voice it was.

Find a way of his own?

In a storm of anger he left. He felt himself transformed into a violent gust of wind. He half crawled and half rolled back to his own house. Covered with mud, he burst in through the kitchen door.

Dengmei wiped him off with her sleeves. "What happened?"

Aling heaved a sigh as if he had witnessed the scene himself.

Ahan's anger vanished as quickly as it had come. He was gladdened by the fact that he could spend the night of a typhoon with Dengmei. He had spent so many stormy nights alone and afraid in the past. But now he had a wife, a woman of his own. Even if the roof were lifted by the wind or blown away, he would not be afraid. He would fear nothing as long as Dengmei was by his side, for him to hold and protect.

After night fell, the typhoon seemed to increase in strength, judging from the sound of the wind and rain. At daybreak, the storm reached the height of its ferocity. Then it began to slacken, and within six hours the worst had passed. There would be a period of light breezes before the storm would pick up again.

When the lull finally came, everyone rushed outdoors, first to inspect the damage to their houses, then to see how others had fared. Peng Aqiang's house was largely undamaged. Su Ajin and Xu Rixing had lost their roofs; Chen Afa had lost his kitchen; the foot-thick walls of Xu Shihui's woodshed had collapsed on two sides and the roof had fallen in. All the other houses were fine. And with the exception of some losses of poultry and animals, no one had suffered any harm.

No one could afford to remain idle. They rushed about stopping up holes and tightening ropes. About two hours later, as they finished making repairs, the rain began to pour. The typhoon was picking up again. Within an hour the rain ceased, but the wind increased. The storm could be expected to reach the same intensity, but the damage was likely to be much greater. After three or four hours the wind decreased, but a pelting rain began to fall.

The rain was of the like seldom seen before. When it began it was like any other heavy rain as it struck the ground. But very soon the sound deepened, as if giants were treading nearby. The rain sounded like the pounding footfalls of a distant army on the march. The rain fell, flattening everything in its path, shaking the earth.

For some reason, Ahan suddenly thought of his grandmother and father. Their graves must have been filled with water, their bodies soaking in the muddy liquid. The image of his mother also flashed through his mind: a tiny woman with a weather-beaten face; a thin and frail woman on the verge of tears. He wondered where she was and if she was safe.

At break of day the following morning, the rain still showed no signs of letting up. Water had long since seeped into the houses and now covered their feet. The water was moving fast. Outdoors, the gray forest was shrouded in a curtain of rain. No other sound could be heard save the beating of the rain that poured mercilessly from the sky. The rain seemed to be suspended in the sky, forming torrents upon touching the ground.

"It's a flood! The mountain is flooding!" shouted Aling.

Their house had been built near the stream, which was now swollen with mud and water. The foundation of the house was already under water, and the stream was still rising.

Aling rushed into the house, snatched a child up in each arm, and, shouting, led the way to the Pengs' house. Ahan and Dengmei were quick behind him, carrying their bedding, their trunk, and two cook pots. Aling returned for the farm tools. His wife was howling as she squatted with one child.

"There's no time to cry!" shouted Peng Aqiang. "Hurry up, you must get to the threshing ground."

A large group of people could be seen squatting on the threshing ground through the gray curtain of rain. The entire Peng family was huddled together there. The large family house was gone; all that remained was a confusion of broken bamboo mixed with mud that had once been part of the walls and roof.

Aling's wife stopped wailing. The scene was too much for her. The women and children squatted in silence, their heads lowered and their hands clasped behind their necks. Aling's wife and children joined the group. Dengmei was also there. Renhua held a piece of thatch over his head, but the rain still poured over his face and body. Peng Aqiang and Renjie were standing, their arms folded. They were expressionless as the rain poured down their faces. Ahan and Aling were also standing. Aling's eyes were fixed on his house in the rolling floodwaters below. The water had already risen two feet up the walls.

The sky remained unchanging; the rain continued falling and turned into torrential floods that rolled down the mountain. The ravines were full and the water spilled over the banks, flooding the fields, swallowing them, sweeping away the topsoil.

"I'm going to take a look," said Peng Aqiang suddenly, his voice constricted and hoarse.

"No. It's too dangerous." Lanmei stood up. Peng Aqiang shouldered his hoe and, with a quick glance behind him, strode away from the threshing ground. Renjie picked up another hoe and followed him. Ahan in turned followed Renjie. They passed the temple on their way to the fields below the cliff, but the water had already reached the temple. Another three feet and the gods would have to learn to swim. They looked at the expanse of yellow water that covered what was their fields. Even the weed-covered banks between the fields were under water.

Peng Aqiang heaved a sigh of resignation.

"Let's have a look at the fields higher up," said Renjie gently to his father. They proceeded up to the high fields. The steep mountain path was now a conduit for swift-flowing water, and the ground all around was covered with puddles.

Soon all the able-bodied men of Fanzai Wood had mobilized to widen the stream beds and dredge out the sand and gravel deposited by the floodwaters in hopes of quickly draining the fields to save them. But it was too late: not a trace of the fields remained; the crops had all been swept away. It would have been a different matter if it were only the banks between the fields that had been eroded, but nothing was left. The topsoil had been washed away. The rain was still falling and even the sub-soil seemed in danger of being stripped off.

Gradually and almost imperceptibly the rain began to slacken. The distance once again was streaked by falling drops. The clouds rose and the mist began to drift away, revealing the landscape. Blind Man's Pool and the cliffs seemed to float and drift in the air. The high clouds rolled away to the south, while the even higher white wisps of vapor drifted off to the north.

The rain had nearly ceased, and the situation at Fanzai Wood was clear to the eye. Only two houses remained largely unscathed: Xu Shihui's five-room bamboo house and Chen Afa's three-room thatched house. The recently constructed houses of Fan Qian and Xie Atan had lost their roofs. Aling and Ahan's house near the stream still had its roof, but the mud walls had been damaged. The houses of the Peng, Chan, Xu, and Su families had all been destroyed.

"It's all over."

"What is all over? None of us has been hurt. How can you say that it's all over? And stop sighing. What can you accomplish by sighing?"

"What else can I do but sigh?"

"Start over. Start again from scratch."

"Start over again for another typhoon?"

"We have to begin again."

"We'll starve. The fields have been washed away."

"We won't starve if we have land."

"What are we going to eat, mud? The topsoil has been washed away."

"There are weeds, and as long as there are weeds we won't starve."

By two o'clock in the afternoon, the rain had let up. A ray of golden sunlight pierced the dark clouds, striking the cliffs and fields and forests of Fanzai Wood. The dazzling sunlight seemed to revive everyone's spir-its. They heaved a sigh of frustration and inhaled a breath of courage. Wiping the mud and water from their faces, they started laying the foun-dations of their homes again using hoes, sticks, and even their bare hands. The first step of rebuilding had been taken.

SEVEN

Change

*I*t had been the most devastating typhoon in thirty years, but the residents of Fanzai Wood did not complain, did not curse. They accepted their fate in silence. At the end of the eleventh month of the same year, snow fell in northern Taiwan. In the middle of the twelfth month, snow fell not only in the high mountains but also on the fields and villages of the coastal plains. Under several inches of snow, the land looked more like someplace in northern China. The rare and unusual snowfall killed many people and animals.

The elderly and the very young were especially hard hit. Xu Rixing's emaciated wife and Chen Agu's elderly mother both died of starvation. Their hunger was apparent in their deeply furrowed lips, and their bodies looked more like those of monkeys captured but forgotten in hunters' snares, where they ended up dried and shriveled by the sun.

Increasingly the young people left the fields and drifted south, only to discover that hunger was as widespread there as in the north. The seasons and the weather seemed to have changed. It was as if the beautiful and fertile island of Taiwan had left its mild latitudes and shifted to a place where bitter cold was followed by unbearable heat.

The people were affected by the weather; only their struggle for survival remained unchanged. Soon the mountains were filled with bandits who came down to prey on travelers along the highways. They were mostly after food. Under these circumstances, farmers and artisans could barely get by. Having suffered the devastation of the typhoon, the people of Fanzai Wood were now confronted with one of the greatest challenges they had faced since they undertook opening up the land.

Nearly all the families in Fanzai Wood had given up cultivating the land; instead, they went out foraging for wild potato leaves, wild spinach, and other mountain herbs to assuage their hunger. Lanmei, who had once been hale and hearty, was now visibly aged and feeble. In three years she had suffered the death of a son, the devastation of a typhoon, and now the pangs of hunger. Although she was only fifty-seven, she looked more like seventy. Every day she gritted her teeth and without a sigh went out and cut firewood and carried it home. The fear-less expression never disappeared from her face, even when she was alone. Hunger made her back numb, and time seemed to weigh on her, giving her an aged stoop. She had always disliked old crones with stooped and bent backs, and this was a fate she had always hoped to avoid. She would rather have been laid out flat in her coffin than end up a bent-over old lady. Thinner by the day, she tried her best to keep her straight posture.

Peng Aqiang was also getting thinner and his skin darker, and he was losing his hair. But he seemed not to have lost his health and looked to be in better shape than when Renxiu had died. After the typhoon and rains had wiped away his fields, he was disconsolate and seemed disori-ented for a while. But soon he acted as if filled with a sense of liberation and exhilaration.

Peng Aqiang thought of how they could no longer be robbed; no one could take anything from them. Heaven had taken it all. He laughed to himself and then wondered why he was laughing. After the storm had passed, he had gone with a hoe on his shoulder to examine his fields and terraces. The topsoil had been washed away, leaving only gravelly subsoil.

Everyone agreed that the subsoil would not yield anything for a year or two. But by the far the biggest shadow hanging over them was that the land had been officially tenured to Ye Atian. If they wanted it for themselves they would have to struggle to pay the taxes in addition to rent. How could they manage that with such poor soil?

Renhua once again suggested that they give up. Peng Aqiang slapped his son's face. That night Renhua quarreled with Qinmei, who had recently given birth to a daughter. The next morning he said he was going to Great Lake.

Two weeks later, the Fan and Xie families slipped away from Fanzai Wood without saying good-bye to anyone. Three days later, as Peng Aqiang and Renjie were working in the fields, they saw Qinmei, baby on her back, walk by carrying a large bundle. Peng Aqiang and his son crossed the stream to the road, where they came face to face with her just after she had finished praying to the gods at the temple.

Taken by surprise, Qinmei went white.

"What are you doing?" Peng Aqiang tried without much success to control himself and keep his voice down.

Qinmei raised her eyes and gritted her teeth. "I'm going to look for Renhua."

"We will look for him," said Renjie.

"Why bother? Just pretend he's dead," said Peng Aqiang.

"No, he's not dead. And he can't just abandon us here," said Qinmei, regaining her composure.

"My brother and I will deal with it. You go home."

"You're going to deal with it? He's gone and you don't know where he is. How are you going to deal with it?"

"We won't let you or your children starve."

"But you want me to be a widow?"

"Be quiet," shouted Peng Aqiang.

"Why do you insist on provoking him?" said Renjie, also annoyed.

Qinmei was fit to be tied and her temper flared. "If Renhua doesn't want me, I can go. If he can run away, why can't I? My name is not Peng!"

"You are married to a Peng, so you are a Peng," said Renjie, looking away.

"Very well, Zhang Qinmei, you can leave." Peng Aqiang was furious; his neck swelled and his white hair seemed to stand on end. "But leave your little bastard child here, she belongs to the Pengs."

Qinmei was stunned and speechless.

Renjie just stared at his father in astonishment.

Peng Aqiang seemed to sway on his feet. "She is shameless."

"All right, Dad, leave her be. Let's go," said Renjie, steering his father away. "Get out of here, Zhang Qinmei, and take your bastard with you. Be out of Fanzai Wood by noon. I want never to lay eyes on you again. If I do, I'll strangle you both."

"Fine. I'll go with my little bastard." Qin Mei was not ashamed to leave on her own. She cried but faced her future calmly. "I've never lied to anyone. You Pengs just couldn't find an unblemished woman for your daughter-in-law. You had to take me with my child. We have all suffered."

Qinmei did leave her daughter, Jinmei, behind in Fanzai Wood, but carried her three-year-old son, Desheng, along on her back.

The drought lasted until the fifth month. The small vegetable plots, the paddies, and the fields were all parched and cracked. Even the grasses and the stubborn weeds died for lack of water. The riverbeds were dry and exposed, the cliffs were grayish white, and the land all around was brown. But just after the Double Fifth, a sweet rain began to fall. It seemed too little, too late. Pale green shoots emerged from beneath fallen leaves and withered roots after the parched, cracked soil had been moistened by the light rain.

Relief seemed to be at hand, and everybody sighed as if a weight had been lifted from them. Everyone in Fanzai Wood was busy. It soon became apparent, however, that the Pengs were short of manpower.

Renxing's wife, Azhi, was big with child and expecting soon. Good-natured Renxing was excited but also fearful. He knew there was nothing he could do, so he redoubled his efforts at tilling the soil. In spite of the typhoon and the drought, he was still strong as an ox. Not hunger, not hard labor, not even his wife's condition could dampen his spirits. Since moving to the Xus', he seemed to have become even more good-natured. With Azhi he was perfectly happy. But even with her intoxicating smiles and the pleasures of the marriage bed, something still troubled his heart. He always felt he owed something to his own family. He tried desperately to think of something he could do for them. One day he came up with an idea, and that night he told Azhi his plan.

"Your father has me working during the day, but he has said nothing about the nights."

"Yes, but no one works in the fields at night."

"I work all day, but I still have a lot of energy."

"I don't want you to," said Azhi as she snuggled against Renxing.

"I'll just do a little work in my father's fields at night. They are really short of help."

Azhi was silent for a moment. "Who do you mean when you say your 'father'?"

"My real father," said Renxing loudly.

"Then is not my father also your father?"

"I didn't say that. I was talking about my father who lives over there."

"Does that mean that the father living here is only my father?"

"He's my father too, but it's not the same. Peng Aqiang is the man who fathered me and raised me." Renxing was growing hoarse.

"All right, all right! I was just joking." Azhi couldn't bear to tease him any longer. "If you want to help out over there, that's up to you. Just remember that a man isn't made of iron. If you exhaust yourself from working too much, then what?"

"I won't overdo it."

"Going without sleep to go work in the fields at night, isn't that overdoing it?"

"I won't work the whole night—I'll still get some sleep."

"I won't agree to it," said Azhi firmly.

"I want to go."

"If my parents knew, they wouldn't be pleased."

"If you don't tell them, they won't know."

"And if I tell?"

Renxing took several deep breaths. "You won't tell, will you? You've got to think of me."

"You've got to think of me and the baby."

"I'll work hard. Don't get me wrong."

"I'm thinking of your health, Renxing."

In order to help his father, Renxing frequently overworked himself at night. Often he would not stop and go home until first cockcrow, especially on nights with a full moon. Within a few days, Renxing's father and brothers became aware of his nighttime activities. Peng Aqiang scolded him several times and said he would not tolerate such behavior, but Renxing continued to help out at night. Peng Aqiang threatened to expose him to Xu Shihui, but Renxing remained as stubborn as ever, refusing to listen to all objections and persuasion.

One night under a silvery moon, he plowed one furrow after another in the potato field. But cutting firewood and pulling stumps during the day must have taken too much out of him, because he kept yawning and could hardly keep his eyes open. *I was no good*, he thought, but he still wanted to finish five or six more furrows before turning in for the night. But he just couldn't go on; he had to stop and rest, just nap, as he had done more than once before.

He put down his mattock, stood up straight, and stretched as he yawned. Suddenly he was overwhelmed by dizziness and fell heavily to the ground. As he fell, he heard a scream from across the field. He passed out as a shadow rushed toward him. It was Azhi. Being so big with child, she had stumbled and fallen into the ditch between the fields. Holding her belly, she struggled out of the ditch. Renxing was still lying motionless in the field. She crawled to him, shouting his name. He had fainted. He was lying face down; Azhi wanted to turn him over, but she couldn't budge him. She burst into tears.

Xu Shihui and his sons suddenly appeared behind her. "What's the matter?" Her father's words startled her. She was crouching in the furrow, crying. With the help of his sons, Xu managed to turn Renxing over. He put an ear to his chest; his heart was still beating—faintly.

"He won't die," said Xu, turning to his daughter. "He's been ruining his health at the Pengs' for a long time now, hasn't he?"

Azhi shook her head.

"No? Don't you care what happens to him?"

"I don't know anything."

"You mean to say you didn't know that he was ruining himself, and us in the process?"

Renxing came to as the old man was scolding his daughter.

"I'm all right now. Go on home, Father."

"All right? Just like that?" said his father-in-law.

"Are you saying that you're not coming home?" asked one of Xu's sons.

"I'll do my work as usual during the day."

"You might as well go back to work for the Pengs during the day."

"No, this won't interfere with work on the family's fields."

"Which family is it that you're referring to?"

"My family, the Xus, of course."

"Right, the Xus and not the Pengs."

"For one more year," he blurted out without thinking.

"That's in one more year," roared the old man. "How are we to settle accounts tonight?"

"Let's go home now," pleaded Azhi. "We'll talk tomorrow."

"No, we're going to get things straight right now."

"Helping my father at night won't affect my work during the day."

"You yourself just said 'one more year.' Don't forget that one year also includes the nights."

Perhaps exhausted from scolding Renxing, Xu Shihui finally allowed himself to be coaxed and persuaded by his sons to go home.

"I'm sorry, Renxing. It wasn't me who told on you."

"Let's go home. It was my own fault."

"Your health is important, Renxing."

"I know. I won't work at night anymore. The dew is so heavy." Renxing walked over to help Azhi to her feet.

Azhi stood up with some effort, but she screamed as she felt a stabbing pain in her abdomen.

"My stomach hurts!"

"Did your fall hurt the child?"

The stabbing pains continued. Renxing was in a panic. It was well past midnight, but Azhi agreed when Renxing insisted that they wake her mother. They were both afraid that the fall had injured the child, because it wasn't due for another nine or ten days.

"It's all my fault," said Renxing. "What are we going to do?"

"What can we do? It's all your fault. If anything happens to Azhi, we'll see how you manage."

"It's all my fault. I beg you, Mother, is there anything you can do?" Sweating in fear, Renxing knelt before his mother-in-law.

"Mom, don't scare him," said Azhi. "Look at what a state he's in." She tried to comfort him in spite of her own pain. "Don't worry. Even if the baby's early, it's just a few days. It's not important. Stop being a nuisance and go to bed."

Azhi's pains came more quickly. The labor pains were normal, but the incessant bleeding was not. It couldn't be stanched. Quite clearly it was the result of her fall. Her first delivery was not going to be an easy one.

Xu Rixing's wife, the midwife at Fanzai Wood, had died of hunger during the famine. No one had come to take her place. Renxing knew that his own mother had delivered many babies. In the darkness, he went for her and brought her back to the Xus.'

The sky was growing light, and Azhi's pains had increased, but the baby still had not turned.

"This is bad."

"If she can't deliver within three hours . . ."

Peng Aqiang had also hurried over. The sky was bright, and the parents decided to send four men to Great Lake for a midwife. They were also charged with obtaining from the temple there two paper talismans of the kind that are burned and the ashes swallowed by women in labor. Renxing begged to be allowed to do something to help, but his mother-in-law refused his pleas. His own father said he could be of no help.

Xu Shihui had no energy to argue with Renxing. His resentment was slow to fade, and every time he laid eyes on Renxing's helpless, puppy-dog look, his temper would flare up anew. When no one was looking, he grabbed Renxing by the collar and dragged him outside behind the house.

"If my daughter dies, what are you going to do?"

His mind calm, Renxing replied without a moment's hesitation, as if he had long since made up his mind: "I'll die with her."

Xu Shihui was completely taken aback. Dumbfounded, he stared at him. He felt ill at ease, but also grieved, perplexed, and displeased. His feelings soon gave way to anger and annoyance. He was suddenly his old self again, and barked, "There's nothing for you to do here. Go and do some weeding in the sorghum field."

"I have to stay with Azhi," stammered Renxing.

"There's no need! If and when the child is born, someone will fetch you. If the child is not delivered, don't bother coming back."

Renxing dared not talk back. Without stopping to look in on Azhi, he set off with a hoe to weed the sorghum field. His father-in-law's words rang in his ears. His loud voice had softened as he spoke; his command ended more like a plea. But it wasn't a plea, either. How could he describe it? The old man, he decided, wasn't all that fierce. He was just angry or very worried.

As he was thinking, Renxing put down his hoe and sat in the middle of the field, flattening a stalk of sorghum on which a head of grain had just set. On this day, he'd do no hoeing; for once in his life, he was going to be disobedient. He was going to sit down and think. But think about what? There were too many things on his mind, making it impossible to think anything through to his satisfaction. The sun was hot and shimmered on the long, swordlike leaves of the sorghum, illuminating the tender green. Where the leaves grew thickest, the green was of a much deeper shade. The south wind blew, momentarily transforming the leaves into thousands of brightly fluttering ribbons.

He thought back to the year before, to when he lay bare-chested on the rain-moistened grass and Azhi came to him as if in a dream and lay with him. She was so soft and warm. He recalled how at that wonderful moment he felt himself at one with the earth. After that, whenever he was having difficulties or he was so tired he felt ready to drop, he would think of that sensation. Strangely, whenever he thought of that moment his difficulties would vanish and his weariness would retreat.

"Hey, Renxing! What are you doing?" Someone yelled from behind him. "It's a boy!" It was Renjie shouting. "Mother and child are fine. What are you sitting around for? You'd better get back."

The sweltering heat of summer was once again upon them. Would there be another typhoon and flood? No one was willing to make predictions. The families of Fanzai Wood had more or less rebuilt their houses; they had thrown them together using old materials, so the houses were not nearly as strong as before. Another natural disaster and there would be no recovering for the people of Fanzai Wood. But the signs were good: the pigeons and crows had built their nests high in the trees, there were few spiderwebs among the rafters of the houses, and the hornets swarmed in great numbers and showed no signs of dispersing. These things indicated that there would be no excessive wind or rain.

Summer also brought success on another front: the people of Fanzai Wood happily arrived at a satisfactory agreement over rights to the land after several months of bitter haggling and negotiating. Shortly after the typhoon had passed, Ye Atian sent his steward, Renxian, to inspect the damage to the fields. After Renxian departed, the villagers, with the exception of Chen Afa, decided after much discussion to send Xu Rixing to negotiate with Ye Atian. They felt that if he wanted to take possession of the land then he would have to put up money for each family to help them restore it. If he did produce the silver, they would acknowledge his position. Otherwise he had best just leave them to their poverty-stricken slopes, and they would willingly compensate him for the losses incurred in obtaining the land patent.

At first Renxian refused the plan. "Our master does not pay out silver for no reason."

"Will the boss leave us alone, then?" asked Xu Rixing.

"So you do acknowledge your position."

"So what? We can just as easily abandon the land and open up fields in aboriginal territory near Big Southside."

"Aren't you afraid that they'll go on the warpath? Don't you care about keeping your heads?"

"The natives give warnings before they attack, unlike you murderers," replied Rixing, gritting his teeth. "What protection has the imperial government given us? We ourselves are half savage. We get along with the natives and offer them food, salt, and rice wine each year—not even a tenth of the pound of flesh you demand!"

Renxian had not expected this development.

"How about it? Ask Master Ye Atian to give us an answer. For the moment we are not going to work the land."

Three days later, Renxian delivered the news that Ye Atian would give up the land. The sum for "compensation" was fixed after a great deal of haggling. Having no silver readily available, each household made out a promissory note to Ye and agreed to pay in fixed installments. Ye Atian ended up with promissory notes worth eighty pieces of silver and became the creditor to all the residents of Fanzai Wood. Eighty taels was a frightful sum of money. Payments were due every six months at an interest rate of 1.5 percent a year. When the agreements were drawn up, the interest rate did not seem inordinate; no one could foresee that the promissory notes would become a chain that would strangle them.

The people of Fanzai Wood were elated. Peng Aqiang was the only person not satisfied, primarily because the agreement was strictly a private one. Ye Atian had generously drawn up a document agreeing to yield his land patent and allowing them to apply for their own. However, before they obtained their own patent, they had to furnish the money for the taxes Ye was responsible for paying.

They were unable to obtain a patent under Xu Shihui's name, so they begged Chen Afa, who had become the headman, to use his name. Still they got nowhere. At that point, Ye Atian became even more generous. He drew up another agreement allowing them to pay the taxes in perpetuity using his name before they obtained their patent, for which he would charge no commission.

The situation by then was clear and fixed. Peng Aqiang was still ill at ease. He was told not to be overly concerned. After all, the mountains would always be mountains, the rivers would always be rivers. He just had to have more faith in the laws of Heaven and the goodness of men. After all, officials and landlords were people too. They were subject to the laws of Heaven and had consciences to listen to. Would Ye Atian, once he had his hands on their silver and his interest, all without lifting a finger, go against his conscience, denying what he owed? No, that was impossible.

Peng Aqiang remained nervous and was unable to take part in the general rejoicing. In addition, there were all kinds of problems at home that often left him short-tempered. He was becoming a moody old man.

Liu Ahan had learned a few farming skills, but he was still a softie, unable to accomplish even half of what Renjie could. He seemed to have lost what value he had had; he was just a superfluous addition to the Peng family. He had no illusions about the situation and worked as hard as he could, but his efforts always fell short of what was required. He was already accustomed to the scorn and abuses of his old in-laws. He was not insensitive to their contempt but bore it nonetheless for the sake of Dengmei and the child she was carrying. He often tried to comfort himself with the fact that the old man and his wife weren't bad people; they had suffered a great deal, and it had affected them.

"Ahan, if it weren't for me, you wouldn't have to suffer like this," Dengmei was always saying to him. He wouldn't let her talk that way. But after hearing her words he could tolerate even greater sufferings and humiliation. He would always do so for her and the love he felt for her, and for the sake of their unborn child.

No typhoons hit that summer, and the few storms that came did not result in any disasters. The sorghum, millet, and potato crops were especially good that year. Even the seed scattered at random among the tea bushes and the terraced fields all sprouted and by autumn was bursting with golden ears of grain. The old saying that if one survived a disaster, blessings were sure to follow did indeed appear to be true.

One day as the sun was setting, Renhua, Qinmei, and Desheng reappeared in Fanzai Wood. They were seen coming around the Earth God Temple. Renhua was in the lead; behind him was his son. Twenty yards away stood a hesitant Qinmei. Renhua kept beckoning to her and even pleaded. Finally she stamped her feet as if she had given in, rushed forward, and picked up Desheng.

The Pengs were in the middle of eating when Renhua, Qinmei, and little Desheng arrived. They were now having potatoes instead of the wild herbs they had survived on for so long.

Liangmei was the first to speak. "Hurry, come and have something to eat."

Renhua stopped on the threshold and called to his parents.

Peng Aqiang and his wife sat motionless. Lanmei was holding sallow little Jingmei. Somehow the child gave a feeble cry.

Qinmei put down Desheng and rushed to her mother-in-law.

Little Jingmei cried, but she was very weak. Qinmei reached out for her daughter, but Lanmei turned and carried Jingmei away out of her reach.

Qinmei fell to her knees with a thud.

Desheng suddenly recognized his grandfather; he shouted his name and ran toward him.

Peng Aqiang reluctantly reached out and took his grandson in his arms.

Renhua also knelt.

Jingmei's cries grew hoarse and short. Qinmei moved forward, still on her knees, and reached out for Jingmei.

Peng Aqiang motioned for his wife to give the child to its mother.

Finally Qinmei had her daughter in her arms. She hugged and kissed her as she swallowed her own sobs and tears ran down her face.

"Father," said Renjie, as if to remind the old man.

The old man was saying something, but his voice was hoarse. He cleared his throat and said, "Get up. Have something to eat. Hurry up, now."

Renhua and his wife had returned home. Their attitude was greatly changed: they were no longer so dissatisfied and full of complaints. They rose early and went to bed late, quietly doing their work like the other people of Fanzai Wood. Renhua never mentioned the days after they left home nor what they did. They said nothing, and no one asked.

Summer passed and autumn arrived. The days of autumn were long and dry. As autumn gave way to winter, Dengmei gave birth to a baby girl as the sun was fading. The baby was small and pale, like a newborn rabbit. They were anxious because they discovered that the baby's left foot was shorter than her right, and it always seemed to fall limply to the side as if she couldn't put her feet together.

"She must have been touched by a demon when she was in the womb," said Lanmei.

"She's bound to grow up a cripple."

"I think you should cut your losses—don't tie the umbilical cord," said Peng Aqiang.

"It has already been tied."

"Then don't feed her."

"No!" shouted the young couple, but Ahan occasionally glanced at the old man and his wife. Dengmei's face was covered with tears, because she remembered how her foster mother had told her how she had been thrown into a pigsty, her umbilical cord not tied.

Ahan had long been worried about the health of the baby, even before she was born. Renxing's Zuwang and Renhua's Jingmei were both extremely weak, and Shunwei and Aling's baby was stillborn. He had also heard that the babies recently born in the area had been stillborn or crippled, or died shortly after birth. These babies had all been carried during the months of famine. Among poor mountain families, weak or crippled infants, especially girls, did not have their umbilical cords tied or were abandoned in some corner or placed in a nightsoil bucket until they expired. Then they were buried so that the child might seek another incarnation. In that sense, Peng Aqiang's suggestion was not at all unreasonable; it was the common-sense way out. But once the parents had seen their child and bonded with it, they could not be so hard-hearted.

"This is our child, Dengmei," said Ahan, his eyes growing misty.

"Yes."

He held her hand. "It's not that bad. Her left foot is just a little off. Even if she is a little crippled, I want to bring her up."

"I'm afraid, Ahan." Dengmei hid her face in her bedclothes.

"Don't be afraid, I'll think of a way. Don't cry."

Ahan went to the new vegetable plot to find Peng Aqiang. There the turnips and rapeseed were already a mass of green. The old man was thinning the rapeseed when Ahan told him his intentions.

"It's bound to be a cripple. How can we afford to keep it?"

"A cripple is a person and has a life too. I will raise her no matter what happens."

"And how are you going to raise her?" Peng Aqiang had been determined not to lose his temper, but he couldn't help roaring. "You can't even pay for your own keep; I never expected you to be so useless."

"But it was you who begged me to stay," said Ahan, also getting angry.

"At that time you were going to be captain of the guard, but what are you now?"

"It's not that I didn't want the job. At any rate, I'm doing my best."

"All right, all right! Rear the child yourself. You can live in the house, but you'll have to supply your own food."

"You mean you're asking us to leave?"

"I'm asking you alone to leave."

"Let Dengmei leave too."

"You're dreaming, you fool. Let Dengmei leave? Right, then bring me two dozen silver coins. It's that simple."

"You have no heart."

Peng Aqiang actually seemed to calm down a bit. "No heart—I have no alternative, Ahan. Apart from the potatoes and greens to fill our stomachs, we have no money. You know that weak and crippled babies, those malnourished in the womb, fall ill all the time. They cost money."

Ahan thought for a long time but couldn't come up with a concrete solution. "Then can Dengmei and the baby stay in Fanzai Wood? I'll leave and do whatever it takes to make some money to care for them. Will that do?"

"Where are you going to get money?"

He thought for a while. "I don't know, but I have to try. Taiwan is a big island, and there must be a way for someone like me to make money."

"I can't stop you," said Dengmei after she heard his plan. "You are risking everything for me and the baby, right?"

He reached out and stroked the baby's cheek.

"Your hands are dirty, don't touch her. If you must go, then I beg you to take care of yourself."

"I will."

"You must keep out of harm's way."

He again reached out. "I know. I'm not a child."

"What are you going to do? What kind of work?"

"I don't know."

"You can't do that. I beg you not to." Her face shone with tears. "You know I don't want you to do that. You must promise me that you won't."

"Okay, I won't. That's final."

"Ahan, look at me. Why won't you look at me?"

He raised his eyes shyly, but without looking her directly in the eye. "What's the matter?"

"Look at me when you agree," said Dengmei. "You mustn't, not even if it means that the child and I will starve."

"Okay, I won't." He gently stroked Dengmei's soft, smooth arm. Softly he cleared his throat, blinked, and said, "Look after our child. I'll be back soon with some money."

The following day, Ahan left his beloved wife and child and set off from Fanzai Wood. Dengmei had begged him over and over again not to do a certain job, one that she never mentioned by name. Dengmei certainly knew what kind of work he would seek. Why was she so sure? He himself had no idea what he was going to do. Did his wife understand him better than he understood himself?

Was he really ignorant of what Dengmei was referring to? Had he already made up his mind? Hadn't he had an inkling but refused to acknowledge it? Was he lying to himself? That must be the case, and Dengmei could see it. But why hadn't she mentioned the job by name? Perhaps she was afraid of giving him a hint if she guessed wrongly. Was that the case? He kept asking himself these questions.

He was full of uncertainty and felt bitter and bewildered. He felt everyone on the road to Great Lake was staring at him, but they weren't; they were all indifferent. It was the plants and trees beside the road that were staring; it was heaven and earth, the mountains and rivers that were staring at him. He vaguely heard what sounded like sighs as well as the cheerful sounds of encouragement. He also heard a faint sobbing. It was the child; it was Dengmei. When he thought of his wife, her face and the sound of her voice filled his mind.

He didn't want her to worry. He would take care of himself. He would come back a proper husband. He was preoccupied with his thoughts. He had decided to throw in his lot again with the soldiers at South Lake.

Three Chops was sitting alone drinking rice wine; he was already drunk. Three Chops probably didn't recognize Ahan, but as soon as he saw him he started mumbling as if he were complaining about something. At the same time, he handed Ahan the bottle of wine and insisted that he have a drink. He didn't remember Three Chops drinking that way.

Ahan took the bottle and started gulping down the wine. After pausing a few times to catch his breath, he polished it off. He was drinking on an empty stomach, and when he put the bottle down he could scarcely stand on his own two feet. Everything began to spin. Then someone seemed to lend him a hand. No, he was being carried by someone; then he was tossed on some hard planks. And there he fell asleep.

EIGHT

The Japanese Arrive

It was a year of fair weather, and Taiwan's wet and dry crops saw bumper harvests. The temperature dropped dramatically with the arrival of winter, and by the time the Lantern Festival rolled around in the new year, snow remained on the high peaks. The old people said it was a sure sign that the harvests would be good that year. But on the sixteenth day of the first lunar month, the birthday of the Earth God, bad omens began appearing.

The first occurred on the night of the god's birthday; a rooster in South Lake Village started crowing at eight o'clock in the evening. Then all the other roosters in the area took it up, eventually upsetting everyone. The old people said that such a strange event hadn't occurred in more than two generations.

Second, the moon rose a dull green color, and for three nights in a row, a comet appeared beside the green moon and remained for half an hour. It was said that the comet was a sign of rightful power being threatened. The bad omens continued: a woman at Great Lake gave birth to a two-headed baby; some people saw a pack of hideous three-legged dogs dig corpses from their graves on Tortoise Mountain, tear them apart, and devour them; rumor had it that nine pregnant women up north had had their babies ripped from their wombs; and down south several young boys had gone missing.

"The times are changing," said the old soldier Agou.

"Is there going to be another flood?" asked Ahan, the memories of the last still vivid in his mind.

"People are going to die in droves," said Du Shuihuo.

"Die? Are the natives going on the warpath, or will it be the plague? Must you be so ominous?"

"I don't know how it will happen; all I know is that people are going to die." Du was showing off his knowledge based on past experience. "These old bones of mine have been through a great deal. Trust me, this time people, no, whole villages will perish."

Ahan was on the point of saying something, but he felt too tired to open his mouth. He walked alone under the banyan tree, adjusted his collar, and sat down feeling numb.

"The situation is unstable: the government might be going to war."

Everyone was stunned. "The government going to war?"

"The defenses here in Taiwan are being strengthened."

"Are soldiers being sent to wipe out the natives?" asked one soldier, gesturing as if someone's head were being chopped off.

"I'm not sure, but I think they're going to fight with the savages of the Eastern Sea," said Three Chops, somewhat unsure of himself. "In any case, it's a foreign enemy."

Savages of the Eastern Sea? Foreign enemies? These were things they knew nothing about.

As events unfolded, rumors about the savages spread, and people developed an image of them: they were barbarians who lived on the islands to the east. They did not wear shirts and covered their nakedness with leaves; their hair was long and disheveled; they were small in stature but very strong; they were skilled in the use of razor-sharp swords; they were natural-born killers, and it was said that they ate human hearts.

Everyone was afraid. "Will they invade Taiwan?"

On the night of the fifteenth day of the seventh lunar month of the twentieth year of the Guangxu era (1894), Three Chops arrived with some news: China's war with the savages of the Eastern Sea had started at the beginning of the month. The savages were also known as the Japanese.

"Who won?"

"China, of course! The savages still hide their nakedness with leaves."

In the eighth month, rumors continued to fly. It was said the Chinese and the Japanese had fought battles on land and sea, but the outcome was still unclear; China had not been victorious, and the fighting continued. It was also rumored that Liu Yongfu, the Chinese general who had defeated the French, had arrived in Taiwan to recruit men and requisition horses. A force was put together and called the "Black Banner Troops." Everyone's hearts began to feel heavy. It looked as if Taiwan was going to war.

The summer sky was overcast, but there were no typhoons or floods. Autumn was dry, but there were more crows than normal and the gibbons were unusually hungry. The winter was mild, but the crabs refused to leave their crevices and the hornets came out stinging.

The strangest rumor of all came: China had been defeated. Could the great and mighty Qing dynasty have been defeated by naked savages who ate their food raw? The soldiers laughed and cursed as they argued. In the midst of widespread confusion, the governor of Taiwan was posted elsewhere. Tang Jingsong, who had been in charge of aboriginal affairs, was elevated to the position of governor. The first thing he did upon assuming office was to move part of the troops stationed in the mountains to the coasts.

In the Miaoli area, the system of shared responsibility for military outposts between the people and the government had long since broken down. The rifles remained the property of the government, but the local residents supplied the soldiers with ammunition, pay, and money for other expenses. At the end of the year, the authorities ordered Three Chops to turn over the soldiers' guns, thus putting the military entirely under the control of the local people. The soldiers at South Lake were now short twenty rifles. How were they to cope with the situation? It was announced that the soldiers' pay would not be affected by the change, but everyone knew that their jobs wouldn't last.

With a heavy heart, Ahan returned to Fanzai Wood for the new year. Over the last few months, the Pengs had been entirely dependent on him for their cash income. He soon discovered that his position in the family had become more secure. He was also comforted by the fact that Dengmei's health had improved; it was even better than before her pregnancy. She glowed with youth and a more mature beauty. He had never seen Dengmei so beautiful. As for their daughter, Ayin, her appetite was good and she smiled and was active in spite of being pale and thin. She was a delight.

At the new year, word came that the soldiers' pay would be reduced by half. Recently, their wages had risen, as had prices in general. But now the pay for a dangerous job like theirs was no different than for any unskilled laborer.

"At that rate, it'd be better not to go back," said Dengmei hesitantly.

Anger rose up in him. "What are we going to eat if I don't go back?"

"The old people couldn't have spent all the money you earned."

"With so many mouths to feed, I'm afraid they have."

"Everything is chaotic these days. There's sure to be danger."

As far as Ahan was concerned, everything was in the hands of fate. But he couldn't bear to look into Dengmei's worried eyes. He went to

Peng Aqiang and told him he wanted to quit the service. Peng Aqiang's color changed. "You'll have to come up with two silver coins for me each month."

"There will only be one silver dollar a month," he reminded the old man.

"Fine, that's better than nothing."

Ahan objected vociferously.

"Ahan, it's not that I don't treat people like human beings, but can't you just bear with it a bit longer? Can't you hang on for six months, until harvest time? Renxing's time with the Xus will be up and I can ask him to become a soldier. If you don't want to do it then, you can quit."

The old man's words were tough, but he had a soft heart. The old man was putting a lot of pressure on him. Ahan would just take it as a personal plea. Could he refuse then?

In the end, Ahan returned to the garrison at South Lake. Upon arriving, he heard it rumored that the garrison was to be disbanded. The wealthier residents of South Lake had moved out at the new year. Most had gone to Long Hill to avoid the fighting. By the second lunar month, rumor had it that the Japanese were going to attack Taiwan. Later it was learned that the target was the Pescadores, which were occupied by Japanese forces by the middle of the second lunar month. The people living in the hills and mountains didn't know what to make of the situation.

In the third lunar month of the twenty-first year of the Guangxu era (1895), the Chinese government sued for peace. On the seventeenth day of the fourth lunar month, both sides met in Japan and signed the Treaty of Shimonoseki, which, among other things, ceded Taiwan to Japan. From that moment on, the fate of the people of Taiwan was no different from that of an abandoned or orphaned child.

Japan sent Admiral Kabayana Sukenori as the first Governor-General of the island. He arrived in Keelung at the end of the fifth lunar month. On the second day of the sixth month, in a ceremony aboard ship in Keelung Harbor, Li Jingfang, the representative of the Qing court, handed over possession of Taiwan to imperial Japanese authority. Taiwan was severed from the motherland.

The arrival of the Japanese occupation forces in Taiwan brought turmoil. The tragedy began in the north and spread south as society fell into utter chaos and upheaval. Once it became clear that Taiwan had been ceded to Japan, the initial astonishment of the island's three hundred thousand inhabitants turned to anger. They did all they could in hopes that the Manchu court would take up the fight again. But the court was weak, and all the people could do was turn to the international community for help, to no avail. The sad and angry people of Taiwan found that they would have to rely only on their own efforts.

On the twenty-second day of the fifth month, a Formosan Republic was proclaimed, with Tang Jingsong as president. Independence was proclaimed the following day. The old imperial *yamen* was made the office of the new president. And with an eleven-gun salute, the Formosan flag—a yellow tiger on a blue field—was raised on the ramparts. Although the Republic was short-lived, it was the first in the history of Asia.

On the third day of the sixth lunar month, the Japanese attacked in the area of Keelung, which fell the following day. Once the northern districts were pacified, all semblance of order farther south vanished. On the night of the fifth day, the President of the Republic vanished out the back door of his office. He fled Taiwan for Xiamen, in Fujian province, on a steamer flying the flag of a foreign power. The following night, the Japanese entered Taipei. The Chinese officials who had gone north to defend the island all fled for the mainland. From then on, defense of the island and resistance to the Japanese occupation came from the people of Taiwan themselves.

It had grown quiet in the border areas between the Chinese and the native inhabitants. The people of Jialihewan and Tabelai villages near South Lake had sent emissaries to the Chinese outposts for news about the fight against the Japanese. Even the native inhabitants had become aware of the Japanese occupation.

"Perhaps we can fight the Japanese," suggested one of the emissaries.

"Do the Atayal people also hate the Japanese?"

"Yes. We get along with the Chinese. There will be too many people and nothing to eat if the Japanese come."

"Are you going on the warpath?"

"We made peace with the Chinese, so we'll kill the Japanese."

Word that the Atayal tribespeople had joined them against the Japanese was welcome news. As a result, many people expressed the desire to reduce the expenditures for the guardsmen. It was eventually decided that the force at South Lake would be cut in half, leaving twenty men. Ahan had been the last to sign up, so he was the first to be laid off. How was Ahan to maintain his position in the Peng family, since he had lost his job? He gave the matter a lot of thought.

It was at that point that Three Chops brought the astonishing news that the people from Miaoli, Xinzhu, and Taoyuan had decided to form a volunteer force to fight the Japanese. Three Chops told Ahan that the volunteers would be paid a monthly wage as well as a signing bonus of six silver dollars up front—the equivalent of six months' wages as a guard. But this time they were going to war against the fearsome Japanese and not as a defense force against the natives. The value of a man's life had been set at six dollars.

"Dengmei, little Ayin, what am I going to do?" asked Ahan confusedly. He grew warm all over when he thought of Dengmei. She was the thin, dry girl he had purchased two years ago—now she was an attractive woman in the full bloom of life. Her smiling face suffused with the glow of love and her gentle manner filled his mind. He didn't want to lose his wife or his daughter. That was all he could think of.

"Come with me and fight the Japanese," said Three Chops.

"No," he answered automatically. "I must return to Fanzai Wood."

Three Chops, who was very fond of him, threw him a sympathetic glance, then set off for Miaoli with seven or eight young guards. Ahan left for Fanzai Wood, his heart filled with uncertainties and worries.

"I heard you were coming back," cried Dengmei with joy.

He had run into Dengmei in front of the temple. She had Ayin on her back as she paced back and forth.

"What are you doing here?" he said reproachfully.

Dengmei's cheeks flushed red as persimmons.

He was right to return. He would willingly suffer any humiliation to be able to spend his days eating potato soup with Dengmei and Ayin. He was afraid of death and gladdened by his decision to return. But Peng Aqiang's face was grim, and Renhua was full of sarcasm. Renxing had returned home with his wife, Azhi. Their first child had died, and she was pregnant again. Ahan really did seem superfluous in the Peng household.

News about the turmoil up north never stopped coming. First they heard that the rich people had all fled north, then that they had fled south, preparing to flee the island from Anping and Dagou. The north had been pacified and the Japanese colonial government had been set up in Taipei, under which a Miaoli Administrative District had been formed. The Japanese army was moving south on its way to Great Lake and was already near Xinzhu. No longer were the Japanese, with their guns and cannons and uniforms, called savages.

In the middle of the sixth month, Wu Tangxing rallied more than two thousand volunteer troops. They vowed before the Matsu temple in Tongluo to march north. Since all the Chinese court-appointed officials had fled to China, all resistance came from local volunteers. Wu, along with two other imperial degree holders, led the troops north to engage the Japanese at Taoyuan, Longtanpo, and Xinzhu.

Several typhoons hit the island that month, after which the weather remained overcast without a breath of wind. The land seemed dull and heavy. In the stifling, humid weather, the bloody fighting progressed southward. A path of burning homes was nearing Miaoli.

One day near the end of the seventh lunar month, Ahan, Renhua, and Renxing were shoring up the terraced fields behind the house and adding soil for the sorghum crop. Ahan was preoccupied with his daughter's illness. At first it was just diarrhea, but later she began to vomit. After using herbal remedies unsuccessfully for several days, Ahan had taken some of his savings and bought some medicine. After she had taken the medicine, Ayin's diarrhea and vomiting stopped, but her temperature rose within a matter of hours. The next day her fever continued to rise; her little body was as hot as a stove. The fever showed no signs of breaking even after three days. She started having spasms, and her face was flushed bright red.

Ahan went to Great Lake by night to buy medicine, but the fever persisted. On the fourth day Ayin lost consciousness. Peng Aqiang seemed indifferent, but Lanmei was concerned. Aling and his wife asked Master Xu Rixing, the exorcist, to come and drive away the evil spirit that had taken possession of the child, to no avail. They then asked Xu Shihui to get a banner from the temple to the Righteous Lords and let Master Xu Rixing arrange for a séance with a boy spirit medium in order to discover the cause of the illness.

The boy spirit medium spoke clearly, entirely unlike the garbled frenzy that characterized most mediums. "Beacon fires burn for days. Jackals and wolves will roam the land. The star of fate is weak. It will be difficult to survive the turmoil of fire."

Ahan had been silent since Ayin had slipped into a coma. Dengmei wept with her head lowered, not daring to look at her husband. Peng Aqiang tried to get everyone back to work. "Death is a decided fate. It makes no difference what you do, and praying is of no use. Go and add soil to the sorghum terraces. We've got to make sure that the adults don't starve."

When it came to handling a hoe, Ahan was not very good. Besides, he was worried about his daughter, who could very well breathe her last at any moment. A fury burned in his guts too, and he was afraid he would lose control. He could not rid himself of the resentment he felt. Dengmei became the target. After losing his job, he had asked her to run away with him. He wanted to get away first, then worry about reconciliation and earning the money to pay the Pengs for their freedom. But Dengmei had adamantly refused. Without looking him in the eye, she had replied to him without a moment's hesitation. And look what had happened to his poor, sweet daughter. He was determined to save her, his daughter, his own flesh and blood. If he, her father, didn't save her, who would? He wondered why he was so obedient to the unreasonable Peng family. He swayed on his feet.

Little Ayin's face took on a purple cast and looked vaguely unreal. Dengmei was crying without restraint. Ahan took the child in his arms;

he hugged her close for a long time. He couldn't lose his own daughter. His feelings as he hugged her would stay with him for the rest of his life, forever. He would always hold his daughter close to him, and never again would he feel the same kind of doting love he felt for this child, regardless of how many children he might have. Perhaps such an intense love could never be experienced in such totality again.

He would let no one take his daughter from him. Dengmei tried unsuccessfully, as did others. He refused to let go of her. Later he heard that Ayin had been buried in the cemetery on the rise behind the temple. He refused to believe it. He laughed contemptuously because his daughter was still in his arms. But little Ayin was stone cold; no, she was feverish. Perhaps the fever had passed.

He didn't leave the house for several days. His cold-hearted wife was busy cooking or washing. She didn't care for Ayin. Dengmei was getting on with her life.

"Ahan, you can't go on like this," said Dengmei.

Ahan wondered where he was.

"Everyone is angry with you and cursing you."

Angry with him? Why? As long as Ayin was not angry with him. . . .

"Ahan! Did you hear me?"

Dengmei shook him. He pushed her away. Dengmei staggered and fell on the bed. She struggled to her feet but started vomiting. Why was she vomiting?

Early the following day, Peng Aqiang walked in and spoke loudly, cursing him. Liu Ahan sat silently without replying or defending himself, his face expressionless. Peng Aqiang stomped off angrily. Dengmei was standing by his side in her apron. She was pale and her eyes were red.

Dengmei tried to screw up enough courage to tell him what the old man had said. Yet when Ahan looked at her, she could not speak—she knew his temper. Despite his mild appearance, he had a violently explosive temper. He could maintain the outward appearance of putting up with anything, but once he found himself in a situation that ran counter to his desires, he might explode. She feared that if she told him what the old man had said, he might get his hackles up and quarrel with her. But if she didn't talk to him, how could she face her foster father? He had told her that if Ahan didn't go to work in the fields, he need not expect to eat supper.

All she could do was sweeten her voice to temper the old man's harsh words. "Ahan, Father says you really should go back to work in the fields."

Ahan's eyes remained vacant.

"Things will be difficult if you don't work—they won't give us anything to eat."

She went outside, retrieved the hoe leaning by the door, and thrust it into Ahan's hands. Ahan looked at her as if he had suddenly awakened. He put the hoe over his shoulder and went out. But as he reached the bamboo bridge over the stream, he stopped and again stood stock still.

Dengmei seemed to choke on her words but soon regained her voice. "Go on, Ahan. Father said that if you don't work in the fields you needn't expect to eat supper."

This time Ahan heard her. He moved off toward the slopes, hoe still over his shoulder. She breathed a sigh of relief and quickly went to water the vegetable garden.

The work in the fields was hard, and the meals had increased from two to three each day. The fields were close by, and the Pengs returned home to eat at noon. But Ahan did not come home. Dengmei stood waiting for him.

"Tell him he can't have lunch," said Peng Aqiang.

"Didn't Ahan go to work?" she asked, astonished.

"He sat on a rock and did nothing."

Panting, Dengmei hurried up the slope. At the top she found him lost in thought, sitting on a rock, his hoe laid to one side.

"Ahan, what are you doing?" she complained.

"I'm hungry," he said confusedly.

She gently whispered to him, then coaxed and pushed him back to the house. She went to get some food from the Pengs' kitchen, but unexpectedly Lanmei was standing in the doorway. Aling and his wife had returned to the fields, so Dengmei went to their room and secretly took a couple of potatoes out from under their bed. She peeled them and gave them to Ahan. As Ahan ate, he muttered how delicious they were.

"You must do some work this afternoon."

"I will," he agreed without protesting.

"We have to put up with the situation. You said so yourself. Okay? Someday we . . . but this afternoon you must work with everyone else."

That afternoon, Ahan followed Renhua to the fields behind the temple to fertilize the jute, a crop recently introduced to Taiwan. Jute was the perfect crop for the poorer fields. The work was light, just right for Ahan.

They stopped working at dusk. Everyone put away their tools and baskets, changed out of their work clothes, and washed their hands for dinner. Only then did Ahan slowly make his way back.

"Did Ahan work this afternoon?" Dengmei asked Renhua.

"No, he slept in the fields," said Renhua resentfully. "He just lay there staring at the mountains."

Dinner was served. Ahan appeared to be his normal self. He had washed his hands but not his face. He sat at the table waiting for his elders to sit down and for the meal to begin.

Dengmei, who had just brought in the last dish—lettuce soup—stood at the kitchen door watching Ahan. The old man and his wife sat down and everyone picked up their chopsticks. The centerpiece of dinner that night was fried spotted grouper fry, considered the most delicious of freshwater fish and a real delicacy. Renhua and the Xu brothers had caught a number of the fish the day before using a weir trap. That night she had hidden a small one in their room with the intention of giving it to Ahan, as he was particularly fond of that kind of fish. She had assumed that Ahan would not have the nerve to eat the fish served at dinner. But there he was, helping himself to the fish even before Peng Aqiang, the head of the household, had touched it, against the custom. He had clearly forgotten his place.

Ahan must have been really hungry and his mind confused. The smell of the fish must have made him forget everything else. Ahan held a three-inch baby grouper, the largest on the plate, in his chopsticks.

Peng Aqiang roared and stood up abruptly. He snatched up the plate of fish and threw the contents on the floor. He stood there still holding the dish. The room was filled with the delicious smell of the fish.

Dexin and Desheng were just about to pick up the fish from the floor. "Grandpa, I want some to eat."

"No," Peng Aqiang roared, "you are not to touch it, because it has been eaten by a beast."

Ahan trembled and his whole body swayed. He made a sound, turned from the table, stepped over the bench, and ran out of the house.

"Look after Dengmei," shouted Ahan as he rushed out the door.

As Dengmei reached their house, Ahan came charging out of the bedroom.

"I'm leaving," he said in a forced tone of voice.

"No, Ahan! Don't go!" She was unable to stop him—Ahan avoided her grasp. She turned to pursue him, but Renhua and Renxing were there to stop her, one in front and one behind.

"Ahan! Ahan!" she shouted.

Ahan had already been swallowed by the dark night. Dengmei's knees gave way and she sank to the ground.

Like a man possessed, Liu Ahan took off down the mountain path, disregarding the dangers of an attack by the natives or a fall from a cliff in the dark. He arrived at Great Lake at cockcrow.

When it was light, he saw many notices posted on the walls by the roadside. He could read a few words and phrases, such as "volunteer" and "Wu Tangxing, leader of the volunteers"; he had picked up a few words when he was a guard at South Lake. Without his being aware of it, his feet had carried him to the garrison located next to the Temple of the God of War at Great Lake. It was breakfast time and gruel was being served. The aroma made his stomach growl, and then he realized that he hadn't filled his belly in several days.

It turned out that soldiers were being recruited not to fight the natives but to battle the Japanese around Miaoli or Xinzhu.

"The garrison at South Lake was disbanded," said an old soldier. Ahan had hoped to get his old job back.

"Why not sign up?" said a recruiter. "When you get to Miaoli, you'll be given three silver dollars."

"Wasn't it six dollars?"

"You'll get three more dollars when you've completed training and marched for the front line."

Ahan's mind was blank, but there was a fire in his belly: he wanted to crush something, to knock something down; he saw red and wanted to kill. He signed up. The same afternoon he and about twenty other former soldiers marched for Miaoli. It was the eighth day of the eighth lunar month, the first day of autumn.

At the beginning of the eighth month, after a break, the nine thousand Japanese troops had regrouped in four battalions. With battleship support, they moved south. The region south of Xinzhu soon fell to the Japanese forces. On the morning of the fourteenth, the Japanese army pushed toward Miaoli, west from the sea and south by land.

Ahan and the other volunteers arrived in Miaoli on the thirteenth to a scene of total chaos as the troops prepared for the Japanese attack. The recruiting station that had been set up outside the old yamen was empty. The volunteers from Great Lake took off at once when they realized there was no hope of getting the three silver dollars owed them.

Shaking off his sadness and anger, Ahan wondered what he should do. He tried to keep his mind off Fanzai Wood by thinking about his old home of Tongluo Bay. Wu Tangxing, the commander of the volunteers, was also a native of Tongluo. Ahan also recalled the worn and weather-beaten face of that thin, frail woman.

He had not thought of his mother in a long, long time. He was an unfilial son. Whenever he thought of her, his heart ached. What had happened to Tongluo Bay? What had become of his mother? He couldn't stay in Miaoli, so he started west toward the coast. He wanted to get back to Tongluo Bay and figured he could make it there before daybreak.

Arriving in the hills to the west of Miaoli, he met six or seven men with torches. They were armed with swords and metal bars, and one of them had a bird gun. They prevented him from passing.

"The road is cut off. The Japs are swarming all over Zhonggang."

"What are you doing here?" asked Ahan.

"We're going to fight. What are you doing?" asked one of the men. "You can't get through. What about joining us?"

Ahan didn't want to join them, but the way ahead was blocked. He had to turn back. The change of guard appeared at that moment, and to Ahan's surprise he recognized one of the former soldiers from South Lake.

"How did you get here?" Ahan asked, smiling.

"It's a long story. I came with the sergeant."

"You mean Three Chops? Is he here?

The soldier pointed behind him.

"How many men are there?"

"Six or seven hundred. You should go have a look. The Japs will attack Miaoli through the hills, maybe tonight. We might be safe if we hide in the hills."

Ahan was led to a large banyan tree that was used as a temple to the Earth God. Three Chops, in uniform, sat at a stone table talking.

"Sergeant He," said Ahan.

Three Chops looked closely at him and then recognized him. "So it's you. Liu Ahan, right?"

"I never expected . . ."

"To see me here. Ha ha." Three Chops laughed till his unshaven face shook.

Later that night, Three Chops came and woke him from his nap. "Ahan, this is one fight you don't have to join. Lie low and take off."

Ahan rubbed his eyes. "Not fight? Why? Everyone else is going to fight."

"You are young," Three Chops replied haltingly. "You are young and have a wife and daughter."

He had a wife and daughter? He stood up abruptly and with his eyes wide open said, "I want to fight! Sergeant, I just want to kill someone."

Three Chops was about to say something, but there was no time. Daybreak had come with the sound of cannon fire, which seemed to be getting closer.

Three Chops gave the order to prepare for battle. He also ordered the cooks to prepare all the rice, which he then distributed to the volunteers.

"Will we be able to hold our position?" Ahan asked a soldier beside him.

The soldier didn't reply but handed him a gun and asked him to fix it. It was a bird gun, one of those that had been collected from the local people. Ahan knew from experience that that type of gun tended to jam after being fired a few times. Three Chops was carrying one of the new repeating rifles.

The red sun had risen above the peaks, accompanied by the sound of cannon fire. Below, the volunteers defending Miaoli had opened fire, but the shooting faded quickly. Gunshots were heard and yellow dust was rising along the river by Zhonggang all the way to Tortoise Mountain.

A soldier arrived seeking orders. Were they to charge down the hill?

"Hold your position," ordered Three Chops. "We will wait here for the Japs to come from the sea."

"What if they don't come from the sea?"

"They will."

"If Miaoli is going to be lost, what is the point of waiting here?"

Three Chops made no reply. True, if Miaoli fell, what was the point of holding the hills?

The sun had risen high overhead. There was no movement along the road from the sea and they had received no intelligence reports about the Japanese having entered Miaoli. But sporadic gunfire continued to be heard north and east of the city.

Suddenly Japanese soldiers appeared above them on the hill. Three Chops was the first to plunge downhill—it was each man for himself. Ahan crouched in a hollow beneath a mossy outcropping of rock. Something blocked the sunlight in front of him and he nearly let out a shout. He saw two legs bound in puttees. He knew they were not the feet of a Taiwan volunteer or those of a Qing soldier. He watched as the feet walked away, stopped, and started to turn in his direction. Holding his machete with both hands, he lunged, plunging the blade into the soldier's belly.

The Japanese soldier screamed, and Ahan quickly threw himself into a large clump of grass. Hitting the ground, he rolled away and crawled into another clump. At that moment a hail of bullets ripped through the first clump of grass he had landed in. He ached all over, especially in his chest and legs, but he knew it didn't matter. His instinct for survival was heightened vividly; he was resolved to fight. He couldn't die. He would escape. He had to live. He had to be master of the moment.

He hid in a gully. Suddenly, a sickening smell rose around him, and he touched something sticky. It was nearly dark and he couldn't see anything down in the gully, but he knew he that his hand was covered in fresh blood. He broke out in a cold sweat but realized that he couldn't have lost so much blood. It must have flowed down the hill from their old position. He wondered how many of the six or seven hundred troops had been killed.

It was August 14, the twenty-fourth day of the sixth lunar month. In the dark of night, the gunfire on the hill had ceased, and none was heard below along the road. Ahan could no longer bear the overpowering stench of the blood. He climbed out of the gully and hid in a dense tangle of creepers.

In his knapsack he still had some of the rice he had been given, but his mouth was so dry he couldn't eat a thing. He fell into an uneasy sleep, only to be awakened by the predawn chill; it was raining. There was not a star in the sky and the moon was a faint yellow glow behind the clouds.

He was still alive, but he wasn't sure how he should proceed. He wondered if Miaoli had been occupied. Then his thoughts turned to Great Lake and Fanzai Wood. He tried to avoid thinking about Fanzai Wood and shifted his thoughts to Tongluo Bay. He was concerned about the fate of his poor mother. He no longer hated her, nor did he feel any resentment; everything was fated. He felt sorry for her and wanted to kneel before her and beg forgiveness. He longed to see her. He was twenty-five and had learned something about life. He regretted the way he had treated her. From that moment on, he was preoccupied with her safety.

The sky was gradually growing lighter. Taking advantage of the light, he made his way down the hill and took the road toward Miaoli, to hide in the hills southwest of the city. There he met with a number of his comrades who also had survived the attack, as well as some volunteers who had been defending Miaoli. He learned from them that the city had fallen the previous night. As for the volunteers on the hill, he learned that the Japanese had attacked from three sides and massacred more than four hundred. There were at least that number of corpses lying exposed on the hillside. A large number of enemy soldiers controlled the hill and shot anyone on sight.

After a day of hunger and exhaustion, more and more people fled Miaoli. From them it was learned that the Japanese were going from house to house searching for "bandits" and any young, able-bodied men. Anyone possessing a knife, a gun, or a fishing spear was without exception taken prisoner. Ahan also learned that due to the large number of volunteers fleeing along the road to Great Lake, checks were more stringent there.

Ahan decided to lie low for a while. He and a few others in the same situation made their way to the other side of the hill, where they built straw huts. They also collected wild herbs and fruit to assuage their hunger. On their fourth day there it began to rain, and on the fifth day, they saw a group of about forty people coming down the path from Tongluo Bay. They looked as if they had traveled a long way and staggered from exhaustion.

They were invited to rest. All of them were old men, women, and children. They were emaciated, dirty, and ragged as a band of beggars.

"Where are you from?"

"Tongluo Bay," replied a hunched-over old man.

"What happened at Tongluo Bay?" asked Ahan, deeply concerned. "Are the Japs there?"

"They torched almost all of the town."

"Why did they do that?"

"They said it was a nest of bandits and Wu Tangxing's home."

Then in a flurry of voices they told about the massacre. First the Japanese had sealed off the city; then they proceeded to pour kerosene over the houses—most of which were made of bamboo and thatch—and set them on fire. The old and the very young were allowed to run away, but all young men were bound and blindfolded and taken to the open space in front of the Matsu temple. The Japs then asked a volunteer by the name of Wu, whom they had taken prisoner, to point out the "bandits." "Each young man was led before him and he was asked by a Jap who spoke our language if he was a bandit. If Wu nodded his head, the young man was taken to the edge of the river, where he was beheaded. If he shook his head, the prisoner was released. Wu realized this, so he just kept shaking his head. Then the Japs got pissed and started beating him on the head with a stick. Unable to bear the pain, he started nodding his head."

"Then all of them must have been killed."

"Almost all of them," replied an old woman. "When we stole quietly out of the town we saw . . ."

"What did you see?"

"The river that passes through Tongluo was flowing red with blood."

At that point they all sighed and fell silent, staring blankly ahead. In the quiet, their thoughts turned to their own sons and husbands. They began to cry one by one.

Ahan had a strange feeling and his heart leaped. He couldn't think, but his heart reverberated with a familiar cry. He had been having these feelings for days, but never stronger than the previous night. What did they signify? He felt he was on the verge of understanding, but at the bottom of his heart he really didn't want to know. Listening to these people, his own compatriots who had fled as refugees, he wondered if the Japanese intended to kill all Taiwanese who resisted them. They had not killed the young and old, nor the women. When he thought of the women a cold shudder ran down his back.

"Hey, aren't you . . . ?" an old woman with thin white hair asked Ahan.

"What? My name is Liu Ahan."

"Ahan! Of course. You came to ask me to witness your marriage."

"Auntie Agui, is that you?" he asked, suddenly recognizing her.

A smile started to appear on her wrinkled face but then froze. She looked down. "Oh, child."

"What is it, Auntie Agui?" He thought for a moment and then was nearly overcome. He rushed forward, grabbed the old woman's arm, and shook it. "It's not true, it can't be."

Auntie Agui glanced up at him.

"It can't be. Didn't you say the women were not harmed?" he asked, seeking to deny any possibility that she might have been hurt.

"That Xu Ameng."

"What about Xu Ameng?" Xu Ameng was his mother's husband.

"Beheaded. He was probably the fifth one."

He screwed up his courage and asked, "What about my mother?"

"Your mother is fine. Nothing happened to her."

"Hey, wasn't Ameng's wife the one that was shot when she tried to put out the fire?" interjected a small, thin woman.

"What? Did you say she was shot?" Ahan turned toward Auntie Agui. "Tell me! Is it true?"

Auntie Agui nodded and looked at him with pity in her eyes.

He didn't believe them! They didn't know what they were saying. His mother couldn't be dead. They were so scared they didn't know what they had seen. They were talking nonsense. He didn't believe them. He denied it over and over. "I don't believe it," he roared. "I'm going to find her."

He thrust a knife someone had left lying on the ground into his belt. His eyes burning, he stared at everyone, then set off down the hill. He was quite clear and rational. Avoiding the main road to Tongluo Bay, he took paths through the hills instead. Brushing aside the branches across the paths and avoiding the thorns, he boldly but cautiously made his way to Tongluo Bay.

The evening sky was a deep orange color by the time Ahan had stealthily made his way to Tongluo Bay by way of the hill paths. Located on the west central coast of Taiwan, Tongluo Bay had been one of the earliest Hakka settlements on the island. It was surrounded by mountains on three sides. From the beginning of winter to the end of spring, the town was shrouded in a thick fog every morning and evening. That year, the fog was especially thick and moved in more quickly than usual. Ahan saw that a dense curtain of fog had completely covered the houses, roofs, and thorny hedges, and those unforgettable longan trees. The air was filled with the acrid smell of the burned town and a faint stench of blood.

He strode into the darkening fog to his heartbreaking old home. Desperately but fearfully trying to verify what had happened, Ahan forgot that Japanese soldiers might be waiting in ambush. The sky was dark, and there were no lights by which to orient himself. But it was impossible for him to lose his way—he simply let his feet guide him. He headed in the direction of the village center. He couldn't see clearly, but it seemed that the little shop and tea pavilion had changed and that nothing remained but tumbled-down walls. The wood smoke was so thick he nearly choked. He neared the end of the village and turned up the slope. His home, that mud-walled cottage, was there. When he had come back five years ago, and later to offer sacrifices to his ancestors, this had been his first stop. Only a portion of the walls remained standing, and the roof had fallen in—no, it had been burned off.

He wondered if there was anyone left alive in the village with whom he could talk. He thought of the big brick house that belonged to the most senior member of the Liu clan, his uncle Bingrong. The village was small and he quickly located the house. The two-storied main hall could be seen even in the dark. Wisps of black smoke rose from the still-smoldering house timbers.

"Uncle Bingrong! Uncle Bingrong!" shouted Ahan, his voice trembling.

Silence reigned as if it were the land of the dead. Not a chicken or a dog was heard, not even a rat scurried.

"Is anyone here?" Ahan thought for a while, then shouted, "It's me, Ahan. I'm back."

There was a loud thud as a smoldering timber fell, sending embers shooting through the air. The flames flared up a ghastly red the color of blood. The thick fog seemed to hamper the flames as they struggled upward in the wet air, only to trail off in faint blood-red licks and then vanish in the empty darkness.

Ahan stepped back, his hair standing on end. "Hey, come out!"

No one replied. Ahan shuddered with fear, then turned and ran. He was confused. He wanted to have a look at the front of the Matsu temple, but in the dark he ended up at the temple of the Earth God. The ten-square-foot temple looked undamaged. The mud walls and bamboo roof were intact. But upon entering the shrine, he tripped over something. He had fallen over a huge stone slab; it was the stone altar of the god that had been pulled down.

"Who's there?" someone yelled.

In the dark, he could not see who had spoken. "It's me, Liu Ahan," he said, steadying himself.

"You're not from this village, are you?"

"I was. Now I live at Fanzai Wood near Great Lake."

"What are you doing in this bloody hell?"

"I came back to see . . ."

"Get out of here. The Japs will be back when the sun comes up for the young who have not escaped."

"I wanted to find out something." He was afraid to ask for fear that his worst fears would be confirmed.

"Did you say you were from Fanzai Wood?" asked the aged voice. "Then you must be Liu Alai's son."

The name held in his memory was Liu Tianlai. Aside from his grandmother, no one had ever mentioned that name buried deep in his heart. "His real name was Liu Tianlai."

"That's right, it was Liu Tianlai. He's been dead a long time. So what brings you back?"

"I've come back to . . . What is your name, sir?"

"I'm Liu Goushun, your uncle."

"You've come back too late, young man," said a woman's voice.

"She's your aunt," said Liu Goushun.

"Auntie, what do you mean by too late?"

"Your mother, Ameng's wife, is gone. She left us before Ameng."

"How did she die?"

What Ahan had heard was true. She had been shot while trying to put out the fire after the Japanese had torched the village. She had already been buried in the mass grave along with the villagers who had been beheaded. "I lost my third and fourth sons. They both had their heads cut off."

"Uncle Rongbing's case was the saddest of all—every last one of his boys was killed."

Ahan sat on the fallen altar of the Earth God. At some point, a vague shadow appeared in the damp, inky darkness. It was not a shadow but a woman—a thin, careworn old woman with a wrinkled, weather-beaten face.

"Look at him, he's still a child." Those were the very words that his mother had spoken to Auntie Agui some years ago.

At that moment Ahan was filled with anger.

"Come back, Ahan!" his mother had shouted to him.

"Why should I listen to you?" he had said.

"Do I have to kneel before you to make you listen?"

"You . . ."

"Your mother is truly sorry. I know you hate me. I don't blame you."

How could his mother have been made to speak like that? He no longer hated her. He couldn't bear her silence, the look in her eyes, her tears. He hadn't forgotten his promise that she would live with him and his family after Xu Ameng passed away. She could help Dengmei look after the grandchildren. They would live together and he would put the ancestral tablets on the family altar. *I know you had no choice but to remarry. I bear no grudge. If you have time, you can stay with us so that your son and grandsons will be able to look after you. But now you have left without knowing. . . .*

In the depths of his numbed mind he knew his mother was dead. He didn't know where the night had gone. Goushun and his wife seemed to have said a great deal about his father's youth and his mother's remarriage. He didn't manage to take any of it in. His mind remained fixed on one thing: he would kneel at the mass grave where his mother was buried and keep a vigil there for her. He hoped that after her sad life of suffering she could at last find peace. She had had no choices in life. She was a bod-hisattva who gave life to others; that was how Ahan saw her. Always he would carry with him the anger and regret he felt then. His heart would be her soul's resting place. He was determined to avenge her. But how?

Not once did he utter a cry, but his tears flowed without stopping. His cheeks were cold and numb as the sky grew light.

"Go to the front of the Matsu temple and have a look. You can help me find the heads of all the victims."

"You ought to go to the big grave pit."

He did not follow any of their suggestions. By the time the sun had penetrated the morning mist and reached the tops of the longan trees, he was on his way out of Tongluo Bay. His heart full of sadness and anger, he returned along the route he had come. Hunger slowed his steps. He had grown accustomed to it and had learned to eat whatever was at hand to quell his empty stomach. In the forests and at the springs, he met groups of refugees. In addition to the women and children, he saw sol-diers, straggling volunteers, and remnants of government troops. His sole response to their questions was to ask them where they were going. He followed the refugees north.

Near noon he found himself in the hills west of Miaoli. He was hun-gry again. He saw two recently deserted farmhouses and went to look for something to eat. He noticed five or six other men standing around silently eyeing the scene; apparently all of them had the same idea.

"The Japs are coming!" someone shouted.

About twenty Japanese soldiers in yellowish uniforms with bayonets affixed to their rifles could be seen in the camphor wood behind the farmhouses.

Shots rang out. The Japanese soldiers pursued them. There were real-ly more than twenty, and they seemed to be coming from all sides. The refugees were surrounded. They had been ambushed.

Ahan and a number of others took off as fast as they could run for a plateau to the southeast. The Japanese soldiers stayed right behind them and seemed to be making a flanking movement to hem them in. Bullets whizzed by as they ran, and occasionally one of them would fall to the ground, struck by one.

The Japanese kept shouting for them to surrender. But they couldn't give up; they ran without looking back. If they could make it to the next hill, they could hide in the undergrowth near the temple. But as they got to the hill, there suddenly appeared Japanese gendarmes clad in black.

Seeing the gendarmes, the refugees headed for Tortoise Mountain. They would be safe if they could make it through the pass to Great Lake. There were several dozen of them now running for the pass. If the Japanese had posted soldiers there, they would be finished. Rather than risk it, they took off through the brush to the bridge. Nearing the bridge, they dared not move any farther. Gunfire could be heard from the direction of Miaoli. But soon they heard the Japanese gendarmes closing in on them.

Ahan decided to take the risk. He crawled out of the brush, followed by the others. He looked at the bridge and up and down the river. Emboldened, he leaped onto the bridge. All he had to do was cross the forty-foot span to the safety of the opposite bank, but he would be completely exposed to enemy fire. He could see a number of volunteers on the other bank. Ahan hesitated.

"Look out!" someone shouted. Suddenly a black shadow hurtled through the air and fell on him. Ahan was unable to dodge, and they fell together on the bridge and rolled off onto the ground and down the bank into the water. At that moment, shots rang out and some of the men cried out and fell. Upon hitting the water, the man in black let go of Ahan and the two of them swam for the opposite bank, bullets whizzing around them. Reaching the riverbank, they crawled out of the water and took cover under the bridge.

Only then did Ahan have a chance to look at the man. He seemed even bigger than he had in the water; he looked half again as big as Ahan. He had a large head and a red face with pronounced features. He was a forceful presence. He laughed aloud and his shoulders shook; apparently he was amused by something.

"You saved me," said Ahan.

"I had to act fast; sorry I surprised you."

"No problem," said Ahan. Suddenly his face froze. "The Japs are crossing the bridge."

"Let's get out of here," said the big man. The dense reeds and grasses provided plenty of cover, allowing the two of them to escape.

The man who saved Ahan was named Qiu Mei, and he was from Changshan, Henan. He had been a bodyguard for Tang Jingsong, the President of the Republic of Formosa. When the Japanese took Keelung, the defeated Chinese soldiers fell back to Taipei. The deserting troops ended up fighting with the local volunteers. They set the presidential residence afire and looted the treasury. The presidential bodyguard scattered and fled. The president, disguised as an ordinary citizen, fled Taipei with his son and a favorite concubine who had dressed like a boy. When the looters and other soldiers met, they fought, and the casualties from those exchanges were greater than those on the battlefield.

Qiu Mei had relieved one looter who had had his hands cut off of a bag of silver. With the silver, he slipped home to his wife and sons. They had just arrived from Changshan six months earlier and had been renting a house in a small alley. When he arrived, his wife and sons were gone. He found his wife—dead—in the empty house of a neighbor. He searched all of Taipei for his two sons, one of whom was three, the other four. He buried his wife but never found his sons.

"How did your wife die?" asked Ahan.

Qiu Mei ignored his question and continued with his story. News of the looting had spread and local residents were raising the alarm as soon as they caught sight of a deserter. By then the Japanese had entered the city. He joined a group of former bodyguards and left for the south, stealing food as they went. Eventually they arrived in Miaoli, but because they did not speak the local dialect they were thought to be spies for the Japanese. The people of Miaoli tried to track them down and kill them and did beat several of them to death. He even heard that some women had cut the flesh from their bodies and had cooked it and eaten it.

"You say you can't speak the local dialect?"

"We were all from Henan. That's why we were also known as the Henan guard."

"The Henan guard was composed of big, strong guys with great martial arts skills, right? How is it you can speak Hakka?"

"There have always been Hakka in Henan. My wife was from Haifeng."

"Well, Brother Qiu, what are you going to do?"

Qiu Mei said he was going to stay in Taiwan and look for his two sons. He would go back to the mainland only if he found them or proof that they had died. Ahan then told him his own tragic story. Sharing a similar pain, they soon formed a strong, fast friendship.

They passed the night in weariness and fear. When the day dawned, they found that there were about sixty young men gathered in the area. Some were still in uniform and carried guns and swords.

"Where are you going?" asked Ahan.

"We're trying to save ourselves. We're going anywhere there are no Japs."

"I heard that they are recruiting over at Great Lake," said one of the men.

"Recruiting for what?"

"To fight the Japs and recover Miaoli and Xinzhu."

At a loss, Ahan and Qiu Mei looked at each other. The group started off. They lived off the land, eating whatever they could. One of the men suggested that they leave the riverbank and take the main road to Great Lake. At that moment, Japanese soldiers appeared at a bend in the river. There was a burst of heavy gunfire. It happened so fast that they were left numb with fear. The panic was greater than on the previous day. Many of the men's knees gave way and they fell to the ground, unable to move.

The enemy soldiers' shouts were followed by more gunfire. Men were screaming all around. Ahan gathered his wits and ran back along the riverbank, but that would expose him to more fire.

Qiu Mei was already standing on the other side of the river at the margin between the brush-covered hill and the sandy shore. "This way, across the river. We've got to hide in the hills."

Ahan half crawled and half rolled in Qiu Mei's direction. Bullets whistled above his head. He rushed ashore. As he hit the soft sand by the river he stumbled and fell.

"Hurry! Hurry!" Qiu Mei was shouting.

Everything became a blur and began to shake. He thought it was all over. He struggled but couldn't move his hands or feet. He wanted to cry, but he seemed to choke on something. He whined like an animal. Suddenly something flashed in front of his eyes; then all was dark. Then something lunged toward him. The next thing he knew he had been seized by the collar and heaved into the high grass beyond the sandy shore.

Shots continued to be fired.

Ahan heard a sharp cry and a heavy object land beside him. It was Qiu Mei.

"I've been hit!" Qiu Mei's voice, like his body, trembled. Qiu Mei's leg was already a patch of bright red.

"Where are you hit?"

"In my right leg. It's my thigh, but the bullet seems to have passed through. It's a huge wound!"

Qiu Mei pulled a long metal box from his waistband. In the box were about twenty long, thin needles. With a trembling hand he proceeded to insert eight of them into his leg above the wound and where his leg joined his torso and along his back.

"Don't move me. You go on. I have to rest." Having spoken, Qiu Mei passed out. The sound of gunfire was moving away down the road and river. This meant that the Japanese were pressing on toward Great Lake. Ahan calmed down; they would be safe there.

Qiu Mei's face was as white as wax, but his breathing was steady. His wound was not bleeding so profusely and merely oozed just a little; the wound was scabbing over. They were about twenty feet from the sandy shore, sitting under a tree that had been strangled by the lush creepers covering it. It was a good hiding place. Ahan sat there in silence staring at Qiu Mei, who still appeared unconscious.

"Oh, are you still here?" said Qiu Mei as he came to.

Ahan heaved a sigh of relief.

"Brother Liu, you will have to help me find some herbs, then you can get away."

Qiu Mei instructed him about the half dozen herbs he needed. They were the sort of herbs that all the people living in the mountains used. Ahan was familiar with them all but was unable to find two.

"That's okay," said Qiu Mei, pulling some herbs from his pocket.

"Why do you carry herbs on you?"

"I'm the kind of soldier who knows more than just guns," he said with a smile on his face as he pointed at his bag. "In addition to a change of clothes, I have some books, including the *Analects*, Mencius, a book of Tang and Song poems, and some elementary textbooks. You get me?"

"No, I don't."

"One day I'll teach you and you'll understand." Then his face darkened. "We're talking too much. When I'm done here you can go. There are so many people in this big world, who knows if we'll ever meet again? Ha ha, I must be talking in my sleep."

"No, I'll wait for you," said Ahan, throwing a glance at Qiu Mei's brightly colored wound. "We'll talk about it when you get better."

"There's no need to. Leave the herbs and be on your way."

"I owe you my life," said Ahan. "Now what do you want me to do?"

"Get something to eat, Brother Liu," said Qiu Mei, also becoming serious. "You think you owe me something just for pulling you off the riverbank? Forget it."

"That's my business. Besides, I don't have anyplace to go. The Japs are everywhere."

Even as Ahan spoke, Qiu Mei dozed off. Ahan made up his mind that they would just live off the land. Having decided, he felt happier and in higher spirits.

After taking Miaoli, the Japanese army remained there just a few days. The army proceeded to divide and spread out in different directions to sweep the countryside. The main force advanced south. In the middle of the tenth lunar month, Japanese warships bombarded Kaohsiung as Japanese troops stormed ashore to attack Tainan city in a pincer movement with the troops coming from the north. There were no Chinese or local forces capable of continuing the fight. On the nineteenth day of the tenth lunar month, General Liu Yungfu and his son bid a tearful farewell to Taiwan. Within two days, the Japanese forces entered Tainan. Anti-Japanese resistance in Taiwan entered a new phase.

The might of the Japanese army began to be felt in the small villages and settlements in the remote mountainous areas. The Japanese were determined to wipe out all resistance. At this time, their colonial government divided Taiwan into administrative districts; Miaoli was part of the central district of Taichu, with Taizhong as its capital. All villages of a certain size within the district were in turn to have an administrative official.

Great Lake was one such village, but the official dared not take up his duties because all resistance in the Miaoli area was centered there. The remnants of several armies had taken refuge to escape the onslaught of Japanese forces.

Liu Ahan remained by Qiu Mei's side as he recuperated. They passed a whole month in their hiding place below the vine-canopied tree, and they survived by living off the land. Qiu Mei's medical skills and his ability to use herbs were impressive; his severe wound healed rapidly. The two of them, united by their common plight, then slipped away to Great Lake and very quickly joined up with the volunteers because they ran into Three Chops there.

"Ahan, this time I demand that you and your comrade stay."

Qiu Mei fixed his wide-open eyes on Three Chops.

"Sergeant, isn't the situation . . ." started Ahan.

"The Japs have Great Lake and South Lake surrounded," said Three Chops, looking a bit worried.

"Great Lake sits on the edge of a huge mountainous area. Can they surround it?" asked Qiu Mei.

"They don't have to, in the mountains there are natives who hunt heads," interjected Ahan.

"Not anymore," said Three Chops. "We've made contact with the people in the mountains, and they've said that they won't kill us Chinese from the plains." Three Chops remained silent for a time. "Of course, if you want to get away it's easy enough to do. But why should you? Why leave? This is the land our forebears opened. I hate the idea of them eating our grain. I heard that all of Taiwan along the main north-south route is under Japanese control."

When they were alone together, Qiu Mei tried to persuade Ahan that the right thing to do was go back to Fanzai Wood for his wife. Ahan refused. Qiu Mei continued to try to persuade him. Ahan asked him to accompany him, but Qiu Mei thought it best that he remain with the guerrillas. "I can help them, because I have no family to worry about. I hate the Japs because they killed my wife and children and destroyed my home."

"If you want me to go, then come with me and take a look," replied Ahan weakly.

Qiu Mei eventually agreed to accompany him to Fanzai Wood. The following day, after a breakfast of rice gruel, they set off. Qiu Mei had even provided money for a set of clean clothes for both of them. As they approached Fanzai Wood, Ahan's heart was filled with bitterness and his nervousness increased. On the hillside, Ahan paused before the huge kulian tree.

"What a giant tree. How strange," said Qiu Mei.

Ahan recalled the words of Peng Aqiang, the heartless old man and foster father to Dengmei. He had said that when widows, old people, lonely travelers, and failed farmers could go no farther, they would come here and put an end to it all. Peng Aqiang had also said that the settlers couldn't fail because there was no way back for them. Ahan braced himself.

"I don't want to go back," mumbled Ahan to himself.

"You have to go back," Qiu Mei corrected him.

Ahan squatted by the path. Qiu Mei tried to reason with him, but the more he spoke, the more determined Ahan became not to return. Finally, losing his patience, Qiu Mei grabbed him by the collar and pushed him forward.

Ahan laughed, remembering the scene at the bridge by the pass at Tortoise Mountain.

The two of them made their way by fits and starts as Ahan continued to have doubts about returning. Passing Blind Man's Pool, Ahan stopped again. The sun was already above the bamboo and Qiu Mei was on the point of losing his temper when someone hurried their way.

"It really is you," said the man.

"Oh, it's you, Brother Renhua," said Ahan, unable to contain himself.

"Who's your brother?" spat Renhua.

"Renhua!"

"It's a good thing Chan Agu warned us, otherwise you would have sneaked in."

"What do you mean?"

Renhua sneered. "Chan Agu saw you and warned us. What do you think I mean? You're not allowed here in Fanzai Wood."

"Do you own Fanzai Wood?"

"Don't even think about coming to our house. And don't think about taking Dengmei away from us."

"Peng Renhua, what are you saying? You're being ridiculous!"

"I'm telling you that Dengmei is no longer your wife."

"What?" He stepped back, straightened up, and rushed at Renhua, grabbing him. "What do you mean?"

"You have no official proof that you married into our family. And when you left, you forgot to take the contract."

Qiu Mei stepped forward. "Friend, what is this about his wife?"

"I'm saying that his marriage is not valid."

"Not valid . . ."

"Go away. Dengmei doesn't want you."

"She doesn't want me?" Ahan released Renhua.

"No. She's going to remarry."

"Remarry?" Ahan backed away, swaying on his feet.

Qiu Mei caught hold of him and Ahan sagged in his arms. Renhua continued on in his sarcastic manner. Ahan slowly shook his head, then turned and walked away. Qiu Mei quietly suggested that he go back to Fanzai Wood and get to the bottom of what was going on. Ahan just walked faster.

"Ahan, Liu Ahan! Where are you going?" shouted someone behind them.

Ahan stopped and looked. It was Peng Aqiang, that cruel man.

"Ahan, come back! Renhua, what did you say to him?"

In a daze, Ahan continued on. Peng Aqiang and Renhua were both shouting. Ahan thought he was going to collapse. His ears were buzzing and he could hear nothing of what they were saying. He didn't want to listen. What was the point?

Ahan and Qiu Mei returned to Great Lake to take part in the last stand against the Japanese.

Winter had arrived, and the weather was getting colder. The greatest problem for the guerrillas was the lack of a clear chain of command. In the tenth lunar month there were nearly a thousand men in the area of Great Lake and South Lake. The men came from the defense unit led by Three Chops; others were deserters. By the end of the year, there were fewer than three hundred left. The new year began coldly but with no wind. The Japanese army and supporting gendarmes began to advance on Great Lake.

The guerrilla force led by Three Chops withdrew to the outpost in the hills outside South Lake. With the exception of the well-to-do, the people of South Lake, like the people of Great Lake, remained in their homes. The residents were unable and unwilling to provide Three Chops and his men and horses with provisions. Everyone knew it was only a matter of time before the Japanese arrived. And the Japanese army had posted proclamations forbidding anyone to aid the "bandits." As a precaution, so as not to be accused of doing so, the people shut their doors and stopped trading.

Three Chops and his men were in a difficult situation. All that was certain was that they had enough guns and ammunition. They didn't want to run away, but they had come to be seen as bandits in some people's eyes. They were encouraged by the arrival of a number of aboriginal leaders who sought to make pacts with Three Chops to fight the Japanese.

As Qiu Mei became apprised of the situation, he again tried to persuade Ahan to leave.

"I've got no place to go, but you should leave as soon as you can," Ahan said to Qiu Mei.

Though he felt dejected, Qiu Mei was resolved to stay. "I'm from Changshan, aren't I? My children are missing and must be dead. I buried my wife here in Taiwan. I have no desire to return to Changshan alone."

Ahan smiled coldly. "Then we might just as well be bandits together."

On the third day of the new year, the sky cleared and the temperature rose. The Japanese army stationed in the hills south of Great Lake began a campaign to mop up what remained of the bandits. They started by bombarding South Lake for thirty minutes. The thatch-and-bamboo roofs of the houses in the village caught fire immediately. The shelling also initiated some movement. At that point the Japanese soldiers began their advance.

Those who opposed the Japanese had already withdrawn beyond the old guard post line to make a stand at Linlai Plain. Every man, woman, and child of Jialihewan had left for shelter with the natives on Malabang Mountain. Within an hour, the Japanese had taken possession of South Lake village. They managed to burn down half the village and kill about thirty residents but not a single bandit.

Eventually, the guerrilla forces joined the natives on Malabang Mountain to fight the invaders. After five days and four nights of fighting, Three Chops had been killed, as had all the native leaders. Most of the men ended up dead.

New leaders stepped forward immediately to take the places of the native leaders slain in battle or executed by the Japanese. All the tribes from Wen River to South Lake united to go on the warpath against the Japanese. The alliance of natives created a force the size of which hadn't been seen in forty years. As a result, the Japanese garrison at Miaoli was dispatched to Great Lake.

NINE

Endless Wintry Night

On September 21, 1896, the twenty-ninth year of the Meiji era, the Bureau of Industry under the Governor-General's Office in Taiwan issued a proclamation stating that all lands without complete documentation of ownership would be confiscated by the government. Those that did have proof of ownership would be subject to heavy taxation. This proclamation was one of many issued by the colonial government to control the land for long-term economic planning. Thus, the land of widows, orphans, illiterates, and all others without complete documentation was confiscated by the Japanese. The proclamation also forbade the people of Taiwan to open land or collect anything from land for which they did not possess ownership documents. All violators of the order were to be treated as criminals.

The battles of 1895 had been fought and the turmoil of 1896 had been quelled. The bones of the dead defenders lay white in the fields; the wounded had recovered; and the Japanese who had served meritoriously had received commendations. The colonial government had laws for everything, but there were just as many waves in the sea, and the island was as beautiful as ever. The inhabitants of Fanzai Wood were struggling for a living as usual. Indeed, their life wasn't all that different from that of the indigenous people; perhaps that was why the place had been spared and remained as peaceful as ever even after the natives had united to fight the Japanese.

The biggest worry for the people of Fanzai Wood was the notes signed by everyone now in the hands of Ye Atian. The 1.5 percent interest to be paid semi-annually was literally choking the people like a heavy chain at their throats. The new laws protected the rights of those with the law on their side more than ever and punished violators more swiftly. Not only would the people of Fanzai Wood never be able to free themselves, but they were also falling ever deeper into debt. It seemed that the harder they worked, the poorer they became. Some decided to abandon their land and run away. But when it came down to it, they were unwilling to leave the land they had struggled so hard to open. Su Afa, the oldest inhabitant of Fanzai Wood, was unable to pay the interest. It was said that officials would be arriving to survey the government lands. Su Afa was so troubled by all of this that he actually took a hemp rope and secretly went to the hanging tree to end it all. Unfortunately, or fortunately, the rope was too short and he was too feeble to climb the tree. Eventually someone stopped his attempts.

These were the worries of the men; the women and children didn't concern themselves with them. Instead, their primary concern was to make sure there was enough food on the table to fill their bellies. Dengmei was secretly happy, gloating over the worried expressions on the men's faces. But she could not let anyone know how she felt, because that would spell disaster for her.

But perhaps that was not the case. A few days before the Double Fifth festival, Ahan had appeared suddenly in the Pengs' fields. After he had had time to catch his breath, he found that Peng Aqiang and Lanmei were all smiles. "Oh, you're back," said Peng Aqiang. Didn't the word "back" imply acceptance?

Ahan had returned with Qiu Mei. Both men were dressed in native garb and carried long-handled native knives. The moment Ahan saw Dengmei, he flushed red with excitement. And almost as if he were picking a fight, he asked her about their child.

She wanted to smile, but a wave of pain swept over her and she was unable to hold back her tears.

"What, again?"

"Is there something wrong with the child?" asked Qiu Mei, as if he already suspected the truth.

She pointed toward the house. Ahan threw a glance at Peng Aqiang and his wife and then rushed over to the house. He brusquely pushed aside Aling and his wife, who had come out to greet him with open arms. On the bed was a baby boy. Ahan looked like an eagle about to swoop down on the child. He approached the baby but then stopped and stepped back.

"Fine-looking boy," said Qiu Mei. "What's his name?"

"We just call him Aming because no one has given him a proper name yet."

"How old is he?" asked Ahan as if he had suddenly awakened.

"Almost four months."

Of what was he suspicious?

He explained that while in the mountains, he had run into Xu Dingxin, youngest son of Xu Shihui. Dingxin had told him about Aming's birth. This news, together with what Renhua had said about Dengmei not wanting him anymore, had increased his suspicions.

The previous year when Ahan was driven away, he had had no idea that Dengmei was pregnant. Add to that Renhua's words and a new baby, and no wonder he was so suspicious. Considering the situation, Dengmei felt sorry for him but then had to laugh.

She recalled how the old man greeted him and how Renjie and Renxing tried to make him feel welcome when he came back to stay. Even Renhua was no longer wearing that nasty expression of his. Actually, Peng Aqiang had had many regrets when Ahan had left Fanzai Wood in anger. It was no easy matter for the old man to smile now.

Everyone had noticed that Ahan and Qiu Mei both had gleaming new rifles slung over their shoulders. After seeing his son, Ahan explained that they had taken them from the Japanese when fighting alongside the natives of Malabang. The old man was stunned, and his three sons went white with fear.

"You've cut off Jap heads?" asked Renhua, his voice trembling.

"No avoiding it; it was war," said Qiu Mei.

"Quick, hide the guns," said Peng Aqiang. "Don't let anyone see them."

"They should be buried," said Renhua.

Renjie thought it a pity to bury them, but Peng Aqiang, his wife, and Renhua all insisted so as to avoid getting into trouble.

"All right, we just won't let anyone find them."

Nobody spoke again, but their eyes betrayed their fears and worries. Late that night, Peng Aqiang and his wife called Aling over and asked him to tell Ahan and Qiu Mei that they hoped the two of them would leave Fanzai Wood as soon as possible.

"We can't leave right now, but we will leave in a few days," said Ahan.

The following day Peng Aqiang asked Dengmei over and announced that for six dollars she and Ahan could buy their freedom, and he would allow her and Aming to leave Fanzai Wood with Ahan. Ahan agreed with alacrity. However, Japanese soldiers had already been garrisoned in the area. Anyone entering or leaving the mountains—Fanzai Wood was now designated part of the mountain areas—was carefully searched. Qiu Mei, who had gone out to reconnoiter the area, returned and said that it would be impossible to move.

It was then suggested that they go to Big Southside because they were on friendly terms with the natives there. But that road was impassable as well because the Japanese army had stationed a huge number of troops in the area to counter the threat from the natives of Tabeilai village, who were constantly on the warpath. The soldiers would no doubt see through their disguise in daylight, on the road—Ahan and Qiu Mei had put on native clothing and had made their way to Fanzai Wood under cover of darkness.

"It will do the Pengs no good if we are taken, because Ahan is a member of the family," Qiu Mei reminded the old man.

Absurdly, out of fear, the Peng menfolk asked Xu Rixing, Xu Shihui, and Su Ajin to meet with them. None of them thought it necessary to panic—hadn't the Xu boys been early and vocal opponents of the Japanese at Great Lake? And hadn't they also taken an active part in the resistance? In the end, the Pengs decided to sever all ties by making Ahan pay the six dollars in freedom money and publicly declare that he was now on his own and no longer a member of his wife's household. Since the marriage had never been registered at the *yamen*, the contract was burned. In any case, Ahan and Dengmei had no blood ties to the Pengs. The demand for freedom money was not considered proper, but Peng Aqiang reasoned that it was his due because Ahan had never fulfilled his duties as captain of the guard; nor had he, as promised, given his salary to the old man.

"You will also have to move out," ordered Peng Aqiang.

"Where are we supposed to go?" asked Dengmei.

"Fanzai Wood is full of cliffs and rocky outcroppings. Find a cave or something for the time being."

"Yes!" Dengmei's eyes shone with delight.

In the end they went to stay under a rocky overhang at Black Rock Cliff above Fanzai Wood. In a few days, Qiu Mei, who was something of an expert at geomancy, located an ideal site for a house opposite the cliff. Qiu Mei, along with Aling and his wife, helped the couple put up a thatched hut with a small kitchen. Qiu Mei also gave Aming his new name: Mingqing. While he was at it, he thought up names for another half dozen sons they might have.

"This is a great place for a nest, and it'll be perfect for you," said Qiu Mei.

"What do you mean?"

"It's not for someone who wants to get rich, but it is ideal for someone who wants to live in privacy. It's a lucky place; you'll be safe here. You will have many sons and grandsons, but fame and fortune will come to your family only after two or three generations."

"What a bunch of nonsense." Ahan laughed. "And what about you?"

"This is not the place for me," said Qiu Mei. "I'm a loner and I'll have to find a high, open peak to live on." Qiu Mei was serious. A few days later, he did find a piece of land high above Fanzai Wood on which he erected a thatched hut.

It was in this way that Ahan, Dengmei, and little Mingqing finally came to have their own home. Dengmei was afraid that the natives would attack them, but Ahan reassured her by pointing to the native clothes he had deliberately hung under the eaves. The Pengs, for their part, treated the young couple well: they gave them a bowl, two pairs of chopsticks, and a pillow stuffed with straw as well as their old bedding made out of hemp sacks.

"Will Father and the others really let us go?" asked Dengmei, still somewhat fearful.

"They're afraid of getting in trouble on account of me."

"You think its' funny. One day we will have to . . ."

"Have to do what?"

"Repay them properly. After all, they did raise me."

"Properly?" The tone of Ahan's voice was at once both joking and annoyed. His expression was also odd, making it difficult for Dengmei to guess what he was really thinking. Ahan had no sense of gratitude even for the sake of his wife and son. He had changed so much in the months he had been away. He used to be shy and timid. Now he walked with his head high and his back straight. His eyes were proud, and when he spoke, the words that rolled out! But something had not changed, regardless of whether he was laughing or sighing, and that was the look of loneliness that would appear and vanish again just as swiftly.

There was something else that was new. He got a piece of wood and asked Qiu Mei to write some words on it, then made an incense burner by cutting a short piece of bamboo and putting some sand in it. He put both objects in a small basket, which he hung on the wall of their house. It was probably meant to be an ancestor tablet for the Lius. But strangely, soon after he hung the basket at noon, he began to look worried. That evening he took down the basket and tossed the contents into the fire.

"Where is your mother now, Ahan?" asked Dengmei. She recalled that he had mentioned her several times after their marriage.

"My mother is dead," replied Ahan, breathing with difficulty. "From now on you are not to speak of her; I can't bear it." Indeed, even years later, when they had a brood of children, his parents were never mentioned.

Aside from that one instance, Ahan always seemed very happy after they had moved into their new house. He busied himself catching shrimp and crayfish and hunting pheasants and foxes, none of which required any money. Dengmei was constantly busy: she had borrowed a hoe from Aling, and apart from grubbing wild potatoes, she had without a word begun to clear a patch of weedy ground in the woods. When

Ahan saw this, he happily lent a hand. They had only one hoe, so Ahan cut the grass with the aboriginal knife he had brought back. Then they took turns turning the soil and holding Mingqing in their arms. Although they were poor, life had never been so good for either of them.

"Ahan, I think it is really nice like this," said Dengmei, trying her best to express herself.

"What do you mean?"

"I mean that even though life is not easy, it is still good."

"Oh."

"At least you don't have any worries now."

"Oh." He smiled ruefully.

"But it's hard on you."

Ahan looked at their son in her arms. "You mustn't say that. It's hard for him."

"It doesn't matter. If one has a hard life as a child, it will be better later."

"I once wanted lots of kids, but I wouldn't dare under these circumstances."

"As long as we work hard, we'll do fine." She suddenly blushed.

"Living like savages? Like wild pigs? How will we ever improve our lot?"

It was obvious that the life they were leading was too difficult for Ahan. Although he came from a humble background, no one had ever really looked after him. He was accustomed to a life of restless wandering, doing as he pleased, with long spells of ease. There was nothing more difficult for him than clearing weeds and digging the soil. Even dangerous jobs were easier. But Ahan never complained.

Dengmei tried her best to do as much of the work as possible. She was always the first to tackle the heavier jobs, as she had been her entire life. Although she was small in stature and she had to feed Mingqing, she still felt that she had enough energy to work from morning till night. Something bright was burning within her.

"Dengmei, don't wear yourself out." Ahan knew there was no alternative, but he looked embarrassed.

"I'm fine, really."

Later, Ahan borrowed some money to buy a mattock, an earthenware rice pot, and a medium-size cast-iron pot. Dengmei wasn't entirely pleased about laying out so much money; but it was a nice feeling to be the owner of a metal pot.

One evening before going to bed, she heated a pot of water in which to soak her feet. Bathing her feet in the hot water, she was filled with a beautiful sense of ease and comfort. She lifted one foot from the water and gently rubbed it. Then she noticed how dirty it was. She set to scrubbing away the dirt, but it seemed never to end; it just kept coming off. She was surprised and felt strange. Maybe her whole body would be stripped away if she went on scrubbing. She was a little uncomfortable but also vaguely pleased. The soil was life, and life came from the soil. Life was not the same as the soil, but ultimately life was the soil. Life could be free and active, but it was also lonely. The soil was the lowest thing, but it was firm and steady.

She woke from her reverie. "What am I doing thinking such wild thoughts?"

She heard Ahan's soft voice. "Who are you talking to?"

"You frightened me," she said, slightly annoyed.

"Oh, you are in a temper!"

Ahan, who was so shameless, had actually taken her in his arms just like that. She was so ashamed she scarcely had the strength to struggle.

"Let go! Let go of me! I want to put on my sandals."

"No way!" Ahan didn't let her go and even went so far as to carry her over to the new bamboo couch, where he wiped her feet dry.

"What are you doing?" She was surprised and ashamed to the point of tears.

"I want you." Ahan hugged her even closer.

"No, don't! Aming is still awake."

"Aming will look away. Ha ha."

"You're mad."

He was a dog. No matter how hard she struggled, he refused to let her go. He was completely out of control; no wonder he got on so well with the men from Tabeilai village. Not only had they not cut off his head, they had actually fed and sheltered him for several months. What really frightened her was that when he set his mind on something he was like a mountain dog that, once it had sunk its teeth into someone, wouldn't let go short of being struck by lightning. Was this tenacity a virtue or his stubborn temper? He could ruin his whole life as well as that of his wife and son.

"Who were you talking to just now?"

"I was talking to my lover!" she said. Her own words surprised her.

"Oh? Where is he, I'd like to meet him."

"My damn bully of a lover is right here beside me," she swore, surprised at her own audacity.

"Not true. So who is he?"

Ahan would never let go of anything. She decided to tell him the strange thoughts she had had while scrubbing her feet.

"Man was made from the earth," said Ahan adamantly. "He is made from the earth and so cannot leave the soil. He loves it, lives by it, and can't live without it. Man is always trying to wrest a living from the soil. And he'll return to it."

"I never dreamed you understood so much about the soil, you bumpkin."

"I've come to realize that the soil is something that men both love and hate. Right? Farming is awful, but it's also the most reliable occupation."

She understood some of what he was saying.

"The soil is also the source of the greatest suffering."

"What do you mean?"

"When there's a lot of people and not very much land, the landowners live well from the rent, but those who have no land can only meekly beg from their betters and work like beasts."

Suddenly Dengmei felt afraid. "Ahan, you're strange and you frighten me."

Ahan began to laugh.

"That's the way life is, but you can accept it. Look at you, look at how you are clenching your teeth."

"The way it is? Everyone comes into the world naked. Then why are some born to be called 'master' and others born to be called 'dog'?"

"I don't want to hear your nonsense." Suddenly she thought of something else. "Are we going to have problems because of the land we're clearing on the hillside?"

"Isn't everyone saying that it's government land?"

"Yes."

"Well, the Jap officials will show up sometime and fine us and make us stop. But do you think we are the only ones?"

"What are we going to do?"

"What can we do? We'll just wait and see."

"Stop trying to upset me."

"I'm not trying to upset you," said Ahan, becoming impatient. "It's just that we have no control over the situation. We'll do whatever the officials tell us. If we can't pay the fine, then we'll leave."

"Leave?"

"Yes. We'll just go deeper into the mountains and clear some land, only to be driven deeper into the mountains again in three years."

"But won't they . . ."

"Sure, but they can't cut all our heads off. We'll just have to go deeper and deeper into the mountains. That's the way life is."

"How long do you think we'll be able to stay here?"

"Who knows? Five years, three years, or maybe a few months."

Ahan's words were like hot irons that branded her heart. But more annoying was that they came true in less than two months. The people were notified by the government that the survey of government lands would be completed in six months, at which time all who had cleared land they did not have title to would have one month to appear and complete the paperwork to continue working the land. Those who failed to do so would not be allowed to continue and would also be subject to severe punishment.

Dengmei was on the point of tears. "What are we going to do?"

"What are you scared of? We'll go report our barren cesspit of a plot, get processed, pay some taxes, and that will be it."

She hadn't expected Ahan to be so law-abiding. "Then you'll go?"

"What else can we do?"

He was right. In Fanzai Wood cases like Ahan's were easily handled. He and Aling had no trouble, but the cases of all the other residents of Fanzai Wood who had voluntarily reported were dismissed because, as they were informed, they were working land owned by Ye Atian. The people had never obtained a patent certificate for the land, and the title was still in the hands of Ye Atian. The people of Fanzai Wood protested, saying that they had an agreement of transfer with Ye, and presented the receipts for the payments made to him. Ye Atian, however, countered by producing the loan agreements for money borrowed from him, the records of interest charged, and the receipts for the taxes he had paid on the land. Although the people had all paid their share of the taxes, Ye Atain had remained the taxpayer of record, and he had all the receipts in his possession.

The people of Fanzai Wood were livid with rage. Then Ye Atian made them an offer: in light of the situation, he was willing to transfer title to the land if they could clear their debts with him and pay all interest within three months. For those who did not pay in full, he would draw up tenancy agreements and, failing that, would prosecute.

Only Xu Shihui and Chen Afa had been able to pay off a portion of their debt; the others had just tried to keep up with the interest payments. Eventually, tempers cooled, and the people of Fanzai Wood acknowledged the hopelessness of the situation. They decided to ask Ye Atian to return the interest they had already paid—which had vanished without a trace—and sign tenancy agreements. Ye Atian refused to return the money, saying that the interest had been accepted in lieu of rent and that government fines had to be paid.

That summer, the sky was often cloudy and the long days were hot and humid. After getting up in the morning, Peng Aqiang sat, lost in thought, on a pile of stones under the eaves.

"Dad, we're going up into the mountains," said Renxing.

Renjie was also standing there, looking worried. Sadly, his tanned and wrinkled face made him look forty or fifty rather than thirty-six years old.

"What about Renhua?" asked Peng Aqiang, looking for his second son, who never looked like a farmer.

"Here I am," said Renhua with his mouth full of potato. "What's up?"

"You boys take off," he said, glaring at Renhua, "but make sure you fill in the taro patch first."

"Dad, it's . . ."

"Let's go, Renhua!" said Renjie, glaring at him.

Watching his sons depart, Peng Aqiang sighed. He had always disliked men who sighed, but that's just what he had become in the last two years. He was sixty-five, and if he had been rich he would be enjoying his wealth right now. Lanmei, his wife, was sixty-one. He recalled how just the day before—on her birthday—he had announced that they were going to celebrate. But the very same day, Ye Atian had notified them that their interest payments were overdue and that Peng Aqiang had to appear at his house within ten days to sign a tenancy agreement or face prosecution. Renxian, Ye Atian's steward, had personally delivered the message to Fanzai Wood.

"Now listen carefully!" said Renxian. "The Japanese are not like useless Qing officials. When they say they will prosecute, they mean it, and they won't waste any time."

"What will they do?" asked Renhua.

"They'll tie you up, take you to the yamen, and cut off your head under the banyan tree. That's what they'll do."

Peng Aqiang cleared his throat. "And can't allowances be made?"

"We've been making allowances for years, and you want us to keep on doing it?"

"No, we'll go to Master Atian's house and plead on our knees," said Peng Aqiang to himself.

"You can forget that!" said Renxian in a rage. "I'm telling you that if anyone shows up they'll be reported as bandits."

Bandits? Who was the bandit? The word was like a nail driven into the foreheads of all those at Fanzai Wood. For three days, the heads of all the Fanzai Wood households, with the exception of Chen Afa, met together. Even Ahan and Qiu Mei were there. Since Xu Shihui was now seventy and had lost some of his vigor and sharpness, Peng Aqiang was naturally pushed forward as the leader.

Peng Aqiang was still in favor of trying to reason with Ye and to inform the Japanese. If no results were forthcoming, then they'd fight Ye Atian to the end.

"All right, let's ask Master Xu to go," said Peng Aqiang.

"No way," said Xu Rixing. "I don't want to be tied up and taken to the yamen and have it said that I'm a bandit."

Qiu Mei, who was standing in the corner, stooped to whisper something to Ahan; then he stepped forward.

"The way I see it, why not let an outsider like me have a try?"

"What do you suggest?"

"I'll go in secret to have a talk with Ye Atian, and if it doesn't work, I'll deal with him."

They all looked at each other in silence; they knew that Qiu Mei was an expert at martial arts.

"That might be a good idea, let someone of experience . . ." said Peng Aqiang, deep in thought.

"No," said Aling suddenly.

"I don't think it's a good idea," said Xu Rixing. "It won't work."

"Why not?"

"There are too many people who know Ye Atian's connections with Fanzai Wood, and if someone loses their life, we'll . . ." said Xu Rixing.

"What's more, as someone from Changshan living in Fanzai Wood, Qiu Mei will be suspected."

"After it's done, I can always slip away and never come back," said Qiu Mei.

"It won't work, Brother Qiu Mei," said Ahan, whose words were probably not audible to everyone.

What were they to do? They were back to where they had started. The people of Fanzai Wood were convinced that nothing could be done. Peng Aqiang had no idea what to do, but he couldn't just give up. He felt he had been pushed to the edge; his mind was a blank.

The people were torn between fighting and peace. The ten days allowed by Ye Atian slipped by, and they still did nothing. This time Ye Atian seemed a little kinder and sent Renxian to warn them of the possible consequences. His steward also brought along the tenancy agreements as he had done before. No one was willing to sign them. It was said that Chen Afa had long since signed his. Xu Shihui and Su Ajin, the two oldest residents, favored admitting defeat and signing the agreements, but their children were against it, which created a lot of conflict between generations.

"If you don't respond within ten days, don't blame the master," warned Renxian.

"What will happen?" someone asked timidly.

"He'll prosecute. He'll ask the police to arrest you," said Renxian. After a moment's thought, he added, "He'll take you to court. He'll have you arrested and locked up in Taizhong."

"Taizhong? Where is that?"

"Taizhong is the district capital where the court that handles Miaoli cases is located. It's far, far away, to the south. If you end up there, don't ever expect to see your wives and kids again." Renxian left these frightening words as a parting shot.

Sure enough, on the very day the Big Snow period of the traditional agricultural calendar began, the weather turned cold. It was also on that day that Peng Aqiang and the heads of six other households at Fanzai Wood received summonses to appear at the Office of Rural Affairs in Great Lake village. They were to appear to resolve the problems of tenancy and rent. They learned that Chen Afa's and Xu Shihui's and Su Ajin's families had already signed tenancy agreements with Ye Atian. Liu Ahan had been exempted because he had cleared government land. But Huang Aling had also been named. The six families felt isolated and powerless. However, Xu's sons and Su's sons had torn up the tenancy agreements and had informed Ye Atian that they would not abide by them.

The following day was bitterly cold. Peng Aqiang rose before the sun and sat in the main room of the house preparing to go to Great Lake. Lanmei tried to persuade him to stay and let Renjie go. But he insisted upon going himself because it was his name that was on the summons; he couldn't very well have his son go in his place.

"I think it would be best if I were to go," said Renhua. "Father's temper is too quick and big brother is too much of a country bumpkin. I've seen a bit of the world, and I won't get in a fight with the officials. It would be best if I went."

"In that case, let us brothers deal with it," said Renjie.

"It won't do. You can't and that's that."

At daybreak, the five heads of the other households arrived. Peng Aqiang was determined to go by himself, but Renjie and Renhua insisted upon going in order to protect their father. Unexpectedly, the Xu and Su boys also turned up, but just to see them off and get an idea of what was going to happen. Ahan and Qiu Mei also hurried over. Nearly all the younger men in Fanzai Wood had turned out.

Initially, both sides in the case had planned to argue in a reasoned way. But after they arrived at the Rural Affairs Office, the actual situation was far different from what they had expected, and most of their plans came to naught. First, the order of the questions did not correspond to the order of the issues raised in the summons. Second, the person questioning them was a Japanese official whose position was unclear. His command of the local dialect was rudimentary and he had to rely on an interpreter. The inspector who presided over the hearings wore a black uniform with silver buttons, riding boots, and a sword at his side. Peng Aqiang was the last to be questioned.

"All the others are law-abiding people and have acknowledged their wrongdoing," began the interpreter. "What do you have to say?"

He had not expected that the official would sound like a buzzing mosquito. "We are farmers, and we are all law-abiding," said Peng Aqiang, trying to keep his voice down. "We have done nothing wrong."

"Nothing wrong? You won't pay your debts; you won't pay the interest you owe; and you won't sign a tenancy agreement. And you still say you have done nothing wrong?"

"We don't owe any money. We never borrowed any money, so where does the interest come from? It was Ye Atian who took over the land we opened and then cheated us into signing IOUs." He could no longer keep his temper in check.

At that moment, the inspector, who had been keeping a disinterested eye on the proceedings, suddenly roared something in Japanese.

"The inspector says that you are a Manchu slave and very cunning."

"What does 'Manchu slave' mean?" asked Peng Aqiang, dumbfounded.

"You're a slave left over from the Qing dynasty."

"I am not!"

"What? You dog!" The inspector rushed forward and slapped Peng Aqiang violently on both cheeks.

Peng Aqiang swayed, but his feet remained firmly planted. His apparent stubbornness infuriated the inspector, who then laid into him with fists and feet as he shouted in a mixture of Chinese and Japanese.

"You are not a human being, and you will be treated as an animal," said the interpreter as he conveyed what the inspector was yelling. "We will treat Manchu slaves the same way we treat animals."

"Go home and think it over, and then hurry up and sign the tenancy agreement; otherwise you'll be executed, you criminal."

Peng Aqiang slowly picked himself up off the ground.

"Get out of here!"

Peng Aqiang clenched his teeth and slowly walked out of the yamen. He tried to keep his mind focused and smile at the villagers, but blood trickled from his mouth.

Renjie stepped forward to give him a hand.

Renhua was scared out of his wits. "Dad, you're bleeding."

"Leave me alone; I'm all right," he said as he walked away with his head held high.

At that moment, a small, thin man stepped forward from the crowd of onlookers. He looked familiar. Peng Aqiang rubbed his eyes and focused his gaze on the man.

"What's the matter, Peng Aqiang? Don't you recognize me?"

"I know who you are, you blood-sucking opium addict."

"What did you say?"

"I said I'll never forgive you, you opium addict!"

Renjie and his brother came over to steady him and persuade him to go home at once. The little man roared with laughter behind them. Peng Aqiang struggled free of his sons and turned around. The people of Fanzai Wood surrounded him and wouldn't let him do anything. At that moment, Renxian, Ye Atian's steward, spoke up. "You people from Fanzai Wood, get this clear before you leave: you've got to sign tenancy agreements at the master's house, right now."

Everyone was taken aback.

"No!" exploded Peng Aqiang.

"You refuse to sign? Then I'll ask the inspector to have you thrown in prison."

"It's not that. We don't have our seals with us. We'll come again some other day."

"And you other Pengs also refuse to sign today?"

"We don't have our seals with us either," replied Renhua.

"No, we won't . . ."

"Then you want to sign another day too?"

"Yes, that's right, some other day," replied Renhua, hastily pushing his father away.

"Fine. Be at the master's house in three days."

"You had best come to Fanzai Wood," said Xu Rixing.

"Yeah! You come to Fanzai Wood," added Peng Aqiang.

"Fine! We'll see," said Ye Atian, panting with anger. "Do you think I'm afraid of you? We'll see if you dare do anything."

"Then come," said Peng Aqiang.

"I mean what I say. I'll come in an eight-man sedan chair in three days' time. I'll show you."

No one said another word. When the men got back to Fanzai Wood they parted in silence, each going to his own house.

Upon arriving home, Peng Aqiang once again took his seat on the stone under the eaves. His face was flushed, his cheeks twitched, and he stared blankly ahead. Although his wife and children implored him to go inside and rest, he refused. When the women brought him food to eat, he remained stock still and as mute as a wooden statue. All that afternoon, Aling, Ahan, and Qiu Mei remained at the Pengs.' Qiu Mei had taken the old man's pulse and had given him some herbs to "reduce the fire element."

Peng Aqiang seemed to have regained his calm; perhaps Qiu Mei's herbs had had the desired effect. He wondered how they were ever going to resolve the situation with Ye Atian. But whatever was to happen, he wouldn't give up his land, which was as dear to him as his own flesh and blood, without a fight. He was not overly concerned about not being able to find a way out; after all, a path was laid one step at a time.

Fanzai Wood was in tumult; like ants that had seen their nest destroyed, the people were in a turmoil. Xu Shihui and Su Ajian were running around chattering like fools.

"I've gone soft? I'm mad as hell," said Xu Shihui.

"I haven't been able to sleep a wink since that day," said Su Ajian.

Peng Aqiang laughed somewhat sarcastically. The two had changed a great deal since the Pengs had first arrived in Fanzai Wood. Perhaps it was age. But Peng Aqiang thought of his own situation and could only feel contempt for them.

"We can fight," asserted Xie Atan.

"Like the last time?" asked Peng Aqiang. "Not one of you has any balls."

The younger men denied Peng Aqiang's claims.

"I'll never give in on this," said Peng Aqiang, "but I'm not going to get involved with a bunch of guys with no balls; I'll go at it on my own."

"That won't work. Our strength lies in unity."

"You guys are useless. When the time comes, you'll all hide and leave me on my own."

He realized that he should have tempered his words. What was the point of hurting people's feelings? But what could these guys do?

Three days passed in no time. The day before Ye Atian's expected arrival, Peng Aqiang ordered that two chickens be killed.

"What for?" asked Lanmei, her eyes wide with surprise.

"I feel like having something good to eat. Everybody can have something good to eat."

"But it's not the new year or a festival or the birthday of a god. What are you up to?"

"I said I wanted something good to eat," he said in a rage. "Won't that do?"

That afternoon, Peng Aqiang went to the fields with Renjie, but he was still agitated. He picked up his machete and set off to inspect his fields. He tried not to think of what might happen the following day, but his mind kept returning to the subject. He couldn't think of any way out of the situation. He left his fields and walked through Fanzai Wood, and before he realized it, he was standing in front of Ahan's house. He felt like talking to Ahan, but the wooden door was shut, which meant that the couple was probably out. When he thought of Ahan, he experienced an overwhelming sense of guilt. He wanted to tell him to forget the redemption money. Then there was Dengmei. He had always been fond of her, but he had also been a harsh, distant, and severe father. How could he demonstrate any kindness to her in front of his own children and their wives? He had always loved her like a daughter, but she would never know it. None of his own daughters was as quick as Dengmei. He left without seeing if they were home. He had thought about visiting Qiu Mei, but as he started walking, his feet led him down the mountain.

Dinner was even more splendid than what Peng Aqiang had requested. Lanmei was really understanding. Besides the two boiled chickens, fried eggs and salted turnips, prawns, and fried fish and peas were on the table.

"What's the occasion?"

"Grandpa, I want a chicken leg," said Dexin. Peng Aqiang served chicken to his sons, grandsons, and daughters-in-law, but he saved a chicken breast for his wife. Lanmei asked him if he would like to borrow a pot of wine from the Xus. He shook his head and smiled. He couldn't understand why Lanmei began crying and ran to the kitchen when he smiled. He asked his grandson to bring her back to the table, but she refused to come. Finally, he went after her himself.

"Lanmei!"

"Go away. Do you want the children to laugh at us?" Lanmei pushed him out of the kitchen. Peng Aqiang scratched his head, unable to explain his wife's tears.

"Come back to the table and have something to eat," said Peng Aqiang, also beginning to cry.

"Tell me what you are going to do tomorrow."

"Nothing. I'm going to argue with that animal Ye Atian like everybody else."

"I've spent my whole life with you, and I have never asked you for anything."

"Fine. If you have anything to say, wait till we go to bed." He took her by the arm and led her back to the table.

That night after the meal, as they were turning in, Lanmei again spoke. "Tell me what you are really going to do tomorrow."

"Didn't I tell you already? I'm going to try to reason with Ye Atian."

"But Ye is unreasonable, isn't he? You want to fight, don't you?"

"I don't know. Wait and see."

"If you get violent, you'll end up in jail. It'll all be for nothing because the land will still belong to someone else."

"Right."

"Don't take the lead in anything. Forget it!"

"Forget it?"

"Remember, my health isn't very good; I'm getting old. You have to help me. The children will have their day." Lanmei began to sob.

"Why are you acting so silly tonight, old woman?"

Peng Aqiang spoke making light of the situation, but his heart bled.

It was bitterly cold the next morning, but bright, beautiful sunlight fell over the roofs of the houses in Fanzai Wood, the fences, the trees, the bamboo, and the vegetable plots on the slope. But a whistling north wind cut right through everyone's clothes, chilling them to the bone.

Peng Aqiang, with his wife behind him, walked toward the temple. They both shivered with cold. Lanmei was transfixed by the sight before them: all the men, women, and children of Fanzai Wood were gathered in the open space in front of the temple. With her dim old eyes, she could make out Renjie and her other sons among them. She rushed forward.

Peng Aqiang also hurried forward. "Renjie!"

"Everybody has stopped work and come," said Renhua.

But Renxing was nowhere in sight. He was inflexible, knowing nothing but hoeing his own land. Even if the sky were to fall, he would not notice. Peng Aqiang looked around. Everyone was there save Chen Afa and Renxing. All those assembled looked at him expectantly. He knew what they were thinking. He ordered all the old people and the women and children back to their houses. It wouldn't do any good to have them in the way.

"It looks like it's getting serious," said Renhua.

Peng Aqiang paid no attention but looked up to see how high the sun was. "Quickly, all of you put your tools away."

They were all astonished. Some were opposed and began to argue with him. He was on the verge of swearing when someone shouted, "They're here!" It was Liu Ahan. Renhua quickly informed his father that Ahan and Qiu Mei had brought their Japanese rifles and hidden them in the grass. As Peng heard this, his expression changed. He yelled for Ahan to come over.

"Ye Atian is here. What's the matter?" he asked, observing Peng Aqiang's angry expression.

"Remember," said Peng Aqiang, keeping his voice low, "if you don't want everyone in Fanzai Wood killed, you had better not show those rifles. Even if it comes to a fight, we must only use our machetes and fish spears."

Peng Aqiang turned around and was just about to order them to put their tools away again when a group of people appeared below the temple. At the head of the group was tall, thin Renxian. He was followed by eight or nine men in worker's clothes.

"Ye Atian is coming in his sedan chair," shouted Qiu Mei, who was standing on the ridge separating the fields in front of the temple.

Ye Atian was indeed riding in a sedan chair carried by two men. The mountain trails were so narrow that a two-man chair was the most impressive show he could muster. Ye's entourage was the same as last time, save that there were a few more laborers. Ye Atian remained sitting in his sedan chair, not deigning to get personally involved.

"So all of you, even the old and the women and children, have come out to welcome us," said Renxian, looking at everyone as he walked up the slope accompanied by his escort.

Not a one acknowledged his words with even a grunt. Peng Aqiang looked around and realized that although the people of Fanzai Wood had concealed their tools, the old people and the women and children were still there.

"Are you all here to see Master Ye? Where are the heads of the households?" Renxian maintained his smile, but it vanished when no one replied.

As he had done on the previous occasion, Renxian removed a bundle of papers from his black bag. "You have to get this straight. Have you all brought your seals?"

"No!" replied one of the villagers.

Renxian was taken aback. He looked around him, scowling in anger. "Who are you? Are you planning to kill someone with that spear?"

It was Fan Aqian who at that moment emerged from the crowd, five-pronged fish spear in hand. One by one the villagers took their tools out from behind their backs.

"What are you doing? So you really want to cause trouble," said Renxian, retreating to the protection of the escort. Again he turned and roared, "Come out, all of you!"

At that moment it became apparent that Ye Atian had an army ready—twenty men emerged from the grass behind his sedan chair. One carried a metal bar and others carried machetes. All the men except for the five or six in front of the sedan chair rushed the temple.

"So, are you bandits of Fanzai Wood sure you want to fight?" said Renxian, somewhat bolstered. "If not, kneel and beg for mercy and affix your seals; there's still time."

"Forget it! Come on!" said Fan Aqian, ready to lead the others down the slope.

Peng Aqiang shook his head and waved his hands. "Stop! Renxian, does Ye Atian want to force our hand? There will be no turning back."

"It's your decision; no one is forcing you."

"Hold on!" said Peng Aqiang to the people of Fanzai Wood. Then he addressed Renxian. "Call off your men."

"Only when you affix your seals and then kneel and beg for mercy."

"Then you will be responsible for any bloodshed." Peng Aqiang was trying to hold back the villagers, who kept pressing forward.

"You're the ones making trouble."

"Renxian, quit talking and get on with it," said Ye Atian impatiently.

"What do you have to say?"

"After today, there will be no more Fanzai Wood."

"Let's get them," said Xie Atian and Lai Ahe as they rushed down the slope.

"Kill them, kill them all for me!" shouted Ye Atian, who was now standing in front of his sedan chair with a knife in his hands.

Both sides rushed at one another. Some of the women wept; some tried to hold their men back; others cursed. Peng Aqiang was confused and his heart pounded. He suddenly regain his calm and with all his strength roared, "Stop!"

"Well, have you seen the light?"

"I'm coming alone," Peng Aqiang said as he moved toward Renxian. The escort tried to stop him, and one of them started to lunge at him, but his steps faltered. Peng Aqiang walked toward where Ye Atian was standing.

"What do you want?" asked Renxian, hurrying down the slope after him.

The people of Fanzai Wood stood where they were.

"I want to have one last talk with Master Ye."

"I don't talk to bandits," said Ye Atian, approaching him knife in hand.

"You have to talk," he said, just six feet from Ye.

"My knife will do the talking," Ye said as he lunged at Peng Aqiang.

The villagers were in an uproar. But Peng Aqiang managed to dodge the knife thrust. Then, lifting his arms, he turned to them and said, "Leave it to me. Stay right where you are."

His words had come from the bottom of his heart; they bore the force and dignity of his life. The villagers were moved to silence. The whole place had grown deathly silent. Then he addressed Ye Atian. "Ye Atian, your whole life you have occupied other men's land with the backing of the officials. I have even heard that you abducted other men's wives and raped their daughters. Can you have a clear conscience?"

"What are you talking about?" asked Ye, taken aback by the accusations.

"Good is always rewarded and evil punished. You know that someday there will be retribution?"

"Crap!" Ye lunged again.

Peng Aqiang again dodged Ye's thrust. This time, the worker with a metal bar stepped forward to lend a hand, but Ye Atian waved him away, saying that he would personally cut the bandit down.

Ye's knife just missed Peng Aqiang's belly. His head swam and he felt queasy. He thought perhaps he had been wounded, but realized he hadn't eaten anything all morning. He thought how good it would be to eat a potato to fill his stomach. But his potato fields were going to be snatched away from him by the thief in front of him. The pale, scrawny thief in front of him.

"I'm going to chop you down, you bandit!"

Peng Aqiang again dodged Ye's knife. He then leaped and seized Ye's thin shoulders in his strong arms. He sunk his teeth into Ye's neck. Ye screamed.

Ye fell from his arms. Peng too fell to the ground. He and Ye rolled down the slope to the edge of the dry paddy field.

Ye's men were shouting to kill Peng Aqiang but dared not move for fear of injuring their master.

They rolled down the slope; soon Ye had grown limp. Peng Aqiang's face was covered with blood. It was quiet, like in the middle of the night. Peng Aqiang slowly raised his head and stood up.

Someone was wailing loudly; it was a shrill, monotonous sound. Suddenly he was surrounded by reddish shadows. He wiped his face, but smeared more blood in his eyes. He realized that he was covered in fresh blood. Then his mind started to clear.

The men surrounding him were part of Ye's escort. He saw a glimmering knife on the ground beside him. He reached down and picked it up, his body aching all over. The men surrounding him began to step back.

"Father!" yelled someone running toward him.

"Stay where you are!" He waved his knife. "Don't come any nearer."

He suddenly heard a familiar voice. "Master Ye is dead!"

"His throat has been torn to pieces!"

Peng Aqiang smiled and walked slowly toward the temple, but blocking his way were a row of armed men. His mind was clear now and he understood what he had done. He was afraid, disturbed. He felt cold, oh so cold. He had no choice but to step back. As he did so, the armed men advanced. He retreated along the path to Great Lake.

"Catch him! Don't let the murderer escape!"

But not one of them dared to advance farther than the others. When Peng Aqiang brandished his knife and ran at them, they scattered in confusion. But as soon as he showed signs of weakness, they swarmed toward him. They kept pushing him in the direction of Great Lake. More and more people gathered around. He was growing more confused but he knew that he couldn't let the thieves do anything or let the Japanese seize him. Again he brandished his knife and charged them. He threw his knife at them and fled off through the bushes.

"After him! Don't let him get away!"

"Kill him!"

Peng Aqiang hid in the thick creepers that covered the moutainside so thickly that even the birds had trouble making their way. His pursuers didn't hesitate and entered amid the creepers. The Office of Rural Affairs had already received urgent messages and the garrison had dispatched a number of soldiers to assist in the search. They were all armed with rifles and made for a fearsome sight. Night fell, but the murderer remained at large. The garrison detachment placed sentries on the paths out of the mountains and waited for daybreak to continue their search.

It was a cruelly cold night. The villagers dared not show their faces. Renjie and Renhua lay hidden in the mountain undergrowth. They dared not hope for a thing but could not bear to abandon their aged father. It was a long, cold night. The sky was a deep blue without even a wisp of cloud. The air was still. A heavy dew fell on the vegetation and rocks by the roadside.

Liu Ahan and Qiu Mei were also out after dark to see if they could locate the old man. Ahan had a strange feeling that he knew where the old man might turn up. He led Qiu Mei, hurrying through the night. They went swiftly in the direction of Great Lake, skillfully avoiding the sentries. They went along the mountainside, feeling their way in the faint light from the sky. Patrols were everywhere, and they were forced to take to the brush.

"Will he be there?" asked Qiu Mei.

"I'm pretty sure that's where he's headed. We have to get there and stop him."

"Why stop him? Do you think the courts should be allowed to do their worst?"

It was past midnight. The frost cut like a knife and their bodies would grow stiff if they paused. They arrived at Kiln Corner and headed up the slope. The silhouettes of the many camphor trees were visible against the backdrop of the night sky. Beside the path was the huge tree, its top nearly leafless. Nothing hung from the thick branches ten feet above the ground. Ahan scrambled to the tree. Qiu Mei shook his head and followed.

Only low weeds grew near the tree. There was nothing under it. Ahan stood there for a while in silence.

"Here," said Qiu Mei. He had discovered something on the other side of the tree. Ahan stepped forward and his eyes met with what he had been expecting to find. Peng Aqiang was sitting upright at the base of the tree, a rope in his hands.

"He's cold," said Qiu Mei.

It was true. Peng Aqiang's dead body was already quite cold. He had not hanged himself but had died at the bottom of the hanging tree.

Ahan suddenly recalled what the old man had said when he and Aling had first accompanied the Pengs past this place.

Why did the old man have a rope?

Had he bled to death from his wounds?

Who knew? The old man had no way out, and perhaps he had died of natural causes. He had chosen to die there, and he had chosen how to die.

"It's cold," said Ahan.

Qiu Mei heaved a sigh and said that it was cold enough to freeze a man to death.

"He froze to death, but we won't," said Ahan.

"True, we're not dead yet."

It was to be a long winter's night, one that would go on and on, for one era of suffering had come to an end and a new era was about to begin.

PART TWO

The Lone Lamp

ONE

*T*he Sound of *W*eeping

*N*ot a drop of rain had fallen since the middle of summer. The fields were cracked, the streams had long since dried up, and the earth had been baked white by the sun. The wind had swept away the withered grass and wildflowers by the roadside. The bushes at the feet of the mountains had withered and were near death. Even the great mountain forest seemed to droop and sigh.

Just after dawn, Liu Mingji and Peng Yonghui left Fanzai Wood for Hawk's Beak, a mottled gray rock formation that much resembled a hawk and stood high above the middle of the forest. They carried a bag of dried sweet potatoes, a bamboo container of spring water, and long-handled machetes. Hawk's Beak was a mysterious place that most people avoided, because a number of those who went to climb it never returned. It was an old tale, but the people of Fanzai Wood preferred not to test its veracity, mainly because on more than one occasion strange noises were heard coming from the place.

The sound of sad, broken-hearted weeping was heard there on clear evenings when the last remnants of sunlight fell across the rock, and on clear moonlit nights, and even on drizzly afternoons.

Mingji and Yonghui were now boldly venturing there. It had been decided the day before when the old people of the village had come to say good-bye to them. Mingji was the son of Dengmei and Liu Ahan; he was twenty-five. Yonghui was the eldest grandson of Peng Renjie; he was twenty-seven. In a manner of speaking, the two young men were related.

Being related and having been conscripted for service in the same place, they would in all likelihood both be sent to the same place in the

Pacific. For this reason, their families had prepared a farewell banquet for them. In those days, everything was in short supply, so each member of both families contributed something, a pot of hoarded rice or a chicken. They were able to put together a feast for an afternoon of talk, which was the best kind of send-off.

"That ghostly weeping on the rock has been clearer than ever recently," said Jiansheng, Mingji's nephew.

"I've heard it frequently,too," added Yonghui.

"What's so strange about it?" said Mingji, unmoved.

"Did you say the sound of weeping?" asked Mingsen, Mingji's brother. Mingsen, who usually stayed in his room, had crept out and stood giggling behind his brother.

Mingji stood up. He and his brother Mingcheng pushed Mingsen back into his room. Then they all fell silent.

"Mingji, what do you really think of that weeping?" continued Yonghui.

"Pure imagination," said Mingji. "I don't believe it." He looked depressed. Clearly, Mingsen's appearance made any cheerfulness on his part impossible.

"Have you ever heard it?"

"Often. So what?"

"The strange thing is that when I hear it, other people don't, and when other people hear it, I don't."

"That's why I say it's pure imagination."

"Imagination? That doesn't explain anything. Do you think everyone in Fanzai Wood has an overactive imagination?"

"Most likely," said Mingji dryly.

"I've heard it every night for the last two or three days," said Yonghui as if talking to himself. "It was very clear. I heard it starting around midnight and then all the way till cockcrow."

"Then you didn't sleep all night?"

"Of course he didn't. How could a loving couple like him and his wife sleep?" said Jiansheng.

Yonghui pretended not to hear. He looked at Mingji as if to say something else. At that point, he really wasn't thinking of his wife or month-old daughter.

"Mingji, let's go to Hawk's Beak. Do you dare?"

"Why not?"

"Before we leave Taiwan, let's go and have a look."

"Don't go. You won't come back."

"In any case, what do we have to fear?"

So it was decided. After eating, Mingji told his mother of his intention. Dengmei looked at him for a long time with her tired old eyes. He could see that she was holding back her tears, but he let his own fall. He knelt down like a small child, looking up at his mother. He laid his head on her lap and she caressed it. He was her youngest son. He had been born when his mother was forty-six. His father, Ahan, who had spent his entire life fighting the Japanese, died shortly after being released from prison, when Mingji was eleven.

Compared to his four brothers and two sisters, Mingji was most like his father in both appearance and character. Whenever Dengmei saw him roaring with laughter or in a fit of rage, she would fall silent, sigh deeply, and turn away.

That evening, Yonghui told his wife about his intention of going to Hawk's Beak.

"You seem to be glad to get away from me and your daughter," said Azhen softly. She did not lift her head from her sewing to look at him.

"Don't work in the fields. That patch of potatoes will be enough for you and the baby. All you have to do is dig them up."

"Don't worry. It would have been better if we had had a boy."

That night, Yonghui and his wife talked the same way they had the night Yonghui received his conscription notice. To lessen the overwhelming misery they felt, they tried to hide their pain by talking about the small pleasures of the past and their hopes for the future.

Leaving Fanzai Wood, they passed the temple of the Earth God. Yonghui wanted to say a prayer for their safety. Mingji agreed with a smile. Mingji was the only person in Fanzai Wood who had received a higher education: he had a diploma from a technical college night school. He no longer believed much in the gods and spirits, except for the spirits of his ancestors, the Earth God, and the Righteous Lords.

After a prayer, Mingji followed right on Yonghui's heels. Both were accustomed to the slopes and took long strides as they chatted. Suddenly a flock of Fanzai birds rose from the grass, circled around them, and, twittering, disappeared into the forest.

"I wonder if there are Fanzai birds elsewhere in the Pacific?" asked Mingji.

"Who gives a damn what kind of birds there are in the Pacific?" said Yonghui in a sudden burst of anger. His wife's pale cheeks and his daughter's rosy softness flashed through his mind, but their faces remained vague.

Yonghui had been conscripted into the Taiwan Youth Labor Corps, which was probably the same as the Southern Peasant Volunteers, which had conscripted Mingji's brother Mingsen.

Mingsen, who was thirty-four years old, had been sent to the South Pacific at the beginning of the previous year. On the tenth of September of this year, he had been brought home by a man from the Rural Affairs Office. He was emaciated, and his skin was dry, cracked, and darkened by the sun. He scarcely looked human. It was hard to imagine that he had once been a burly young man. After a month's convalescence, his health returned, but he seemed to have lost his wits for good. Sometimes he flew into a tantrum like a child; at other times he laughed insanely.

How wonderful it would be to have his conscription rescinded. Yonghui began daydreaming that the war had ended and that the Japanese army had won or been defeated. He wondered why he thought of such things. Suddenly his mind turned to more serious matters: What if he were to become blind in one eye or break a leg? No, the authorities were on to such ploys to get out of serving, and he would probably end up being beaten to death.

"Let's take a rest!" This time it was Mingji who made the suggestion.

Upon looking around, they realized that they had already reached Upper Fanzai Wood. From there, the path ascended to the King of Hell's Ridge, and then it was another four hours to Hawk's Beak. Before them was a plum orchard overgrown with weeds. The trees were bare and one could tell at once that it was not due to seasonal change or a lack of water but because the roots had died. They sat down in the shade under a tree beside the trail.

Their eyes met, and they smiled and quickly shifted their gazes.

"Mingji, how are things with you and Ahua?"

"How should they be?"

Ahua was the only daughter of Su Yongbao, who had moved to Great Lake from Fanzai Wood. She and Mingji had had a tacit understanding for more than two years. When the Taiwan Youth Labor Corps was recruiting in the sixth month, the Miaoli office of the National Oil Company, his employer, had volunteered him for service. When Ahua heard the news, she said that she would find a way to have the order rescinded. On July 16, the day before he was to report to the training camp at Flag Hill, he received notification that it had been rescinded.

Surprised, he had asked Ahua how she had managed it. Ahua rather coolly informed him that she had done so with the help of friends. He pressed her further, and she evaded his questions. He couldn't stop thinking about the matter but couldn't say anything. He had received a second notice just five days ago. When he walked into the machine shop, the Japanese supervisor handed him a red form notifying him that he was to serve with the Airplane Factory Technicians in Manila, and that he was to report to the garrison at Kaohsiung on December 18.

The evening he received the second notification, he told Ahua. Her face went white. She told him that she would do everything she could to have the order rescinded again.

"Do you really have so much power?" asked Mingji.

"I'll do all I can," Ahua said. Her smile had always charmed him, but now her normally sweet smile was filled with sadness and bitterness.

Two days passed and there was still no news from Ahua. It was an official holiday, so Mingji went to see her at the Rice Distribution Center where she worked. He chanced to run into her as she was coming to Fanzai Wood. The two of them talked in the grassy area behind the temple at Great Lake.

"No go?"

Ahua shook her head as she choked back her sobs.

"Don't worry. Everybody has to go."

"You shouldn't have to go. That's what he said. . . ." Mingji's mind was filled with doubts and his heart ached. He too shed tears, seeing the girl he loved weeping broken-heartedly. But after they parted and he returned home, he thought about what she had said, thought about it all night long. The more he thought the more confused he felt. He finally decided that whatever happened, he was going to the South Pacific. He knew there was no point in thinking about the matter since nine out of ten who went never returned.

Yes, better not to think of such things. He couldn't help laughing. Ignoring Yonghui, he stood up and started up the slope.

The path grew narrower and steeper as they climbed. Soon the King of Hell's Ridge lay before them. The path was overgrown with tough grass that was slippery to walk on; soon they were both using their hands to climb.

"It's hot. I wonder if it's this hot in the South Pacific?"

"There you go, talking about the South Pacific again!"

"Okay! I won't mention the lousy South Pacific again."

"Let's sing a song."

"Good idea. It's been so long since I last sang that I probably sound like a duck."

They climbed to the top of the King of Hell's Ridge, and before them was a level area shaded by trees. They sat down to rest, wiped their brows, and took a drink.

Although Yonghui was a rough young man, he was a first-rate singer:

Maple leaves dye the mountains red;
When my love smiles, the mountains smile too.
As the dragon boat is pushed downstream,
Who knows when we will meet again?

Mingji was a good singer, but he hadn't mastered the subtle art of Hakka folk songs:

Spring water is cool, the mountains are high;
My love has no choice but to leave;
When a shrimp from the stream finds itself in the southern sea,
How long must it swim to see the hills and streams again?

The echoes of the songs were carried on and on for a long time. Mingji's eyes were fixed on the distance. Yonghui's throat felt constricted and his eyes moist. Mingji thought that Yonghui was mocking him, so he glared at him with a grunt.

Yonghui was suddenly overcome with the desire to hug Mingji, but at the same time he felt like giving him a thrashing. Quickly he put these wild thoughts from his mind. He wondered if a woman would be able to resist such feelings. He thought of Azhen, her round and soft breasts. He hadn't touched her in months, and it had only been a month since she had given birth. Soon he would be leaving for the South Pacific, and there would be no chance after that. He shook his head.

"Did you hear that?" Yonghui stood up.

"What is it?"

"The sound of weeping. I heard it just now, shrill and faint, floating on the air."

"Soon you'll be seeing ghosts in broad daylight. It's not even dusk or a moonlit night."

Mingji said nothing more, and both men stood up. They started off at a good clip, both intent on the climb they were to make. After they crossed a level area, the ground began to rise again. They climbed the steep slope until they hit another level, grassy area where a hut had been built facing west.

The sun seemed to be at eye level, and all they needed to do was reach out to touch it. Where had such weather come from? Both men felt as though they had been wrung dry. They decided to sit down and have lunch.

"This potato really hits the spot."

"Mmm. . . . They don't seem as bad as usual today."

At last, they arrived at their destination; the huge rock formation rose before them. They looked up and could see the perpendicular formation of the hawk's beak thrusting out into the air. The hawk's body seemed to form a huge column attached to the sky.

"Let's climb to the top. The sun is going to set soon."

"We'll never be able to climb that steep, slippery face."

"Let's climb up to those trees by the hawk's wings."

The crag rose above all the other peaks; they only had to go a few steps before they felt themselves to be halfway up in the sky. The sun was going down and the air was starting to feel cool.

The wind picked up and they risked being swept off the crag at any moment. But what had appeared to be barren rock was actually covered with small plants with tough leaves that provided them with handholds. Upon reaching the trees, the crag leveled off slightly to form a shelf of sorts. The whole scene seemed to change as they were confronted by a dense pine wood. The soil was rich and, except for a few clumps of ginger, the undergrowth was sparse. There were also some purple flowers, which they did not recognize, shaking in the wind. They suddenly felt a cold draft. After they caught their breath, their senses seemed sharper; it was a new sensation for Mingji.

Looking down, he saw himself surrounded by the small purple flowers. He could feel the earth under his two bare feet; he could feel the beat of his heart in his feet. He felt connected to the land—his blood seemed to flow into the earth, from which it flowed back into his four limbs. Feeling at one with the world, he saw himself standing on the earth, connecting the earth with heaven, providing nature with consciousness. Mingji's mind achieved an unusual clarity and detachment, but this enlightenment brought him a pained rapture.

The trees went partway up the slope, where they were replaced by creepers that produced a dense shade. There were jagged rocks and monstrously shaped boulders overgrown with moss. It was becoming increasingly cold.

"What a place! I'd like to live here forever!" shouted Yonghui.

"I hope you have that kind of luck."

Yonghui grunted unenthusiatically in reply. Just then, Mingji lost his footing and fell head over heels down the slope.

"Are you all right? Did you hurt yourself?" said Yonghui, sliding down to him.

Before them stood a big cave that opened to the south. Inside it was quite dry and there was a large, flat stone the size of a table. Farther inside was a heap of dry straw apparently piled there by someone. The two men stood close together at the entrance, reluctant to leave but not daring to enter.

"Someone—man or demon—must have lived here."

"Maybe it was an escaped convict like Uncle Amei."

Mingji recalled that his mother had told him that Uncle Amei and his father, who were in the same resistance group, had hidden deep in the mountains for a fortnight evading the police. And what about Mingji's own missing brother?

Mingji tried to climb up, but a clump of bamboo obstructed his path. As he reached out, he looked to the left of the cave, where he saw something white between the stones. He lost his grip and slid down the rocks, landing at the mouth of the cave again. He had glimpsed a complete human skeleton. The skeleton was covered with a piece of wood that protected it from the rain.

Yonghui too had seen it, from above, and motioned to Mingji. Mingji climbed quickly up the slope, and the two of them set off in haste and in silence through the pine trees.

"There was a huge rusty knife, like those used by martial artists," whispered Mingji.

"I saw it," said Yonghui, his voice quavering. "There must be some-one else around here."

"They must have died a long time ago," said Mingji.

"Who do you think it was?"

"Must be one of us."

"You think it was someone who ran away from the Japanese?"

"Probably, huh?"

"My father told me that Ahan, your father, was also . . ."

"Let's get back." Their enthusiasm and curiosity had been complete-ly dampened.

"But the sound of weeping . . ." said Yonghui. "I really want to find out for sure."

"I'm not interested anymore, and that's that."

The sun was a dull yellow disk standing above the hills to the west of Great Lake. The wind was cold and blowing strong. Autumn seemed to have arrived.

Before leaving Hawk's Beak, Mingji suddenly raised his machete and brought it down on the purplish-gray stone. Sparks flew as the end of the machete bent from the force.

"What's the matter with you?"

Mingji took no notice of his friend and struck again. This time he chopped off a few small pieces of stone. He picked up two small slivers and stuffed them in his trouser pocket. He picked up two other pieces and handed them to Yonghui.

"What's this for?"

"One piece is to take to the South Pacific, and one piece is for Ahzen to keep."

"Then I'm still short one piece," said Yonghui, smiling innocently. The two men gazed at each other. Neither would be the first to look away, but finally Yonghui blinked. Turning, he strode off in silence.

It was already dark and getting colder. Mingji seemed to see a faint image of his father in the red sky to the west. Then he saw his missing brother, good friends, and Ahua, the girl he loved. But there was still his mother, the mainstay of his soul and the light of his life.

He remembered his father's final words, as relayed by his brother: "If it wasn't for your mother, the family wouldn't exist; you'd have no brothers and sisters." He had long kept those words in his heart along with the vague impression of his father's voice. The following day he was to leave his homeland and his family.

"Good-bye, but I shall return," said Mingji to himself, full of confidence and determination.

The return trip was faster than the trip out, but they found themselves in complete darkness before the moon had risen. They had to feel their way as they went down the slope. They slipped and slid at every other step, but their progress was quick. The moon rose over Hawk's Beak behind them; their long shadows flew before them, sliding down the mountainside. They found themselves engulfed in the forest, the trees and grass swaying in the wind. Everything had taken on a grayish-white softness in the moonlight.

The King of Hell's Ridge looked like a straight snake in the moonlight; the greenish black of the ridge was covered over with a layer of frost, the color of dreams.

Then they heard it: the sound of weeping. The sad and bitter weeping came softly from afar. The sound poured over them, flowing from Hawk's Beak down over the King of Hell's Ridge, over the dense forest, over the hollows below, and in every direction. Everything seemed to respond to the weeping; it was soft and loud by turns, then shrill and deep, as if it floated down from the moon. When they listened carefully, it seemed to vanish. The weeping seemed to have entered their ears, permeating their minds and their hearts.

"I'm going to find out about this," said Yonghui.

Mingji shook his head and sat down, muttering to himself, "Don't bother, you'll never find out."

Mingji sat up, thrust his legs forward, and abruptly slid down the path on his bottom. Yonghui looked around him and then slid down too. The sound of weeping, the low, sad weeping, like weeping in a dream, covered everything.

Good-bye

December 18, 1943, the eighteenth year of the Showa period.

The cock crowed twice; it was four o'clock. The clock on the wall struck four times. The entire Liu family, except for Mingsen, had gotten up as early as their mother, and they were standing or sitting in the living room.

When Mingji had returned home the night before, he had bathed, but his mother would not allow him to speak and told him to go to bed. Though he was unhappy about the situation, he intended to cast all worries aside and have a sound sleep. Yet he had to give up and instead gave free rein to his thoughts, letting them run wild.

Saying good-bye was no longer something to be anticipated with fear, something painful left to the realm of the imagination; it had now assumed a form that was gradually pressing toward him. Saying good-bye was inevitable. He had to accept it and experience it. He finally drifted off to sleep just as the cock crowed.

He got up and quickly washed, doing his best to pretend that it was his normal routine. Then he went to see his mother, who was sitting in the living room. The two tables that stood together to form their dining table had been moved. One of them now stood against the wall. In the middle of the table was placed a small basket containing the ancestors' spirit tablets, dark with age. Normally the tablets were hung in a corner of his mother's room, where they were covered with several stalks of dried mugwort.

His mother was standing before the makeshift altar with three sticks of incense in her hands. Behind her stood Mingji and his brothers, and behind them their wives and children. Mingji was in the middle, right behind his mother. He bowed three times with all his heart. His mother indicated that he should kneel, and she knelt beside him, her hands folded, muttering a prayer.

Mingji knelt for a long time, his eyes closed and his mind focused. He wasn't praying; he breathed in the light scent of his mother's body and remembered when he was small. In those days, when she chopped firewood on the mountain or worked the soil, a sour smell emanated from her body, but he found that smell comforting. For years now his mother had not labored hard in the mountains, and her smell had become barely perceptible. Yet regardless of how faint it might be, he found it very special.

His mother stood up. "That will do; your ancestors will protect you."

He also stood up. His mother held his hand tightly in hers. Her hands were trembling.

"I'll be careful, Mother." He gently pressed his face against his mother's shoulder.

"When you go overseas, you must take care of yourself." She was still telling him what to do.

"I will." He wondered when his mother had become so thin.

Suddenly Dengmei raised her voice. "Mingji, you must come back in one piece."

"I will, Mother. Don't worry."

His mother fumbled around in her sash for a while, then thrust something into the palm of his hand. It was a silver ring. "It's not worth much, but I want you to take it with you. It'll be like having me at your side." His mother, who had always been so strong, suddenly broke down crying.

"Mother . . ."

"Remember, bring the ring back with you and give it to me." Dengmei suddenly smiled. "That ring was given to me by your poor father the day we were married. It was the only thing he gave me."

"I'll bring it back safe and sound for sure."

His eldest brother, Mingqing, patted him on the shoulder, telling him it was time to go. His brother insisted that his mother sit down.

By then the sky was growing light. In Fanzai Wood that day, four families had sons who were being conscripted, and people were already moving about outside. His eldest brother's wife handed him his backpack, which contained a change of underwear, his favorite songbook, a leather flask that held a pint of water, and some dried chicken wrapped in cooked rice flour—food that would keep for a long time.

"It's getting late; you'd best get going."

"Where are you going so early?" asked Mingsen, coming out of his bedroom yawning, with his hands on his hips. The scene before him startled him awake.

"What are you doing?"

"It is of no concern of yours, Mingsen."

"No! I don't want to go! I don't want to!"

His sister-in-law tried to console him. "Why don't you go back to bed?"

His brothers and his sister-in-law pushed Mingsen back into his bedroom. They could hear him sobbing, sobbing without stopping.

The conscripts and their families who had come to see them off had gathered outside the temple of the Earth God. When the young men met, they talked and their hearts began to feel a little lighter. The group set off. By the time the sun had risen in the sky, everyone had arrived at the square in front of the Office of Rural Affairs. To the right of the office was the police station, which was avoided like the plague by one and all.

The conscripts and their families had all gathered in the square; they milled about, heads moving, children crying, men and women cursing and complaining. Several large banyan trees stood opposite the office, and a number of people had gathered there. Ahua was also present, standing in the doorway of a shop. Although she was a bold girl, she dared not approach Mingji; instead, she just watched him take care of the formalities incumbent upon new conscripts. She saw him squeeze his way through the crowd and enter the office where he completed his registration, emerging ten minutes later wearing a red sash on which was written BEST WISHES TO THE VOLUNTEER LIU MINGJI.

His brother Mingqing was already waiting for him outside the office. He led him to one of the banyan trees where the people from Fanzai Wood had congregated. After a while, Ahua walked over to join them, and Mingji quickly took off the sash. Yonghui and Azhen were standing at the back, talking earnestly, their heads close together.

"Ahua . . ." Mingji started to speak when he saw her. He wanted to tell her to go home, but he couldn't bring himself to utter the words.

"It's okay," said Ahua, who understood completely what Mingji was trying to say.

It was almost ten o'clock, but still there had been no call to assemble.

"I heard that there are some naval technicians here," said a middle-aged man.

"Naval technicians?" asked Mingqing and Jiansheng simultaneously.

"What's so strange about that? Some of them have been sent out four or five times."

Jiansheng's face suddenly went white. Blinking, Mingqing looked at his son. Both had been keeping quiet about the fact that Jiansheng, just graduated from a technical school, had been volunteered to compete for the chance to become a naval technician. He had been selected and just three days before had received notice that he was to report to the garrison at Kaohsiung on January 15. Like all other "volunteers," he was to be sent straight to the South Pacific. They didn't want to tell Dengmei about it; nor did they want to add to Mingji's worries. Fearing that Jiansheng's mother would let the cat out of the bag, they had even refrained from telling her. Thus, Jiansheng, a young man of eighteen, had to bear the burden alone. Every time Mingqing thought of it, he wanted to cry.

A man with a shaved head who was wearing a yellow armband used a megaphone to order all the conscripts to assemble. The people in the square said their hasty good-byes as the volunteers fell in. Within five minutes they had assembled. The volunteers, their heads shaved, were divided into four groups facing the office. On the left were twenty men already in uniform; next to them was a column of forty teenage boys. Mingji was in the third group, which numbered about one hundred, and Yonghui was in the fourth group—the Taiwan Youth Labor Corps, which numbered close to two hundred men, all a little older than the other soldiers.

All the families had left the shade of the banyan trees and stood near the volunteers. An inspector, sword at his side, was yelling for them to maintain order. He struck out with fist and boot at anyone who pressed too close to the columns, but in a matter of moments, they had edged back again. The sun was high overhead, the air was still and muggy; everyone was sweltering, but no one complained.

Azhen and Ahua found themselves standing next to each other. They were intent solely on finding their men. They had a hard time keeping track of them in the sea of red sashes. Mingji was standing there at ease—he would look down at his arms, then turn to look in their direction. Yonghui stood at attention, but did take advantage of the chaos to look longingly in their direction.

Several swaggering fellows emerged from the office, one of whom wore a khaki uniform and carried a sword. He was no doubt the commanding officer. The order was then given for the volunteers to march before the officer and his shaved-pate assistants.

The family members who had come to see off the recruits were ordered out of the way, to take their place on the other side of the square behind the grade school students, the Agricultural Brigade members, the Youth Corps, and the union representatives. It was total chaos as everyone ran to get a good place.

Azhen pulled Ahua behind her as she struggled along that wall of people. Ahua was a little shy about pushing and shoving and had decided to stay put. But as soon as a chance to be near Mingji presented itself, she forgot everything else.

Azhen, for her part, was not willing to let a chance to see Yonghui pass. She hoped to shout his name as he passed by. With this in mind, she threw caution to the wind: she rushed to the front, followed by Ahua.

Azhen kept telling herself aloud that she mustn't cry.

"What did you say?"

Azhen shook her head, scattering her tears. Ahua appeared to have steeled herself against sadness, or perhaps she was troubled by something else at this moment of parting, perhaps for life. Her face was a ghostly white; her dry, empty eyes stared into the distance, as if she had lost all feeling.

The sound of a familiar martial song was suddenly heard from the direction of the office. Immediately, several inspectors strode over and ordered everyone to sing. All the streets of Great Lake seemed to have been set afire by the poisonous flames and sank into raucous, violent song:

> For Heaven we fight the unrighteous;
> Soldiers loyal and true are we.
> In glory we depart,
> Leaving the motherland,
> Never to return unless victorious.
> Bravely, we vow to fight to the death.
> Banzai! Banzai!

Nearer came the volunteers, and Azhen strained to find Yonghui. All the faces were dripping with sweat; everyone was wearing a red sash. They were passing her by. She wanted to rush over and find him; she wanted to see him just once, even for only a few seconds. Azhen was nearly mad, waving her arms, trying to get across, and shouting Yonghui's name. She wanted to go with him.

"Azhen! Azhen!" It was Yonghui. He gripped her hand, but she seemed not to see him. "Don't be this way."

"Yonghui!" She could see him now, vaguely, through her tears. She suddenly heard someone yell, and then she was struck. Yonghui disappeared.

They were gone, all gone. Azhen's friends and family lifted her to her feet and comforted her as she sobbed. In the confusion, Ahua disappeared around the bend in the road.

THREE

*T*en Thousand Miles of Sea and Sky

Dear Mother,

    (ask one of my nephews, Jiansheng or Jiantang, to read this for you)

    I spent five days at the garrison awaiting orders. On the night of   we set sail and finally arrived safely at Manila in the Philippines. At the moment we are on the outskirts of   I am well. Everything is fine so please set your mind at ease. Tell my brothers and sisters.

    Having just arrived, we have not yet been assigned our duties. I haven't left camp, but I'm told the scenery is beautiful. When I get a chance to see it, I'll tell you about it.

    Don't worry, Mother. You are in my prayers day and night. Although I am ten thousand miles from home, we share the same ocean and sky. The distant clouds drift as they please; my heart is with you. I hope this letter will make you smile.

    Blessings and peace be with you.

Your youngest son,

Mingji

DECEMBER 28

The letter had been through the hands of the military censors.

After Mingji polished off the remaining grains of rice from his gruel, he sealed the letter. He could feel the tears on his cheeks.

The row of huts in the camp had been constructed recently. The huts consisted of nothing more than a straw-and-twig roof supported by wooden pillars over a sand floor. The "walls" were straw mats that hung down three feet below the eaves. Inside each hut, an aisle ran between two rows of beds. The beds were made of rough-cut wood with the bark still on it. Straw, not entirely dry, was used for bedding.

For all intents and purposes the beds were in the open air—sunlight entered at a thirty-degree angle. Afternoons, a misty rain would soak the bedding and leave puddles of water in the aisles and under the beds. Often the men walked ankle-deep in mud. Since many of the beds had tipped over or collapsed, most people just took some straw bedding and slept out in the open.

They were stationed at Pandacan Oil District, an Air Force oil depot ten kilometers south of Manila. In addition to supplying oil for military needs, the district was also responsible for the repair and maintenance of transport vehicles and the training of technical personnel. The Emergency Rescue Team was also stationed there; they were billeted opposite the huts.

The Pandacan Oil District was situated on a flat grassy area of red earth. To the east was the town of Teweiga, on the south side of Manila Harbor. But the beautiful harbor was not visible from the district— coconut palms and bushes with fiery red flowers formed a natural wall over the rolling hills to the east and also to the west along the road that ran north to Manila.

The air was a little cool just before dawn on New Year's Day 1944, but once the sun came out, the clouds burned away, leaving the azure-blue sky. It was another brilliant day.

Mingji had lost contact with everyone from Fanzai Wood at the garrison in Kaohsiung. On the ten-thousand-ton transport to Manila, he caught a glimpse of Yonghui, but before he had a chance to say anything, he had been swept away in the crowd.

Mingji was attached to the First Squadron, which was commanded by Masuda Shoichi, a second lieutenant in the reserves. The squadron was not a regular air force unit; it was a reserve unit organized along the lines of the marine corps. The squadron was divided into four units. Mingji was part of the second unit, which was led by Sergeant Aoki Kumizo. Each unit was in turn divided into four squads of ten men, the leaders of which were selected on an ad hoc basis. The First Squad, to which Mingji belonged, was led by Zhong Renhe, a Hakka from south of Xinzhu. Another Hakka in the squad was Huang Huosheng, who was from north of Xinzhu.

A number of troop trucks, engines idling, were waiting to set off for Manila. The duty officer took roll call and found that the entire First

Squadron had turned out and that there were not enough trucks. The First and Second Squads were ordered onto the trucks.

"Better go and have a look; there will be no time later," said Masuda.

"You're strange, Liu Mingji—seems you've got a lot on your mind," said Zhong Renhe.

"What do you mean?"

"I've noticed it over the last few days," said Zhong, slapping him on the shoulder. "Relax, we're in a war zone."

"Don't I know it. I really don't have anything on my mind."

"Are you married? Do you have a girlfriend?"

Mingji didn't reply, but his cheeks flushed. What was the point of lying?

Zhong was not an observant person, so he didn't notice Mingji's embarrassment. Zhong informed him that he had been married less than a month. His family made him marry the girl he had been going with for years. The girl was willing, and his relatives said he should think about continuing the family line.

"Everybody is going to be dragged into this big war, this mess," said Zhong. "All the young men from Taiwan will end up dead, so what do the private feelings of men and women matter? Who can care about a woman's happiness? Who knows how to be happy these days?"

"What do you mean that all the young men from Taiwan are going to die?" asked Huang Huosheng, turning around.

"I didn't mean it," said Zhong, his face going white.

"Forget it, Huosheng," said Mingji. "We are among friends—we all come from the Xinzhu area."

"Don't call me Huosheng; my name is Nozawa Saburo."

"Forget it, it was just a manner of speaking."

"That won't do; you're jeopardizing morale."

It was a pointless argument, but it drew everyone's attention.

"Hey! Look over there," shouted someone in delight. Manila appeared before them, and the argument was forgotten.

The harbor city of Manila lay on the east shore of the Manila Bay. A splendid bridge spanned the Pasig River, joining the northern and southern parts of the city. This was the best part of town: the Manila Hotel was located here, and large Spanish-style buildings ran along the curving sea wall. The headquarters of the Japanese navy for the southwest Pacific was located near the bridge. Several cruisers and destroyers were anchored out in the bay, as well as several transport ships. But there was no sign of the ship that had brought Mingji from Taiwan; perhaps it was transporting troops to places farther south.

It was a bright, clear day with especially good visibility. The whole of the bay could be taken in, and several radio towers could be seen to the north.

"It's beautiful, just like a painting," exclaimed Mingji in wonder.

"You've got to see it—it's quite different from what the books say," said Zhong Renhe.

Time flew for Mingji and his group. After admiring the view from Naval Headquarters, they crossed the bridge and wandered along the famous Manila promenade. Then it was time to assemble again. At 11:30, they reluctantly climbed back into the trucks for the drive back to Pandacan.

The transport that had brought Mingji to the Philippines was in a convoy with three other transports, escorted by cruisers and destroyers. They were heading toward New Guinea under an air escort. But as they passed Mindanao, the convoy was ordered to abort its mission and head northward, as it was not possible to proceed farther.

Days earlier, the American forces had attacked New Britain, where the Japanese had suffered one of their worst defeats: hundreds of planes and ships had been destroyed or damaged. The American forces had gained the upper hand in the Pacific and the Japanese were on the defensive. As a result, to avoid attack from the air, the convoy had been ordered to head north with no fixed destination. No one, not even the commanding officers, knew where they would put in to port.

One morning it was announced over the public address system that third-degree rationing was to be implemented for the sake of the Japanese Empire. What this meant was that each man was restricted to one solid meal a day and a second meal of thin gruel. In addition, three cups of water were provided for drinking and washing. But that first day, no wash water was issued in the morning, and by lunch the mystery was solved: they were to be issued one cup of water to use as they wished and one mid-day meal of thin gruel. No other rations would be provided.

The four hundred troops to which Peng Yonghui was attached had been confined below deck. The dismal hold was filled with the noxious smell of oil and illuminated by just three feeble battery-powered lights, which were lit only at the time of rising and during the one meal. The smell of sweat, vomit, and urine mixed with the smell of the oil created quite a stench. But as the amount of food and water was reduced, the smell of urine decreased.

Most of the men had been sick, but they only vomited saliva or bile. One man went into convulsions after vomiting. The convulsions had resulted from spasms in his intestines. He vomited, but nothing came up, causing him to retch even more, which in turn caused even more violent spasms. It seemed as if his innards were being ripped apart. By the time the gruel was issued, he was lying motionless. Only then was it discovered that he was dead. The body was dragged out and thrown into the sea. On the third day of rationing, another man died; on the fourth day, three men died.

At some point, all the men began to go around without clothes; some went entirely naked, others covered their shame only with a towel in the Japanese fashion.

No one talked or walked around the hold, and gradually even the groaning stopped. Amid the silence, some men fell into a half-comatose state, a vague, dreamlike state. Consciousness had shrunk, as had physical awareness. Occasionally the ship would roll violently and loud thuds would be heard like distant cannon fire. But all of this was far away, as were the war and their families.

Yonghui couldn't help thinking how wonderful it would be if the black ship were to take them back to Taiwan. He knew he was dreaming and that they would more likely be taken to hell. Images of Azhen, his sad, loving wife, floated before his eyes. She was a strong woman, but sometimes seemed fragile and easily moved to tears.

Yonghui then turned his thoughts to his baby daughter, Amei. He often thought of how odd women could be but how wonderful his daughter was. He knew he was a rough country boy, as thick-skinned as an ox and as tough as the rind of a bitter melon. He often thought that he had never really taken anything seriously until after he was married, but especially after he had a daughter. All his thinking, which was something new to him, revealed just how much he had changed.

His wife and daughter were a source of strength for him, but also of weakness—his courage had diminished and his worries grew by the day. He had begun to fear death. He felt his fears made him a coward, but they also gave him the will to survive. As long as the ship wasn't sunk and he wasn't killed by bombs, he was stubbornly determined to survive and struggle on. The thought made him happy. He hadn't ever thought so much about anything in his whole life. Maybe he wasn't that dumb after all.

Time seemed to have stopped. The progression from day to night no longer held meaning. But time was ticking away, minute by minute. After sailing for another eleven days, the transport was finally ordered to put the workers ashore on Cebu Island.

Cebu Island lay sixty nautical miles west of Leyte Island. A mountain ridge ran its entire length; the military base was located on a plain slightly southeast of the mountains. Originally, the base had been the site of a secondary airstrip. But now that there had been a shift in the direction of the war, it had taken on new importance. Leyte Gulf was the door to Luzon, and Luzon could be used as a springboard to Japan. If Leyte were lost, the Philippines would fall, and Japan would be next. The strategic importance of Leyte was not lost on either the Japanese or the Americans.

They were taken ashore at dawn. An unexpectedly stiff and cold southwest wind blew in the faces of the famished young men. They were emaciated and sallow and looked more like skeletons. Having been physically inactive, most found it difficult to stand up again after they jumped into the water or were pushed off the boats. Many were swept away by the waves. Every man who managed to stagger or claw his way onto the beach lay on the sand unable to move. The officers kicked them and struck them as they lay on the ground. They didn't even have enough energy to ward off the blows. They finally got up and walked to their destination. About twenty barrels of water and some grain was ordered from the base.

Azhen nearly died waiting for Yonghui's letter, which at long last arrived. Azhen had four years of schooling to Yonghui's six. To understand all of his letter, she had to read it several times and read it aloud to try the sounds. Azhen hid in her bedroom, smiling to herself. It was only in the last few days that she had discovered that Amei could smile, and she looked so pretty. She was smiling the day the letter arrived. Azhen smiled too but suddenly broke into tears. She held Amei in one arm and the letter in her other hand, and without shutting the door headed for her uncle Defu's house. She had taken just a few steps before she changed her mind and set off for the Liu household. She thought it would be more interesting to talk with the Lius because Mingji had also been conscripted.

The Lius' house, which lay opposite Black Rock Cliff, was roofed in red Taiwan tiles and had yellow walls. The Lius had lived there for fifty years, since they had left the Peng family and set up their own household. At first their house was built of straw and thatch, but after typhoon damage they rebuilt with bamboo. After the children began working and could contribute their earnings, the house was roofed in tile. It was a typical Taiwanese farmhouse with a main hall and two side wings, but the house was unique in Fanzai Wood.

There had been two other such farmhouses in the village. One belonged to Chen Qian, the head of the village, and the other—the oldest—belonged to the descendants of Xu Shihui. But none of the branches of the Xu family that remained in the village flourished. Most moved away or died; their fortune dwindled and their numbers declined. Then a large part of the Xus' roof came off in a typhoon, and it looked like it would never be rebuilt to its original state. Fanzai Wood, after all, was a typical mountain village of little means in central Taiwan. A half dozen or so families had settled there fifty years ago in the days when the land was first being opened, but the population had barely doubled in that time.

When Yonghui's wife, Azhen, arrived at the Liu house, she found Dengmei sitting in the sun on the threshing ground as she kept a watchful eye on her grandchildren.

"I just got a letter from Yonghui, Grandma. He says he's fine, that his living quarters are okay, the food is all right, and that he is safe."

Dengmei smiled and looked quietly at Azhen as she poured forth a torrent of words. For some reason, whenever she saw Azhen she would think of her own distant youth, those dark, bitter days of sweat and blood, pain and exhaustion. Azhen's days were so much better than hers, but they shared a similar passionate character: they were both impatient, sensitive, and delicate, but also stubborn and unbowed. But she had never expressed her own character the way Azhen did. In contemplating Azhen, Dengmei obtained a sort of compensatory satisfaction.

Azhen had a husband who adored her, but now he was somewhere in the Pacific. Certainly a bleak future. Ahan had once loved her the same way. He had taken dangerous jobs to keep their hunger at bay. Then when the resistance to the Japanese occupation had begun, he was often far from home or in prison. He had almost died in jail. In the end he died at home, where he wanted to be. He had left her with a tumble-down shack, a bunch of children, and a piece of land on which to grow potatoes. Actually, she had cleared that piece of land herself, with her own sweat and blood and with her children in tow. She hoped Azhen's life would be better than hers.

FOUR

The Clouds and the Moon

As of February 1944, Japanese military capability in New Guinea had been obliterated. By April, American planes from the base in Rabaul, New Britain, started attacking Japanese bases and the Japanese fleet in the Pacific. Now the seven airfields near Manila, especially those at Labao, and Cebu, which was being expanded, took on greater importance in the coming decisive battle. The thirty-fifth division commanded by Lieutenant-General Suzuki Shuusaku was based at Cebu.

Because the expansion of the Cebu airstrip was being carried out in secret, the runways and hangers had suffered little damage. A second runway had been built along the shore, at night, by the Taiwan Youth Labor Corps and some local prisoners. There were a few small bulldozers and steamrollers, but almost all the work was done by hand. Their first task had been to clear the nearby hills to park the airplanes, which were camouflaged with leafy tree limbs.

The small town of Cebu where the base was located had been remade to serve the troops—stores, barber shops, bath houses, and comfort stations appeared. Of course, the facilities were for the use of officers and pilots.

The residents of Cebu had all been conscripted into the Service Corps to help with growing and cooking vegetables. All able-bodied men, without exception, were forced to do heavy labor. Two hundred and fifty of them were attached to the Taiwan Youth Labor Corps, with whom they lived and worked. They seldom spoke and they stared coldly at the Japanese with their large eyes. They had a similar attitude toward the Taiwanese.

The second runway was nearly complete. The part that had been finished was well camouflaged with tree limbs, but the air raids had increased, as had the death toll and damage. The workers were divided into two groups: one group worked on the runway near the aircraft parking apron, while the second kept the first, as well as the soldiers, supplied with everything, including ammunition. Manpower had been greatly depleted by air raids, illness, and sheer exhaustion, and many more men had been beaten to death or had died in work-related accidents. The medicine had long since run out, and the food supply from August onward was limited to local produce—vegetables, sweet potatoes, beans, coconuts, and yams. Their only source of protein was the small fish they caught in the ocean, but even that ceased after headquarters issued an order prohibiting fishing.

Peng Yonghui had been at the Cebu base for two weeks. His strength and energy had been adequate for him to meet the demands of the heavy labor. He had been able to maintain his mental balance by focusing on thoughts of home, his parents, wife, and children. But the endless labor took its toll, and as his food decreased, his body and mind underwent many changes. In the end he was reduced to an instinctive level of existence; like everyone else, he worked like an automaton, never making voluntary movements or exchanging a word. Their minds were blank.

"Hey, get moving! Watch out! Watch your head!" yelled Murakawa, waving his stick as he energetically supervised the men. He was only about five feet tall, dark-skinned, and thin-faced, with a mustache, a shiny nose, and staring eyes. He looked more a beast than a man.

While on the job, the men were in constant fear of the squad leaders' sticks and the officers' leather whips. The men were frequently cursed, beaten, and treated like beasts of burden. At first they were so scared their bodies trembled, and the moment they heard the whips cracking over their heads they would wet their pants in fear. Gradually they came to take no notice of anything, to the point of having little or no feeling. Yonghui, Zhou, Fu, Xie, and Xu were all from Fanzai Wood. Their legs were black and blue from the blows from the sticks and whips, and they were covered with scratches from the thorny brush.

Yonghui became like all the others—numb to the abuse, incapable of understanding or resentment. In the end, they stopped running for cover when the Allied planes dropped their bombs. They simply laid their tools aside and slowly left the work site to find a bush or a coconut palm to lie or curl up under while their supervisors shouted at them. Apart from the shouting of the squad leaders and the officers, no other human speech was heard. Only after the planes had screamed past did the men seem to awaken. They would inspect their own limbs and then look about for their friends and countrymen.

"Hey, isn't that Fu Zhichang?" The lower part of Fu's body was mangled and covered with blood. It didn't look like he'd make it.

"Hey, Thin Savage's head was blown off."

Then came the most solemn of times, when almost all of them were fully conscious: they carried the mangled bodies to the control tower and buried them on the slope near headquarters. It was a task that they had become accustomed to. And it was at that time that someone from the same area in Taiwan would clip some nails or hair to take home in the future.

$\mathcal{M}$isfortune

$\mathcal{B}$y mid-September 1944, the clouds of war were threatening the Philippines. On the twenty-first, the American army bombed Manila and, in a surprise attack, bombed the Japanese bases on Mindanao and Labao. It was clear that the final battle was approaching. The Japanese could see that the Americans had set their sights on the Philippines.

Field Marshal Count Terauchi, the commander of the Southern Japanese Army, therefore put the Japanese forces on alert on October 10. Two days later, when the conditions for battle appeared ripe, he issued battle plans "Victory 1" and "Victory 2." "Victory 1" was for the Philippines, "Victory 2" for Taiwan and the Ryuku islands. "Victory 3" was the unissued battle plan for the last stand on Japan itself.

At the time, Liu Mingji—who had spent only three months at Pandacan—and the other technicians had been transferred to Nichols Field. At first Mingji's duties were to train young technicians for the navy in basic repairs, welding, and maintenance work. Later their duties included mixing a highly toxic lead compound into highly volatile aircraft fuel as a stabilizing agent to prevent war planes from exploding during high-speed flight or from shocks during combat.

In mixing the lead compound, the technicians were required to wear protective gear. The compound was very toxic, and if even a centimeter of skin were exposed to it, the nerves or the brain could be affected. There had been more than one tragic case of a technician losing his mind as a result of exposure.

At the beginning of April, the Pandacan Oil District had been shut down in order to reduce losses and casualties. The facilities and personnel had been moved elsewhere. Having graduated from a technical college and being a trained mechanic, Liu Mingji was sent to the One-Three-Six Machine Works for Nichols Field. The machine works was located in the northern part of Manila. It was widely touted to be an iron works, but in reality it was a weapons maintenance facility under the army.

On September 21, the night of an air raid on the facility, Mingji was working in North Building, No. 4. Only at the height of the bombing were they given orders to leave the building and seek shelter outside.

He didn't know what time he regained consciousness or if he had even been unconscious after being swept away by a violent blast, nor did he remember how he climbed out of the debris that had covered him. He couldn't stop coughing and the back of his throat had a salty taste; his nostrils were filled with the smell of gunpowder. He coughed and retched repeatedly. Enveloped in a thick smoke, he could faintly see a bright, yellow light. The light changed from yellow to orange to red to gray. It was the sun, he thought.

He wondered if he had died. He looked down at his chest, his stomach, then his arms, hands, and fingers. Then he moved his legs, carefully examining himself. He wasn't dead; he hadn't even been wounded. He was becoming more conscious of his surroundings. Then he stood up.

Suddenly an air force ambulance appeared, and he was pulled in. The people in the ambulance had all been wounded. Huang Huosheng— Nozawa Saburo—was there; his calf was a bloody mess and his face a deathly white. Mingji quickly turned away, then looked back.

"Broken?" he asked.

"I don't know."

Huang Huosheng was the only other person from Taiwan left from Pandacan Oil District—the others had all been sent elsewhere. And now he was half dead. Mingji had also run into Squad Leader Aoki Kunizo and Squadron Leader Masuda Soichi.

Since August, the Taiwanese workers had received military training and were called "War-Zone Volunteers." Liu Mingji had been given the rank of Soldier, Second Class, and his pay had been increased from $60 to $140. In actuality he received $70 each month, with the other $70 being deposited in an army postal savings account.

Mingji's duties were light and he had plenty of time to talk with people, get homesick, and think of his family and friends. Aside from the twenty-odd fighter planes that were usually kept camouflaged, no other planes ever landed at Nichols Field. Mingji had been in the war zone for a year and was already twenty-six years old. The year he had spent there seemed more like ten; he was no longer the immature technician he had once been.

Mingji lived in a barracks close by the meter-high, beaten red-earth perimeter wall. The roofs and sidings of the buildings were all of rough-hewn, pale-gray ash planks. The October sun was still scorching hot and seemed intent on cooking a person's skin. In the morning, after a meal of yam and vegetable gruel, there would be no work to do. Mingji and a half dozen companions such as "Squid" Wang, "Crooked Mouth" Li, and Old Man Jiang would drag out their bed planks or old bedding and sit around and chat idly.

"There's been no sign of an enemy plane for twenty hours now," said Squid Wang.

"Perhaps the fleet has attacked them," said Crooked Mouth Li.

"There's nothing to bomb here," said Mingji.

A couple of months earlier, such idle chatter would have been unthinkable. Now they could talk about whatever they wished.

The weather was good and the sky cloudless, save in the south. It was from that direction that the sound of big guns could be heard. It was no longer just rumor: war on land and at sea were near at hand. During the early air raids, the shadow of death hovered over one and all, but the enemy hadn't been seen and the war still seemed far off. The situation had changed: war and death were in the air around them, but they managed to achieve a certain detachment from their fears and trepidations and to savor their new sense of freedom. Inevitably, they were disturbed by the insecurity and emptiness they experienced, but such feelings would disappear as soon as they were together.

"I wonder how much longer this will last," said Crooked Mouth Li.

"What are you talking about?" asked Huang Huosheng as he hobbled forward.

No one took any notice of him. Squid Wang turned his back to him and said, "When the bombs begin to fall, all you have to do is hide and save your skin."

"Mr. Wang, how can you have so little confidence?" said Huang Huosheng, frowning.

"The Americans have too many planes, their bombs are huge, and their machine guns are merciless," said Old Man Jiang. He wasn't really that old, but he seemed to be the most mature member of the group. "Nozawa, are you really that confident?"

"Old Man Jiang, you . . ." said Huang Huosheng, struggling to his feet.

"Are you going to report us again?" asked Mingji.

"Forget it. You're one of us, not a Japanese officer."

"How can you say that Nozawa Saburo is the same as the rest of us?"

"I am Nozawa Saburo, and don't you forget it," said Huang Huosheng as he hobbled away.

"Better watch out—he really is going to report us."

"Don't pay any attention to him."

"Hey, Nozawa," called out Mingji. Mingji approached him and in Hakka asked, "Tell me in Hakka, are you really going to report us?"

"Why? Are you scared?"

"If I'm not afraid of bombs, what is there left to be afraid of? Don't waste your time. Hang on to the life you have and make it back to Taiwan."

"Stop being sarcastic. I understand you."

"Fine," Mingji said, turning to leave. "Just don't go near the airstrip during the raids or you might not manage to get away."

Mingji felt sad. Since his arrival in Manila, he had spent more time with this collaborator than anyone else—ten months all together. Mingji had seen and heard about all of Huang's misdeeds; he had even been beaten by him. The blood flowing through their veins ought to have been the same—they were from the same area of Taiwan and both spoke Hakka. Sometimes he saw something of himself in this man and wondered if he might not be like him if the circumstances were different. He felt a certain contempt for himself.

He assured himself that he would never be like Huang. He also thought about how his father had suffered and how he himself had lost a brother.

The thought of his father calmed his mind. He felt more secure being the son of such a father, and it enabled him to look with scorn on a person like Huang. Then he thought of Chen Qian, the headman of his village. Why did the bad side of such people always come to the fore when they were given a position of authority? It seemed that such positions were created to bring out the worst in people.

All the spying, betrayals, and capturing and torturing of people in Taiwan had been done by the Taiwanese themselves! That's what his mother had told him. She often repeated his father's words that most Taiwanese were collaborators.

Were most Taiwanese collaborators? The very thought pained him.

Had the geography and climate of the island influenced the character of its people? No. Had the three hundred years of Taiwan history distorted the character of the people? No. That was an insult to the Taiwanese. Then was it the situation in Taiwan that brought out the worst in people? It was in a plant's nature to turn toward the sun; it was in the nature of an animal to possess the instinct for survival. But man, who was endowed with a free will, could choose between good and evil, life and death. Man also possessed the instinct for survival and the desire for a better life. Perhaps it was this combination that was the source of humankind's tragedy and the root of evil.

Mingji's thoughts raced on—he thought about the island's past, he thought of being called a "Chinaman" by the Japanese; he thought of the motherland, mainland China, a vague, dark shadow.

He wondered if all the people of his island were collaborators. Not a happy thought. Perhaps it arose due to the doubts he had about himself and his origins, which seemed to exist like a riddle or a dream. He was always comparing himself to the Japanese, comparing the Taiwanese with the Japanese. There were differences, but they were differences that were difficult to articulate.

He remembered an incident that had occurred when he was working at the One-Three-Six Works, an altercation that had arisen between the Taiwanese and the Japanese in a restaurant one day. Headquarters had sent some men over to have a look at the engines for Zero fighters and pick out a number of them. Those responsible expressed satisfaction with what they saw, and the officer in charge of the workers had given them a half day off. It was the only break they had had in months.

"Let's go blow our money!" They hadn't been able to send money home and hadn't had a chance to spend a cent, so they all had a good deal of cash on hand. After some discussion, about thirty of them decided to go to the club for a good time. Their group also included Sergeant Aoki and four Japanese soldiers. Normally the two groups never mixed socially, but since they had all been awarded time off, the gulf between them seemed to have narrowed.

Sergeant Aoki and his men sat at one table and the Taiwanese at two other tables. The Japanese had taken off their shirts and sat there barechested. They were soon singing and dancing, telling dirty jokes, and making obscene gestures.

The Taiwanese were also laughing and joking loudly, and there was a nonstop stream of dirty jokes. But they did maintain a degree of sobriety and controlled themselves. After they finished their wine, they remained alert and seldom abandoned themselves completely. The food was ample, but they remained unsatisfied. Soon they were playing finger games. Then the games became a competition between tables.

"Hey you bums, we challenge you if you dare!"

"Why not? You scared you won't win?" The challenge was taken up quite readily.

"We're not scared of you Manchu slaves," jibed Koiso, a Japanese soldier.

"Koiso, why call us Manchu slaves?" objected Mingji in a proud tone of voice.

"You are Manchu slaves. So what?"

"Shut up!" shouted Mingji in anger.

"Enough! You can't call people names!" Mingji's companions spoke up one after another. The epithet "Manchu slave" produced a great deal of shame among the Taiwanese. In fact, the Japanese had forbidden the use of this insult.

"Manchu slaves! That's what you are. So what? Come over here."

Koiso was a small fellow and usually quite timid. But now, in the company of his fellows, he was a strutting sparrow who thought himself a hawk.

"Wake up, Koiso," said Mingji as he straightened up and went forward to meet him.

Mingji had been involved in one fight since his arrival in Manila. His opponent had been a Japanese soldier. A fair fight was permitted by the army during off-duty hours as long as there were witnesses present. At that time, the diminutive soldier had suddenly lost his nerve, apologized, and left. Mingji had been pleased and soon began to regard the loud-mouthed soldiers with contempt. Koiso's loud behavior would probably end up being a lot of thunder with no rain. Mingji was happy to risk the fight, as Koiso was outmatched. He pressed forward.

"Manchu slave. You shit!" shouted Koiso as he retreated.

"Dog!" said Mingji contemptuously.

"Mr. Liu, how can you insult us like that?" asked Aoki, stepping forward. They knew that the Taiwanese privately referred to them as "dogs" or "animals."

"What about Koiso? He called us 'Manchu slaves.'"

"That's his business."

"He insulted all of us."

"It doesn't matter. You can't talk to us that way."

"But he can't insult us that way."

"Liu Mingji," said Aoki with the air of a superior officer, "what kind of attitude is that for you to take with me?"

"Sergeant Aoki, please remember that we've been drinking," said Mingji calmly. Mingji knew that the army tended to look the other way if men got into fights after drinking, as long as they weren't too excessive.

"So, Mr. Liu, are you saying we should settle this with a fight?" said Miyamoto, who had been egging them on. Mingji had heard that Miyamoto was an accomplished sumo wrestler.

"Koiso started it."

"This no longer has to do with Koiso alone."

"What do you mean?"

"It's us Japanese against you Taiwanese!"

Mingji fixed his eyes on them, but inwardly he felt depressed. Normally the Japanese were rational and clear-headed and knew the difference between right and wrong. Then why did they act so crazy when they were together?

"Well, gentlemen, what are we going to do?" asked Mingji sadly.

"We'll settle this with a fight."

"How?"

"All of you against the five of us."

"No, we'll choose five too," said Mingji.

"There's no need; we'll take on all of you."

Mingji insisted that five against five was fair. In the end both sides agreed to return to base and meet at the sandy area behind the No. 2 Metal Shop. Aoki led the four other Japanese downstairs first. After descending a few steps, he turned around and spoke to Huang Huosheng, who just stood there gaping.

"Hey, Mr. Nozawa, whose side are you on?"

"Of course I . . ."

"Nozawa, you go join their side!" interrupted Mingji.

"Are you saying . . . Yes, I'll join the commander's side."

"No, we have enough. One more might prove to be a spy. Then what would we do?"

After Aoki left, the Taiwanese began discussing how to respond to the challenge. The more they talked, the more they blamed Mingji for going too far and creating their current predicament.

"How can we fight them?"

"Why not? The officers won't do anything," said Mingji.

"There will be no end to the trouble later."

"But we're not just going to take this lying down, are we?"

"Just act like nothing happened."

"Sure. When something big is downplayed it just goes away. What's the point of forcing the issue? Just look at the mess."

"A nice break ends in a fight."

"It's not worth it."

"Not worth it!" said Mingji, between tears and laughter.

"It's strange. Mingji, you are usually so quiet and keep to the background. Now look at you—some horse piss to drink and you change completely."

"In that case," said Mingji despondently, "I started this, I'll go and fight it out alone. I hope that some of you will join me, though."

In the end, four others volunteered, for a total of five. Feeling somewhat bolstered, they all went back to the base for the fight. Only Nozawa hid.

Later, whenever Mingji thought about that fight, which had so much significance for him, he would feel miserable and become quite emotional. For as they approached the sandy area at the appointed time, his companions—including the four volunteers—all stopped and would proceed no farther.

"Ha ha! Just one man?" laughed Aoki as he stroked his moustache knowingly.

"You're going to have the tar beaten out of you."

"One man is enough," said Mingji indifferently.

"You'd better give up now," said Iwami.

"You Taiwanese cowards have no courage," said Matsushita.

"There's one Taiwanese here. Come on!" said Mingji proudly.

"Come off it, Mr. Liu, you can't be Taiwanese—you've got backbone," said Aoki.

"I'm a regular Taiwanese guy."

The outcome of the fight was a foregone conclusion. When Mingji came to, he saw several faces crowded around him, all looking worried and at a loss.

"Feeling better, Mingji?"

"We've been worried stiff about you."

He quickly closed his eyes, unable to look at those around him, but he was even more afraid of crying. And he would rather die than let them see him cry.

"This should be a lesson to us—we don't want to get into another row with the Japs."

"Shut up!" shouted Mingji, summoning his breath. He sank back into unconsciousness. It had been a lesson—one more painful than the blows he had received, and one that would torment him the rest of his life.

And now most of his companions at the One-Three-Six Works were either dead or wounded—only Nozawa was left. He wondered about the loyalty of men like Squid Wang, Crooked Mouth Li, and Old Man Jiang.

After the fight, he became more distant. He often reminded himself that his attitude was wrong, but he couldn't change. If only his friend Zhong Renhe were there—he would be able to help. He also thought of his mother and his home, and Ahua, but he immediately banished those thoughts. They were his only joys, and he was unwilling to take them too lightly. He would save them for when he was alone and could concentrate on them. He hadn't had any news from Ahua in a long time. A few days earlier a strange letter—more like a riddle—had arrived. Then there were no more.

The battle for Manila was now imminent, and he might die in a day or two. He had trouble keeping calm, but what was the point of getting worked up?

Then a surprising bit of news came to Nichols Field: a *kamikaze* force had arrived.

The pale moon, which was as round as a bowl, was gently setting behind Negros Island. The blood-red sun was rising from behind Leyte Island, and the red clouds over the sea were tinged gold. Four kamikaze planes touched down quietly at Cebu Base.

The current situation had forced Onishi Takiji, the commander of the Japanese First Naval Air Fleet, to implement his unprecedented kamikaze strategy. Of the fewer than 450 planes in the Philippines—including both the first and second squadrons—less than 100 could be put in the air at any one time. Through this inhuman plan, determined pilots could fly their planes and crash them into enemy warships, especially aircraft carriers. Such human bombs, it was thought, could never miss their targets. By sacrificing the life of one pilot for each ship, it was hoped, a miraculous victory could be achieved.

Prior to the enemy landing, all that could be seen from the Cebu lookout posts was a layer of dense smoke over Leyte Island, sixty nautical miles to the east. By nightfall the sky flashed intermittently and was streaked with shafts of light as enemy warships bombarded Cebu. The Labor Corps had ceased working, and the 240 men were ordered to take cover under the trees around the airfield and not to move. The squadron leader joked that it was a way for the laborers to reduce the calories they burned.

Peng Yonghui, on account of his honesty and his good health, now found himself the leader of a squad. Day or night he was usually together with his buddies from Fanzai Wood—Xie Tianding, Xu Akang, Zhou Shengxiang, and Zhuang Mingsheng. Originally they had been in different squads, but the whole system had broken down and they naturally gravitated together. They had received few orders in recent days, and rations had ceased to be issued. The main task for everyone was finding something to eat.

Xu Akang had died during one of their foraging trips.

They had crossed some weedy fields to a coconut grove where there were several thatched huts on stilts. Strangely, the coconut trees had all died, and their huge gray fronds rustled eerily in the wind. The men all slowed their steps before proceeding. One wall and the floor of one hut had collapsed. Not a sound was heard and not a person was seen, but the stench of decay hung over the place.

"Help! Help!"

Xu Akang came running out of one of the huts.

"What's the matter? Calm down."

Yonghui rushed forward and spread his arms to stop Akang, who nearly knocked him down.

"Ghosts! There are ghosts in there!"

Indeed there were. Three skeletons were found inside the hut. The bones, from which all flesh had been stripped, gleamed white. There were still several ravenous maggots squirming around amid the bones. The men suddenly lost all thoughts of food.

Xu Akang was sitting on the ground looking at his left foot. In the middle of the arch of his foot were two small puncture wounds, still oozing dark blood. There was also some swelling.

"A snake bit me! See, it was a poisonous snake!"

Xu Akang's face had gone white from fear. Yonghui knew a little about herbs and how to treat snake bites, but what could he do there? Xie Tianding suggested that they carry Akang back to the base. Yonghui opposed the idea because moving Akang would only make the poison spread more quickly. Besides, there was no antidote at the base.

The sun had just moved past its zenith; the whole morning had slipped by without their being aware of it. Their drinking water was gone. Everybody was at a loss as to what to do.

"I feel dizzy," complained Akang.

Everyone tensed. Despondently they sat down, heads hung low. They didn't know how to treat a snake bite and could only sit around Akang in silence. Blood continued to ooze from the wound, which never formed a scab. The swelling had not increased, but Akang kept complaining about the pain. After a while, Yonghui thought of a way of dealing with the situation. He took off his puttees and tore them in strips to use as a tourniquet.

"How do you feel, Akang?"

"Very tired, and dizzy. I can't think straight."

"Is there anything you want?"

"I want to go back. I want to sleep."

"I'll carry you back," said Yonghui loudly. He seemed to have forgotten that he just stopped the others from moving Akang. He stooped down and put Akang over his shoulders. Yonghui couldn't see very clearly in front of him and he swayed about.

Akang began to struggle. "Put me down," he said.

The others helped Yonghui put him back on the ground. Akang's hands and feet trembled and his cheeks twitched. He remained fully conscious.

"How do you feel now?"

"I feel fine. I just want to lie down."

They were all thinking the same thing. They had been surrounded by death for the last six months, but they had never seen anyone die from a snake bite. Death was a strange event, and regardless of how it came, it was always recognizable.

"Akang, don't you want to go home to Fanzai Wood?"

"Yes, Fanzai Wood is a nice place. Where is Ashu?" Ashu was Akang's wife.

"Akang, don't think too much." A smile seemed to flicker over Yonghui's lips.

Akang smiled, but his smile froze and his brows contracted. His white lips twitched.

"Akang, don't be afraid."

Yonghui stroked Akang's cheeks with his left hand; Akang's hand, which he was clasping in his right, soon turned cold.

Yonghui snipped some of Akang's hair and some of his toenails and fingernails. Together the men dug a deep hole and buried Akang. Only then did Yonghui burst into tears. The others also cried without restraint. They all stood there turned away from one another, crying their own tears.

They returned to base as darkness was falling. That night, after a meal of palm hearts, they crowded together under a coconut tree, but no one slept. Exploding shells flashed at intervals to the north and east. Not long after midnight, they heard something scream overhead, exploding with great force at the end of the runway. More and more shells fell as daylight approached. The ground never stopped shaking. Several direct hits put craters five feet or more in depth in the second runway. The buildings near the control tower had also been hit and were burning, sending up billows of black smoke. The men all got up and blindly searched for shelter.

Suddenly the public address system came on and all the workers were ordered to gather by the second runway.

They were there within three minutes. Unexpectedly, they were not given orders to fight but to fill in the craters as quickly as possible. Shells from the enemy ships were raining down from the sky, and as soon as one crater was filled, another, even bigger and deeper, appeared.

Four Zero fighters were then pushed from the parking apron onto the runway.

"How can they push out the planes when the shelling has scarcely stopped?"

Three officers approached the runway at a trot. A long, narrow table had already been set up, on which had been placed a white cloth that trailed to the ground. Then came three soldiers carrying white vases of flowers, followed by another man with a sake jar. An open truck carrying four men approached from headquarters. All of them were wearing white headbands on which was a red sun insignia. They were dressed in snow-white kimonos. The man who led the group wore a long sword at his side. The workers watched as they approached.

"What's all this?"

"I've heard that that's how the Japanese dress when they are going to commit *hara-kiri.*"

"Are they going to kill themselves?"

The three officers and the four men stood facing one another. Colonel Imoto, the commander of the base, stood in the middle with Captain Tsuruyama and Warrant Officer Sakai on either side of him. Colonel Imoto looked pale in the light of the sun. His mouth was tightly shut and he was extraordinarily solemn. Yonghui and his friends couldn't see the faces of the four men because they faced away from them. But they stood there rigidly, as if they couldn't move.

"Gentlemen, today we decide the fate of our nation! The fate of millions of people. I earnestly pray that you will succeed and that your sacrifice will save our country." Colonel Imoto paused, and after a long silence continued, "Gentlemen, the spirit of our country . . . you will find eternal peace when you attack."

There was another moment of silence. The officer standing to the left of the colonel picked up the sake jar and poured five cups. The colonel stepped forward, took up one cup, and raised it to the white-clad pilot on the left.

"Captain Seki, would you be so kind."

"I'm off, then."

The colonel then drank with each of the other pilots in turn, as did the other officers. They all stood facing one another for some time, then they all turned to the north and bowed deeply—no doubt to their country and kinsmen. Then a song was heard softly on the wind. It was that well-known popular song, "Cherry Blossoms." It was a sad song and a favorite among the pilots:

> *We are cherry blossoms of the same season,*
> *Together we flower in the air force garden;*
> *The southern sky was aglow with fire from the sun,*
> *You shall never see a plane return.*

After a few minutes they climbed into their planes. The ground crew pushed the planes onto the runway. The engines were started at the same time, and within a matter of minutes they had all climbed into the sky.

At the same time, five other, similar planes appeared from the north, circled around and took up defensive positions behind the four fighters, and then disappeared into the smoke and fire to the east.

"They are going to their deaths."

"Yes, to their deaths," said Yonghui. It was half past seven on the morning of October 25.

At ten forty-five, Captain Seki led his kamikaze force in an attack on the U.S. carrier fleet. One aircraft carrier was sunk, another badly damaged; and one cruiser was sent to the bottom.

In mid-November, Colonel Imoto gave orders that both runways were to be destroyed, all buildings burned to the ground, and all aircraft fuel and oil dumped at the south end of the runway where it would be set afire when the enemy attacked. That day, the forty remaining members of the Labor Corps, along with fifty natives, were ordered to fall in in front of headquarters, of which nothing remained but a heap of ashes. They were to receive orders from the notoriously ruthless Captain Tsuruyama.

"The natives of the island will remain here. The members of the Labor Corps can decide if they wish to accompany the Imperial Army or remain on the island. You must decide right now. Those who wish to accompany the army should meet here within thirty minutes."

Evacuating Cebu! Had they ever dared dream such a thing?

The captain continued, "Cebu is now entirely surrounded. The only way off the island is to break through the enemy blockade. Without the protection of the Imperial Army, your lives will be in danger!"

What were they to do? The members of the Labor Corps looked at one another. Yonghui and his friends decided to discuss the matter. Some were indecisive and others were not in any condition to move.

The natives for their part gave a whoop and disappeared. The Taiwanese continued to argue the point but could come to no immediate decision.

Yonghui heard the words, "Let's go back to Taiwan; let's go back to Fanzai Wood." Like words in a dream, they echoed in his ears. He shook himself and broke into a cold sweat. He hadn't dared to think about going home in a long time. But there he was, thinking about it.

Arguing about what to do was fine, but they had to make up their minds quickly. After thirty minutes had elapsed, the Japanese soldiers marched off, followed by those Taiwanese who had already made up their minds. With seemingly no other choice, those who had not decided began to follow. They felt that to remain was hopeless and that their best chance for survival was with the majority. Yonghui, Zhou, and Xie brought up the rear.

As they walked along, a Taiwanese nicknamed "Foul Mouth" spoke. "Hey, Peng. Are you really going with them?"

"I don't know." Yonghui smiled.

"Fuck it! I think we ought to take off."

Five or six others stopped and came back to listen to what was being said.

"Yonghui," said Zhou, breathing sharply, "forget about us wounded, and get away while you can."

"Don't talk like that," said Yonghui seriously. "I didn't really want to follow them and end up as cannon fodder. It's just that everyone else went with them. I wasn't thinking clearly and was just following along. If we are going to survive, we'll have to do it on our own."

As they spoke, the sky to the northeast darkened. The noise of airplane engines increased above them. In the past they had always heard the drone of approaching aircraft, but this time, the sound seemed to fall suddenly from the sky above them.

"B-24s, B-24s!"

Bombs began to fall, shaking the base. The sounds of machine-gun fire, exploding bombs, and shouting were heard from the direction of the departing troops. Even if they had wanted to, Yonghui and the others could not catch up with them. They took cover amid the many low-growing palms in the area. Finding themselves safe, they gathered palm hearts and ate. The hearts of the palms, which had been a lifesaver for the men, were tender and sweet.

The day slipped away. Yonghui suddenly found himself in piercingly cold water. He tried to climb out of it, but he couldn't move. He shouted. Then he opened his eyes—it had all been just a dream. It was pitch dark all around him, but in the sky he could make out the Southern Cross glowing dimly. He wondered what time it was.

His companions all lay nearby. He fumbled for something with which to cover himself, but could find only dry grass and stones. They were outdoors and it was cold, really cold. He hugged himself, drew his legs up under his chin, and curled up on his side facing south.

Through his clothes he could feel the secret pocket he had sewn in his underwear. The pocket contained a photo of his wife, Azhen, and four of her letters as well as the letters he had written to her but he had not posted. The men had received no letters from Taiwan in six months. His secret pocket was his only contact with his family and home. He knew Azhen's four letters by heart, and when he closed his eyes, he could visualize each poorly formed character. Her letters were short, written in pencil, and full of eraser marks. And although they were badly smudged now, he would always be able to read them.

Light was beginning to show in the east, and his companions were waking one by one. Xie was still sleeping at his feet.

Yonghui gently prodded him with his feet. "Hey, you'd better get up!" Xie remained motionless. "Xie . . ." Yonghui shook him by the shoulder.

Xie's skin was stiff and cold. Yonghui hurriedly knelt to listen to his chest.

Dead! Yonghui felt a sharp pain in his heart. Another companion from Fanzai Wood was dead. Yonghui placed Xie's head on his thigh and stared off into the distance. Zhou tried to persuade him to let go of Xie's body, but Yonghui seemed numb and impervious to his words. Finally Zhou pulled Xie away from Yonghui. At that moment, Foul Mouth ran to them in a panic, yelling that the Japanese were back.

Three Japanese soldiers suddenly appeared—it was Yamada, Tsuguchi, and Otaki, three squad leaders of the Labor Corps. They were armed with hand grenades and rifles.

"Aren't you going to evacuate with the army?" asked Yamada as he gestured to indicate that they should remain at ease.

"We couldn't keep up," replied Foul Mouth.

"If you had kept up, you'd be lying dead on the beach at this moment," said Yamada gloomily.

"The enemy attacked?"

"Our transport ships were torpedoed, and then there were the American heavy machine guns."

"Are you here for us?" asked Yonghui, feeling uncomfortable.

"Come for you?" asked Tsuguchi with a knowing smile.

"The commander has ordered all of you to report," said Yamada.

"You mean?"

"All of you . . ." Tsuguchi sighed and looked at them without finishing his sentence.

The three Japanese soldiers huddled together to speak. Their expressions were even grimmer that when they beat someone. No one dared move. They suddenly seemed to reach some conclusion, and Otaki announced, "We have come to carry out the commander's orders."

"To prevent the enemy from obtaining any intelligence information," said Tsuguchi smiling weakly, "we have orders to clear the battlefield."

"Clear the battlefield?" Yonghui's voice trembled.

"We are supposed to eliminate you," said Tsuguchi, pointing to a hand grenade.

It had to be a dream. How could such a thing happen? Were they, the few fortunate survivors, to be killed by soldiers on their own side?

"Is that final?" asked Yonghui.

"The commander made the decision a long time ago."

"But what do you think?"

"You understand," said Yamada as he fumbled with a grenade.

"You can let us go."

"Is what you are planning to do right?" Yonghui's throat was so dry he could scarcely speak.

"We know . . ." said Otaki.

"Please! We beg you!"

"Let us go."

"A good deed will be rewarded."

Otaki and the others hesitated. The men from Taiwan continued pleading with them, and even knelt before them.

"Will a good deed really be rewarded?" asked Tsuguchi, smiling bitterly.

"It will! It will!"

"Okay, okay," said Otaki, laughing. He motioned with both hands that they should keep quiet. "Actually, we had come to the same decision on our way over. Six hundred of you labored against the odds of ever surviving here on Cebu. You have done enough."

Yonghui felt the blood surge through his heart.

"There aren't even forty of you left. Nearly all of those who were evacuating with the army were killed on the beach."

"Heaven will not allow us to carry out our orders."

"Go home. We will pray for you."

"We will always be grateful to you for sparing us." Yonghui and the others thanked them repeatedly with tears in their eyes. They went their separate ways.

Suddenly an explosion was heard from where they had just escaped with their lives. They stood motionless, in shock.

"Otaki must have used his grenades."

"How could they go back and deal with their commanding officer?"

They were now confronted with a new problem. The Americans were nearing Cebu from the south and perhaps had already landed. Would it not be certain death to go in that direction? But if they stayed where they were, might they not run into more grenade-wielding Japanese? And chances were that other soldiers wouldn't be so compassionate.

"Let's get out of here," said Foul Mouth.

"Who knows which way the Americans will be coming?" said Yonghui.

"Let's head north and try our luck there."

They argued for a long time. In the end they decided to head north, sticking to low ground. There was no path to follow, and they simply made their way along where the grass had been trodden down earlier. As Yonghui reached the top of a rise he couldn't figure out which way to go.

Suddenly Yonghui was overwhelmed by terror; it was an instinctual reaction from deep within. He turned to go back down to where his companions were waiting. At that moment a horrifying sight appeared before him: human feet hanging in a bush. He crouched down instantly. Apart from the breeze it was silent on the hill. The slanting sun turned the dried grass a soft, dreamlike golden color. As he approached the horrible sight under cover of the vegetation he discovered two corpses lying on their backs not far away. On closer inspection he saw that they were each missing a foot, and both were dressed in the same kind of khaki work clothes he himself was wearing.

He wondered if it might not be a trap set by the Japanese, so he immediately lay prone on the ground, motionless.

Suddenly he heard someone groaning. One of them was still alive. He crawled swiftly toward the bodies. What he saw next was even more shocking: a third body lay below him in a grassy hollow. All three were the same—their left legs had all been chopped off below the knee. It was clear that whoever had cut off their legs hadn't intended to kill them, because the stumps had all been bandaged. Emboldened, he crawled forward. Two of the men were lying motionless, but the third was moaning and tearing at his hair.

"Who are you?" asked Yonghui in Hakka.

The man moaned.

"You must be a native." The man was blind in his right eye. Who was blind in his right eye?

"Are you Murakawa Tadao?"

The man moaned again.

"Is it really you, Murakawa, you animal?"

"Peng Yonghui!" said Murakawa, recognizing him.

"Who cut off your feet?"

"Nishihama and Safu. They overtook us on the path and did this to us."

"Cut off one of your feet," said Yonghui, sneering.

"Please take me back to Taiwan."

"If it had been me, I'd have sent you to hell with one blow."

"No, don't kill me." Murakawa's one good eye stared at him while the other rolled in its socket. "Don't kill me. Take me with you."

"Take you with me?"

"After all, we're both imo."

Some say that Taiwan is shaped like a banana leaf, but because the island produced potatoes—which are called imo in Japanese—the Japanese began to refer derogatorily to the Taiwanese as *imo*, or potatoes. Although the potato didn't look as nice or taste as good as rice, it was still a filling and nourishing food. Also, potatoes could survive even in the harshest conditions, flourishing and multiplying beyond anyone's expectations. As a result, the Taiwanese took no uncertain pride in referring to themselves as *imo*.

"Are you still an *imo*?"

"Yes, I am."

"You're just saying that to save your skin, you stinking, rotten *imo*."

"Stinking or rotting, I'm still an *imo*."

Yonghui gritted his teeth and cursed the man and his way with words.

"Take me with you and I'll be forever in your debt." Murakawa's one good eye misted over and he began to cry.

"I don't want a collaborator's gratitude. You're shameless. If you were to die, even the King of Hell would be afraid of you."

"I know I'll never make it back to Taiwan. Just don't leave me." Murakama took no notice of Yonghui's curses or sarcasm. "If you stay with me, I won't be afraid."

"No, Murakama. You can just go stay with the Japanese Imperial Army."

"Yonghui, I want to die among people from Taiwan." Murakama was sobbing now. "It's a request you can't deny."

Yonghui's heart was pounding violently. Murakama—or Chen Zhongchen—was a worthless animal. Looking at his pale, bloodless body, which was more like a skeleton, Yonghui figured he couldn't be scheming anymore but was indeed speaking from the bottom of his heart. Yonghui was reluctant to help the collaborator, but he couldn't take revenge; nor could he save him. He made up his mind.

Weeping and moaning, Chen continued pleading with him. Yonghui took two gulps of water from his canteen and handed it to Chen. He looked at him with mixed emotions and turned to leave.

"Fine, Yonghui. Thanks," said Chen in a distant, indifferent tone of voice.

"What?" said Yonghui turning abruptly.

"Thanks for the water. Let bygones be bygones. Since I'll be buried here on Cebu, forget me when you get back to Taiwan."

"What do you mean?"

"Let everyone forget a Taiwanese like me; erase all memories of me. There will never again be people like me on Taiwan; we should all be forgotten." That look in his eyes—how it flickered and dulled as he gave up all hope of living.

Yonghui tightened his belt, rubbed his hands, hoisted the thin, maimed body over his shoulders, and hastened back along the path on which he had come.

The sun was setting, red and bright; the wind blew, stirring the desolate grass. As the wind rose, Yonghui had difficulty locating the way back to where his companions were waiting.

Suddenly he heard the whiplike sound of a gunshot. He saw the shapes of several men running toward him—they were his companions.

"The Americans are behind us. Run!"

Amid the sound of machine-gun fire, bullets whizzed past in the air. Each man ran, trying to save his own skin. They ran about like mindless animals; their shouts were scarcely human.

"Peng Yonghui, you want to get killed? Run for it!" shouted Foul Mouth as he rushed by.

"Put me down!" Chen struggled from Yonghui's back. Holding his bleeding leg, he rolled away from Yonghui's grasp.

"Hurry and run. I'm staying."

The machine gun continued firing. Someone at Yonghui's side was hit, and the hot blood splattered Yonghui in the face. Chen had rolled away from him. The blood on his face quickened Yonghui's instincts for survival. He bent forward and rushed off.

Yonghui heard a soft explosion as a flare burst overhead in the sky. Several more flares exploded, bathing the area in light. He caught sight of Chen, who was sitting in the open waving his arms. Yonghui felt bad about having deserted him.

His thoughts turned to his parents. He had to escape and return to Fanzai Wood. Then he thought of Azhen; he wanted to see his wife and daughter again. He told himself that he could get away from the American soldiers.

Another flare burst in the sky; a machine gun roared; a grenade exploded. Yonghui found himself hurling through the air. He fell in a grassy hollow. He shook himself, climbed out of the hollow, and crawled forward, scurrying in heaven only knew which direction.

Yonghui now recalled that when he had hurtled through the air, he had seen a man's head blown from his body and dashed against the trunk of a tree. Who was it? It looked like Chen, but maybe it wasn't. Was it Zhou, Xie, Xu, Zhuang, or a native man? Perhaps it was he himself. No, he was still alive and thinking. He had to keep running.

Fire rose to his left, and he saw a lot of people. He was being pursued by soldiers and they were yelling for him to surrender. No, he couldn't stop. He saw no fire or people to his right, so he half crawled and rolled in that direction. His mind was very clear; he felt no panic. He seemed to see himself running and crawling madly ahead. There before him were his parents, his wife and daughter, the houses, streams, and plants of Fanzai Wood. He saw everything, even his childhood, in a flash. He seemed to live in all those different moments of his life at once. As Yonghui rushed toward the open slope, bullets fell thickly around him, and the soldiers drew nearer and nearer. . . .

SIX

Good-byes on the Grass

December 20, 1944 (Showa 19)

Just after midnight a heavy rain started falling; it showed no signs of letting up at seven in the morning when it came time for their departure. Manila was entirely shrouded in rain. Two days earlier, rumors that the decisive battle for the city was imminent and that some of the personnel were being evacuated to northern Luzon were bruited about.

Liu Mingji was sitting motionless on his bed. He held a piece of plywood above his head to shelter himself from the rain that was dripping through the roof. The plywood was soaking wet and the water ran down his arm to his armpit. Mingji seemed to be oblivious and sat there without moving.

Liu Mingji was combating an identity crisis. Wang the Eel and Crooked Mouth Li were sitting back to back, also motionless without speaking. Old Man Jiang had died a few days earlier in an air raid. One of his arms and half his back had been blown off and never found. Later his broken body had been buried in a mass grave. Wang and Li were Liu's only acquaintances who were still able to work. Nozawa's wounds had healed and he seemed less combative than before. Whenever he ran into Mingji and the others, he would smile in an embarrassed fashion and lower his head.

The sky was growing lighter and the rain fell less heavily, but still it didn't look like it would stop anytime soon. The order to fall in had been given, for all personnel were asked to prepare their weapons and gear and make ready to leave.

The ground crew had never been issued any weapons, just a blanket, a canteen, and an old helmet apiece. When the orders were given that morning, each man was also given a five-pound bag of rice as rations along with a package of biscuits and salt. They were ordered to assemble in full gear with their rations and personal belongings stowed in their packs.

They were already soaking wet before they even stepped out of the barracks. No one said anything, and no one was in the mood to complain. A large group of men could barely be made out through the rain in the dim light. The commanding officer was shouting through a megaphone because the public address system was on the fritz.

The mustered men began to move in formation. There were a few new faces in the ranks. Second Lieutenant Masuda appeared. Now they could make out some of what was being said: they were being put in the Kose Regiment under Major Kose Kenzo. The regiment consisted of 640 men, including the ground crew. The regiment was divided into four detachments, each of which was broken into four units with four squads of ten men. Nozawa was again made their squad leader; Aoki commanded their unit, which was part of Masuda's detachment. Mingji found himself with the same superiors; they were still alive. He felt something between fear and foreboding.

"Mr. Liu, here we are together again," said Masuda.

"Sir, I await your orders," was all Mingji could say in response.

"We are ordered to retreat," said Masuda, smiling wryly and shaking his head.

Masuda and Aoki had been issued new rifles; everyone else was issued two hand grenades and given strict instructions that they should protect them as they would their own lives. Losing one would result in a court martial.

The temporary force was soon on its way. The men left Nichols Field through a bombed wall on the north side. Traveling north on the highway, they passed through the northern suburbs of Manila. The road was filled with Filipino refugees, groups of soldiers, and noncombatant military personnel.

The heavy rain had let up and a muddy yellow sun hung in the gray eastern sky. The water on the road was knee-high. The road had been badly damaged and was heavily cratered. The craters were filled with muddy water, making them into fearsome traps: if someone in the fleeing crowd fell in, they often went unnoticed, or were rescued with much difficulty.

The column Mingji was part of continued north; although at one point they found themselves in the middle of a massive air raid, they suffered few casualties. At the Pampanga River they found that the bridge had been largely destroyed, and only two piers remained. It was dusk by the time all 640 men managed to cross the river. The commanding officer decided he would rather face guerrilla attacks than air raids and ordered the men to march at night.

They reached Clark Air Base, which was the hub of the air force of the southwest Pacific, but their destination was Bamban Field, twenty kilometers north. Fortunately they met with no guerrilla activity or air raids. They arrived in Bamban Field on the morning of December 24, 1944.

Upon arrival, the regiment was disbanded and the men of the four detachments found themselves reassigned to different work units. Masuda's detachment still served as the ground crew. They were quartered in low buildings behind the first parking apron. Their first task that morning was to turn in what was left of their salt and rice marching rations. In the three days and four nights of their forced march, they never once stopped to cook. So when they felt hungry, they would pull a fistful of rice from their packs and chew on the dry grain. At noon that day, they enjoyed their first cooked meal in days: potato soup seasoned with ginger.

Potatoes had always been a regular part of Mingji's diet. Since being conscripted, each man had been issued five spoonfuls of rice every other day—hardly enough for a child. Potatoes became highly prized, and now they were eating potatoes from Taiwan. Mingji felt he could detect the aroma of Fanzai Wood in his potato. As he ate, Mingji became more animated.

"Today you may eat your fill and rest in the barracks," announced Masuda.

Bamban Field was a rather simple and crude airfield. Besides a command post under camouflage netting, there were some low, gray barracks hidden behind some trees. Two short, narrow runways ran north and south and were largely hidden by weeds. This had saved the airfield from being attacked. Although the runways were intact, large planes such as medium and heavy bombers were unable to land there. On the parking apron, several Zero fighters were camouflaged with netting and palm fronds. To the left and to the rear of the command post, three large black planes were parked; they looked like light bombers. Such planes had not been flown in combat in ages and were used mainly for training. What were they doing there?

After eating, Mingji decided to walk around and take a look. Finding the place pretty boring, he headed back to the barracks for a nap. As he walked, someone called his name. Lifting his eyes, he saw a tall, pale, thin man with two shorter companions.

"Liu Mingji, is that you?" The tall man hurried toward him.

"Who? . . . Oh, is that you, Zhong?"

"Don't you recognize me? It's me, Renhe." The two friends embraced. Then they stepped back to look at each other. Talking as they walked, they were in their own private, happy world. They sat down on the grass near the parking apron. Only then did the taller of Renhe's companions speak. "Uncle Mingji!"

Mingji trembled and nearly leaped to his feet.

"Uncle Mingji, don't you recognize me?"

Mingji didn't know the teenager in front of him, but a glimmer of recognition flickered in his eyes. "Are you Su Xiumin?"

"No, he's my cousin," the young man replied, blushing. "I'm Su Xiuzhi." He smiled slightly.

He was Ahua's cousin. Seeing Su's gentle, open smile, Mingji was overwhelmed and felt like crying.

"What's the matter, Mingji?"

"Nothing," he said, smiling bleakly. "How is that you came here?"

"I arrived three days ago. I joined the Air Force Preparatory Training Course," responded Su gloomily.

"But aren't you still in school?"

"At the beginning of the year, I volunteered for the naval technicians, but later they told us to join the Preparatory Training Course."

Since December of the previous year, the Japanese had been conscripting school-age children into the service. The so-called Preparatory Training Course was in fact an air force cadet corps. Mingji never imagined that the policy of making the Taiwanese "the Emperor's People" would mean making youngsters air force cadets.

"Who is your friend?" asked Mingji, remembering Su's companion.

"My name is Lin Mingzhu." He looked even younger than Su.

"Like me, Lin is from Zhu'nan," interjected Renhe. "Yesterday we ran into each other, and the kid recognized me. He and Su are in the same company, and they're both from Taiwan."

It turned out that this group of air force cadets had received little more than six months of basic training and just sixty hours of actual flight training—some as little as forty-five. The cadets who had arrived in the Philippines to take part in the war were all stationed at Bamban Field. The last contingent was to arrive soon.

In his conversation with Su, Mingji learned news of home. His own nephew Jiansheng had "volunteered" for the naval technicians at the same time. Peng Yonghui and all his cousins had been conscripted, as had the young men from the dozen or so other families he knew at Fanzai Wood and Great Lake. In fact, nearly all men between the ages of seventeen and thirty had been mobilized. The younger ones had become laborers in the army and navy; the older ones had been sent to the Labor Corps or the Combat Support Troops. The full-scale mobilization of Taiwan had begun on August 20. On August 22, a formal policy of mobilization was implemented after the wartime situation had grown more desperate, and a Women's Corps had been set up on September 15.

They had been talking for about an hour when a whistle blew for the cadets to fall in. Su spoke quietly to Mingji as he went to leave. "I heard that Ahua is also here in the Pacific."

"What?"

"She might be here in the Philippines."

Ahua in the Philippines! There were so many islands, but when someone spoke of the Philippines, they usually meant Luzon. That was the very ground on which he was standing. Mingji wondered it if could be true that Ahua was on the very same island. His heart swelled with emotion, and he felt bewildered.

But where on Luzon could she be? Why was she there? He desperately wanted to see Su again and ask him for news of his cousin Ahua. He would surely ask him the next time they met. Then he began to worry that Su would climb into one of the special fighter planes and never return.

When he was at Nichols Field he had heard how the Commander of the 1st Air Fleet had personally seen off the *kamikaze* pilots. He had seen the kamikaze pilots wearing their rising-sun headbands taking the ritual farewell drink.

He also recalled how, one evening when he was walking with his head down on the low earthen rampart behind the barracks, he had nearly collided with a young officer. The man had close-cropped hair and a sturdy physique, and was wearing a white shirt. Mingji knew he was a pilot at first glance. The young officer was standing facing north, his head held high as he gazed at the horizon. Mingji did not want to disturb him and risk a few blows across his face. So he hastily tried to sneak away before being seen.

"Hey, come back," ordered the officer.

"Sir! I have disturbed you. I beg your pardon!" Mingji stood at attention, saluted, and apologized.

"Don't be afraid. I'm a pilot, and not one of your superiors. Don't worry."

"Sir! What are your orders?"

"Just to chat. How long have you been here?"

"About one year."

"Where are you from?"

"From Taiwan, Xinzhu County."

"Oh, you're Taiwanese. Taiwan is not far, just north of here," said the officer, heaving a sigh. "Are you homesick?"

"No, I'm not," said Mingji, biting his lips as he spoke.

"Liar! Who are you kidding?"

"Sir! I'm not lying."

"I'm not accusing you. Are your parents alive? Your wife?"

"My mother is well. I have a fiancée."

"Do you know what I am?"

"You are an officer in the Japanese Imperial Army."

"Ha ha! Really?" The officer gave a short laugh, and a questioning look flashed in his eyes.

"I wouldn't dare lie."

"Ha ha. You know what? Tomorrow a ball of flame, some ashes, the sky, the sea, all gone."

"You are a kamikaze warrior, guardian of the Japanese Empire." Mingji bowed low before him.

"Ha ha. It was nice meeting you today. Let's shake hands."

"Sir!"

The officer shook Mingji's hand heartily. His hand was soft but powerful, his palm smooth and warm. Mingji felt dazed.

"Good luck, Mr. Taiwanese."

"Sir, what is your name?"

"A Japanese—a ball of flames and some ashes. Ha ha. That's my name."

"Good luck to you. Please take care of yourself."

"And may you return home safely."

"Thank you, sir."

"That is all. Wave to me tomorrow as I leave."

The strong, handsome pilot never gave his name, but Mingji would never forget his face and voice. The next day at dawn, Mingji stood carefully on the roof of the barracks—he was afraid of damaging the roof—looking in the direction of the runway. As he had expected, four Zero fighters were waiting to start their engines, and four men dressed in white were being escorted to their planes by a group of officers.

Mingji waved both his arms and kept waving long after the planes had risen high into the sky. He was still waving when they were but small specks in the distance. Following behind the four planes were two other Zeroes and four large black planes of a type he didn't recognize.

Then another group of men dressed in white appeared. He couldn't make out clearly how many there were. He just waved his arms. He won-

dered which one was the man he had met the previous day. Why distinguish between them—a ball of flames and some ashes. . . .

December 26 was a special day. At around 3 P.M., it was announced at
Bamban Field that the Japanese forces on Leyte Island had been annihilated and that the island had fallen. It was said that 8,500 Japanese troops
had been killed and only about 800 taken prisoner. Almost all of the 14th
Area Army troops in the Philippines had been committed to the defense
of Leyte Island. It was also said that not one soldier of the infamous 16th
Division—responsible for the Bataan Death March in which 25,000
Americans died—had survived. Like their victims, they were now buried
in a foreign land.

The second and last time that Mingji saw Su and Lin was on the
evening of December 26. Both men were neatly dressed: black flight hats
with white earflaps, cream-colored uniforms, and brown boots. Their
figures both looked strong and handsome and commanded respect, but
they themselves looked numb.

By chance, Renhe had shown up. At first, Mingji suggested going to
the canteen for a chat, but Su thought it inconvenient. They ended up sitting on the grass where they had first met.

"Leyte Island has fallen."

"It was all over for Mindanao a long time ago. The Americans who
landed at Batagas are already pushing toward Manila."

"That swine of an officer said that this was the last chance."

Lin kept his head lowered and said nothing. He seemed to be a different person from two days ago.

The winter sun had gone down behind a mountain, throwing a
huge shadow over Bamban Field. A dreamlike golden light seemed to
hover over the grassy plains to the east.

"Uncle Mingji, I'm glad to have seen you before leaving," said Su,
maintaining his cool.

Mingji found it difficult to hold back his tears.

"Uncle Mingji, I want to tell you about Ahua, but I don't have the
whole story."

"No, let's not talk about that now."

"What do you want to talk about?"

"Well . . ."

"Something happened to her not long after you left."

"What happened to her?"

"I'm not sure. It seems that during a speech at school, she started to
make a commotion."

"What happened?"

"I heard that she started cursing somebody in front of everyone who was in the hall for the speech. She was shouting and cursing."

"Who was she cursing?"

"I don't know. She passed out. They carried her outside. After she came to, she disappeared for several days."

"Disappeared? She died?" said Mingji, leaping to his feet.

"Great-uncle Yungpao and Uncle Changqing asked everywhere for her, but they couldn't find out anything. Later, when I was conscripted, my father said that she had written."

"A letter?"

"It arrived through the military post. I heard that Ahua had gone to the South Pacific."

"How could that be?"

"She volunteered to be a nurse's aide. I heard that she was in the Philippines someplace."

"Does my family know about this?"

"I'm sure they know. I remember Uncle Mingqing came to our house once or twice."

Mingji stared fixedly at Su through the darkening evening light. His mind was in turmoil, but he could bear it stoically. He wanted to die, to explode into a million pieces, but that would have to wait until he had said good-bye to the young men. He could not be so selfish as to take all their time for his own affairs.

At that moment, Renhe produced some dried potatoes and some water. "We have some biscuits," said Lin, speaking for the first time. The two young men took the biscuits out of their pockets. They were the high-class foreign kind, something inconceivable at that time.

"Let's have something to eat," said Renhe with a forced cheerfulness, trying to raise everybody's spirits. "Who knows, pathetic creatures like us with our little lives are all the same. Sooner or later death must come. But we're still alive and we're here now, so let's eat and drink."

"Uncle Mingji, what are your feelings for Ahua?"

"What's the point of asking?" said Mingji, trying to act light-hearted.

"You two are the envy of many people."

"Really?"

"Don't despair," said Su. He seemed to have aged prematurely. "If you have feelings for each other, you'll get married one day. You'll see her again."

"Thank you," said Mingji from the bottom of his heart.

"When you see her, remember me to her."

"I will. I wish you good luck on her behalf." What more was there to say?

"When you get back to Taiwan, would you look in on my mother and father when you have time?"

"Of course I will, if I'm still alive."

"You'll make it back alive," said Lin.

Mingji's heart was filled with pity for Su. He wished he could die for both of them. By dying he could offer a chance to those younger than himself. He wasn't being heroic, he just couldn't bear things the way they were.

He never saw them again. The two seventeen-year-olds had gone. Mingji couldn't believe it. Every morning and evening when he heard the roar of an aircraft engine, he would rush out of the barracks expecting to see them. He was doomed to disappointment. Every time the airplanes took off, he could only wave his arms with all his might, just as he had done for that unknown kamikaze pilot at Nichols Field. Every night he and Renhe would go to that grassy place where the four of them had sat together. They both hoped for some miracle for the two young men, that Su and Lin would appear before them. But they never did.

$\mathcal{M}$isty Spring Days

$\mathcal{F}$anzai Wood was shrouded in mist from the tops of the persimmon trees halfway up the slope to the Earth God temple, from the stream to the precipitous cliffs. Drops of mist hung thick in the air; the green bamboo and the battered eaves and rotting roofs of the houses were all dripping wet. The sun glowed above the mountain behind the cassia bamboo, turning the dense mist white. The mist thinned a bit, then began to move, surging toward the cliff and then rolling back. The scene was silent save for the chanting of Buddhist sutras coming from the house of the Liu family near Black Rock Cliff.

Dengmei, Liu Mingji's mother, was reciting the Lotus Sutra as she did every morning. "If there is one who keeps the name of the bodhisattva Kuanyin, even if he should fall into a great fire, the fire would be unable to burn him, thanks to the imposing supernatural power of this bodhisattva. If he should be carried off by a great river and call upon this bodhisattva's name, then straightway he would find a shallow place." Although Dengmei could not read, she could recite "The Gateway to Everywhere of the Bodhisattva Kuanyin" chapter of the Lotus Sutra and the Amitabha Sutra. Alian, a holy woman, had taught her the texts line by line. It had taken her years to learn them by heart, and then only with the help of Alian's explanations.

In Fanzai Wood, Alian's tragic life, the strange events that befell Huoxian and his wife, Uncle Amei's martial arts skills, the sutra chanting of Dengmei, and the pickles made by Auntie Pickles were all well known in their day. Alian had long since passed away. Amei was old and decrepit; he had long ago lost his youthful vigor for wielding his staff and was more likely to be seen toiling in his potato patch or looking for herbs in the mountains with which to fill his belly. Huoxian had once taught Chinese, but since it had become a forbidden subject under the Japanese, he had become a priest at funeral services. He was assisted by his beloved wife, Angmei, whom he affectionately referred to as "my fat piggy." Auntie Pickles had no more pickles in her jars because of a shortage of salt, which was rationed.

Only Dengmei continued to recite sutras, wind or rain, morning and evening. He voice still rang clear, rising and falling but never ceasing. Her chanting and the weeping from Hawk's Beak were the two predominant sounds in Fanzai Wood.

Shortly after Liu Ahan died, Dengmei had stopped eating meat at her morning meals and on the first and fifteenth of each month. After chanting her sutras this morning, she went to the kitchen for her breakfast of sorghum porridge, which her daughter-in-law had prepared earlier. This was a special treat just for her; the rest of the family had potatoes.

Dengmei's third son, Mingsen, sat on a low stool in the courtyard. He had been home for more than a year but still had not recovered. Although he no longer suffered from sudden outbursts of tears and laughter, he was often dazed and confused.

The rest of the family, both young and old, had gone to the fields. Air raids were increasing in frequency, and often, as soon as the flag was raised at school in the morning, the air raid siren would start wailing. Classes were rarely held, and the children who skipped class were seldom punished. Instead of going to school, the children of Fanzai Wood stayed home and helped with the chores, picked wild fruit, or caught shrimp. In this way, the lonely villages seemed a bit more lively. The youngest grandchildren in the Liu family were about nine years old and since they didn't go to school, they often helped out around the house and in the fields.

Having had her porridge, Dengmei came out to the courtyard to sit in the sun. She was very thin and her face deeply wrinkled. She stroked Mingsen's hair and cheeks with her deeply veined hands. Tears welled up in her eyes, but she held them back. Her mind often drifted back to memories of the past, and she frequently had to make an effort to keep her thoughts on the present.

It had been a long time since she had had any news or letters from Mingji or Jiansheng. None of the sixteen families in Fanzai Wood had heard from their sons who had been conscripted to work in the Pacific in six months. She was actually afraid to receive any news, because that usually meant only one thing. A month earlier, Peng Desheng and Lai Ahe had been summoned to the Military Affairs section of the Rural Affairs

Office and picked up two foot-long boxes wrapped in white cloth—the ashes of their sons. No news was good news.

It had been years since Dengmei had done any work. Her one task was to cross the wooden bridge over the stream and climb up to Black Rock cliff at around ten o'clock in the morning. Facing the cliff, she would still her mind and then recite the section about Kuanyin in the *Lotus Sutra* thirty times. She recited the sutra for the sake of her youngest son and her eldest grandson and for the safety of all the sons of Fanzai Wood. She wanted to ward off evil, ward off the arrival of any government official.

Dengmei never claimed a profound understanding of fate, but she felt she had found her place in the natural order of things. Nevertheless, she did still have some doubts about life. Had her husband and son been right in their activities? Did their deeds have any value, or had they sacrificed everything, including their lives? Why had Ahan and Mingding died? Why were so many people of the same mind, willing to sacrifice everything? Why had there been so many? Why were there still so many, and would there always be so many?

Dengmei thought it amusing that she could be so indifferent to the passing of life but could not be indifferent to its value. She understood the reality of life, but she could not fully understand her own place in the events that made up her lifetime. Perhaps Ahan could. Ahan was more intelligent than she was. Ahan understood things; that was why he had boldly pursued his ideals. Was he satisfied when death came? It was good. But everything to do with Ahan was in the past, and soon all that was hers would be in the past too. That was life.

She was still bound to her life by love. Or was it an unwillingness to let go? No, it wasn't that. It was simply that she still had feelings and could not bear to see her sons and her grandchildren—and all the people of Fanzai Wood—suffering so. It was her lot in life, and she couldn't relinquish it. Scarcely could she bear it, but then it would all soon pass away. She prayed that her children would be safe. Safety was what counted most at that time. She prayed to Kuanyin Bodhisattva to protect her children, who risked their lives for the sake of feeding themselves, and to protect those suffering overseas.

She deeply felt the lack of security in life and the hardships, and her heart was filled with feelings of pity and grief. Without much thought, Dengmei began to murmur the *Lotus Sutra:* "If there should be a thousand-millionfold world of lands filled with *yaksas* and *raksasas* who wish to come and do harm to others, if they should but hear the name of the bodhisattva Kuanyin, these malignant ghosts would not be able even to look upon those others with an evil eye, much less inflict harm on them!

"Even if there is a man, whether guilty or guiltless, whose body is fettered with stocks, pillory, or chains, if he calls upon the name of the bodhisattva Kuanyin, they all shall be severed and broken, and he shall straightway gain deliverance."

At that moment, Mingqing and his brother and a few others came down the slope singing. They were all carrying sweet potato vines or plants, which were used as feed for pigs. Wrapped inside was the meat of a wild boar that they had taken illegally.

"They're back safely," said Dengmei, sighing with relief.

At some time or other, Mingsen had come to stand beside her. He was leaning against her like a child. She sighed again, feeling sore all over and very frail.

Two days after a rather subdued Lantern Festival, as the sun was shining on Blind Man's Pool, a government functionary arrived to visit the Xie, Xu, and Peng families.

Young and old alike were convinced that he must have news of Tianding, Akang, and Yonghui. The functionary informed them that they had to appear at the Military Affairs Section of the Rural Affairs Office at eight o'clock. He told the heads of the families that they could send their wives in their places if they couldn't go—after all, allowances had to be made since all the young men had been conscripted. The closest relatives could go, but they had to appear with their seals and identity papers.

"What for?"

"Just to pick up something."

"What are we picking up?"

"You'll find out when you get there. Remember, you must have your seals and your identity papers."

The people listening to the functionary, especially the Xies, Xus, and Pengs, insisted that he be more specific.

"I don't know. I'm not allowed to tell you anything."

"Can't you give us a hint?"

The man would not say.

"Can it be?" said someone softly while outlining the shape of a small box with his hands.

"Think what you like," said the man as he turned to leave. "If it weren't that, do you think I'd be here?"

Fanzai Wood was thrown into turmoil. The white boxes containing the ashes of Tianding, Akang, and Yonghui would be brought home the next day.

Yonghui's wife, Azhen, and Akang's wife, Ashu, burst into tears and began wailing. Tianding was a bachelor. His elder brother had died a long time ago, and his father was an invalid at home. His mother, when she heard the news, fainted away. Her mother-in-law, Auntie Pickles, was there to bring her around with some ginger juice.

Ashu, baby on her back and son in tow, ran to Azhen's house. Akang's mother had died many years earlier. But his elderly father rushed to catch up with them because he was afraid that something might happen to his daughter-in-law and grandson.

Peng Yonghui's parents were drying their tears and trying to comfort their daughter-in-law Azhen. With three branches, the Peng family was the largest in the area. Having heard the news, all the members of the family rushed to Peng Yonghui's parents' house. Just two months earlier, Peng Desheng and his wife had gone to pick up the white box containing their son's ashes, and now it was feared that their nephew was being brought home the same way. They were overcome with grief.

Azhen was still wailing. She was bathed in sweat and trembling. She hugged little Amei to her breast. Amei stared at her mother with her big, gleaming eyes. Tears soon gathered in her eyes and she too began wailing. Her daughter's cry tore Azhen's heart to pieces. Her body throbbed with pain as she recalled how she had spent every day of the last year in misery, longing for her husband's return. She had hoped he would come home, and now he had, but in a box! She reproached herself, feeling that perhaps her wishes had been a curse on her husband. She had been a bad wife. She had tried to prepare herself for just such a day, and it had come. She felt bad about herself.

Just as she had feared, he really was coming back in a box. She felt guilty for having thought of that possibility. Bad women always anticipate the worst.

"I can't stand this!" Azhen suddenly opened her eyes wide, put Amei down, stood up, and went toward the door with her head held high.

"What are you doing?" Uncle Defu and his wife stopped her at the door. At that moment, Ashu, Akang's mother, and the others came in weeping.

Darkness had fallen, but no one lit the lamps. All was darkness in their hearts and before their eyes, but in that darkness they could see their families and the people of Fanzai Wood, who shared their grief. The sound of wailing went on and on; the sound of weeping filled the house, filled the mountains.

Suddenly a torch appeared. The light cut through the night like a knife and shone so brightly that everyone had to squint. The sound of wailing died down.

"Dengmei is here," said someone softly.

It was Dengmei. Small and slight, she was dressed in her padded jacket, work pants, and cotton shoes. Her white hair strayed from under her headcloth. Mingqing and Mingcheng stood beside her, each holding a cassia bamboo torch.

Everyone greeted her in their own way as befitted their age. She softly acknowledged their greetings as her eyes moved from one person to the next. Lastly her eyes rested on the group of weeping women who stood there holding one another.

"Auntie!" cried Azhen.

Then the weeping rose again. Dengmei began to cry, but she gestured for them to be quiet.

"You must all control yourselves." She herself was the first to do so. "Although it has come to this, you must look after yourselves. Tomorrow a man from each family must go and bring them home." She swallowed with difficulty and glanced around as if looking for someone.

"Here I am, Auntie Dengmei," said Huoxian, standing by the firewood outside the door.

"Huoxian, you must perform the funeral services."

So it was decided. Escorted by Mingqing, Dengmei was the first to depart. Then each family left without saying a word. The three families who had been charged with sending representatives to the Rural Affairs Office held a discussion. Peng Dexin and his wife asked Peng Zuwang to go because all the young men had been conscripted. He himself had no sons, but there had been no bad news about his sons-in-law. Xu Dingxin decided to go himself. Tianding's father couldn't go, so they asked Huoxian to help them, because he was related by marriage.

After everyone left, Azhen remained sitting on the floor of the main hall, still hugging her daughter. Tears flowed down her cheeks as she wept in silence.

It all turned out as expected. Huoxian and the others returned to Fanzai Wood bearing three white boxes at ten in the morning. All together, thirty-two boxes had arrived at the same time at Great Lake. The road to Fanzai Wood was quite busy, as nine other boxes were being borne in the direction of Big Southside. In such a small corner of the mountains, everyone was related in some way. Thus those who had gone to pick up the boxes did not find themselves alone. No words were spoken, and all that was heard was the sound of footsteps and muffled sobs.

Huoxian had left incense and a small gong that he used in rituals in the grass outside Great Lake. As they passed along the road on their way home, he lit the incense and banged the gong to summon and lead the spirits of the departed.

"Xie Tianding! Spirit and soul, fear not, come forth." Huoxian then turned toward Peng Zuwang and Xu Dingxin.

"Yonghui, be not afraid, come forward!" said Peng Zuwang hoarsely.

"Akang! Akang! Come home!" Xu Dingxin could scarcely pronounce the words.

"You have to call his full name," said Huoxian.

"Xu Akang, come here. Your father is here to take you."

Huoxian beat the gong as they walked back to Fanzai Wood.

The people from Big Southside also beat a gong as they turned onto the mountain road. The filial children in the procession wore the flax headgear and clothes of mourning. Some held incense and spirit tablets. At each turn in the road stood a few old women and children, staring at them. Some asked what family they were from and where they lived, and some even asked if they had seen a conscripted loved one.

"Excuse me, my son Qiu Mubin was conscripted. Have you seen him?"

"What about Zhang Ayin? Has anyone seen him?"

"What kind of question is that? You fools, you may as well ask him," said Huoxian, pointing with annoyance at the box in Angmei's hands.

The mourners made their way back along the road to Fanzai Wood. When they arrived in front of the temple, Huoxian raised his gong stick high above him, then sounded the gong three times to announce their arrival.

"Here we are! Xie Tianding, ascend the slope!" said Huoxian, instructing the spirits.

"Peng Yonghui! Up the slope, you have arrived!"

"Xu Akang! Go up the slope to Fanzai Wood!"

"Yonghui, take care at the bend in the road!"

"Akang, the road turns, take care!"

"Xie Tianding, you have arrived. Cross the bridge!"

"Yonghui, be careful as you cross the plank bridge!"

"Akang, when you cross the bridge, you will have arrived. Take care as you go."

A makeshift mourning hall had been erected in the Pengs' courtyard. It was twenty feet long and fifteen feet wide, made of a bamboo framework with straw from the chicken coops and piles of kindling for a roof and fresh-cut banana leaves for walls on three sides. The hall, which was for the whole village, had been erected hastily and without much planning. After the work had begun, the village headman, Chen Qian, expressed his concern by saying that the colonial officials might object and some people might end up in jail. But no one took any notice of his warnings as they quietly hastened to complete their work.

The mourners had returned with the three wooden boxes. Everyone was silent. But their silence was tinged with anxiety that Chen might bring in an inspector to arrest people. It was to be expected; after all, the erection of private structures for mourning and funeral rites had been forbidden by the Japanese for years.

After a whole night spent grappling with the situation—a time that seemed interminable for her soul—Azhen was resolved to stay calm and keep her composure when Yonghui's ashes were brought home. But she gave a violent start at the actual sight of Peng Zuwang carrying the white box. As the box neared her menacingly, she trembled violently and staggered; as she reached out to take the box, she gave a short scream and collapsed in a dead faint.

By the time she regained consciousness, she could hear the steady rhythm of the gong. She smelled a scent that she could not mistake. That was what brought her around. She turned sharply. "Mother!"

"Lie still." Her mother had rushed over from Big Southside. Her mother held her close.

"Azhen." Someone was sitting on the edge of the bed.

"Father! Father!"

"Lie down. Don't move," said her father, trying to calm mother and daughter.

"Don't worry. What matters now is your health," said her father. "Everyone will look after you. Your mother and father are here, and soon little Amei will grow up."

"Listen to your father," said her mother as she tidied her daughter's hair. "There is nothing you can do. It is fate."

Fate? Was it fate? Azhen remembered how Dengmei described fate— she said that it could not be explained, that it worked of its own accord and often suddenly, and that there was no escaping it. She wondered why it was that way. Because she was human and that's the way people were. That's what Dengmei had told her. Then there was no meaning to life. Azhen felt angry. But that's what gave life meaning, Dengmei had said. She didn't understand, but Dengmei had told her that one day she would. And she would have fewer grievances when she understood life for what it was—fate and the suffering. But Dengmei also told her that perhaps it would be better if she never understood it.

She realized that many women in Fanzai Wood, not to mention Xinzhu and the island of Taiwan, had exactly the same fate. There were thousands and thousands of women just like her.

Yonghui was gone and never again would she have his love, but that didn't mean life was over. Yonghui wasn't coming back, but she couldn't say that he didn't exist; and what had been would always be. She had to go on living for Amei and Yonghui. Suddenly her heart was suffused with light. Yonghui was dead, but he was still with her, and he would cease to exist only when she herself had died.

Azhen suddenly raised her head from her mother's lap and sat upright. The comfort of others was also a ray of light to her heart, and it was strengthening her. She felt that she had aged considerably in just twenty-four hours; she felt ten years older.

She drank down a bowl of thin gruel and led Amei out to the courtyard. There in the middle of the mourning hall were five white wooden boxes. Ashu was there, baby on her back, and Atian's wife was there too. She guessed that the other two boxes contained the ashes of Lai Ahe's son and Peng Desheng's son. No service had been held for them since they had been brought home. It looked now as if they were going to be given the proper rites.

Azhen had calmed down considerably: she wanted to fully take in the service for Yonghui's soul. In her calm state, she felt so near to Yonghui, almost able to touch him; it was painfully exhilarating.

She stared at the wooden boxes for a long time. Did that box really hold Yonghui? Yonghui was back, but he wasn't in a box. He was in the wind and the light, or in some corner of the mourning hall. He was everywhere. She was certain that he wasn't in the box. She felt completely in control of herself, and was in fact more calm and rational than she had ever been before.

It was three o'clock in the afternoon. The sun was hidden by the clouds and a chill breeze blew. The mourning hall was very simple. All of the deceased were under thirty, and naturally there were no portraits of them for the altar, nor were their any photos suitable for enlargement. There wasn't time anyway. The white boxes were placed on the altar, and in front of each box was a spirit tablet Huoxian had made out of cardboard and a bamboo incense burner. Huoxian's ritual paraphernalia was placed on another table. Huoxian himself was busy writing ritual inscriptions.

Huoxian was the star of the moment. He began with an invitation to the gods. He knew the names of all the gods and spirits in the three realms: the gods in heaven, the spirits in the mountains, and the demons in the ocean. But on this day he was very disturbed and actually forgot some of their titles. In the end he could only offer a prayer of apology: "Gods, spirits, and demons, I, Yang Huoxian, a teacher and follower of Confucius, find myself in the midst of these turbulent times. Fanzai Wood has been plunged into misery, my heart has been consumed, and thus my invocations have not followed the proper order. Those whom I haven't summoned by name are all invoked. Have pity on the young who have died unjustly, their bones in foreign places, their pain everlasting, their lonely spirits wandering."

The sun had sunk behind the bamboo, filling the mourning hall with a pale green light. And although Huoxian was incomparable in his recitation of the sutras, his mind was elsewhere. He thought of Yonghui. He had seen him grow up into a young man as strong as an ox. But he had been cut down without reason. What were Yonghui's wife and little daughter to do now? Tianding had departed, leaving a lame father and an ailing mother. Even his grandmother, whose bones were as brittle as charcoal, was there kneeling with the rest of the mourners. Akang also left behind a widow and a child. The Xu clan had declined rapidly since so many of their menfolk had been conscripted. How many were left? Akang's idiot brother would be safe from the government, but he couldn't even feed himself. Now that Peng Shuncai was dead, his branch of the family was finished. He left no one but his elderly parents. Qingtian was gone too. He was handsome and lucky, but he had died in the war. Huoxian remembered bouncing him on his knees when he was an infant and how he had wet his trousers. He remembered how as a child Qingtian had said that he would one day read Chinese books. A man's fate and the ways of Heaven were unpredictable.

He asked that the wandering spirits return. He hoped that the other young men would return alive: Lin Ahuai, Qingping, Mingji, and Jiansheng. He knew his invocation was incorrect and he hoped that he had not cursed the young men. If they lived, he prayed that they would prosper; if they had died, he would summon back their spirits. His conscience was as clear as the sun and moon, but his heart was filled with hatred and rancor.

He invited the Earth Store Bodhisattva and the lords of the ten hells to take their seats. He reminded them that they were the ones who apportion praise and blame. He urged them to allow the five young men who had been unjustly slain to ascend to heaven. He also asked them to protect the young men of Fanzai Wood who were still alive. He demanded that they punish the guilty and execute their leaders. Huoxian's thoughts galloped on, ascending to heaven and descending again to earth.

When he finished reciting the *Sutra of the Earth Store Bodhisattva*, he suddenly felt lonely and weak. All men, he felt, were drowning together in a sea of suffering. He wondered when peace would ever come. He wondered who could save the people of Fanzai Wood.

Huoxian felt as if a huge weight were pressing down on his shoulders; his chest felt as if it were about to burst. Tears welled up in his eyes and flowed like mountain springs down his wrinkled face.

"Huoxian is crying too," said a child standing outside the mourning hall.

The midnight service had ended, but Azhen remained in the mourning hall. Her parents and in-laws had to drag her home.

Azhen's mind stubbornly clung to the white box. Then the cock crowed and a new day began. She finally decided on a fearful course of action. She took a pair of scissors from her basket, walked out of her bedroom, opened the door, and crossed the courtyard to the mourning hall. No one was keeping vigil there. The two small oil lamps were still burning. She approached the altar and stared at the box with Yonghui's name on it. She felt her heart fill with anger and pain, but again she controlled herself.

She decided to open the box, to see what was really inside. If Yonghui was there, she would accompany him to the Western Paradise. If he wasn't inside, then her doubts would be resolved and she would be able to live with more courage. She unwrapped the box with skillful hands as if she were doing something completely natural. Finally, she opened it. It was filled with the fine white sand from a riverbed or a beach. Her grandfather had been cremated, and she knew what human ashes smelled like. There were no ashes in the box.

She sat down on the floor beside the altar, somewhat disappointed. She felt so tired and weak. The energy she had had a moment ago had vanished entirely.

EIGHT

Sacrificial Rites

The last fifteen *kamikaze* planes took off from Bamban Field at three o'clock on January 6, 1945 with an escort of five planes. What was left of the Japanese army and air force had begun their retreat. Liu Mingji and the others stationed at Bamban Field were no exception, and they were pressed into a forced march west.

Straggling troops were everywhere, usually in bands of five or six and sometimes in groups as large as twenty or thirty. These were not formal military units but groups composed of friends and acquaintances. Mingji and Masuda found themselves in a group of twenty that gradually dwindled in size. By dark there were only seven or eight of them left. They found a half-toppled house behind a windbreak of trees. After a careful inspection, they found no evidence of booby traps inside the house or outside, so they decided to spend the night there. It had once been a two-story house and was much larger than they originally thought. They searched the house in the dark and found a package of salt in what appeared to have been the kitchen. Out back they found potable water in an open cistern.

Masuda and Matsushita both had rifles, the only two possessed by the group. In addition, they had only about twenty rounds of ammunition between them. Masuda handed his gun to Nozawa, who, along with Matsushita, took up positions at the front and back doors. The others quickly fell into a deep sleep. Mingji had no idea how long he had been asleep when he heard the floorboards creak. He also heard voices and saw a light coming from the main room.

"Hey, get up," Mingji prodded Renhe with his elbow.

"I heard them," said Renhe.

The two of them got up at the same time. They could clearly see that there were several people who looked like Japanese soldiers in the main room. A light was coming from upstairs as well. They woke the others and, crouching low, made their way out the back door. Matsushita and Nozawa were on the back step sound asleep—they had most likely been too scared to stand guard alone and had ended up asleep together.

"Which way did they come in?"

"I don't know," said Mingji as he woke Matsushita and Nozawa.

Suddenly they heard voices coming from upstairs.

"Let's go and have a look," said Masuda. "What is it? Some kind of poetry reading?"

Mingji and Masuda felt their way along, followed by Matsushita. The three of them tiptoed up the wooden stairs on the outside of the house. Just as Masuda's head reached the top of the stairs, he stopped at the sight of two stout legs through a broken window. Mingji, who was standing below Masuda, could see everything clearly through the window. Inside, sitting in the middle of what appeared to have been a bedroom, was a man sitting cross-legged on the floor, his back straight. He was a middle-aged man with a shaved head. He wore a dark green uniform, on the collar of which was affixed the insignia of a major. His gleaming buttons were undone; strangely, he seemed not to be wearing any undershirt, and his dark chest was faintly visible. His stomach was completely exposed. His belt and fly were also undone, exposing his white loincloth.

Masuda's legs were shaking as he reached out to grasp Mingji, apparently to get down the stairs. But Mingji did not move. As footsteps were heard below, Matsushita did not dare move either. Only then did Mingji notice that two soldiers were standing at attention in the shadows behind the major—one appeared to be a lieutenant, the other a sergeant. There were also two armed guards at the door and two others at the head of the stairs. In front of the major was spread a green army blanket, on which lay a wooden board holding two white candles and an overturned wine bottle. Also lying on the blanket was a piece of white cloth—perhaps from a parachute.

"He's going to commit hara-kiri," said Mingji. "But he looks different from the way they are described in books."

The descriptions contained in novels glorifying hara-kiri by military men made it seem so solemn, so awesome, even holy. But obviously the major had drunk a great deal of sake, and his face was smeared with tears and snot. His wildly protruding eyes were filled with hatred. He had nothing in common with the descriptions of ancient warriors who viewed death as a return home of sorts.

The major laughed coldly as he stroked his hairy chest. "I can't stand it. And I've killed at least two dozen men with my own sword."

In front of the major and to his left lay an unsheathed sword, the blade of which had been wrapped with a white cloth about six inches below the tip. He was obviously meant to grasp the blade there.

"We've done our share of killing here in the Pacific, ha ha."

There was another bottle of sake by his side that he seized and gulped down noisily. He dropped the empty bottle and it fell with a crash, striking the other empty bottle in front of him.

"This is life? What a joke." There seemed to be a kind of self-satisfaction in the major's ugly laugh. "I'm a born killer, but I haven't killed enough! And now there are no more enemies to kill. Ha ha, I can kill myself!"

Was that the final testimony, the final speech before committing hara-kiri? Mingji's heart burned with a fire of anger. He wasn't afraid, but instead stared fixedly at the drama unfolding before him with the sharpness and stillness of an old eagle.

"I'm tired, and I'm ready." The major turned to look at the two soldiers behind him with swords slung across their backs. "You must assist me properly. Don't be afraid."

"Yes, sir!" So the two subordinates were his seconds, who were responsible for cutting off his head. As Mingji realized this, shivers ran down his spine.

Finally, the major took up the sword in front of him, holding the part wrapped in white cloth in his right hand. He rubbed his belly with his left hand. Was that to make the blade go in easier? The major turned the blade toward his belly, lowered his head to look at his belly, straightened his back, and plunged the blade in. He grimaced and gave a hoarse shout that penetrated the house and floated out into the dark night.

The major groaned. The tip of the blade had penetrated his belly and he had cut a couple of inches to the right. His hands and the cloth around the blade were soaked with blood, as was his loincloth. He had lowered his head, and it was clear that he lacked the strength to finish.

"Quickly, help!"

The major was calling for help. Help? Was he expecting to be rescued? The two subordinates had drawn their swords and stood ready.

The major gave a sharp cry and unexpectedly pulled the blade out of his stomach. He shouted again for help. The two soldiers slowly lifted their swords. They were shaking visibly; their legs and arms trembled. In the end they both swayed and dropped to their knees.

The major was lying in a pool of blood, screaming and writhing like a wounded boar.

"A gun! Shoot him!" shouted one of the men to the guards.

"Yes, sir," the four guards replied in one voice, but not one of them moved. There was no sound. The guard standing in front of Mingji seemed to be trembling so violently that it looked as if he would fall over at any second.

Masuda suddenly rushed forward, snatched a gun from one of the guards, and shot the major.

Bang! One of the guards had pulled the trigger. *Bang!* Another had shot.

The major stopped moving at last. He seemed to heave a sigh of relief when he was shot.

Masuda looked at the six soldiers, who were standing there numbed and motionless. Masuda turned and walked back to the stairs. Mingji could feel that his body was trembling violently. Mingji offered him his hand in support and he took it. They made their way back down the stairs. Matsushita had long since disappeared.

"That was Major Tani Nobunari," said Masuda, breathing heavily.

Mingji felt dazed and confused for a while. Then he began to ponder what had transpired. It was a shock to his soul. He had never before so clearly seen a man die—an ignoble death, or better, the final despicable act of an ignoble life. He took comfort, sad as it was, in the fact that he had seen through that rose-colored fantasy, the Japanese army's view of death as a return home. He realized that only those who hated their own lives were capable of inventing the kamikaze, that inhuman means of total destruction.

> The cherry blossoms all flower together
> and they all pass so quickly.

That was the opium of the Japanese army. An illusory beauty given to life. In actuality it was evil and diametrically opposed to life; it was the very root of the world's ruination. But was this evil inherent only in the Japanese army? Or was it inherent in all Japanese? Or was it something inherent in all of humanity?

Mingji's sense of bewilderment was tinged with sadness and a feeling of helplessness. But at the same time he experienced a sense of liberation: the brainwashing he had received in six years of primary school, two years of high school, and three years of technical school seemed to slide away. He felt contempt for his past illusions, and his own certitude at that moment made him more self-assured. He no longer felt he had to be defensive about the contempt shown to the Taiwanese by the Japanese. The tables had turned now.

At daybreak, Masuda divided the salt among the men. He told each of them to look after themselves.

They ended up joining the exodus southward. It was blind flight—they decided the enemy had landed in the north, so they headed south. Yet they were all aware that the enemy had long ago landed at Batangas, and since then Manila had perhaps fallen. If that was the case, weren't they throwing themselves into the very maw of death? But if they didn't go south, where were they to go? Eventually the scattered troops formed bands. The group led by Mingji and Masuda grew to sixty; even the half dozen men who had been with them at the beginning stayed with them.

They stuck to the main road, foraging for provisions as they hurried south. Near Tarlac, they realized that they were back on the road to Bamban Field. Dead Japanese soldiers lay all along it. A few had been shot, but the majority had had their throats slit or their heads staved in.

"The guerrillas must have done this!"

Only Masuda and Masushita had guns; the rest had bayonets that they had picked up along the road. There were swords, but they found them too cumbersome. If they met with a well-armed band of guerrillas, they would be finished.

They decided to change their route and head directly southeast to San Fernando and in that way avoid Calumpit, which might be in the hands of the Americans, and avoid crossing the Pampanga River. From San Fernando they would turn north along Highway 2 and again avoid running into the Americans. It seemed the best route, based upon hearsay and their own estimates of the situation.

They were all intent upon getting home; none of them wanted to die in a foreign land. This fervent wish soon took control of the hearts and minds of all the men.

"Remember, never abandon the hope that you will return home," Mingji told one and all, "for only with that hope will you have the determination to go on."

They crossed an open plain and decided that San Fernando could not be far off. In the hope of lessening casualties, they divided into two bands during the day and regrouped at night.

As the sun set, the wind picked up and rain began to fall. They were just entering the rainy season. They didn't know if the rain would continue the whole night, so Mingji decided to look for a sheltered place to rest. They entered a bamboo forest. It was dark and gloomy. Mingji recalled the bamboo groves of Fanzai Wood.

"Mingji! Are you looking for mushrooms, or what?" Chen chided him in their Hakka dialect.

Chen's words reminded him of something his mother might say. He slipped into a reverie, but soon was brought back to himself by a sense of lurking danger.

Suddenly they heard a gunshot.

"Guerrillas!"

The gunfire increased.

"Give up! Give up!" shouted a group of guerrillas, rushing them.

The only idea Mingji had was to flee. With all his strength, he ran, he jumped, he fled. Soon the shouting and gunshots were left far behind. Suddenly he found himself on level ground, in a garden of ferns and jasmine.

There were many others there; some he recognized, others he did not. But they had all succeeded in fleeing their captors. They were all exhausted and lay down to rest near a huge rock. They woke after the sun had risen high in the sky. They went back to search the bamboo forest for their companions who might still be alive but found only eight bodies, including Chen's.

Chen had taken a bullet through the throat, which had broken his neck. Matsushita had also been shot several times, and the back of his head had been bashed in. As they picked him up, gray brain matter fell out of his opened skull. Masuda ordered them to place the bodies in the garden where they had spent the previous night. Mingji picked some jasmine flowers and placed them on the breasts of each of his companions.

"What are we to keep as a remembrance of them?" asked Masuda.

"Sir! Their ashes would be best."

Masuda considered the situation for a while. He ordered half the men to collect firewood and the other half to arrange the bodies in a row and dig a hole for each body. A great deal of firewood was collected, and one man even found a can of gas.

"Fall in in two ranks!" ordered Masuda. "Let the service begin!"

A huge fire was soon leaping, giving a red cast to everyone's face. Chen's eyes were wide open, and regardless of how he tried, Mingji couldn't close them. They remained wide open and glaring.

"Close your eyes, Chen. I'll take you home," said Mingji.

"Mingji, fall in. We are all waiting for you."

It was a simple yet solemn ceremony. After Mingji had taken his place, Masuda took over.

"Attention!"

"Salute!"

"We pray that you will be happy in the next world. Three minutes of silence."

In the end, Mingji wept. At first he had thought it impossible. He thought of all their quarrels and of Chen's father, the village headman. He didn't want to cry, but he couldn't stop. He quit trying and let his tears fall, sobbing quietly.

He and Chen had often joked about carrying each other's ashes home. Now it had really come to pass. But Mingji couldn't be certain if he himself would return alive. Today he was burying Chen, but might he not die tomorrow with no one to bury him? Life was so precarious, and he felt so vulnerable, so helpless. There was no way of putting off fate. Could the gods in Heaven intervene? A living being today, a corpse tomorrow. The same tragedy had been played out thousands of times in the Pacific and in every corner of the world. And what then? The situation would never change.

As Mingji stood thinking, he didn't hear what Masuda said. He suddenly noticed that Masuda and several others had moved to where the bodies lay. They stood with their legs apart, swords in hand.

"Mingji! Are you going to take care of Chen yourself?" asked Masuda.

Mingji knew what was being asked of him but didn't know how to do it. He took a sword and walked over to where Chen's body was lying.

"Matsushita, beware of this blow," said Masuda in a low voice. He swung his sword and severed Matsushita's left arm. Then he stuck his sword in the ground, lifted the severed arm high, and tossed it into the flames. Then the others lifted their swords.

"Well, Mingji?"

Mingji tried to shake off his confusion. He pulled Chen's arm away from his body so as not to harm it any more than need be.

"Let me do it." Masuda pulled at Chen's arm, which came off at the shoulder with a snap. Mingji took the arm and lifted it high. He knelt, facing the fire, and kowtowed three times before putting the arm in the flames.

As the arms were consumed by the fire, the men dug the graves a little deeper and put the bodies in. Mingji spread a layer of jasmine flowers in the bottom of the grave, and then with the help of Crooked Mouth Li and Nozawa, he lowered Chen's body into the hole.

He prayed for Chen to rest in peace and for his soul to accompany him back to Fanzai Wood, and if Mingji too should lose his life, he said that they would return together.

"We have to remove the flesh from the bones," said Masuda.

They removed the burned arms from the ashes. They were still hot and emitted an acrid odor. After allowing them to cool, each man grasped an arm and with rags or handfuls of grass stripped the flesh from the bones. They kept the white bones.

It was a cloudy, chilly morning, not in the least like spring. The thirty of them passed north through the empty main street of San Fernando. They could hear the faint thud of cannon fire; their futures seemed uncertain at best. The ground seemed to shake at intervals, but they didn't know if it was due to air raids or tanks.

They wondered if their homeland was safe.

Women of the Mountains

On January 3, 1945, several hundred Allied planes bombed Taiwan. Hundreds of planes flew bombing raids on January 4, 9, and 14. Two hundred planes bombed Taichung, Changhua, and Kaohsiung on the fifteenth. Casualties from fire were especially heavy in Kaohsiung. Eighty B-29s bombed Xinzhu, Miaoli Station, and the Nanmiao Sugar Factory on January 17. On March 3, island children were organized into a defense corps. Island women were forced to take military training.

That year, the first cicada chirr in the tree behind the Earth God temple was extremely loud. Rain had been more abundant than usual, and the abandoned fields were thick with weeds. The margins of the fields were covered with reeds that stood pointing at the sky like a forest of blades.

Summer had begun. Amei was nearly three, but she was small and stunted and looked more like a one-year-old. She could stand only by clinging to the bed; otherwise she crawled like a feeble puppy. Her mouth hung open and saliva ran from the corner. She hiccupped constantly.

"She is sick again," said Dexin's wife. "I will go get some peanuts."

Azhen immediately put Amei on her left leg and, supporting her daughter with her left hand, started pinching the skin on her neck. She continued pinching and pulling the skin on the child's throat. Already her throat was bruised in several places, and soon another red bruise appeared. This was how country people attempted to cure, or as they put it, "capture" the *sha* syndrome. Over the last few years, bruises had appeared on the throats of the people of Fanzai Wood, young and old alike.

"I don't have any more," said Dexin's wife, "not a single peanut left."

In consternation, Azhen continued pinching Amei's throat, shoulders, and back.

It was felt that people suffered from the *sha* syndrome, as it was called in Chinese medical terminology, due to a lack of fat in the diet. In those days few people could afford to fry peanuts. Peanuts were hoarded as if they were a treasure, and when someone felt the condition coming on, they would chew a few raw peanuts until the symptoms disappeared. However, the Pengs had long since consumed the peanuts they had stored the year before. Azhen asked that she be allowed to give her daughter some of the seed peanuts, but Dexin's wife said that was what they had been using.

Dexin's wife herself was hiccupping. Azhen put Amei back on the bed and went to give her the same treatment. Dexin's wife told her that she would do it herself.

There were so many purple bruises on her throat, one on top of another, some darker than others, that it was impossible to tell how many she had. Gritting her teeth and knitting her brows, she pinched and pulled her skin.

Azhen herself felt a tickling in her throat. She too hiccupped, and her mouth filled with saliva. She suddenly panicked; she trembled, and her hands and feet felt numb. She had spasms in her stomach and her belly twitched. She realized that she too had caught the syndrome. She quickly started to pinch the skin of her throat. Saliva filled her mouth and rolled out of her quivering lips. The symptoms seemed to vanish, and she quickly finished sweeping the house and doing the wash. She then asked her mother-in-law to look after Amei and feed her when she awakened. After talking with her mother-in-law, she set off for the temple. Akang's wife and Minseng's wife were already there; to her surprise, fat Angmei was also there.

The women had agreed to meet at the temple to catch frogs. The field frogs, like the snails, had all long since been caught, but now word had it that a different kind of frog—a mountain frog—could be caught among the rocks in the stream behind the temple. Mountain frogs had become the catch of the day. The frogs were tender and fat and if boiled, would produce a fatty broth. That was what everyone was saying.

But there was one problem with catching mountain frogs. The place under the cliff where they were found was thought to be "unclean." In the late afternoon as the sun was setting, a cold wind would rise there, standing one's hair on end. Some people said that they had heard strange noises and seen furry, black shadows there too. Nevertheless, the lure of mountain frogs proved much stronger than any fears and superstitions.

Just the day before, Azhen and Ashu had been talking about the idea of catching mountain frogs. Minseng's wife had overheard them.

"We can go together to catch them, if you really dare," said Mingsen's wife.

"Okay! But do you dare?" they both replied.

They quickly arrived at a dark and gloomy spot high up along the stream. The shrimp and crayfish had long since been cleaned out, and even tadpoles were a rarity. The stream was low and flowed very slowly. The stones were covered with moss, making it very difficult to walk. In the end, the women found it easier to walk in the stream.

"Gotcha!" shouted Angmei, who was walking ahead of the others. "Come and look."

"What did you get? Goodness, an eel!" said Azhen, nearly falling into the water.

Angmei was holding it in her right hand, and it had coiled up her right arm. Actually, it was a poisonous snake, a variety quite common in the area. It had red spots and was about as thick as a person's toe.

"Did it bite you?"

"Look," said Angmei, holding the snake firmly at the base of its head while showing the others how it had opened its mouth.

"Throw it away. Do you want to die?" said Mingsen's wife, her voice quavering.

"It makes the best tonic," said Angmei in a whisper. "My old man always eats them. It's such a delicacy, he eats them bones and all. Don't tell him about it; I'm going to eat this one."

As Angmei spoke, she squeezed her fingers together, crushing the life out of the snake. She really was an expert at dressing snakes. She broke the fangs off in a branch, then tossed the lifeless body into a cloth sack she was carrying.

"Angmei," said Ashu, slightly embarrassed, "if we come across another one, will you catch it for me?"

"All right. But there aren't many of them left."

They did not find anything else edible as they made their way. They were harassed constantly by huge mosquitoes, and occasionally a bat would swoop down through the trees.

"Wow, a big one!" said Angmei, who had made another catch.

"You caught another one?" they all said in disbelief.

This time, Angmei had managed to knock a bat from the rock overhang along the stream. It was a good-sized bat, about as big as a fist.

"Can you eat it?"

"Idiot! There isn't a thing that can't be eaten," said Angmei with satisfaction as she threw another item into her sack.

Now they began looking for anything and everything edible. It was said that Angmei could make anything palatable. The things that other people thought were useless—the bones of wildcat, gibbon, or boar— found a place in Angmei's pot.

"Aren't you afraid of getting sick?"

"I boil everything for a long time and even the bones are soft. How can I get sick?"

Everyone in Fanzai Wood was thin—except for Angmei. She didn't seem to know hunger like everyone else.

"You are laughing at me," said Angmei, frowning. "With a husband like mine, what else am I to do? Huoxian has never worked for his meals—I provide them all."

"You're better than us," said Azhen, smiling sadly.

In the past, everyone in Fanzai Wood had looked upon Angmei with some contempt—she was thought to be fat, messy, and unkempt. But now her status in the village had risen. Yet Angmei never thought of herself as being better than anyone else; she was always humble and modest, and felt herself to be inferior to the other village women. She was a natural survivor—she didn't have to think about it or work hard at it; it was her nature.

"Azhen, why are you so absent-minded? We're here!" shouted Angmei up ahead of the others.

They had arrived at a long rocky outcropping at the foot of the cliff. The three-foot-high stalks and egg-shaped leaves of the stinging nettles, known locally as "dog-bites-man," were everywhere.

High above, wisps of cloud could be seen in the pale blue sky. But down where they were, the air was damp and cold. The place seemed devoid of life—there were no bats, mosquitoes, or snakes. Azhen was afraid, but her fear was mixed with a sense of awe and reverence. She felt she had arrived at the living heart of the mountains, the very root of their strength, a place that ought not to be entered. But strangely, she also felt it to be the safest place on earth—there were no evil spirits or demons, nor were there enemy guns and bombs. The threat of death did not seem to exist in this place. She thought of Yonghui.

"Mountain frogs!" said Angmei, who had spotted their quarry. "See, there in the crevice."

There in a crevice on a moss-covered ledge near where a spring bubbled out of the ground, was a row of frogs. They were a silvery gray tinged with blue, and their eyes were a watery red. They were bigger than field frogs and had huge round mouths and thick meaty backs. Their bellies were white and they looked so tender and appetizing.

"How are we going to catch them?" asked Angmei, suddenly at a loss.

"Why don't we . . ." Azhen started to speak.

"We can't take too many," said Mingsen's wife.

"I don't dare . . ."

"What are you afraid of? I was just thinking that they will all scatter as soon as we get close enough to catch them," said Angmei. "I think we can get a few if we club them with a stick."

"But we would kill them."

"Are you afraid of killing them?"

They had, after all, set out to catch mountain frogs. They were dying of hunger, so what were they worried about? Azhen still felt that the frogs were not meant for peoples' tables.

Angmei and Mingsen's wife went to look for a stick with which to club the frogs. Azhen hesitated. Slowly she edged closer, lifting her hand ever so gradually. She wanted to stroke their backs. Her fingers were almost touching them when she suddenly caught sight of a monstrous frog squatting in the crevice behind the others.

Azhen screamed and slipped, nearly losing her balance. Suddenly all the frogs vanished from the dark crevice. When Angmei asked her angrily what she had seen, she said that she had seen a huge frog the size of a bowl.

Angmei was angry with Azhen and started thrusting her stick into the crevice, but not a single frog appeared.

"Careful Angmei, or you might pull out a big snake," warned Ashu.

"That would be fine! It couldn't eat me, but I sure could eat it."

They all burst out laughing. Angmei's anger seemed to fade. They started turning over stones in search of anything to eat. To their surprise, they caught a number of crayfish. These were considered a delicacy, so their trip was a success after all. They also caught a large number of fat snails. It was a big haul, and Angmei was beaming.

They cleaned the snails by the edge of the stream. First they crushed the shells with a rock, then they cut the guts away from the meaty bodies. When they got home they would sprinkle them with ashes to absorb any remaining dirty juices and then boil or fry them with chives or celery. It was a favorite dish in Fanzai Wood, and especially good for curing the *sha* syndrome.

All the women managed to gather a huge amount of food, with Angmei getting the most. She was still not satisfied so she took up all the innards, washed them clean in the stream, and put them in her sack.

Azhen was also very happy. Her small sack of food would keep her family from getting sick for another week or more. She also pondered what fat Angmei had said to them that day. She now felt stronger and more confident.

TEN

*T*he Journey of the Salmon

*S*ummer had arrived in Luzon, and the tributaries of the Pampanga and Tarlac rivers were overflowing. Liu Mingji and his companions had left San Fernando, and after a five-day march had arrived at Cabanatuan, gateway to San Jose, the military heart of central Luzon. The Rising Sun Regiment that had been stationed there had long since been withdrawn to the north, and confusion now reigned in the area.

Rumor had it that the American army was making its way south ahead of them, so they again had turned north. All the bridges over the Tarlac had been destroyed, so they had to swim the river. Finally they arrived at San Jose, which was headquarters for the Iron Regiment. But it too had long since been withdrawn. Looking down at San Jose from the hills, they saw not a soul, but all the lights were lit. They wondered if the Americans had already arrived.

Manila had fallen on April 2, so it was possible that San Jose might already be in American hands, or controlled by the guerrillas. They decided to spend the night on the outskirts of town. It was there that they learned from some stragglers that the Japanese army had decided to make a stand at San Jose to stop the American advance, even if it meant total annihilation.

Mingji and his companions decided to risk cutting across the outskirts of town at night. They set off in pairs at fifteen-foot intervals. In that way they bypassed San Jose. By daybreak they had reached the highway and put more than ten miles between themselves and the danger zone. Vehicles came and went along the highway. They decided to leave it and make their way north.

For two weeks they had carried no provisions save the salt they had found in the house. They had foraged for wild fruits, herbs, and young potato shoots. Six days out of San Jose, the going was becoming more difficult and the terrain steeper. Cloud-shrouded peaks now lay directly before them. They were at a loss as to what to do.

"This has to be the southern tip of the central mountain range of Luzon."

"Then we must be close to Baguio."

"No, Baguio is close to Lingayen Gulf. We're going to the north, right?"

"Yes, to Aparri, and from there we'll take a boat across the Bashi Straits."

"And back to Taiwan."

They all smiled and laughed until tears flowed from their eyes.

Groups of stragglers were seen all over the countryside; they were everywhere except on the highway. None of them knew the way north or what their final destination was. They headed north by observing where the sun rose and set. Some just blindly followed other soldiers.

They were entering the mountains. No one dared follow the highway for fear of being bombed or being forced to rejoin what was left of the Japanese army for a certain death. The mountains rose higher and higher the farther north they went. They encountered peak after peak, and narrow passes and defiles. Often, after walking two or three days, they would come to a precipitous cliff, which meant that they had to turn back. Even though they moved in this groping fashion, the paths were filled with long columns of people. The paths were littered with trash and excrement and an occasional corpse, some of which had been there for a long time and others that were quite recent.

At first sight of the corpses, the men felt a mixture of fear and pity. But after they had seen a good number, they didn't give them a second thought. One thing good about the new corpses was that they might provide matches and salt or even clothes and shoes. By now no one carried anything but a helmet, which could be used for cooking, and a bayonet. Their packs were empty save for the bones of their companions. And only Mingji and Masuda still had their packs—the others had long since ditched theirs. When they encountered other groups, the men usually eyed their packs.

"Have you got anything to eat in that pack?" asked one man, already salivating.

"No, just the bones of my friends!" said Mingji angrily.

"Let's have a look." They found themselves surrounded by several men with bayonets.

Mingji and Masuda put down their packs without a word and showed them the white bones. An acrid smell of rotten and singed flesh arose from the bags.

"You eat human flesh?"

"These are the bones of our friends. Don't you believe us?"

"Those bastards on New Guinea ate human flesh. You bastards . . ."

"I think we had better get rid of these," said Masuda, pointing at the packs. "People think we have food. We might be robbed, or even worse."

"How can we get rid of them?"

"Throw them away, or bury them."

"No, I promised him," replied Mingji gloomily. Masuda saw there was no point in talking about it, so they continued on. Aoki and Nozawa scarcely spoke a word these days. Aoki also agreed that the safest thing to do would be to abandon the bones. Mingji didn't even look at him, and Masuda said nothing.

Renhe had been suffering from diarrhea since having eaten some mildly poisonous plants. Mingji, Aoki, and Crooked Mouth Li were bothered by malaria after entering the mountains. Masuda's hemorrhoids were acting up. Masuda and Renhe were having the most difficulty. Nozawa was actually the healthiest of the group.

"We have to stick together," said Mingji. He had become aware of a new danger after the episode with the pack. "It looks like there is safety in numbers."

"That's right. If we had had any food in that pack, one of those bastards might have stuck a bayonet in us."

"We have to stick together."

"We have to watch our health," said Masuda weakly. "There is no need to go so fast."

For a long time now Mingji had wondered by what strange twist of fate he had fallen in with these men, especially with Masuda. He really didn't seem Japanese. Was he unique, atypical? No, Mingji decided that he just had the wrong impression of the Japanese people. But if Masuda was a typical Japanese, what circumstances were necessary for the other kind to exist? He thought of Nozawa, a real bastard, who was stronger than anyone. He hated him. Why had such a bastard survived? Why hadn't he been killed by the American bullets or shrapnel? Mingji prayed that Masuda would make it, that he would get safely home to Japan and father more Japanese like himself.

At around noon that day they had crossed a large open area covered with brambles and creepers. They reached the foot of a gently sloping hill. Halfway down the other side was a group of ten stragglers. The men could see the smoke from what was probably their cook fires. It was surely safe there. They took the path down, picking edible herbs as they descended to cook when they arrived. But it was clear that there was no water on the hill. They would have to locate some water before they could cook anything.

Crooked Mouth Li, Aoki, and Mingji took a winding path through a hollow filled with trees, then through an abandoned pineapple field in search of water. Large white butterflies flitted around them in the hollow and in the abandoned field. They saw water below and made their way down through a gully with steep walls covered with vines. It was clear no one had passed that way before. The butterflies were still fluttering around them. They worked their way through the gully and suddenly a shallow pool of water opened before them. On the other side of the pool was a rock wall about ten feet high.

"Beautiful! What a beautiful place!" exclaimed Aoki.

Mingji felt intoxicated by the shady stream, which reminded him of the one behind the temple in Fanzai Wood. He was still feverish from the malaria, and each time he moved his eyes he felt a sharp pain. The scene before him seemed bathed in a white mist, and there seemed to be another dimension behind everything. Was he penetrating beyond the surface of reality? It was impossible; only what was in front of him was real. The rest was an illusion, a strange and sudden apprehension of another world behind this one that could never be explained by a physics textbook.

Aoki had jumped into the pool and was dipping water up with his helmet and pouring it over himself. He was really enjoying himself. Crooked Mouth Li, after having drunk his fill, was holding two helmets full of water while keeping his eyes peeled.

"Mingji, are you still daydreaming?" mocked Aoki.

Mingji recovered himself and was just about to stoop down and scoop up some water when he caught sight of something out of the corner of his eye.

Then he heard a gunshot.

Crooked Mouth Li staggered forward and fell with a heavy thud.

"Surrender! Surrender!" they heard shouted at them in English.

They were guerrillas. Four guns were trained at Mingji and Aoki. Standing still, they obediently raised their arms.

The guerrillas could speak Japanese. They used simple Japanese and gestures to indicate that they wanted them to cross the pool and ascend the hill.

Mingji's throat was dry, his muscles ached, and he breathed with difficulty. He was aware that his fever had broken. His face and hands were cold and a little numb. He felt a tremor. It was over, all over. They were murderous guerrillas and not some illusion. Mingji forced himself to understand the import of what was happening.

He seemed to float on his feet; the scene before him grew numinous. It was a dream. No, it was not a dream. He wanted to flee but knew it was impossible. He didn't want to die. He wanted to live and return to Taiwan. He didn't want to die in a foreign land.

He obeyed their commands and ascended the hill. At the top, he found four guns pointed at his chest.

"Kill!" shouted Aoki as he rushed the man before him.

The man had no chance to fire as Aoki fell on him. Mingji saw several sudden flashes before his eyes. They entered Aoki's back. He didn't even have a chance to groan. His body twitched as he turned and hit the ground, where he shook with violent spasms.

A gleaming object was pressed against Mingji's throat. He felt a sudden heat, and something flow down his chest. He knew what it was. He was suffocating with despair. A dark cloud fell around him, and Mingji fell to the ground.

"Who are you?" asked one of the men in Japanese.

He nodded his head.

"Are you Japanese?"

He shook his head.

"What about this?" asked the man, looking at his army pack.

"Bones, my friend's bones."

"Really?" The man talked excitedly with his companions.

"Bones! Bones!" someone said in approval.

"Are you Taiwanese?"

He nodded.

"Formosa?"

He moved his lips ever so slightly.

The guerrillas were discussing him as they glanced at him. They examined his eyebrows, his face, and his tousled hair. He closed his eyes.

"Mother," he said to himself.

"What did you say?" asked the one who spoke Japanese, apparently having overheard him.

They stopped talking and stared at him. The man who spoke Japanese felt his forehead.

"Hot! Are you sick?"

"It's malaria."

"We won't harm you, you are our prisoner."

"My mouth is dry; I had a fever; I need water."

"Move! Quickly! If you try anything, we'll shoot you."

Should he move? They might shoot him as soon as he turned his back. guerrillas were known to kill without thinking twice. They were probably letting him live because he was Taiwanese, but it was unlikely that he would ever make it home.

His feet felt heavy; it was as if he were chained to the ground. His legs shook, but his mind was clear. He felt a vague pain in a spot on his back above his heart—that was their target. He wanted to squat in spite of himself. But he continued on with the guerrillas behind him. He put on his helmet and slid down the slope. He knew they were on top of the hill with their guns trained on him.

"I can't walk very fast," he reminded himself as he took off his helmet.

The shallow pool was there. Crooked Mouth Li was lying face down on the other side; the pool of blood beneath him was congealing. Mingji thought it strange that Li could be reduced to such a heap of nothing.

He wondered if he should try to make a run for it. The thought was big in his mind. The fever had subsided again, and his mind was clearer than ever. He felt calm and was certain he would return home. There was no way he would be prevented from making it back to Taiwan.

He suddenly thought of the salmon. He remembered studying the salmon and its strange life cycle in school. He made his way to the bottom of the hill and walked to the edge of the shallow pool. He told himself that he was almost there and didn't want to make them suspicious. They were watching his every move.

He drew a deep breath and turned slightly. He threw his helmet, which he had just used to dip water from the pool, to the right, and then like a mountain goat he leaped into the reeds at the end of the pool. He landed on both feet in the water, then dove head first into the grass on the opposite bank. Bullets whizzed around him. He crawled as fast as he could through the grass up the slope. He suddenly felt a burning hot pain in his right thigh.

He could hear the shots falling all around him. He was certain he had made his escape. He would be out of danger as soon as he put a little distance between himself and the guerrillas. Finally he took shelter behind a large drum-shaped rock. Taking his bearings, he climbed up through the abandoned pineapple field and to the right, where his companions were gathered, or so it seemed to him.

He had escaped, and he was still alive. He felt a pang of joy and sadness. Tears rolled down his face and he smiled. Summoning all his strength, he crawled to where his friends were waiting.

"Mingji? Mingji, is that you?" came the familiar voices of Renhe and Masuda.

"I've been shot. I'm bleeding a lot." Fear welled up inside him and he tried to remain focused. In the end he passed out.

It had taken the men more than a month to reach another sizeable town since leaving San Jose. Wrong turns, backtracking, and avoiding the guerrillas had taken a lot of time. They weren't sure what city it was that they had reached. They thought perhaps it was Panbac. But from a distance they could see that the Philippine and American flags flew over the city.

In addition to Mingji, the only remaining members of the original group were Masuda, Renhe, and Nozawa. However, along the way they had picked up another eight or nine men who had stuck with them. They followed a path that ran parallel to the highway, along which lay corpses and excrement.

In the last few days, they had also encountered a large number of well-printed propaganda leaflets containing wild assertions. One leaflet surprisingly told of how the Allies had attacked the Ryuku Islands on February 19 and had taken them on March 6. The campaign had resulted in thousands of Japanese casualties. The most frightening piece of news was that concerning the bombing of Japan itself. There was even a photo of B-29s bombing Tokyo on March 10. The caption to the photo said that 2,000 tons of incendiary bombs had been dropped on the city, destroying 40 percent of the buildings, with 130,000 dead or wounded. There were photos of the bombed-out shells of buildings.

Mingji's wound had healed—it was actually just a minor flesh wound. But the health of Masuda and Renhe had steadily worsened, till they could scarcely keep up. Worse yet, they were becoming mentally unbalanced; their condition had become quite obvious to Mingji by the time they reached Penablanca.

Renhe was a strong and optimistic man, and even after he began to suffer from hunger and diarrhea, he continued to talk and laugh. One day, though, he began to talk to himself and cry, and behave strangely. Masuda would now go for days without speaking a word, and he would occasionally stumble because he walked with his head up. His face was without expression, and no one knew what he was thinking. He tripped over rocks and roots several times, but he would merely pick himself up without ever looking at his cuts and scrapes and just drag on.

Mingji wondered why a person like Nozawa had escaped. Renhe was the only friend he had made since arriving in the war zone, and Masuda was the only decent Japanese he had ever met. He would have cried for them if he had had any tears left; now his heart was filled with poisonous flames.

Going northeast along the highway, they reached a large open plain—was it the land through which the Cagayan River flowed? They could see the road stretching off over the wide open plain. There was no cover for them there. Military vehicles, including jeeps and tanks bearing the American flag, sped back and forth along the highway.

In their discussions about what they should do, some suggested that they hide deep in the mountains and live off the land, while others were in favor of surrendering. Such suggestions were mere talk. Mingji and his group were like all the others that were fleeing north and looking for a route through the mountains beside the plain.

Although it was the middle of summer in Luzon, they found the heat bearable in the forest, but they were still troubled by the mosquitoes, poisonous snakes, and daily afternoon downpour. The rains slowed their pace, and many groups found themselves mired to a complete standstill. The size of Mingji's group also began dwindling. Two men were bitten when they tried to catch a poisonous snake. Others sat down never to get up again. And others died from eating poisonous plants.

One day when the sun was directly overhead, the rain suddenly began to pour. Mingji and his companions quickly took shelter under a rocky overhang. There was water nearby, so they decided to rest for the evening. The rain was unusually heavy. It began out over the plain and gradually moved toward them; all they saw was a white curtain that gradually blotted out the glorious sunshine. The curtain, which hung suspended between heaven and earth, pushed toward them.

A deep sound not unlike a sigh passed over them, and the ground seemed to tremble. A strong, hot wind rolled over the earth, making it difficult to breathe. The heavy rain continued to pour down. It was just like the spring rains in Fanzai Wood. The rain lashed the land but gradually subsided. Even after it had passed, it still seemed to echo in the ears.

The wind died with the rain. The rain-washed sky looked more like a clear prism, making the scene vaguely unreal, like something out of a dream. Mingji came back to himself. He made sure Renhe was comfortable, then went to pick edible herbs and gather dry grass to make a fire with the others. Their foraging generally consumed half a day and also contributed to their slow progress north. They were surrounded by danger from both man and nature. Being unfamiliar with the land, they had no knowledge about which plants were edible. Mingji, having grown up in the mountains of Taiwan, had become the group expert. Whatever he picked, so did the others. Perhaps that was why Nozawa had stuck with him.

Showa grass, red cabbage, and other bitter herbs he ate at home did not grow in Luzon. Only rarely did he encounter "sow's teat," which was a nourishing plant. Most often he was able to find the wuniu plant, which was common in Taiwan; it grew at the edge of the forest and on the dikes between fields at home. It was a hardy plant, deep green in color, that grew to about a foot in height. It had roundish, serrated leaves about twice as big as kulian tree leaves. It didn't contain much salt and was tough and hard to swallow, but it wasn't poisonous and actually made a good soup. It was now one of their principal foods.

When wuniu was unavailable, they risked eating other plants. Mingji had a few dos and don'ts when it came to selecting them: 1) the plant had to be an herb; 2) he would eat no plant with milky sap; 3) if the leaves or stalks were tinged yellow or red he would avoid it; 4) if it had a strange smell he wouldn't touch it; 5) if it tasted bitter, hot, or acrid, he would not pick it. The more salt it had, the better, and finally, plants that bugs and birds ate were usually tried.

The hunger was hard to bear; they couldn't sleep, and their guts growled and were rocked with spasms. They had to fill their bellies, or it was chaos.

Mingji smelled a faint scent. It came suddenly and was not the smell of food; it was a smell he could not describe. It was a smell at the center of his life, and one that came to him in times of great danger or despair. He touched the thin silver ring that he wore on the little finger of his left hand. He wanted to sleep, but that scent was present. He wondered how long it had been since he last slept. He decided he had to think of something else. He thought of Renhe and reached out to touch his friend sleeping by his side. But Renhe wasn't there. He got up.

Renhe wasn't there. Suddenly a dreadful notion entered Mingji's mind. The wind whistled through the treetops, and insects and the sound of men sleeping could be heard. Where could his friend have gone?

The lake near where they were camped reflected the moonlight, making it easy for Mingji to see in the night. He went in the direction of a cliff above the lake, calling Renhe's name. One of the others suddenly saw Renhe on top of the cliff.

Renhe's silhouette could be seen ahead, but a dark hollow loomed between where he stood and the group. He must have somehow crawled across. In the dark, the rocky cliff seemed to float in the lake, but they remembered that the cliff actually stood at the edge of the water.

"Renhe, come back! It's dangerous there!"

"What danger can there be when I'm at home with Axiang?" Renhe's voice sounded calm, and they sensed a note of happiness in it.

"That's not your home, Renhe."

"Says who? There's a light burning in my bedroom." Renhe reached forward.

"Renhe! Tell me how you got over there, and I'll join you."

"No. You can't come. This is my home. My wife and I are sleeping. Japs aren't allowed."

"We're not Japs! This is Liu Mingji! I'm from Taiwan. I'm your friend."

"Who are you trying to kid? Do you think you can trick me?"

Mingji felt his panic rising, but he also felt hurt.

"Quit trying to trick me. Go home and leave us Taiwanese alone."

"Renhe! We are all Taiwanese!" shouted one of the men.

At some point Masuda appeared next to Mingji. He looked wide awake and seemed to understand their Hakka dialect sprinkled with Japanese words. He suddenly began to cry.

Getting down on his hands and knees, Mingji ventured down into the hollow. He soon could make out objects two or three feet in front of him. He was driven along more by instinct than by strength. He suddenly felt the path was familiar, as if he had been on it a long time ago. It was a long, long time ago, before he entered technical school, before he entered primary school, even before he could walk. He was learning to walk again. He was trying to relax when suddenly a soft golden glow appeared before him.

That scent came again. He also heard a faint cry in the air. Who was crying? He himself? One of the other men? Was it his aged mother or Ahua? It seemed like it was all of them at once. It was the cry of all living things, a cry emitted by the mysterious heart of life.

"Renhe, come back!" he shouted as he moved forward.

"Stay where you are, Mother; I'm coming right now." Had Renhe entered a dream world of his childhood?

"Renhe," cried Mingji ever so softly.

"I'm leaving for home first," said Renhe as he turned to wave at Mingji.

Renhe suddenly leaned forward and with a cry, let himself fall. All they heard was a splash in the water, a splash that was soon swallowed by the lake.

By that time, a thin shaft of light was coming from the east. The light was already touching the trees on the mountaintops. But Mingji and the others were still shrouded in utter darkness.

Mingji and his companions continued to struggle northward through the mountains. When they reached Bontoc, the highest town in Luzon, located in the central mountains, they found the Philippine and American flags already flying there. On that brilliant summer's day, amid the bright green hills, the brightly colored flags were particularly eye-catching.

They had arrived late again. When had the town been taken? The groups of fleeing soldiers were now less frequently seen. Many of them had given up running and had taken shelter in caves and were living off the land. Those continuing north had found that although it was rough going in the foothills near the plain, they were free of guerrillas. They could still reach Aparri, and from there they could get home to Taiwan.

But it seemed that the Americans had occupied the whole of Luzon. It wasn't possible—there were still hundreds of thousands of Japanese troops in the Pacific, and it was just a matter of transporting them to Luzon. The Japanese also controlled key areas in the north of the island—or so they thought—and were preparing to withdraw for the last stand at home.

It was 1945, but no one could say which month and which day. They had an inkling when they saw the propaganda leaflets. Mussolini and Hitler were both dead. The Americans had landed on Okinawa, and after a bloody three-month battle, the Japanese forces of 90,000 troops had been annihilated.

The Allies were already dictating the terms of surrender to the Japanese authorities. If Japan were to refuse the conditions, the Allies would land on Taiwan and Japan. The Americans had ninety divisions and 8,600 aircraft. After reading the leaflets, the men knew the Japanese were going to lose the war, but what would that mean for Taiwan? What would happen to the island and its five million inhabitants?

Mingji, though feeble of body, burned with the desire to return home. The battle for Japan was a Japanese affair and had nothing to do with the people of Taiwan. Mingji's only goal now was to return home, the thought of which made him happy.

They decided to continue northward. One week out of Bontoc, the only good Japanese Mingji had ever met died. Mingji and his companions had been staying at a cave for several days. One day, Mingji managed to coax Masuda into eating some soup made of boiled herbs. His failing health seemed to improve. The day grew hotter. Masuda looked at Mingji and climbed out of the cave.

At the mouth of the cave, Masuda began to gasp. He sounded more like a wild boar panting and grubbing around in the ground. He had been making the same noise for days. Just then, Mingji caught sight of eight or nine wild men—half man and half beast—laughing and shouting as they passed by. Their hair and beards were tangled and matted. They were naked from the waist up, and they were wearing shorts and loincloths. All of them carried Japanese swords, and their eyes glowed with a ferocious gleam.

Masuda instinctively became defensive.

"Hey, you bastard, who are you?" said one of the men in native Japanese.

Masuda grimaced, showing his teeth like a puppy ready to fight.

"Masuda," said Mingji, patting his shoulder gently.

"Are you Japanese soldiers?" a man with no hair asked.

"Why are you hiding here?" another asked.

Neither Masuda nor Mingji replied. After all, the men were Japanese soldiers, so there was nothing to fear.

"What company are you with?"

"I'm not a Japanese soldier!" So Masuda could still speak.

"Then you must be American, you bastard!"

"I'm not a Japanese soldier!" Masuda continued to protest.

"Gentlemen, Masuda is not quite right in the head," said Mingji.

"He's right. Masuda is actually a second lieutenant," said Nozawa, coming forward.

"Well, Second Lieutenant, why do you deny that you are a Japanese soldier?" asked the man with no hair as he grabbed Masuda by his tattered collar.

"I'm not a Japanese soldier; I am a beast," said Masuda in complete confusion.

"Is that so?" said the man as he thrust the hilt of his sword into Masuda's belly.

"Not a Japanese," said another, striking him with his fist.

"Gentlemen!" said Mingji, rushing forward. "Please, he is delirious." Masuda collapsed in his arms.

"Gentlemen, please forgive him," said Nozawa, bowing deeply.

"You're not even Japanese, you bastard!" said the man, aiming a kick at Mingji but missing. "Oh, so you're a strong one. Let's have it out," said the bald guy, growing excited.

Mingji sat Masuda down and slowly stood up. He told himself there was no way out except to fight. The wild men all had swords; today was most likely his last day. If it was the end, then he would make them pay dearly.

While in technical college, Mingji had learned swordsmanship. When he was a young boy, Uncle Qiu Mei had taught him martial arts—the thirty-six movements of the Plum Blossom style. Although he wasn't a good student, he had picked up some rudimentary moves. Boys will be boys and fighting was common among the youngsters of Fanzai Wood, but no one except Chen, who also had studied martial arts, had dared challenge him. When he left for college, Uncle Qiu Mei warned him not to let on that he had studied martial arts so as to avoid any possible trouble. Today he hardly need worry about that. When he recalled the unfair fight at the One-Three-Six Works in Manila, he was determined to have plenty of company at his funeral.

"Show your sword," said the bald man as he drew out his sword with a move totally new to Mingji.

"I'm ready," said Mingji, putting his right foot forward and assuming the "the dragon appears and the tiger hides" position: his hand raised and his sword, still in its scabbard, raised before him in front of his attacker.

The bald man laughed, and his sword gleamed. His overconfidence stemmed no doubt from the fact that Mingji hadn't drawn his sword. The man obviously was not concentrating. He stamped his foot and charged, slashing with his blade.

Mingji countered with his sword still in its scabbard and met the blow. Their weapons clanged, and Mingji made a half turn to meet his opponent, parrying his blow; then he followed with a blow of his own.

The man yelled wildly and stumbled backward, shaken by the blow. He stepped back three paces, gave another loud cry, and rushed straight at Mingji with his sword lowered before him. Mingji had just recovered his balance when he saw the blade coming directly at him. He leaned away, but the blade slashed his right arm. The bald guy had fallen at Mingji's feet, and his sword had slipped out of his hands and lay several feet away. The bald guy pounced on Mingji, but Mingji kicked him with a kick known as "the bright point of the suspended leg," catching him in the groin. The bald guy doubled over and rolled on the ground, groaning in pain.

Mingji's sword had come out of its scabbard. He reached down to pick it up, but his right arm was numb. He switched hands and grabbed the blade with his left hand instead. He lifted his sword and put the tip of his blade on the man's back.

"Stop! The fight is over!" someone shouted. Suddenly a sword blow knocked Mingji's blade from his hand.

Mingji gritted his teeth as he stood there. His right arm felt as if it were on fire, and a dull pain spread over his right side. He could feel the blood dripping from his arm.

"Where are you from?" asked the short guy in a loincloth, who appeared to be the second in command.

"I'm from Xinzhu in Taiwan. My name is Liu Mingji."

"You've got real courage. You're a real fighter."

"A man does not take insults. That is how a Taiwanese responds. Are not the Japanese the same?"

"That's enough, okay?" said the short guy, looking at the bald guy.

"As you order," said Mingji halfheartedly. But it was enough. He was covered with sweat and really couldn't take any more. The Japanese all left, carrying their friend.

Masuda, exhausted, was sitting on the ground. Mingji and Masuda staggered back to the cave to sleep. Only then did two of their new companions emerge from where they had been hiding in the grass to help him into the cave and stanch the flow of blood from his arm.

Mingji fell into a deep sleep. When he woke it was dark. The two men brought him some boiled herbs. He was hungry and realized he hadn't eaten all day. He finished the soup to the last drop. His stomach, like his companions', was distended.

"Masuda. What about Masuda?" he suddenly asked.

"After we carried him back, we gave him some soup, and then he passed out."

"Masuda!" Mingji sat up and leaned on his right arm. A sudden pain shot through his arm and he remembered he had been wounded.

"I'm okay," said Masuda quite clearly.

"No problems? Good, keep it up."

"I'm more or less okay," he replied, laughing.

"Try a bit harder to go on living and make it home."

"Thanks. You do your best too." Masuda coughed dryly a couple of times. "Get some sleep and save your strength for tomorrow."

Mingji wanted to say more, but he felt so tired. His whole body was in pain. He had to sleep, but he had to will his mind to stop thinking and concentrate on sleeping. As on every other night, he remained in a half-waking state. His swollen belly ached and felt about to burst. He was so hungry and thirsty he could down gallons of herb soup. There was no ignoring his body, and his mind was especially restless. But he was suffused with a vague sense of pleasure, no doubt arising from his victory that day. But a sense of despair glittered in his pleasure like stars deep in the night sky.

He could just see a few stars in the sky amid the leaves above. What a beautiful night. He felt the need to go to the bathroom. No, his penis was erect. How strange. It had been ages since that had happened. He hadn't had any such feelings for a long time—not since they had begun their flight. His manhood had died and was there for nothing but pissing. He remembered someone told him about a man who was on the point of dying from thirst in the desert, when suddenly his penis stood up to ejaculate the last bit of his life. Mingji's penis was fully erect, stiff, proud, and angry. Did it mean that his end was near?

On this starry night, in the wilderness in a foreign country, his manhood had reasserted itself. He pitied himself and felt bewildered. He was a man, but what did that mean? Certainly he was fated to return to Taiwan. He gently stroked his penis. He held it tenderly in his hand, his heart full of awe. By the faint light of the stars, he could clearly see his erect member. He vaguely sensed he was seeing life itself; in a flash he had intuited the meaning of life. He seemed to hear himself summoned, drawn into space; he felt himself swell, filling all space. So lonely, so alone. But so real. He was moved to tears. They were the tears of life, rolling through time. He was just one person in the great chain of life. He had to continue on.

"Mingji, are you awake?" asked Masuda.

"Yes," he replied, drawn away from his reverie.

"Can't you sleep?"

"No. How do you feel?"

"I'm glad to have known someone like you from Taiwan," said Masuda, changing the subject. Normally he addressed Mingji using his surname, but by using his given name, he demonstrated greater intimacy.

"Same here," said Mingji earnestly. "You're a real Japanese."

"I'm grateful for what you say, but can you explain what you mean?"

"I mean that not all the Japanese people can be extremists; it isn't normal."

"Thank you for saying that. I thank you as a Japanese and on behalf of the Japanese people."

"I hope there are other Japanese like you." When Mingji finished speaking, he felt he had expressed himself poorly.

"Like me? But I'm dying," said Masuda wearily.

"You can't. You must go on living."

"Thank you." Masuda was quiet for a while as if pondering something. "I have always hated myself for being so weak and cowardly. But after I saw Tani Nobunari commit *hara-kiri*, I realized that it is often hard to distinguish between bravery and cowardice."

"You have always seemed brave to me. You possess true courage."

"You are a strange man, Mingji. You are stubborn and never say die."

"You think I'm crazy?"

"It's strange. You come from an island too, but you have something most Japanese lack. There is something in your eyes, especially when there is danger, that fills me with awe."

"You talk as if it were something special. I just don't want to die. I think of my home, and all I want is to return there."

"It's so simple; it's the instinct to survive, like in migrating birds."

"Like the salmon. Since the beginning of time, it has always returned to its birthplace, even at the cost of its own life."

"The salmon, a noble fish," said Masuda. "I still long for my days in the south."

Mingji had no idea why he had changed the subject.

"I have been happy in this life, because I have known you."

"What's tomorrow's date?"

"Who knows—June or July."

Masuda asked himself if the sun would rise the following day. He mumbled and hummed to himself.

Mingji felt confused and wanted to say something, but was soon overcome with sleep.

He didn't know how long he had slept, but the sun had already risen when he woke. He was being prodded awake by the two new men and that dog Nozawa.

"Masuda is dead."

Mingji turned to his right, where Masuda lay. There was a calm smile on his face. He was gone forever, and they had never been closer. There seemed to be tears at the corners of his eyes.

Mingji reached out and laid his hand on Masuda's heart. He wasn't trying to determine if his heart was still beating, but trying to pass his thoughts and feelings to Masuda. He realized that Masuda was not like the migrating birds or the salmon; he didn't make it home, though he should have. He would be buried in a foreign country. He wondered if Masuda's spirit was still present. He wished to communicate his thoughts. All he could do was offer his tears as a funeral libation. He didn't know where Masuda came from in Japan and there was nothing he could do for him, but he prayed that he would find peace. The war would be over soon. As part of the earth, he would be among the trees and flowers and would then know that the world could be a peaceful and beautiful place. Mingji fell across Masuda's chest and wept.

"Mingji, don't!" His companions pulled him away.

They spent half the day opening up the cave. Inside, they buried Masuda's emaciated body. They gathered stones and heaped a cairn over him. Even Nozawa, who never helped anyone, joined in to raise the cairn.

With his left hand, Mingji lopped off two large branches, which he broke into lengths and placed around the cairn. The others brought a large square stone and placed it atop the cairn to serve as a grave marker. After they had finished, Mingji immediately set off, against the pleading of his friends. He didn't think he could spend another night there near his friend's grave. The other three had no choice but to take to the road with him.

They continued along the forest edge. Occasionally they saw enemy aircraft overhead, but they never encountered a single guerrilla. They could detect what they thought were refugees moving over the plain, but no soldiers. It was as if they had never been there.

In the mountains; they encountered some natives. They were small, dark aborigines, untouched by civilization, entirely different from the Filipinos of the plains. They were unafraid, as if they had never been attacked by the Japanese and never had to flee. Nevertheless, they remained alert and would not approach Mingji and his companions. When they stepped nearer, the natives drew their curved knives.

The groups of refugees gradually dwindled. Sometimes they would not meet with a single soul for days. The few stragglers and solitary soldiers would join a group, and the groups would grow. Two weeks later, when they came upon a group of twenty-five men, only Mingji and Nozawa were left alive. Of the other two, one had died of exhaustion, and the other had fallen from a cliff.

$\mathcal{T}$he Eternal Lamp

It was near the end of July, and the sun, which had just risen above the plains, was huge and white. The whiteness grew more glaring as the sun rose, and by mid-day the entire sky was a bright white. The intense light overwhelmed the dark forest and the plains. Then at one point the forest seemed to sigh and the ground seemed to tremble. A hard-driving rain poured from the sky. Hours later, the punishing sun was riding through the sky, bright and shimmering.

It seemed that the dead bodies lying in the grass outnumbered those who walked haltingly in a group. Fresh corpses outnumbered the skeletons and those that were in various stages of decomposition.

The small groups had merged into a large company of men. If one member failed to stand up when the group rose from resting, friend or no friend, his companions would harden their hearts and abandon him. But if he had firewood or food, he would not be left behind.

Liu Mingji had managed to free himself of Nozawa. At first Nozawa begged Mingji to speak with him, but he ignored him. Finally Nozawa ended up talking to himself, as did Mingji. Mingji's hatred for Nozawa never really disappeared, but it was later replaced—perhaps as a result of habit more than anything else—by an inexplicable feeling of concern for him. One day Mingji dozed off during the heat of the day, and when he awoke, Nozawa was gone. He became quite anxious and almost panic-stricken.

Nozawa reappeared shortly. Mingji was angered by his feelings for a long time, but that would change. As usual, they foraged for edible herbs. That night Nozawa was groaning, but everyone was accustomed to such groaning and paid it no mind. Nozawa seemed to have found a lot to eat and devoured it by himself, and now his stomach was so swollen he could scarcely bear it.

Nozawa was unable to get up the next morning.

Mingji scrutinized him. He was satisfied to see that Nozawa had fallen before he did, that he would probably outlive him. Nozawa's face was red and swollen. He was unconscious. Mingji turned and walked away.

"Don't go!" said Nozawa, opening his eyes. He reached out and seized Mingji by the leg.

Mingji tried to shake him off violently with a kick.

"Animal!" Mingji picked up a stick and struck Nozawa's arm. The blow was sufficiently heavy to leave Nozawa lying there panting with exhaustion.

"Don't leave me, Mingji," said Nozawa.

Mingji started to walk away.

"Mingji, save me," said Nozawa, struggling after him. Nozawa was actually speaking to Mingji in their native dialect. "Mingji, just look at me, and I'll be saved!"

Mingji heaved a sigh and turned to look at Nozawa. He seemed to do so against his will or better judgment. Nozawa Saburo—Huang Huosheng, as he was known in Chinese—was standing about twenty yards away. He looked terrible: his hair was standing on end, his face was red and swollen, and his nose and mouth were smeared with dried blood. His shirt was torn and he was losing his pants. His legs were bent slightly at the knees and he leaned forward, hands stretched out in a beseeching gesture.

"Mingji!" He fell to his knees, back bent, his hands still outstretched.

Mingji closed his eyes and turned away.

"Mingji! I'm dying. I'm afraid. Stay with me until I'm gone. Take my nails and hair home."

Mingji glared at him as if he were a monster.

"Won't you do that for me, brother?" Nozawa had actually addressed him as "brother."

"We are not close enough for you to call me brother," replied Mingji in Japanese.

"Call me Huang, Huang Huosheng."

"No, you are no longer Huang Huosheng; you are a Japanese soldier."

Nozawa seemed to faint from his exertions. When he recovered somewhat, he saw Mingji standing nearby. Perhaps his efforts had increased his blood flow, and his body was able to rid itself of some of the poison. Perhaps his fear of death overcame the poison. Nozawa did not die.

Nozawa regained consciousness a couple of days later, and he saw Mingji cooking something.

"Thank you, brother Mingji."

"Don't call me brother, I don't want to hear it!" Mingji warned him. "We will never be on those terms."

"What did you say?" Nozawa looked at him in astonishment.

"I said we'll never be on those terms," said Mingji, shaking his fist.

"What? I can't hear you. All I can see is your lips moving."

"You've lost your hearing?" asked Mingji, bounding over to him.

"What? My ears are buzzing."

"Hell, the fever must had damaged your ears," shouted Mingji.

"My ears, damaged?" said Nozawa, looking bewildered.

When Mingji shouted into his ears, Nozawa could barely hear what he said. Within a few days, he was stone deaf.

Mingji felt guilty, and somewhat responsible. Now that he was deaf, Nozawa was grateful for but anxious about having Mingji's help. He was more self-abasing and less assertive. He seemed to fawn over Mingji, making him feel very much ill at ease. Mingji's feelings were very confused. He decided he would look out for Nozawa—not something he wanted to do, but something he couldn't refuse.

They walked slowly, hoping to be overtaken by a group of men, but for days on end they saw not a single living soul.

Mingji marveled at the strangeness of the human heart and the capriciousness of fate. He wondered what road his own life and fate would take in the future, if he had one. There was a time when ideas such as a man's "heart," "life," and "fate" were all abstractions spoken of by his teachers or found only in books. Now they had become a palpable reality for him.

There was no point in being surprised, angry, or annoyed with one's fate. A person had to submit. Mingji realized that he had been wrong to think that fate was something one could choose to accept or like or dislike. A person was identical with his or her fate. Recognizing this, Mingji saw that he had to follow the narrow, steep path of his fate, neither hurrying nor lingering.

Mingji was hungry, but his speculations took his mind off his empty belly. A new strength was born from his weakness. Suddenly the barriers and dangers before him seemed less intimidating and easily surmountable. His resolve to go on living was strengthened as well. Every step he took meant that he was one step nearer to Taiwan, his homeland. Thousands of miles might lie between him and home, but it was just a distance made up of so many steps.

"Look over there," said Nozawa, patting Mingji on the shoulder. Mingji at first doubted his own eyes; he rubbed them and took a few steps to get a better look. About thirty yards away were what appeared to be apes like those in a zoo. They were short and hairy but wore loin-cloths. They were in fact men. Mingji looked around. Save for bleached bones and a few rotting corpses, they were alone on the plain with these strange men. Mingji suspected that they were cannibals—he had heard that they existed. His hair stood on end.

The men, who were very scrawny, were coming toward them, swords and knives in hand. They approached cautiously, in measured steps.

"Where are you going?" they asked in halting Japanese.

"We're trying to get away," replied Mingji. "And you?"

"Are you Japanese?" they asked, smiling.

"Taiwanese. We are from Taiwan."

"So are we."

The emaciated men seemed elated, and gathered around them.

"Where are you coming from? What part of Taiwan are you from?" they asked in Taiwanese.

"We're coming from Manila. We're trying to get away," said Mingji, struggling to speak Taiwanese. "We are Hakka from Xinzhu," he said in Japanese.

"You're Hakka?" ventured the smallest member of the group. "So am I. I'm from Nantou."

Mingji had so many things he wanted to ask them, but he didn't know where to start. They told him many things he didn't know. They informed him that northern Luzon had long been occupied by the Americans, and according to the propaganda leaflets and broadcasts, the entire island had been liberated on July 4. The Allies had also issued the Potsdam Declaration laying down unconditional terms for Japan's surrender.

"Has Japan surrendered?" asked Mingji.

"Probably not."

"What is today's date?"

"Who knows? Probably early August."

"Why are you heading south?"

The plains on the west side of the Cagayan River were full of fleeing Japanese. Mingji decided to join the wild men and head south. They objected, saying that the larger the group, the easier the target they became for the Americans. They thought it better to move in twos and threes and rely on their luck to evade capture.

"Then you don't think you will be captured if you go south?" asked Mingji.

"If we don't go south, we'll all be killed by the Americans, who'll be here in another day."

"Are they killing everyone on sight?"

"We don't know, but why take chances? We haven't run into anyone who has escaped the Americans."

Death seemed a foregone conclusion; it was just a matter of sooner or later. They divided into several small groups and started south along the highway. They had no clear destination in mind.

They had no matches left for starting cook fires, and they had been low on salt for a long time. Their health was declining: their vision was blurred and their legs were swollen, as were their faces. If they were overtaken by the enemy, there would be no escape.

The Americans were actually already ahead of them, and the men were playing a game of cat-and-mouse with them. Sometimes they got ahead, other times they fell behind. They hid in high grass and fallen leaves to avoid capture. They often heard gunshots and the screams of the man who had been shot.

After a few days, they decided against going south and headed southwest across the plains to the mountains. Mingji and Nozawa had spent a long time in the mountains and warned the others not to go there. But their advice was not heeded.

"We would rather die in the mountains or be eaten by wild animals than surrender to the enemy."

Mingji had no strength to argue.

"It would be too humiliating for us as members of the Japanese army to surrender."

Mingji was silent and closed his eyes. He could hardly bear the sight of these men who scarcely looked human. They were all young men in their twenties, but having lost so much weight, they looked more like fifteen-year-old boys. What a pitiful state of affairs—even at that point, they clung to the idea of being soldiers in the Japanese army. How far the poison had gone! They were to be pitied, these children of Taiwan.

Suddenly they heard the sound of an approaching engine.

"Scatter! Hide!"

The car came to a halt, and several men stepped out and walked in their direction. Mingji lifted his head to have a look. They were enemy soldiers, tall and vigorous, and fully armed. It was the first time he had ever seen the enemy. He began to tremble.

"Listen! All Japanese soldiers surrender! Your lives will be spared. You are surrounded. Surrender is the only way to save yourselves. Otherwise, you will be killed."

Surrender was being forced upon them: under the enemy guns they would be pursued till exhaustion and death. That was the enemy's plan. There would be no need to shoot them; they would be run to the ground and die of exhaustion. But all Mingji could think of was flight. If there was just one minute to flee, that would still be one minute of life. He had to seize his opportunity and escape. Only by escaping could he hope to stay alive.

The five of them took off in different directions, sometimes crossing paths but always acting on their own, except for Nozawa, who stuck close to Mingji. Eventually, they could no longer hear the car and the broadcast demanding that they surrender. The shadow of the enemy had vanished.

On August 7, 1945, the newspapers in Taiwan printed a brief notice that the Americans had dropped a new kind of bomb on Hiroshima the day before, and that there were apparently seven hundred thousand casualties. On August 8, no newspapers were printed. The people of Taiwan knew that earth-shaking events were taking place. Everywhere, people talked quietly. Opinions were rife, and everybody wondered what was happening.

Dengmei fainted one day and ended up in bed for two weeks. She didn't look sick but was probably weak due to lack of food. But suddenly she seemed to recover and actually looked quite healthy.

The ration system for rice and pork was now operating in name only. People often waited in line for half the day only to be told there were delays in the delivery of supplies. Strangely, though, the black market was flourishing.

On August 16, Mingqing got up before it was light and set off for Great Lake Village. He planned to buy some pork on the black market to make a gruel of pork stock and asparagus for his mother. She had steadfastly refused to eat meat after she recovered without resorting to taking medicine. He had to do something, because her weakness was obviously due to poor nutrition.

For some reason, the roads were unusually crowded. Hardly had he set out than he ran into a large group of people from Little and Big Southside in front of the temple. By the time he reached Garrison Camp and Long Hole, there were even more people. Everyone was talking in hushed tones.

"Where are you going?"

"We're going to Great Lake. What about you?"

"I'm going to town too. By why so many people today?"

"I'm going to buy some pork on the black market."

"Me too!"

Mingqing was dumbfounded. Something must be wrong. Did they all share some secret that only he was ignorant of? He decided to ask someone he knew.

"Brother Akui, what's going on today?"

"Haven't you heard in Fanzai Wood? The news has been all over Little Southside."

"Heard what?"

"That the Japanese are finished," he said in a low voice.

"Finished?" Mingqing's heart leaped at the news.

"They surrendered, unconditionally," said Akui, looking around nervously.

"Really? Is it true?" asked Mingqing, seizing Akui by the hand.

"Keep it down! I've just heard rumors."

The Taiwanese were to be pitied. Even at such a moment, they still had to be nervous and not speak loudly.

"Your family has always been against the Japanese. Especially Ahan, your father. It's a pity the old guy isn't here," said Akui, full of respect and regret.

"Then it is true?"

"It has to be. We'll find out when we get to Great Lake."

Mingqing stepped up his pace until he was nearly running. He was thinking of his father and wiping his tears away. They were the tears of an old man. He felt exhilarated and let his tears flow without a thought as to what others might think.

Great Lake lay before him. There was the public school—the rising sun flag had not been raised. Farther on was the middle school for the Japanese—no flag there either. The rumors must be true. The Shinto shrine, which was usually busy by now, was empty. The houses of the Japanese were shut tight, with not a soul to be seen—and the Japanese were the ones who always had their houses open for the fresh air.

Mingqing was certain that the rumors were true. Arriving on the main street through town, he saw that people were thronging around the Taiwanese shops, which were open. They weren't buying anything, just standing around and talking. They seemed worried about something and spoke in hushed tones.

There was no one in front of the Rural Affairs Office; it was shut tight. There were no flags on the flagpoles along the street either. The rumors had to be true.

"Excuse me, then it's true?" asked Mingqing of a stranger standing nearby.

"It's true," said the man rather warily. "Someone said they heard a broadcast, but there has been no official word here."

"Who will make it official?"

"They'll have to make it official, but until then, we'll have to keep our happiness to ourselves."

Mingqing's heart leaped, but he also felt bitter. He decided that once he had delivered the news to Fanzai Wood, he would go to Miaoli and then to Taipei. No, he would go to Taichung and get in touch with his friends there. He had to confirm the facts. He suddenly thought of fireworks. The shops didn't stock them, but he had to get some to celebrate with. In the end he managed to get hold of the raw materials for making firecrackers.

The sun was rising higher, but the streets were still quiet. Mingqing, with a parcel under his arm, entered the square in front of the Rural Affairs Office. It was the place from which his youngest brother Mingji and his own son Jiansheng had been joyfully seen off. He smiled to himself as he thought of his brother and son, but he smiled through his tears. What a state of affairs. They didn't dare laugh or express their joy. He wanted to hug someone, to shout, to laugh aloud, even weep. But he couldn't, so he set off for Fanzai Wood.

At that moment he saw someone walking toward him down the middle of the street. He seemed to be walking as if in some sort of ritual procession. He was a middle-aged gentleman, fair-skinned and somewhat portly, dressed in a traditional Chinese gown of bright blue silk with a black satin waistcoat. On his head he wore a small black skullcap topped by a red ball. He was wearing the kind of boots one saw opera actors wear. He was waving a fan, and his left hand was placed on his hip. He appeared calm and his steps were unhurried.

Many people in the shops stopped talking or whatever they were doing and seemed to respectfully stand at attention. Some of the women began to whisper.

"Isn't that Umemoto Kazuo?"

"That's Xie Tiansong's son Xie Tianxing."

"What do you mean Xie? His name is Umemoto!"

"That is Umemoto, the head of the Great Lake Committee for Japanization."

"What is he up to?"

"What a strange get-up."

"Is that some sort of ancient Japanese ritual dress?"

"Don't know. Never seen it before."

"No, it's Chinese. My grandfather has clothes like that, which we keep hidden in the bottom of a trunk."

"You're just bragging. How could your family have clothes like that?"

"It looks like the costumes in the opera."

Mingqing felt sick to his stomach. He wanted to vomit. He wondered if he had the *sha* syndrome. He looked away from Umemoto, stepped into the shade in front of a shop, then shortly left for Fanzai Wood.

When he arrived at the temple in Fanzai Wood, he saw Mingcheng and his wife and Dexin and Dechang, as well as Azhen, Ashu, and his own wife, waiting there. They must have heard the rumors.

"The Japanese dogs have surrendered," announced Mingqing.

"Can the men sent overseas come home now?"

"Of course they can."

Azhen breathed a heavy sigh of relief. She turned and left. Ashu followed her in silence.

"Is it true?" asked Dengmei, who somehow had managed to walk up the slope to the temple.

Mingqing rushed to give her a hand.

"Don't worry about me. Are you sure it's true?" she asked, pushing him away.

"It's true!"

"I knew this day would come. Did you find out what was going to happen to Taiwan?"

"What do you mean?"

"You've been in the resistance. I'm asking you if the Japanese are going to leave. Are they giving Taiwan back to us?"

Mingqing laughed until he was red in the face. He handed the materials for the firecrackers to Mingcheng and then picked up all the money there was in the house—about thirty dollars—and set off for Miaoli and Taichung. He didn't return for three days, and when he got back he found out that Fanzai Wood had been filled with the sound of firecrackers until there were none left. No one knew where so many firecrackers had come from.

Mingqing returned with news that Taiwan was being retroceded to China. The Chens and Tangs of Miaoli had returned. He also said that his companions in the resistance wanted him to join them to help keep civil order, because the Chinese officials might be delayed for a time. They wanted to take matters in hand to assure that things were secure.

"I don't think I should get involved," said Mingqing to his mother. "I'm just an old farmer. What can I do?"

"I disagree. You had better do it. If others want you to join, you should," his mother replied with a smile.

"But Mother, you're not well."

"That's true, but I have been waiting for this day for so long."

"You ought to relax. Things will improve in Taiwan now."

"It's a pity I can't wait for my son and grandson."

"What are you talking about?"

Dengmei took no notice of her son's surprise. She waited until her whole family was present before she softly announced, "Yesterday I had a vision of Kuanyin Bodhisattva, and she beckoned me."

The whole family was struck dumb.

"It has been appointed that the day after tomorrow I will go, and Kuanyin will receive me."

"Mother, you are tired," said Mingcheng, trying to lead her home to bed.

"Let me finish," she said, shooting a look at Mingcheng. "You should not grieve; let me depart happily and at peace."

Mingqing wanted to stop her from saying any more.

"It is good," said Dengmei, as if talking to herself. "It's doesn't matter if Mingji and Jiansheng haven't returned to see me off. It will be fine if they simply return alive. Life doesn't always go the way one wants. But everything will be all right."

Mingqing's wife brought her a cup of hot water. She took a sip. When they tried to help her, she pushed them aside.

"Did Dexin take care of the coffin boards?"

"Yes," replied Mingcheng, stamping his feet.

"Don't set up an altar or hold any fancy ceremonies. Just have Huoxian hold three sutra readings. It should be simple since the Bodhisattva is meeting me. I leave all this in Mingcheng's hands."

"I won't do it," said Mingcheng, his temper flaring. "I mean, I don't know what to do."

"Mingcheng, when will you ever grow up?"

"You said tomorrow. Why don't you go rest?" said Mingqing.

"My remains should be buried with your father's behind the temple. Mingqing will handle it." She paused for a while. "Ask my daughters and their husbands to come day after tomorrow to see me off."

"All right. Will you rest now?"

"Okay. Everything must be as normal. You have never gone against my wishes, and these are my last. Do not anger or upset me."

Dengmei pushed away their hands as they tried to help her, and with steady steps she set off to lie down, leaving the entire family stunned.

"Did Mother say that she is leaving us?" asked Mingsen.

"Yes."

"Where is she going?"

"She is going to meet Kuanyin Bodhisattva."

"Then, that means . . ." Mingsen seemed to have recovered suddenly.

"Mingsen, you go rest too."

"You should rest too," said Mingsen firmly. "We have to do what Mother wants."

As Dengmei lay awake, she heard what her children were saying. She could not help smiling to herself. She knew she looked pretty when she smiled, and could almost visualize her own happy expression.

Man's life, like the mountains and rivers, must one day end, thought Dengmei. The scene the previous night had been real and not a dream. Meeting Kuanyin would be easy, and wonderful. Everything had been arranged. She had waited for Mingqing to return before telling everybody, and he had returned in time.

The Japanese no longer ruled Taiwan; the island was once again theirs. From then on they would be their own masters. Ahan would be pleased to know that his wishes had been granted. She sensed him standing there in front of her with Qiu Mei and their other comrades. She thought to herself that she had to leave, and wondered if Ahan knew.

Ever since her encounter with Kuanyin, she felt that everything superfluous had been stripped away. Life, old age, illness, and death were all illusory. To part with loved ones was no parting at all, and sorrow was no sorrow at all. If you strove for nothing, you lost nothing. Form, feeling, thought, formation, and consciousness were all empty.

When Dengmei awoke, she heard the cicadas chirring in the xiangsi trees behind the house. Mingqing and Mingcheng had been standing at her door for who knows how long. Dengmei was feeling lighthearted. When she finished washing, Mingqing brought her a bowl of water.

"I will eat nothing today," said Dengmei.

"That won't do, Mother."

"Don't you understand, Mingqing?"

She did not let him reply. She sent her sons off to make the arrangements. Then she asked her grandsons to take her for a walk.

"Mingcheng and I will come," offered Mingqing.

"That won't be necessary. I'll be all right."

Mingqing and Mingcheng were silent. They knew their mother's temper, and she always meant what she said. They had to do as she wished.

Dengmei took no more notice of them. Accompanied by her grandsons, she walked across the slope in front of the house, crossed the bridge, and went up the slope to the cliff. They sat down on a stone bench that had been placed there for people to rest. Her eyes and ears were sharp. She could clearly see the bamboo, the house, and even the firewood piled outside.

"Grandma, what are you looking at?" asked Jiancai.

"At our brick house," she said, hugging him.

"Grandma, how long have we had this house?"

"Almost fifty years."

"Grandma, how old are you?"

"Don't you even know how old your grandma is?"

"Seventy-two! Grandma's birthday is coming soon."

"You do know."

"Everybody knows except Jiancai."

"Actually, Grandma is just eighteen."

"What are you talking about?" they asked in astonishment.

"Seventy-two and eighteen are the same. Didn't you know that? Grandma is eighteen every year." Dengmei couldn't help laughing at her paradoxes.

"I don't understand."

"You know that Grandma often sits here. Later she will always be here," she said, stroking Jiancai's face.

"Grandma, are you going far away?"

"It's not really far away. Just remember that I'll always be here."

She stood up and started climbing the steps up the slope. Jianting, always a sensible child, tried to persuade her not to make the climb. She said that she could beat him. He reminded her that she had had nothing to eat that morning. She replied that from then on she would have no need to eat. She went on up the slope. The children had no choice but to follow her.

"Grandma, where are you really going?"

"I am going to have a look at our fir farm," she said. Leading her grandsons, she eventually reached the top of the slope where the fir trees grew in profusion. The Lius had planted the slope with trees and the twenty-year lease on the land had expired the year before, but because of the war, they had not yet felled the trees. The trees were all at least a foot in diameter, and each would yield more than ten yards in boards. The Lius had worked hard planting the trees, and now that the war was over, building materials would be badly needed. The Lius would get 30 percent of the wood, the rest going to the landlord. There were at least 10,000 trees, 3,000 of which would go to the Lius.

"Poor children," said Dengmei without thinking.

"What did you say, Grandma?"

"Nothing," she said, pointing at the trees. "I'm saying that it was hard work planting the trees in this forest."

"Yes, it was hard work."

"And what about Grandma?"

"And Grandpa!"

"Yes, and Grandpa."

"I've never seen Grandpa."

"Grandpa looked like your fathers and uncles together."

"I don't understand."

"I mean your father looks like your grandpa, but not exactly. Each one looks a little like him, and if you put them all together, that would be him." She didn't understand what she was saying herself.

As they talked, Mingqing and his wife arrived in haste. He insisted that his aged mother come down the mountain. She couldn't argue with them and finally agreed. At noon she didn't eat but did have some water with a little salt in it. In the afternoon she once again insisted on going out. Accompanied by her daughters-in-law, she set off for lower Fanzai Wood, where the Pengs, Huangs, Xus, and Chans all lived. She said good-bye to each family in turn. It was tiring for her, but fortunately the houses were close together. By the time the sun had set, her visits were done.

"I don't have enough strength to make it back up the slope," she said.

When she finally reached home, everyone came to see her. By the time it was dark, her daughter Qinmei from Long Hole had arrived.

"Qinmei, you haven't been telling everyone, have you?" said Mingqing reproachfully to his sister.

"No."

"Then why is everyone here?"

"I just said that Mother wanted to see everyone," said Qinmei, sobbing.

"Stop crying. What if Mother saw you?"

That evening Fanzai Wood was ablaze with torches. People had converged at the Lius' house. The brothers found the situation difficult and had to stand on the path to turn away the well-wishers.

"There's no need to visit. If you do, you'll only be giving credence to this," said Mingqing.

No one knew what to say.

Mingqing was reasonable and they didn't want to argue with him, but they didn't want to leave without seeing Dengmei. They put out their torches to discuss what they should do.

"Will it be all right if we come tomorrow?"

"No, it won't," said Mingqing.

"Then when can we see the old lady?"

"Do you really think that by tomorrow my mother will have passed away?"

"Don't you believe her?"

"No, I don't," said Mingqing angrily.

"Okay, we'll go home and pray for the old lady tonight," said someone.

After nightfall, Dengmei drank some water and lay down to rest. Her children didn't want her to find out about all the people who had come to see her. But she seemed to know that the neighbors had all gathered outside. She instructed her daughters-in-law that they should tell them all to go home.

"All this coming and going. I haven't gone anywhere. I saw everyone this afternoon, so what are they doing here? We'll see each other again, so why struggle for a few minutes now?" Her words were passed on to those outside. They half understood and they ceased to worry. The old lady had said that they would meet again.

Everyone went away satisfied. Azhen and Angmei managed to slip into the house.

"Azhen, go home," said Mingcheng's wife, pushing her toward the door. "Don't disturb the old lady."

"Wait," said Dengmei from her room, "let them come in. I have something to say."

"Okay, but you should lie down," she said, letting the women in.

Azhen stood solemnly before Dengmei.

"Azhen, take care. You must look after Amei properly."

"I will."

"A hundred years is an instant, Azhen. Live your days one at a time."

"I know."

"Your life is hard, Azhen, but I know you can do it." She was silent for a while before continuing. "Learn from Angmei. The rivers are rivers and the mountains, mountains. Don't be consumed by idle thoughts the way you were with the sand in the box."

Azhen was silent, her tears streaming down her face. She had told only Dengmei about the sand in the box. Just the two of them knew what the old lady was talking about.

"I'll be back tomorrow," said Azhen, crying.

"There is no need to come, Azhen."

"It doesn't matter. I'm going now."

"Don't cry anymore. Even the crying on Hawk's Beak has ceased. You had better go. Take care on the road at night."

"That's right! I haven't heard the crying in days," said Jianting, who had been hiding in a corner of the room.

By the time Azhen had made her way out the door and down the slope, Dengmei was already asleep.

Dengmei rose early. After her sutra recitation in the morning, she walked out into the courtyard. As she looked over the mountains, she did her exercises.

Mingqing and Mingcheng remained out of sight. She still did not eat anything and would drink only water. She thought she saw Mingqing wiping tears away. She spoke to him.

"Have you prepared everything?"

"All done."

"You are the master of the house, now."

"Mother. . . ."

"It has been hard for you the last few years."

"Not really."

"You will have to keep an eye on Mingcheng."

"Yes, Mother," said Mingqing, smiling in spite of himself.

"You will have to be a big brother to Mingsen."

"I will."

"There is also Mingji, when he comes home."

"I was thinking that when we get our share of the timber, we'll have to find a wife for Mingji."

"You're a good brother." She smiled.

"I think we should buy those orchards on the slope. If we don't have enough money, we'll have to find a way."

"It would be a good idea to get some paddy land as well. Wasn't Ye talking about selling his paddy land by the temple?"

"Yes, he did say something. Okay, we'll put half our profits in paddy land and the other half in orchards."

"Mingqing, you and your brothers have to get on in the world. If it means splitting up, don't do so until after Mingji is set."

"Set your mind at ease—we won't split up."

"How old are you now?" she suddenly asked.

"Fifty. How could you forget? Mingcheng is forty-six, Mingsen is thirty-eight, and Mingji is twenty-seven."

"I asked just to remind you!"

"For what?"

"Next year you will have passed fifty, and you will have to have a big celebration. After you sell the timber, you can really celebrate properly."

"Let's do it," said Mingqing childishly. "Shall we have a joint birthday party? Perhaps Mingji's wedding can be arranged for the same time."

"Good! That would be perfect." She laughed happily. She looked at her son for a while. Then she asked her daughters-in-law to prepare her bath.

The sunlight shone on the cliff opposite the house. After finishing her bath, Dengmei put on the blue robe that she wore on the first and fifteenth of every month—it was the robe that the holy woman Alian had made for her. After Mingqing had returned from Taichung, the ancestral tablets that had been stored in a corner of the house for years were taken out and placed on the altar. On one tablet Huoxian had inscribed LIU AHAN OF THE TWENTY-FOURTH GENERATION. It was sad to think that offerings had not been made to Ahan for so many years.

Dengmei sat in a rattan chair facing the altar. She had always wanted an altar painting of the Buddhas or Kuanyin but had never acquired one. She began to recite the *Amithabha Sutra* and a chapter from the *Lotus Sutra*.

Mingqing and the rest of the family were asked to leave the main hall, but they remained by the door. Dengmei's recitation was as clear and as soothing as ever, like the lapping of water in a mountain stream or the sound of the wind in the trees. The old lady was at peace and calm; there was even something about her reminiscent of a religious painting. She didn't appear hungry, even though she had had nothing to eat in almost two days.

It was past nine o'clock in the morning when she finished chanting the sutras. She placed them in a cloth-covered box.

Her grandson Jianting offered her a washcloth, at the instigation of his father.

"Grandma, would you like to wipe your face?"

"That would be nice, but it doesn't matter. Grandma is always clean."

"Mother, you must have something to eat and lie down," said her sons, bursting in.

"No, the time has come." She stood up. "Jianting, take a chair out to the courtyard. Hurry now."

Jianting picked up a chair but didn't seem to know what to do next. Mingqing fell to his knees before his mother. Mingcheng did the same and was followed by Mingsen, who seemed to have recovered completely. Jianting was quick to understand, and he also knelt before his grandmother. Soon the entire family was kneeling.

"Fools, what is this all about?" said Dengmei wearily.

"Please stop, Mother," said Mingqing, trying very hard to sound natural.

"I'm going in any case," she said as she turned to Jianting. "Now take that chair outside."

Tears were streaming down Jianting's face, but he dared not cry. Nor could he disobey his grandmother. He picked up the chair, his face full of fear.

"What's the matter, Jianting?" asked Dengmei. She held her prayer beads in her left hand and stroked his cheeks gently. "It's nothing. You go inside now."

Dengmei adjusted her chair so that she was facing the main hall, and then she sat down. Her eyes were half closed as she chanted her beads. The sun was nearly directly overhead. The air was humid and seemed to brighten. Dengmei's silver hair flashed with light.

Mingqing and Mingcheng got up from where they knelt and rushed over to their mother. With one on either side of her, they tried to make her rise and go back inside the house.

"Fools! You want to carry me inside just as the gods are arriving?"

Mingqing and his brother, without offering a word, forced their mother back inside the house.

"Oh dear, why?"

"Mother."

"It's all the same, anyway."

"Mother, you must not do this."

"You must pray for Mingji."

"Mother, don't go."

The old lady's voice grew faint as she began to detect a fragrant aroma in the air. What was that subtle fragrance? She stopped counting her beads and her lips ceased to move. Her hands opened once, then closed. Her head rolled forward, then she pulled it back, and then it rolled to the right. The sweet scent was growing stronger. The whole Liu family was aware of it. Then it vanished.

Mingji staggered along the northern plains of Luzon, followed by Nozawa. There had been a violent storm and now the dark clouds were moving swiftly, low in the sky. Like a swarm of angry hornets, the clouds rolled on. Gusts of wet wind blew over the plain. It looked like afternoon, but it also looked like rain threatening in the morning.

Mingji's and Nozawa's limbs were swollen and difficult to move. Day and night they had walked, never stopping for the rain or the fierce sun. Even when the lightning flashed, they just kept on walking. It had been a long time since they had felt any pain; now it was just numbness. Mingji struggled on and suddenly opened his half-closed eyelids. A sweet scent. He smelled a delicate and subtly sweet aroma.

He had smelled that scent before. He slowly lowered himself to the ground. On his hands and knees, he breathed that sweet aroma deeply into his lungs. But as he breathed, the smell vanished. It was a smell he associated with his mother. He didn't want to think about it for fear of losing something.

The scent had vanished, but he felt that he would encounter it again. He then lifted his hand with great difficulty and leaned toward it. He touched his swollen and cracked lips to his little finger. He felt a jolt and looked carefully at his blackened and swollen finger. The ring his mother had given him was gone. He had lost the ring!

His body seemed on fire and he trembled. He crawled on the ground looking for it. He looked everywhere.

Nozawa stood beside him, making faint, unintelligible noises.

He had lost the ring his mother had given him. He remembered how she had given it to him on December 18, 1943, just as he was walking out of the main hall of their home. She had pulled it from her sash and pressed it into his hands, saying that it had been his father's and he had given it to her on the day of their wedding. He recalled how he had bit his lips as he held her small, thin hands. She told him that the ring wasn't worth much, but she wanted him to wear it so as to have her near him. His mother, who was a strong woman, broke down and cried. She told him to bring it back to her and to return home safe and sound.

He was so confident about returning safe and sound at that time. And later, in the face of death, he never lost that confidence. For him, his mother represented home; home, Taiwan, and Fanzai Wood were all one and the same. His mother was more than just a woman of flesh and blood; for him she was life itself. She was a sweet smell, a sound, a lamp, all emitting love, a love that knew no distance, a gentle light that penetrated the soul.

Now that sweet scent wafted through the air and disappeared. And that ring that had come to stand for his mother had somehow disappeared. He wondered how his mother was. Had she . . . ? The ring was gone. Did that mean she had gone?

His senses came alive—and the sensations of color, sound, smell, and touch were all extraordinarily vivid. Then they gradually began to fade until they disappeared. Mingji collapsed, a heap of flesh prostrate on the ground.

It was death, death that began in the heart and spread outward. It was a death of sorts.

Dead. His mother had died. Ahua was most likely dead too. He didn't know how she had gotten here, but she had come to the Philippines on account of him. And she had died on account of him. Taiwan and Fanzai Wood had all expired. That sweet scent, the sound, and the light had all vanished along with the ring. Everything had been lost.

Nozawa was still standing there in front of him. No, he was pacing about, but never more than ten feet away.

When had he heard of Japan's surrender? Japan had been defeated. The war was over. The war in the Pacific and Asia was over, but why was he still fighting? He was alive, but he felt dead inside. He had to walk, he had to move on.

He got up; that heap of flesh got up off the ground. The war was over. He had to head north in the direction of Taiwan, his home. He seemed to be empty of feelings and have no will of his own—his feet moved of their own accord. He didn't know where he got the strength to walk. A man comes from the earth and returns to the earth; he was from Taiwan and he would return to Taiwan. He would return to his home in Fanzai Wood, and the balance of nature would be preserved.

There was no familiar scent or voice to follow, but before him, in the direction of Taiwan, there burned an eternal light. It was a light that was not perceptible to the senses, but it burned there all the same.

His mother might have died, but she was still there all the same. She had nothing to do with death; she was eternal. His mother was that light, that lamp, the light of thousands of lamps shining in Fanzai Wood, shining over the Pacific, shining above his own lofty soul.

He stumbled toward the light, keeping his sights set on it. Time and space had become unreal and had lost their meaning. But time continued to flow.

One day vague, flickering shadows appeared before him. Each shadow held a black rod; they trained their rods on him, but he continued to plod forward.

The shadows began emitting strange noises. He did not understand them. He continued to advance. The shadows continued to make strange noises and grunts.

Then he heard an explosion. It was a sound he knew, a bad sound. It must have come from those black rods. The sound had been accompanied by a blue flash of light.

He moved no more. He seemed to have fallen. He wanted to continue forward. He continued northward, following the light. The shadows approached him, still making those strange sounds.

"The war is over. Surrender!"

What? Who was speaking? He seemed to have understood what was said to him. He was held fast by something, and prevented from moving. Then his body seemed to float above the earth. Had he been lifted up? He felt unobstructed, and the light was there ahead of him. He knew he had to head toward that light.